QUEEN
OF THE
MASQUERADE

ALSO BY ALICE QUINN

Queen of the Trailer Park

Queen of the Hide Out

QUEEN OF THE MASQUERADE

A ROSIE MALDONNE MYSTERY

ALICE QUINN

TRANSLATED BY
ALEXANDRA MALDWYN-DAVIES

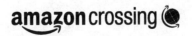

Text copyright © 2016 Alice Quinn
Translation copyright © 2016 Alexandra Maldwyn-Davies
All rights reserved.

Translated from French by Alexandra Maldwyn-Davies. First published in English by AmazonCrossing in 2016.

Published by AmazonCrossing, Seattle

www.apub.com

Amazon, the Amazon logo, and AmazonCrossing are trademarks of Amazon.com, Inc., or its affiliates.

ISBN-13: 9781503939493
ISBN-10: 1503939499

Cover design by Janet Perr

Printed in the United States of America

"The zebra's shadow has no stripes."

—*Eudoxie Bintou Apraksine*

"When you dig in shit, you wind up stinking!"

—*Monsieur Charles*

"I was no longer the love of his life, but a weird little specimen under his microscope."

—*Rosie Maldonne*

Monday:
Lazy Bones

1

It had been some time since I, Rosie Maldonne (or Cricri, as everyone calls me because of my love of crickets), had woken up on a Monday morning with such a zest for life, but as I hopped out of bed in my big, beautiful trailer, that's exactly what I had.

Let me sum up my situation. It's no easy ride bringing up three little girlies on my own, with no fixed income and just my welfare checks to get by. Life can get more than a little tough at times, forcing me to do a fair amount of juggling to make ends meet. But I ain't complaining. Luck is on my side when it comes to the most important things in life: I live in the most magnificent trailer in France, and my daughters just happen to be as amazing as they come.

To be honest, I'd been feeling in pretty fine form since returning from Amsterdam. I know it seems far out that a girl like me, surviving in a trailer with three kids and no permanent job, could get herself and her little ones up to Holland for Christmas on just her welfare money, but truthfully, it's the total truthful truth.

And even though it was starting to feel like ages ago, and the incredible memories of the postcard-perfect medieval houses along the canal were slowly fading away, and despite the unbelievable things that had happened to us while we were there (another story for another time), my life had been on the straight and narrow for six months, and things finally seemed to be on the up and up.

I suddenly wondered what had woken me and then I remembered: Pastis! My cat. The man of the house! The only man who has ever stayed. Sabrina's daddy was just a ship passing in the night—a ship that had sailed all the way from Cape Verde. Lisa's father actually put a ring on my finger but took it off quick enough when he left me for a classier broad. I've never had anything to do with Emma's father because she's not my real daughter. Emma is the daughter of my best friend, who died having her. I was beyond devastated. Emma's been with the three of us since the day she was born. So Pastis has been the only fella to ever live with us in our home sweet home—and we like it that way.

He was standing in front of the window, ready to pounce.

He was making those funny little *nic nic* noises that cats make with their jaws when they're hunting. A little bird must have caught his eye. And that's when I heard the pretty song of a swift. At least, I think it was a swift. I have no idea what the difference is between a thrush, a blackbird, a swift . . . I don't know any birds! But I think the swift has the coolest name. So a swift it was.

I scanned outside. Wild honeysuckle quivered in the light breeze that came over to my trailer to say a quick hello, leaving in its wake the most gorgeous of smells. Magical! A tiny little bird, like a bobbin red chest but without the red bit (honestly, no clue about birds), was jumping from flower to flower, as happy as a clam.

I understood why I had such an incredible level of energy that morning and why my mother had sent me a particular song from beyond the grave.

The sun has got his hat on, hip, hip, hip, HURRAY . . .

Although my mother died when I was just sixteen (over eleven years ago now), she has never really been all that far away. She continues to speak to me as I sleep and sends me hidden messages through songs that get stuck in my head. They're not always easy to solve, these little singsong puzzles, so they get those little gray cells working as soon as my eyes open.

And that particular morning, it was an ode to sunshine she had given me. Perfectly normal.

During the heat wave that had been sweeping France just then, I had been sweating like a pig and swigging water to stay hydrated. When I was out and about, my pumps would stick to the pavement. I didn't mind too much, but the melted tar could be a pain. I don't own skirts unless they're very, very short, but the one I was wearing that day was not quite as mini as I usually like, and my strappy, see-through vest weighed down on me like a sweater. Breathing was becoming a bit of a problem too, in the suffocating humidity.

Everything around me was screaming: *It's summertime!*

That meant there were only a few days left of school.

I peered at the clock. I was fifteen minutes ahead of my usual schedule. Great. Not being late was always a good thing. I would use the time wisely: five minutes to laze around, and then time to gently wake up Sabrina and the twins and take all three of my gorgeous little girlies to school.

When I thought about school, I felt a shudder go down my spine: How was I going to avoid the staff today? I owed a lot of cafeteria money this semester, as always. And then it hit me: I didn't owe a cent! Nada! Oh, what a relief! How light I felt!

Just fantabulosis! I didn't have much money to my name, and there were a few other debts here and there, like the ongoing tab at the grocery store, but there was nothing major, nothing urgent, and, best of all, I was managing to feed the kids.

As I was getting my little munchkins washed and dressed and all packed up for class, I wondered whether there was something I'd forgotten. It was such a weird feeling to have next-to-zero stress in my life that I couldn't bring myself to quite believe it.

The twinnies had grown some that year—I call them my twins because they're the same age, four years old, and although I only gave birth to one of them, they're both my girls, of course!—so they didn't need their huge double stroller any longer. You'd think that would have made life so much easier, wouldn't you? Wrong. You see, I have a couple of little dreamers on my hands who take a long time over things. Over everything, in fact. Especially walking.

Lisa is a pretty timid girl and follows Emma everywhere. Emma is a little go-getter and always ready to give it her all. But when it comes to walking, they're both on the same wavelength. They like to stop every couple of yards to check out a pebble, inspect an insect, dig around for cigarette butts. They call it *looking for lucks*. Anything on the ground is of incredible interest to them. Neither one could ever imagine anything more exciting than heading outdoors and looking for lucks. Before, when we'd used the stroller, we were one superfast little family. But everything now takes at least twice as long.

So there the three of us were, slogging real slow to school. There were no dramas like we'd been prone to encounter in recent history. Nothing in any of the trash cans—I always check them out (let's just call it a reflex)—and no more FBI or mafia types, no big muscly guys following us. No danger on the horizon. Total calm. Zero stress!

First of all, I dropped off the two little ones at the nursery school and then Sabrina at the big school. She was in actual elementary school. Unbelievable! My, how she'd grown—she was seven now! Still full of nervous energy, tall and thin, all arms and legs. Her favorite things in life included bossing Pastis around, tying everything she could get her hands on with bits of string and yarn, and listening to adult conversations so she could chastise those who used any curse words. Observation was her true passion—looking at everything and everyone with her huge peepers. She'd make a good spy, that kid. She didn't miss a trick. And she could read now! Oh my, could she read!

What a fantastic school, I thought, watching her go inside. I must have really been seeing the world through rose-colored glasses that day if I thought that dump was great. The building had once been painted in garish shades, but the walls were now faded and covered in graffiti, the almost-bare little bushes dotting the yard were halfheartedly trying to brighten the place up, the swings in the yard were shabby and rusty, and the whole thing was surrounded by shoddy-looking welfare housing. But it all appeared magnificent to me.

The heat was pounding down, but maybe I was getting into this whole heat-wave thing. What a great mood I was in! All this sunshine, all this free time I had ahead of me . . . Things were turning out well.

I sang to myself, *The sun has got his hat on!*

I meandered back to my trailer, taking some time to appreciate life. I told myself that for once, instead of attacking the housework and the laundry, or heading out and trying to track down work, I'd just enjoy a great long nap. Sleeping when everyone else is at work and it's broad daylight outside. Sleeping when I really shouldn't be sleeping. Was there a more glorious feeling?

Of course, thinking back now, I should have known better.

It was the quiet before the typhoon. However the saying goes . . .

Be careful when the water is sleeping?

A resting volcano . . . does something?

A seagull squawking signals a storm?

A rolling stone gathers no moss? (I know that one has nothing to do with any of this.)

That was the general idea.

2

I did what I'd set out to do.

I attached one end of my hammock to a big hook on the wall of the old railway station behind our little home and the other onto a thick branch of the big plane tree that provided a little shade around our trailer-sweet-trailer.

I kicked off my wedge heels and climbed into the hammock. Softly, softly.

Oh! I was just too supercool for school!

The sensations were simply amazing! I felt safe, comfy, a real sense of freedom. Just as I was approaching full snooze mode, the sun warming my skin, reality came screaming toward me at full whack.

My cricket started shrieking his little head off, startling me out of my slumber. My cricket being my cell. I call it *my cricket* because of the ringtone. As I reached down to pick it up, I almost fell out of that excellent hammock of mine.

Snoozing in a hammock is about as good as it gets, but it's hard to stay graceful in one. When you're rummaging around for your cell and you're far from being fully awake, you can very quickly find yourself flat on your face.

I managed to grab it just before it stopped ringing.

"Hello?"

It was Émilie. Mimi to her friends. She was a waitress at Sélect, the bar where I sometimes worked (but got paid under the table). Her son, Léo, had been under the care of social services for some time. I didn't know all the ins and outs, and Mimi didn't seem interested in filling me in. Maybe she was ashamed? Or it was just too painful? All I knew was, she'd been trying to gain custody for several months.

She sounded stressed out to the max. "Oh, it's a nightmare! A total nightmare! What should I do? Cricri, is that you?"

"Well, of course it's me. You just called me, didn't you?"

"You're the only one who can save my ass. Cricri, please, I'm begging you."

"What happened?"

"What happened? I'm down at the ER! Go figure! I fell off a stepladder. I was cleaning my place, a total top-to-bottom job, because Léo is coming a week earlier than expected, you know? Just as a one-off. The judge agreed to give me a trial period. I can have Léo for the week. All the holidays and long weekends he spent with me went really well, so we're doing a real-life test now to see how things would turn out on a day-to-day basis. I'm fine with it, he's fine with it, the judge is fine with it, and all those social-worker touchy-feely types are down with it too."

"And?"

"You don't get it, do you? He's arriving tomorrow! And I'm at the hospital. I'll be going under the knife in a couple of days. They're operating on my wrist. I can't move, either! I knocked my back out."

"You poor thing! What do you want me to do? Do you want me to call them up? Tell them he can't come?"

"Have you gone craycray, Cricri? If he doesn't come this time, it'll be a never-ending story trying to make it all happen again. I'd have to go in front of the judge and all that crap. That's if they'll even give me another chance!"

"What do you want to do?"

"I don't know. What do you think, Cricri? You tell me what to do. You always know what to do!"

What was this? Someone wanted my advice? I don't like giving out advice. Not even to myself! I'm not the sort of gal whose advice should be followed, either. The ship's better off sailing alone than with me at the helm. But for some unknown reason, my girlfriends always wanted me to give them advice. Maybe it was because I loved reading all those books that Véro's boss wrote. Véro was my other bestie. She cleaned for a shrink—well, for *her* shrink. And she lent me some of the shrink's books from time to time.

"I don't know how good my advice is, Mimi. Sometimes I have some pretty bizarroid ideas."

"That's exactly why I need you, Cricri. You don't think like everyone else. So just tell me, what would you do in my shoes?"

Since the beginning of the conversation, I'd known what I'd do in her place. But telling others to do what I'd do isn't all that simple. Because afterward, they'd have to do what I'd do and see it through. And doing what I'd do might not be what they'd do. Except they wouldn't be asking what I'd do if they knew what to do. They'd just do what they'd do, right? It's getting a bit hard to follow all this "doing" business.

"I'll tell you, but you don't have to follow my advice, OK?"

"Come on, Cricri. Spit it out."

"Well, I'd send Léo to a good friend of yours and tell him not to say anything to the welfare folks, and then see how it went until I was back on my feet again. Nobody would ever need to know, especially because Léo is almost all grown up now, isn't he? He gets all this shit, right? Mimi? You still there?"

A few more seconds of silence followed, and then she babbled on in a rush.

"I was so hoping you'd say that. Thank you! Thank you, my Cricri! So you can take Léo for a couple of days? You'll soon see he's no trouble at all. You just have to make sure he gets his homework done, stop him from seeing those loser friends of his who all deal, and make sure he doesn't get any closer to that other buddy from school who seems to be in some sort of neo-Nazi group. OK?"

"Oh, is that all? And Léo's supposed to be no trouble, you say?"

"Yeah, he's fine. He's very easygoing. It's just that he's always been attracted to the outcasts, you know? And I don't want him getting carried away. It's a difficult age. Teenagers like to belong to something. All the kids in high school have the same problem. And then there's absenteeism, of course!"

"Are you some kind of sociopathogist now, using words like *absenteeism*? Do you mean playing hooky?"

"Yep! You'll see, Cricri. Your gang will be in their teens soon enough. You have to wise up."

"Fine. So, what do I have to do?"

"Nothing! Don't even move a muscle! I'll send him a text message after class tomorrow and tell him to make his way to your place, OK?"

"Do you need anything down at the hospital?"

"Not right now. I'll let you know if I do. The Léo thing is the most import—ouch! Oww! Don't touch me! Don't pull me like that! Leave me alone! No! I can't move! My back! Sorry, Cricri . . . I'm going to have to hang up on you now!"

And click. She cut me off!

I sat back in my hammock. Léo at my place? I'd have to make some room! I could put Sabrina in with the little ones and Léo could go in Sabrina's bunk. Spacewise it was doable, but it would still be a bit complicated, to say the least. I mean, teenage boys . . . They eat a ton, don't they?

I could see the tab at the store getting longer and longer. Anyway. We'd just have to see how it went. Stuff usually manages to work itself out, doesn't it? And like my little Sabrina always says with her trademark lisp: *That'th life!*

I was trying to figure out our new routine when a loud ring-ding-a-linging interrupted my thought process.

It was a message from Véro.

—I need U. U workin 2mrrow? Nxt cpl days?

—Na! Y?

—Gr8! Plz, plz, go work at my boss Rachel Amar's place 2moz. 41 rue Felix Faure @ 10

—Wat 4?

—She aint there. We off with kidz 4 a while. Vacation. And she wants a big clean. Big spring clean. I trust U on this. Call u wen bck. Will tell her ur goin.

—VACATION?

—If at all possible, please take the books you borrowed back to my boss's place. Nil volentibus arduum.

Ismène must have taken the phone from Véro. I'd recognize her style anywhere. She doesn't like text language. And she was obviously showing off by speaking some foreign language too.

It's so weird. Two of my best girlfriends have totally fallen for each other and been in a relationship for months. Ismène, my confident Black Beauty, and Véro, Little Miss Miserable Panties.

They are night and day. Ismène works in local government, loves poetry, Japanese tea ceremonies, secret codes, and brainless bimbos. Véro goes from dead-end job to dead-end job, has had a string of rotten relationships and several longish stays on the psych ward. An unlikely pair, but it seems to be working. The two are inseparable. More power to them!

I couldn't think of a reply, and I'm rarely short of something to say. So they were out of there, was that it? With no warning? And I was supposed to go and replace Véro at work, just like that?

Not cool, chickos, not cool.

How come I'd just wound up with a job all of a sudden? How was I supposed to make that work with the schedule I had? I hadn't organized a thing! How in God's name could I fit it in, what with taking care of all the kiddos and everything else? It was going to be a toughie. Teens like to go out and about at all hours. You don't know if they're coming or going. And then what about all those high-school teachers walking out on strike all the time?

Oh well. No point being a big crybaby about it. I couldn't exactly change anything. School was nearly out for the summer, anyway. Oh, it was all going to get pretty complicated pretty fast.

Well, at least I could now return all those books I'd borrowed from Véro, the ones she'd clearly borrowed from her boss. Heck, there were some weird books in there. Mental stuff! Even crazier than my fave Snoopy comics, half the time! Most of them were written by this Freud guy, who had premonitions. Dreams and shit. I loved reading all that spooky baloney. Well, *reading* might not quite be the word I'm searching for here. I skimmed through them. There weren't very many pictures, but still, I could feel the suspense! And they made me think of my own musical dreams that my mother sent me on an almost-nightly basis.

Véro's boss had written a fair number of books. Fancy stuff for brainiacs. A lot of it was about big criminal types and why they did what they did. I'd seen the broad one time when I went to pick up Véro after work. She was one of those snooty, nose-stuck-in-the-air women. Dressed like a total square in a long-cut skirt, prissy shirt with a stiff collar, flat shoes . . .

One of those.

So, today's big question: Could I face the housework at her place?

I absolutely hated cleaning other people's houses, but it wasn't totally out of the realm of possibility. I knew how to clean well enough! And it's not like I was rolling in cash or anything. I had my checks from the state, but not much else. I wasn't deepio-deep in the red, but all the same.

I replied: OK.

What else could I say? I wasn't about to leave Véro neck-high in the brown stuff. This was maybe the first time she'd ever been on vacation.

I added: Keys?

Immediate reply: Thanks! We owe you. We left a spare key in an envelope at the reception down at city hall. The girl there knows to expect you.

These dames had seen to everything. It was clear that Ismène was good at her paper-pushing-executive job for the local administrative services. Miss Methodical Girl.

My nice easygoing morning had suddenly turned into a swim against the tide.

3

I tried to prepare myself for the upcoming tornado by tidying up the trailer.

I gave it a real good cleaning and changed the kids' bed linens. Despite the fact that every window in the place was wide open in my attempt to get something of a draft running through, I was sweating gallons.

I took the time to slice up half a baguette and dip it in olive oil. It would be enough to see me through to the next meal.

Finally, I took all our dirty clothes and bedding down to the laundromat.

As they were washing and drying, I went to the grocery store and added a little more to my tab (a can of tomatoes and an onion for spaghetti that evening). Grocery Guy was the only one around here who ever gave me any credit.

Bad news. Grocery Guy told me that I'd reached my limit with my tab. Settling up with him was now at the top of my list.

I took a quick detour to Sélect. I wanted to let Tony know there was no point counting on me over the next few days because I had to work for Rachel Amar.

Now and again, when he needed me, I helped Tony out in his café, Sélect. He gave me the odd couple of bills for it. All off the books, of course. Everyone got something out of it. Especially when he let me sing on Saturday nights.

Tony enjoyed a good flirt with me when he could. I never led him on too much. Our relationship had always been a breeze. Easy come, easy go.

Tony was getting ready for the after-work rush. It didn't look like he could cope much without Mimi. He thought I was there to help out. As I don't really like to bite the hand that feeds me, I promised I'd show up a little later on, once I'd picked the babas up from school.

However, there was nothing I'd be able to do for him the following day. I couldn't even think of anyone who was maybe seeking a couple of hours' work. I told him I'd think on it awhile and let him know if I had some ideas.

He offered me a quick coffee and I savored every hot gulp as I stood against the bar next to Antoine, an old regular around sixty, with a mustache and a big potbelly under his tight tee, dressed in cycling gear. Your typical gramps. An upbeat old man who clearly thought he could still kick it! He was wearing Lycra shorts, a fanny pack, and a Coke baseball cap to top it all off. He seemed very pleased with life.

I'd sometimes seen him with his grandson at the bar. It had been a while, though, since we'd seen the boy. I only remembered him because he and my Sabrina used to like playing together. We used to talk about the kids and school worries, their favorite toys, and how their teachers could sometimes get us so stressed and wound up.

That's about it. I hadn't seen him for a while, but we'd crossed paths here and there and given each other a little knowing nod and smile of recognition. He worked in real estate or something like that. I'd heard Tony say Antoine bought and sold properties and that the guy owned entire neighborhoods all down the coast. Rich? With that thick southern-French accent? Always dressed in neon shorts? Doubtful.

Plus, Sélect was hardly the kind of dive that anyone with serious money would be seen dead in.

"Things going OK, Antoine?" I asked.

"Oh, you do what you can. And you, Cricri? Everything running pretty smooth?"

"Sure, life's pretty good these days. I'm more or less in the black. You? Your grandkiddy? Bet he's growing up fast!"

"Smooth sailing! He's head of his class! A real brain! I don't know where he gets it from, but it certainly ain't me!"

He roared with laughter. A kind, hearty laugh.

"Cool," I said. I didn't really know how to respond to such showing off.

He leaned in close and asked in a friendly tone, "Your real name is Rosie, isn't it? I never really understood why everyone calls you Cricri. Cricri isn't short for Rosie! 'Rose' or 'Roro' I could understand!"

Another roar. He considered himself quite the comedian. He was starting to agitate me a little, but I felt obliged to answer him. Elementary politeness, my dear Watson.

"Oh, it's just a family thing. My mother was the only person to ever call me Rosie," I said.

I hate it when people call me Rosie! At least "Cricri" doesn't remind me of my mom. After she died, I decided I didn't ever want anyone calling me by my real name again. She chose the name and it belonged to her. And the fact that she isn't here to say it anymore doesn't change that! I just wound up choosing the name Cricri myself. I thought it was pretty nice sounding. Straightforward. No fluff.

"Fair enough! I have to go back to work now," said Monsieur Cycle Pants as he finished his raucous laugh.

"Oh, do you still work? Not retired yet?"

"No. People don't really retire in my line of work."

He rummaged around in his fanny pack.

"Here! Give this to Sabrina, would you? It's a Happy Families card game. I had them made on the Internet. It's a nice little way of advertising."

He handed me a mini deck of playing cards. On the back of every card was the logo of his real-estate agency, his contact information, and, in a larger font: "RENT or BUY." On the other side were families— little kidlets all the way up to the grampies and grannies. Each family was looking at a different type of property with a "For Sale" sign in front of it: apartment, vacation home, suburban condo, etc. There was even a trailer-trash family!

"Thanks, these cards are great!" I shoved the game into my back pocket.

"It's difficult right now," he admitted. "There's a financial crisis going on. Property prices aren't going anywhere!" He was shouting.

"Wow, I can feel how stressed out you are! You need to take a chill pill there, bud!"

"What about you? How'd you like to buy a condo?"

And now it was my turn to crack up!

"Where do you think I'd get the money? Any bank lending to me would have to have fallen on hard times, don't you think? Anyhow, I'm doing just fine in my trailer. It's the biggest trailer in the whole region! Did you know that it was built for the King of Travel—like, Gypsy royalty or something?"

He took a great big long stretch and clicked his heels together as he jumped a good half a foot off the ground. The other clients gaped at him. He looked like something out of an energy-bar ad. We were all beat just watching him.

"OK, then! See you guys!"

And he skipped out, singing to himself.

I downed the rest of my coffee and followed in Antoine's wake— with a little less enthusiasm, but followed all the same.

"You won't forget about me, will you?" Tony shouted after me.

4

I went by city hall to pick up the keys to Véro's boss's place, which Ismène had left in an envelope with my name on it.

It was then time to go get the kiddos. I gave Antoine's Happy Families game to Sabrina. Next stop was the laundromat to pick up our clothes. If I wanted to keep my promise to Tony, I had no time to go back to the trailer, so I shuffled back to Sélect with the groceries, shopping, and kidlets in tow.

The heat wouldn't let up. Scorchorama. I set the children up at the back of the café with some bread, butter, jam, and glasses of milk all pilfered from the fridge in the kitchen. It was leftovers from breakfast. You can get a good breakfast at Tony's place.

As they all enjoyed their after-school snack, I started helping out.

Between two orders, I managed to clear the kids' table and get out their notebooks. Homework called.

Sabrina was supposed to be learning how to count aloud up to a thousand and how to add together two-digit numbers. Not too difficult. I was able to help her whenever I had a spare moment. The twins each got out a brightly colored notebook. They were learning how to draw straight lines, wavy lines, and circles. It all looked very pretty.

After a while, the little ones had clearly had enough and took it upon themselves to go and explore the café—at high speed, running around like little maniacs. Luckily, Tony was so busy, he didn't notice.

As soon as she'd finished her math, Sabrina spread out all the Happy Families cards on the table and studied the pictures. But she soon wound up bored, so she got out her string and tied the twinnies' dolls and some of her schoolbooks to the tables and chairs. She had always had a thing for string.

I'd been reading (when I say "reading," I may be exaggerating a little) Rachel Amar's books about the brain, and I'd been wondering about this little habit of Sabrina's. String was her thing. Or anything that was string-like. Elastic, rope, laces, yarn . . . anything that could be used to tie two or more things together. Scotch tape was also a biggie. And knots were about as exciting as things got for my eldest daughter. It was why I had to be super careful at my place. Everyone did! You could so easily go splat in my trailer with all those long stringy scraps all over the house! We were booby-trapped to the max!

The child-therapisty person at preschool, back when Sabrina was a real tiny tot, told me that it all meant she was trying to stop the things she loved in life from getting away from her. She wanted to tie together anything she saw as separate—like her father and me, for example.

Back then, I'd thought the therapist was pretty weird to get all that information from a kid's game. All I saw was that Sabrina liked playing with string. Period. But I'd come to know a bit more on the subject thanks to Rachel Amar. I was now totally tuned in to this shit and thought that maybe, just maybe, there was a little bit more to this string theory than I'd first thought.

Of course, I really wanted her to get over this string anxiety nonsense (especially as I kept falling flat on my backside in her knotty little world). So I had the idea of drawing pictures with her, the idea being she could draw lines between these pictures and attach them whatever way she wanted. Who knew? Maybe this could help put an end to it all. It couldn't do any harm, right?

Little by little, the punters at Sélect started going home. Rush hour had come to an end.

As I was collecting the last of the glasses and giving the tabletops all a wipe down with a damp cloth, I heard a yelp and a couple of curse words coming from the back room. It sounded like one or two chairs had toppled over. Maybe Sabrina had gone too far again . . .

And she had. She'd tied two chairs together and left them outside the bathroom.

The guy who had tripped over them was lucky he hadn't broken his nose on the floor. Before the situation got further out of hand, I grabbed Sabrina by the sleeve and snarled, "Emma, Lisa! Here, now! We're going home!" I pushed them all out the front door. "See you, Tony! I'll be back any day now for my pay! I've done two and a half hours for you, OK? OK! Ciao!"

Tony knew the kids had been up to no good and that I was running away from it all. He smiled at me.

"Thank you, Cricri!"

5

As we made our way back home, we ended up trudging behind a teen-age girl who came across as more than a little odd. It seemed like she'd gotten her clothes from a bad gypsy yard sale. Just horrible. I didn't pay much attention at first. She was just ambling along, carrying a ton of plastic bags. But at one point, she stopped at a small building and came out shortly afterward.

The reason I remember this is because it was at the exact moment Emma decided to sit on the ground and refuse to move any farther.

Emma's not a bad little girl. In fact, she's very easygoing most of the time. But sometimes, she fixates on something and there's no budging her. Little jealous fits of rage. It's often hard to understand what exactly is bugging her when she gets like this.

Luckily for me, Sabrina always knows what's going on.

She leaned in close to her baby sister, then stared up at me and revealed the meaning behind the snivels.

"Emma won't walk home with uth becauthe the'th forgotten her Printheth Tharah doll at Tony'th and the won't be able to thleep without her."

"Well, why didn't she just say so?"

Emma loves her doll. She dresses her up as Superman and tells everyone that Princess Sarah has magic protection powers. I was worn out by this stage, so I sat down on the ground too. My other two daughters followed suit.

Emma scrutinized me, and I pulled her onto my lap.

"So, you want Princess Sarah, is that it?"

"Yes."

"Listen, we're a long way from Tony's place now. I'm very tired. It's late and I just don't think I have the energy to go back and pick her up. So I don't really know what we're going to do. We'll have to put our thinking caps on, OK?"

I got to thinking, and just as I did, the teenage girl came back out of the building. She gave us a fixed stare and then continued on her way.

Our eyes had met for only a brief moment, but I could see how beautiful she was. Obviously, she was still just a kid, but her almond-shaped eyes lit up her whole face. She had Eva Mendes's cheekbones, Penélope Cruz's lips, silky black hair tumbling down her back, flawless skin, fine wrists and shoulders. She reminded me of a little doe or a gazelle.

A spooked gazelle. A hunted gazelle. But the vulnerability just made her even more stunning to behold.

We picked up our conversation again. Sabrina had a great little idea: we could draw a picture of Princess Sarah when we got back home. We'd keep it until we had time to get back to Tony's to pick up the real thing.

Emma was happy enough with this idea and we all set off again. At the corner of the street, we saw the same girl. This time, she was leaving a small condo with a little garden out front. She lowered her head and scuttled on ahead of us. I noted that she was now nearly empty handed. And she was springing along more quickly.

So, what was the deal here? She was walking into buildings and coming back out again several minutes later and her plastic bags were disappearing little by little.

She suddenly ran into the courtyard of a group of scruffy apartment blocks and dirty little houses. We followed her. I wanted to take a little peek at what she was up to. It was just pure curiosity, I guess. We got as far as the entrance to the lot.

What in God's name am I doing? My big mouth usually gets me into enough trouble as it is, so why am I now meddling in other people's business? People I don't even know! Normal, sane women don't act like this, do they?

She made her way toward one of the dirty little houses. It was on its own, down a little alley. The front door looked to be boarded up. We moved in closer. It stunk of pee and rotting vegetables. I was betting it was a ratfest here. I saw a "For Sale" sign attached to one of the broken shutters. It had the number of the real-estate agency on it. She stopped. Luckily she didn't glance behind her before looking up at the crummy little house.

A man suddenly pushed me aside on his way past us into the alley. I had a quick chance to scan him. He had a hard face and gave me the willies. Even though he had icy-blue eyes, a sensuous mouth, a five o'clock shadow (but the kind he'd clearly intended to happen), and an angled face resembling Jude Law's . . . Something was off. He looked like the bad version of Jude Law.

He had far too many clothes on for the sticky weather. A gorgeous, presumably expensive white suit, a black shirt, and real stylish leather shoes. He strode over to the young girl, who had her back turned toward us, and as he approached her, he grabbed her arm violently. I thought he was going to attack her, and just as I was about to step in, I heard him speak in a foreign language.

She was examining the ground and didn't react when he shook her arm. She softly responded to his question. He shoved her by the small of her back and it looked like she was going to trip. She just managed to hop onto the first step in front of the house before making her way up the rest.

Just then, I heard a loud ringing sound. It almost burst my eardrum! A cyclist whizzed past me and waved. It was Antoine. I waved back and he cried out, "Yo! Cricri! How's it going?"

He'd distracted me from the teenage girl and the mean Jude Law. I turned back toward them as Antoine rode off into the distance.

The girl had reached the top of the steps and was now clambering through the ground-floor window, over a piece of wood that had maybe been used to bolt down the shutters at some stage. There was no point intervening. These two clearly knew each other, and, even though he hadn't been particularly nice to her, it was their business and had nothing whatsoever to do with me.

Well, at least I know where she's holed up, I thought, as if this information was actually important. I mean, this girl was a perfect stranger, wasn't she? But I felt intrigued by her. So what?

We all did a one eighty and strolled back toward the trailer, singing songs along the way—our usual style. About a hundred feet down the road, the guy jumped out from a little side road in front of me. It was the same hot guy. Jude. White-Suit Man. He was blocking the sidewalk, stopping us from getting past him. The kids jumped up and down and let out little screeches!

"Have you lost it?" I hissed. "What's your problem? Are you mental?"

I shouted the last bit a little too loudly to make up for the fact that he had really gotten me whacked out. I wanted him to think I wasn't the slightest bit bothered by him. Emma pushed him, Lisa hid behind my legs, and Sabrina got out a ball of string and started unrolling it.

"I've got the right of way," the man insisted—not only in French, but with a perfect French accent.

Right of way? He's got right of way? Does this imbecile have a screw loose or what? Since when does the highway code apply to sidewalks and pedestrians?

I stared at him straight in the eyes as I said, "Sabrina, put the string away. Twinnos, you both move back now." And then to the Suit, I said, "You might have the right of way, sure, but I've got the green light. Green light wins."

I was pretty pissed. I must have been—I'd just invented the road version of rock-paper-scissors! I mean, what the hell? When I don't get something, I become wound up. Maybe that's why I'm always so antsy.

He stepped toward me, towering above.

If I'd been on my own, I would have kicked him where it hurts, but I don't want to teach my babies that most problems can, in fact, be solved by violence.

So I stayed where I was, not moving a muscle, for what felt like hours. My daughters could sense the weirdness of it. Lisa pulled at my clothes; her lips were trembling and the tears were only seconds away. Sabrina brandished her nylon string menacingly, and Emma gave the guy what she considered to be her darkest, meanest glower.

Gritting his teeth, he whispered, "If I ever see you around here again, you or your shitty little brats, I'll wipe all of you out. Got it?"

OK, so he definitely spoke good French.

I didn't want to show him that he could intimidate me that easily, even though he totally could. This fella was scary. I delicately and slowly held out my hand and made a sweeping gesture, telling him to shoo out of my way, and I darted forward. Miracle of miracles, he moved.

But his piercing blue eyes continued to glare, and I felt them burning a hole in my back for a long time as we marched off. When I finally had the courage to turn around and inspect the scene, he'd disappeared.

We continued along our merry way without any further dramas. I tried to get my head around what had just happened. But then, little by little, our misadventure disappeared from my thoughts as I started to make plans on my planet.

"OK, so with the job at Véro's boss's house, I'll make about three hundred. Plus my welfare check and my work at Tony's, I'll be able to pay my tab easily. Coolio! We're rolling in it!"

"Mommy, are you talking to yourthelf?" asked Sabrina, which made the twins suddenly very interested in what was going on.

They stared at me insistently, trying to figure out what I'd been yammering on about.

I was saved by Pastis, who came skipping up to meet us all. He looked like a simple alley cat, but he really did have the IQ of Einstein. He was a little screwy, and not your typical cat at all. You'd almost say he had the personality of a dog. For example, he often came out to meet us as we made our way home. Probably because he was hungry, but even so.

He rubbed against my ankles. "Ah! There you are, Pastis! Don't exaggerate! You're not exactly starving!"

He meowed slowly, peeking up at me with his big pussycat eyes.

"Mommy," complained Sabrina, "Pathtith alwayth lookth at you like he lovth you tho much."

"That's kind to say, but I'm sure it's just that whenever he sees me, it's like seeing a big bowl of kitty treats on legs."

As soon as we stepped inside, I asked the kiddies to get their backpacks all ready for the next school day. Yes, I know, not the most fun activity (especially for the twins, who needed virtually nothing at school), but I wanted to take their minds off things.

But it was like they'd already forgotten everything that had happened on the way home. For them, everything we'd just seen with the teenage girl and the big baddie was no biggie. It was as if they'd simply watched a scene in a cartoon.

"Mommy, let'th do a muthical!" cried Sabrina.

"No, we'll do a show," replied Emma.

"A show, a muthical, a play . . . they're all wordth for the thame thing," Sabrina explained, shrugging.

They disappeared into one of the little bedrooms with the radio.

When Pastis noticed I was messing around with the gas stove, he bounced up onto my shoulders. He wrapped himself around my neck, clearly deciding I wasn't warm enough and needed a scarf. He stayed up there and watched as I prepared something to eat for everyone. Hardly practical.

He's a pretty gifted cat. It must be quite some feat to stay balanced on someone's shoulders while they're moving, throwing you around the place like a sack of grain.

I cut up the onion and started to brown it in the pan. I opened the can of tomatoes and set the water to boil for the spaghetti. The onion made my eyes all red and itchy.

Criiiiiii. Criiiiiii. My cricket phone.

I screamed out, "Quick! Hurry! Someone! Phone!"

The kids came running into the room, and Emma managed to locate the phone before it stopped ringing. She passed it to Sabrina, who opened it and held it up to my ear as I continued to cook. This is how we do things.

It was Gaston.

Gaston is like the father I never had, a gallant knight ready to serve my every whim, and my very best friend. All in all, he is someone I can count on day and night. I should also add that he is absolutely rolling in it. He is a poet, lives in an enchanted castle that's half in ruins but reminds me of something out of a fairy tale, and drives an old Jag. It's true that Gaston can get me out of the shit I'm in most of the time at just the click of my fingers, but nothing is as valuable to me as my independence. I'd rather eat old dry bread than have to count on someone else for something. For anything. I know, it's perhaps not the wisest move on my part, but there's no getting away from it. I am what I am. The result of a long line of women. Not always the sharpest of women, but women who've always managed to get by with what (little) they've had.

That particular day, Gaston had called to ask for a favor. Every now and again, he liked to meet up with us, break away from his routine, and get a hit of adrenaline from me and my rug-ratties. Taking care of the munchkins awhile was just like an action movie for him.

"I'm bored half to death, my Cricri! You don't need me to run you anywhere tomorrow by any chance, do you? If so, my services are available!"

"Heck, why not? I'm starting a new job in the morning. Around ten. You can drive me there, if you like! It's up on the coast."

"OK. I can come a little earlier and drop the kids off at school. You'll have your own chauffeur for the day! It'll be some time out for me. Wonderful!"

"Works for me!"

"Also, I've got a really great idea I'd like to run by you. It concerns you, as a matter of fact. See you tomorrow."

I didn't even have time to say good-bye before he hung up.

How did his idea concern me? What was it all about this time? He was always planning some scheme or other that involved me. Gaston liked to go on and on about how my multiple talents were wasted ("multiple talents" were his words, not mine, for the record). He wanted me to learn English, to take my driver's-license test . . . There was always something I should be doing. He should have known by now that I was allergic to learning. I'd repeated tenth grade four times (as far as I can remember) before I'd finally been kicked out.

"That smells yummy, Mommy," said Lisa.

"Why are you crying?" asked Emma.

"Oh, I'm not crying! It's the onions."

They were amused by this. They headed off to one of their mini-bedrooms with some onion peelings. They were taking big long sniffs of them, trying to make themselves cry. I don't know why, but they must have been immune to onions. It didn't work with them at all.

While everything was simmering on the stove, I served myself a small glass of port left over from some party or other. God only knows how long ago. There was only a tiny bit left in the bottle. Pastis, still managing to keep his balance, wobbled dangerously. I thought about the guy who'd threatened us earlier. I was really concerned about the girl. Did she live with him?

"Pastis, try to keep still, would you? Stop bobbing around!"

He replied with a moody meow.

We all sat around the table and wolfed down our spaghetti. The children helped me clean up afterward. We finished later than usual because of all the shenanigans on our way back home. We went through the getting-ready-for-bed ceremony, which included giving Sabrina a quick shower so that we could save some time in the morning.

I put Lisa to bed, and Sabrina helped Emma draw a picture of Princess Sarah dressed as Superman. They put the drawing under Emma's pillow.

After all the pots had been put away and all the clothes folded, I checked that the kiddies had done a good job with their backpacks and then settled down on my bed with a Rachel Amar book and . . . I dropped off.

Pastis settled down on my belly and his purring lulled me deeper into slumber.

And boy, did I sleep that night. I slept like a dead dog and didn't move a muscle until the next morning.

Tuesday:
New Encounters

6

I woke up with a terrible feeling of being suffocated. Pastis was a heavy little kitty, and when he pressed down on my stomach, like he was doing just then, the sensation of not being able to breathe properly was terrifying.

I jumped. I was sweating like a little piggy. I had Patsy Cline's "Crazy" running through my head, but I changed the words: *I'm cuckoo! Nutso for feeling so lonely! I'm bonkers! Loony for feeling so blue!*

How old was that song? Surely not my mother's era. Was she using my grandmother's repertoire now? I was feeling a little pissed at her. Couldn't she put a nice modern song in my head? What about that "Does that make me crazy?" song by Gnarley someone-or-other. That was a little more up my alley.

I squinted at the alarm clock. Oh *God*! It hadn't gone off! We were over a half hour late. And the twins were such slowpokes these days. We were never going to be on time.

I scurried into Emma and Lisa's room, pulled them out of bed, and threw them under the shower as quickly as I could. The shower-head made some noises. A *sqquuuiiirrrrt* and a *schluurrrrrpppp* and a *pliiiippp, driiiippp, droooppp*. About three droplets of dirty water came out, and then it just gave up the ghost.

In the meantime, Sabrina had managed to get dressed all by herself. I ran with the little ones halfway up a nearby street to the public fountain. It was a stunning little structure done in the style of some old king or something. It was a natural source of water, and I had no shame washing my baby girls in it—needs must be met and all that.

I could tell that everyone around me was staring, but there were only a few locals around. The tourists weren't up and about yet. That was something, at least.

The water was cool and clear, and the girls loved it! They splashed around happily and washed themselves, and then we all ran back to the trailer as quick as our legs would carry us. I'd taken two empty bottles and filled them with water, just in case we still had problems later on in the day.

I would have to find a way of dealing with the water issue at some point.

I toweled off the little ones, dressed them, and turned the radio on so I could listen to the news as I got some breakfast going. I had to throw some odds and ends together, whatever I could find. There was a little bread left over from the day before and some milk.

On the radio I heard the words "Full Moon Pyromaniac."

Full Moon Pyromaniac? They were talking about a guy who liked setting fires to libraries and shit. I already knew what a pyromaniac was. I'd read it somewhere. I liked stuff like that. And this one was a specialist in library fires! Good kindling, I supposed. What a weirdo. He'd be no friend of mine, that was for sure.

Libraries are my favorite. I go to the library when I want to chillax or when I feel the blues coming on. The comic-book aisle is where it's at for me.

We just happen to have the world's most beautiful library right in our neighborhood. It's an old villa up on the hill. In fact, it looks like a palace. It was built by the Rothschild family! So you can imagine just how *la-di-da* it is! And now we, the *underclass*, are allowed to go inside whenever we feel like it! We can use the grounds too! We can stroll around, dream, meander . . . Like goddamn royalty, I tell you.

Anyway, this berserko fire-starter guy had been arrested and his trial was beginning. So far, he hadn't breathed a word. He was one of those "silent as the grave" types. Taking the Fifth, they call it over in the States. He was refusing to speak or communicate, which only ever turned out badly in the movies.

Imagine wanting to set fire to such a beautiful, heavenly building. I just didn't get it. I wanted to know what made this guy tick. Maybe I'd find the answer in one of my psychology books. I was sure there was some sort of rational or scientific explanation for such behavior. The idea reassured me as I got everything ready for the school run.

Everyone brushed their teeth and all that jazz using some of the bottled water from the fountain, and then off we scampered. I was praying with every spare bit of energy that Gaston would turn up in his magic Jag taxi machine, but his alarm clock must have been busted up too. He was running later than me.

It wasn't like him not to keep his word, but seeing as he didn't have any family obligations, he wasn't used to getting up at the crack of dawn to see to a big pile of tiddlywinks off to school. And this particular pile of kids had to be in front of the school gates by 8:31 a.m. The school principal is a fascist. He locks the gate at 8:32 a.m. No excuses. He's more than that: he's a sadist. Even if you're right there while the teaching-assistant girl (or whatever she is) is turning the key, she won't open up. She's not allowed. He said so. That school is a hellhole.

It's the only school around here, though, so we can't say or do much about it. Don't be tardy. Rule number one.

Anyway, time was of the essence and I couldn't be worrying about school policies. I knew we had to get our asses into gear.

We got there two minutes early. The little ones at the Little School and the biggie at the Big School. The schools were right next to each other. Thank God! It made a big difference from last year, when they were far apart.

I ruffled their hair, gave them all moochio smoochios, and sent them in. That's when I heard the horn of Gaston's Jag. Beep beep. But haughtier than that.

He was waving to get my attention. I sauntered over to his stunning ride and bounced into the passenger seat, and we headed back to my trailer.

He was feeling frustrated that he'd missed the trip to school and offered to help me with the cleaning at Véro's therapist's place.

"What do you mean? Help me how?"

"Oh, just tell me what to do and I'll do it. It's as simple as that. There's not a chance I want to miss out on another exciting drama like the last time you had a job, Rosie!"

"Cricri!"

He knows I hate being called Rosie, but the poor guy can forget at times. "Sorry! Cricri!" replied Gaston as he pulled in front of the trailer.

"Listen up! It's not my fault if my last boss went and kicked the bucket, is it? There's no reason it'll happen again, knock on wood. Oh, why did you go and mention it, Gaston? You'll bring me bad luck!"

"It's just that I want to fill you in on my idea."

I ran into the trailer to change into a better work outfit. I slipped on a pair of flowery shorts, the lowest heels I could find, and one hell of an ugly T-shirt that covered all my assets. I didn't want to go causing any permanent damage to my good clothes. My good clothes are the super sexy pieces I get from Mimi as soon as she's done with them. And she's a real fashionista!

Before setting off, I made the most of having wheels by heading up to the fountain and filling as many plastic bottles as I had. I liked knowing that my trailer was all stocked up.

After putting all of Véro's boss's books in a big plastic bag, we set off to my new job—to Rachel Amar's place!

The cricket started chirping again. It was Mimi calling from the hospital.

"Hello? Yes? . . . Don't worry, I got it. Loud and clear. Class finishes at four p.m. . . . Sure. I'll keep you in the know, OK? Don't worry about a thing. Chin up, OK? You need your strength and all that for the operating table! Fine! See you then!"

Gaston stared at me quizzically. I didn't really have the energy for it, but I explained the whole deal.

"It's Émilie. She fell. Broken wrist. She's going under the knife tomorrow. Her back's all messed up too. Smithereens. She was supposed to have her kid, Léo, over. But now he's coming to my place until we know how things are."

"But your home isn't suitable! Your place is much too small, Cricri!"

"Too small? Are you kidding me or what? You should know more than anyone else that I have the biggest trailer in France! It was built for a traveling Gypsy king, Gaston!"

"That may well be the case, but I bet the Gypsy king didn't have as many kids as you! Why don't you come and spend a few days with me?"

"At the sleepy magic castle? Oh, I'd love to do that, but you know I hate taking advantage of people, Gaston!"

He sulked for about ten seconds and then launched into a lecture.

"Listen now, Cricri. I've had the most amazing idea. I'm going to make you famous. You're going to be a big famous singing sensation. Even bigger than that what's-her-face who made me as rich as Croesus. What do you say to that?"

"What do I say to that? I'd say that was mega-exciting," I replied sarcastically. "And how exactly are you going to go about it?"

"I've written a collection of poetry. I drew inspiration from a medieval Icelandic saga, and what I'd like to do next is make an opera based on my poems, you see? Your voice is every bit as good as Colette Magny's. Oh! We'll make a killing!"

Colette Magny? Like anyone outside of France or under the age of 106 has ever heard of her.

"You know," he continued, "I used to play guitar a little when I was a young buck! It'll be enough to get started. Enough to play a few chords and get a rhythm going at the beginning. We'll compose the tune together, and then we'll get a real musician."

"Hmm, great," I moaned, not the slightest bit convinced.

He'd come up with yet another silly plan for me to learn something new. And honestly! Has he lost his marbles? Medieval shit? Iceland? A killing? Doubtful.

"Hey! We're here!" I said, relieved I could change the subject. I didn't want to disappoint him, but I could hardly see the pair of us composing an opera together!

He continued, anyway. "Hear me, now, when I say 'opera,' we're not talking *La Traviata*, you understand? We're not talking Benjamin Britten either. I mean one of those big in-your-face pieces you'd see on Broadway in New York or the Strand in London. A bit like Andrew Lloyd Webber. Can you see what I mean? Huge audiences. Very popular. You're going to love it!"

What in the world? What was he on? I realized this was what my mother had been trying to tell me that morning with her song about the crazies! I think she was warning me that Gaston had lost it. *Dippy for feeling so lonely* . . . Either he was feeling lonely and was going to go all screwy on me, or he was going to drive me nuts with this opera business! Whichever came first, I supposed.

7

As Gaston pulled up outside Véro's boss's place, the conversation was forced to an abrupt end.

We read the copper plaque outside: "Rachel Amar. Psychiatrist and Psychoanalyst." It was glistening. Véro obviously did a good job here!

The building had an underground parking lot. Practical. Once we'd parked, we took the elevator to the fifth floor.

Opening the door was like entering another world. Just like Narnia.

There was an entrance hall with gorgeous waxed parquet flooring leading up to a humongous living room with a view over the winding roads of the old town, the Vieux-Port, the region's famous palm trees, and the neighboring islands. Wow. White walls. Next to no furniture. Two big sofas, two armchairs, a large coffee table, and one big-ass blue painting with nothing on it. All blue. Nothing even a bit abstracty. Nope. Nada. Only blue. What a load of crud! Whoever painted that thing was the King of Swindlers!

Gaston sat down in front of it and just gasped. I left him there while I went to explore the rest of the apartment.

A long corridor had a whole ton of doors coming off it. On one side were a shitload of bedrooms, each with its own bathroom like at a hotel. The corridor all looped around and you wound up in the same living area again.

I plodded past Gaston. The living area had an integrated dining space with a high-tech white open kitchen at the far end. I ventured back into the hallway. The other side boasted views onto a calm court-yard with a cherry tree in the center. There was what appeared to be some kind of waiting room with lots of magazines on a table and an office off to the side.

The office.

The sanctuary.

A white leather divan. Two gray armchairs in front of a heavy table made of waxed wood and covered in files. There was a statue thing on there the same color as the ridiculous painting in the living room. Except that this was *something*. A headless woman. She also didn't have any legs. Or arms. OK, so it wasn't much. Poor Rachel Amar. It didn't seem like she was too sharp, paying good money for crap like that. Why was everything the color of Smurfs in this place, anyway?

I tried to mimic Gaston. I sat down in front of the blue statue woman just to see what would happen. If anything. And something did.

Despite the cold, god-awful color scheme, there was something so calming about the room. It was inviting and relaxing. Maybe it was all the books everywhere.

I mean, they really were everywhere. Weighing down the shelves, spilling all over the place, in piles on the floor. In the middle of one of the shelves I noticed a huge plasma screen. Then I saw that some of the books were actually DVDs. There was also a laptop computer. I rec-ognized what it was because it had one of those apples that someone's taken a chomp out of. It was open and a cable linked it to the big TV.

I was attracted to it like a magnet, but rather than give in to my desperate need to watch a movie, I headed off to hunt down a vacuum cleaner. That's why I was there, after all.

On my way out, I noticed that a bowl of candy bars had been left on the table in the middle of the waiting room. The wrappers were the only splash of color in there. I tidied a couple of them away . . . by eating them . . . And whoosh—there go some in my purse for the babas. The bowl was really full and looked a bit messy. That's the excuse I was sticking to, anyway.

On the kitchen counter I noticed a small notebook and a basket. There was a fifty in the basket. The first page of the notebook was filled with small, tight, beautiful handwriting signed by Rachel Amar. It was a list of stuff Véro was supposed to do or know about while her boss was away.

At the top she'd written: "FOR VÉRONIQUE—MEMORANDUM."

As I informed you, I am embarking on a conference tour in the States.

My patients have all been informed of this via text and e-mail. However, please note that I have not had the time to verify whether everyone was in receipt of my messages. I will not always have full access to my e-mails while I am on tour, so please go ahead and read them from time to time, as I showed you. I have unblocked the password on my laptop and linked it to the television screen in my office. It is all very straightforward. I am counting on you to inform me via text of any emergency situations that may arise. Please explain to any patients who may present themselves for appointments that I am absent and will be in touch upon my return.

As far as the apartment is concerned, I have left some funds should you need to buy cleaning supplies and so on. There are some left in the cupboard. Please take the time during my absence to clean the whole apartment thoroughly—the windows, the curtains, the light switches, the doorknobs, behind the furniture, the back of the cupboards in the kitchen, etc.

The whole enchilada, right? I thought.
The note continued:

> I have received a court summons from a lawyer on the "Full Moon Pyromaniac" case. Apparently, the defendant refuses to speak with anyone but me. If the lawyer calls, please explain that I am away on business and will see them as soon as I get back.

"Hey, that's weird. That's what they were talking about on the radio this morning."

Gaston's attention was drawn away from the blue painting when he heard me muttering. "What was that?"

"There's some buffoon who's been setting fire to libraries or something. It was on the radio that he's keeping quiet. The whole *no comment* thing. He hasn't said anything to anyone since he got arrested."

"And?"

"I see here that Véro's boss has written something about him wanting to talk to her."

"Well, she really must be an expert in her field. If she's the only person this man will communicate with, then not only does she know her science, but she inspires confidence!"

"Oh, yeah! She does! She's weirdly on the ball! She writes fantabulous books. I love them."

"You love them? Cricri! Wow! You never fail to astound me! You read psychoanalytical reviews? I thought you were more of a comic-strip kind of girl. I thought you enjoyed those funny videos on the YouTube program."

"Well, sure, I like the psycho books too. I think they're real good fun, but I can't read them in the evening because they send me to Z-land in seconds flat. I can manage them during the day, though. Rachel Amar's books are incredible. They're like action films. It's just a pity there aren't any pictures."

"What's her area of expertise?"

"Criminals. Come on, let's go check it out."

We went into the office and picked up a book. There was an author biography on the last page.

Rachel Amar is a psychiatrist and psychoanalyst specializing in criminology. She teaches criminal psychology at the university level, and is often invited to give expert-witness statements in criminal trials, including the trial of the infamous Bratva Godfather. She is the author of several highly acclaimed works. Psychoanalysis and Criminality met with enormous success and won her the Freudian Psychoanalysis Academy Award.

"The word 'Freudian' means it's about a man called Freud who was also into this mind-reading stuff," I explained.

"Because you now know about Freud too, do you?" Gaston smirked.

I shrugged, not saying a word.

A newspaper article had been carefully cut out, neatly folded, and used as a bookmark. And there I saw *my* big Russian boss man from a previous big crazy adventure—handcuffed, with *my* buddies, Marco and Piotr, on either side of him, and all three were surrounded by a sea of cops as they made their way out of the courthouse. The godfather of the Russian Mafia was staring at the camera lens with pure hatred.

Under the photo was a caption: *The Bratva Godfather claims he's been framed, but Rachel Amar's expert-witness statement sees him sent away.*

"Look at that! It's incredible! Rachel Amar helped bring down my big nemesisis? Nemesi? Nemeses? Do you recognize them, Gaston?"

"Of course I do!"

"We're going to become fast friends, me and this Rachel Amar. We're on the same side!"

"Gosh! They must have it in for her, though!" exclaimed Gaston.

"I know! It's because of her that they're all serving the max!" I added, then nodded thoughtfully. "Yeah. She'll need to watch out with those guys. They don't forget these things easily. I bet she has a contract out on her. Well, never mind all that. I need to get a move on."

"I'll help you out with the dusting in the office."

"OK. Then we'll look through the fridge for any leftovers. No point throwing stuff out. After that, we can split!"

"No, no! Before *splitting*, we can read through my collection together. I want you to decide which poem we start out with. Listen, I think the easiest thing would be if we just started at the very beginning. We'll read it together and then you can take it with you and learn it by heart."

"By h-heart?"

I could hardly get the words out. I was having difficulty not telling him what I really thought about the whole opera idea, but I didn't want to hurt him.

"Um, Gaston, let's go easy on this whole learning-things-by-heart crap, what do you say? I don't have much of a memory!"

"Nonsense!" exclaimed Gaston. "Don't start all this up again, Cricri. I've had enough of you putting yourself down all the time. You have exactly the same memory capacity as everyone else. Take all those foolish pop singers out there! What about Petula Clark? If she can remember her words, then why the devil can't you?"

Petula Clark? His references were getting more and more obscure. Even my mother had never sent me anything by Petula Clark!

"But—"

"No buts, I'm afraid. It's learning it by heart or not at all."

Well, that's exactly it. I'd prefer the "not at all" option . . . But I'd never say something like that out loud to him.

"Do you think you can become a rich and famous star without learning your words? Come off it! Dream on, Cricri!"

When exactly did I say I wanted to become a rich and famous star? Never! What was going on with Gaston? I'd never seen him this excited about something.

"OK, OK . . . ," I whispered. "I'll do what I can, but don't go expecting any miracles."

He was satisfied with that answer. He took out a paperback from his pocket and started making copies of some of the pages using Rachel Amar's photocopier.

I got out what Sabrina calls the *thucky machine* and the rest of us call the vacuum cleaner and gave the rugs in the main rooms the once-over.

I swept the parquet and the kitchen floor before serving myself a strong and sweet espresso. I wanted to sit down and drink it with Gaston, but I didn't even know if he wanted one.

As I headed back to the office, with its books, armchairs, TV screen, and all the modern comforts, I could hear a man's voice. It was calm and collected and pretty chatty. I wondered who Gaston could possibly be speaking with. I hadn't heard the phone ring or the doorbell. I pushed the door open.

Gaston was lying down on the sacred couch, watching one of the tapes from Rachel Amar's private collection.

"Hey there, Gaston! Get a load of you! Is this what you call getting the dusting done?"

He gave me a wink while holding his finger to his lips.
"Shhhh."

At least he seemed to have forgotten that whole idea of me learning a poem. For the moment.

8

Gaston pointed to the video. On the screen was a guy who was the spitting image of James Franco, but an intellectual version, sitting in what appeared to be a real comfortable chair as a journalist interviewed him. He was speaking in a soft voice about an assembly of . . . of students, maybe? Something like that?

He certainly didn't speak very clearly. The female journalist was lapping up every word, though. She looked like she was just about ready to eat him up whole. She didn't know how to hold herself properly. She was drinking in his words, coming across as a bit desperate, twisting her hair around her finger nervously, sticking her teeny boobs out as far as she could manage. I'd never seen such an obvious crush!

I was intrigued and moved farther into the room to get a better look. I sat down in Rachel Amar's chair, behind her huge desk, and put down my little espresso cup.

The James Franco wannabe—tall, handsome, crew cut, cute glasses—appeared distracted, lost in his thoughts, indifferent to the sexual tension surrounding him. He just spoke about his ideas as if he were simply thinking out loud.

"He's not a bad-looking fella, that one. But not my type. Doesn't do a thing for me, really."

Gaston rolled his eyes. "Goodness me! You're in love already! You don't even know who he is!"

"What's your problem, Gaston? Are you deaf? Didn't I just say I couldn't care less about the guy?"

He smiled his knowing smile. My oh my, that can be as annoying as shit!

The pretty young journalist was now speaking directly to the camera.

"Linus Robinson, the famous psychoanalyst, who has just described at length the theory of the Oedipus complex . . ."

She really accentuated her English accent when she pronounced his surname. *Robinson*. She couldn't have sounded more like a snooty hooty snobbity snob if she'd tried.

I couldn't stop giggling. I also couldn't resist imitating her fake English accent.

"Wobinsone! Wobinsone! Wobinsone! Wobinsone! What do you sound like? You sound like a weird little chatty batty birdy!"

She couldn't hear me (obviously), so she carried on yapping.

". . . has accepted our request to respond to our questions and to say a few words which will then go on record at the Freudian Academy . . ."

This snobby little bitch turned toward Linus and questioned him as if her life depended on it. It was all very over the top.

"Doctor Robinson . . . the Oedipus complex . . . blah, blah, blah?"

Linus Robinson answered slowly, and his strong Canadian accent was hard to miss. He sighed between sentences—big long sighs. In his eyes, it was clear to anyone with intuition to see how annoyed he was, bored even.

"As for Freud, he, hmm, wasn't afraid of saying how it is. He explained that there is no distinction between a mother and love. Hmm, not love, but attachment. And this is where the real question lies . . ."

I thought this broad was about to ask for his hand in marriage.

She interrupted him excitedly. "But what about the part about having sex with your mother? Do you think psychoanalysis can be an instrument used to talk about this?"

And that's when I exploded. It came on pretty fast. I was angry! I couldn't hold back! This was a scandal!

"She's coming on to him! My God! And she's coming on strong! I can't believe that! Look at her! I've never seen anything like it! How unprofessional can you get?"

"So what, Cricri? She has every right to be in love, hasn't she?"

I had to agree. What he was saying made sense.

Linus Robinson repeated what he'd just heard. He was dumbstruck—like he was thinking, *But how can someone come out with such garbage?* I couldn't even remember what question the journalist had asked, but I agreed with him 100 percent. That girl just didn't come across as credible. She didn't know her subject. In fact, she was talking a pile of bull, as far as I could tell.

"Sex with your mother . . . Um . . . ?" he repeated. His slight smile turned into a fit of laughter. "I find these terms so amusing, let me think. Excuse me . . . Uhhh . . . It's about a son's *relationship* with his mother . . ." Then suddenly, and fairly aggressively, he added, "It's a lot more complicated than that . . ."

I applauded, delighted by this. "Bravo! That sure did shut her up! All righty . . ."

Gaston had to have his say at this point. "Cricri, you're not exactly being impartial here. And this young man is being more than a little condescending. All things considered, this woman, even though she is clearly under his charms and is not doing her job properly, doesn't deserve to be humiliated . . ."

"Give it a rest, Gaston! Stop taking sides!"

"Me? Taking sides?"

During Gaston's and my brief discussion, Linus Robinson had answered the questions but was no longer making eye contact with the journalist. He appeared precise, serious, sarcastic, and intimidated by the camera. So many emotions in such a short space of time.

Too cute for words.

He gestured to the camera to stop filming and scuttled away before the cameraman had a chance to obey him. It was a kind of natural authority. Firm but gentle at the same time.

He was out of there. The film stopped.

"Gaston, what can I say? This guy's a cutie, sure, but would I really go for him? Honestly, I don't care either way."

"I'm not buying it, Cricri. One doesn't have to be the sharpest tool in the box to notice that you could totally fall for someone like him."

"Whatever!"

"No, really. What did you think of him? Objectively?"

"Just stop it! You're being ridiculous! He's not bad, OK. But me, I . . ."

And the doorbell rang. I went to open up while Gaston stayed sprawled out on the couch.

9

A woman stepped in. She was striking—simply exquisite, with beautiful bronzed skin. She wore a superb long robe cut from a brightly colored, slightly shiny, orange-and-pink fabric. A huge flashy scarf covered her hair like a turban. She gave the impression that she wanted to come across as an African tribal woman. She wasn't one. But to each their own. It even looked like her cheeks were tattooed, but it must have been makeup. On her arm, she had a very expensive Longchamp bag, which didn't go at all with the rest of the outfit.

"Hello there," she said with a strong Parisian accent. "Are you new?"

I didn't know how to answer so I just nodded.

She continued, "Hmm, Eudoxie Apraksine. I have an appoi—"

"Um, with Rachel Amar, I'm sure—" I started to explain, but she just carried on.

"Of course with Rachel. I'm not quite unzipped to the point of not knowing what door I'm knocking at. Not yet, anyway. Yes. I have an appointment with her."

"Well, it's not possible. Listen, Madame Aspirin, I—"

"Apraksine!"

"As you wish. So, I was just saying, Madame Asspiercing, I'm very sorry, but Rachel Amar is absent at the moment. You'll have to call her back in a few days to schedule another appointment. I don't know exactly when she'll be back."

"Oh no! I can't do without her! I really can't!"

"That's just the way these things go. Sorry. Nothing I can do. I'm just the maid—"

She hurried toward the psychologist's office, making a multitude of choking and spluttering noises. She was slightly taken aback when she saw Gaston spread out like a corpse on the couch.

"Am I early or late here? Where's the shrink? She's here, right?"

Gaston stood up hastily. He was clearly embarrassed. "No, it's just that—"

I picked up where I'd left off, speaking drily. "I've told you everything there is to know. Rachel Amar isn't here. She's gone away on business for a few days. I'm the maid, Maldonne. Pleased to meet you. She asked me to make sure all her patients were in the know. She also mentioned something about calling you to set up another appointment when she got back."

"Her maid? Wrong!"

"Wrong? How's that?"

"I know her maid! Her name is Véro. She's shorter than you, petite, brunette, sweet little thing."

I glanced at Gaston. Boy, this was going to take some explaining. She spotted the way we'd eyeballed each other and now appeared to be very much intrigued by the whole situation. She peered over at the desk and saw my coffee cup in front of the big chair.

"Very well, very well. I understand exactly what's going on and I find your attitude very impolite!

"How's that?"

"Is that all you can say?"

Now, I really hate it when people make that sort of remark. If anyone's going to speak like that to others, it sure as hell better be me. Everything was ass-backward here and I didn't like it.

"Listen. This is all a bit complicated to explain. Actually, I'm replacing—"

"I knew it! You're replacing Amar!"

I couldn't get my head around what she was saying and smiled. "No! The other one! I'm replacing Véro! I'm replacing the maid!"

"Of course, sure, I believe you! And you know what? I'm replacing a patient. And this is very good timing, because I love when the couch is already nice and warm."

And without further ado, she banged her butt cheeks down on the exact spot Gaston had just left.

The Patsy Cline song came back to me: "I'm bonkers for trying . . ." That's exactly what this was. No point in trying! It was high time everyone just got the hell out of there and left me alone. They were driving me over the edge.

Gaston studied me, clearly waiting to see how I was going to get myself out of this situation.

I decided to tackle him first. "Gaston, when you've finished getting on my nerves, you let me know, OK?"

I stopped, not saying another word. The woman had closed her eyes. Gaston backed out of the room and made his way toward the kitchen.

"Coffee for everyone?" he cried out from a distance.

Neither of us replied. He tried a little joke.

"Don't all shout out at once!"

Our silence persisted. The woman opened her eyes and saw me just standing there between the couch and the desk, a terrified look on my face.

"Sit down, would you?" she said. "It would be more orthodox, you know?"

"Well, seeing as I've told you that one, I'm not a shrink, and two, I'm not replacing Rachel Amar, I have no place sitting behind this desk."

But something in the way I spoke must not have quite rung true with her. Maybe she sensed that I wanted to play shrink, like little girls play shop. One thing was certain—she didn't believe my protests.

"Now, now! I'm not going to eat you. If this is your first appointment, I can understand that you're a little nervous. Please, take a seat and let me resume telling you what's been happening."

For reasons unknown to me, I obeyed. I sat behind the desk and stirred my (now cold) coffee.

She started yapping. "Well, I'll sum up for you who I am and why I'm here. So, I'm Eudoxie Apraksine, but I have another name, Bintou, if it's easier for you. I don't use it very often, though. I am the unhappy mix of poor white Russian descendants and generous African ancestors who made a fortune in the diamond mines. Apparently they collaborated with the French government *in situ*. This is why I have to have these appointments with Amar. I'm having an identity crisis. Also, I have had some serious burnout issues with my job, but for totally different reasons."

I was starting to get interested in this story of hers. That's always been my problem. I can't resist a good story.

"How do you know when you've burned out? What happens? Do you faint? Go mental? What?"

"Well, I don't really know, actually. I don't know how to explain it. All I know is that I can't even handle going anywhere near my office. As soon as I approach the building, I just start scratching my skin. Scratching, scratching . . . Scratching everywhere. And I feel like I'm going to suffocate. One day, I just told myself that enough was enough. I arrived early one morning, as usual, then spun around and traipsed straight back home again. I couldn't look at their stupid faces any longer, listen to their voices, hand in same old stories, lick the same assholes belonging to the same pricks. Excuse my language. I turned my back on it all. I didn't believe in the job anymore. And it's a real shame, you know. I mean, these people were my friends. I really liked them. I still do."

"What do you do for a living?"

"Journalist. But now that I've quit my job because of my never-ending depression, I have a heap of money difficulties."

"Do you have any money coming in at all?"

"No, nothing at all. Well, no direct revenue. Not a salary as such. I have my shares and the money from my rental properties, but I don't want to touch that any more than I have to."

"I can help you there! I know the ins and outs of the state welfare system by heart!"

"That's very kind of you. I forget that shrinks can also be a bit like social workers too, can't they? It's all part and parcel of the service."

"Oh, I've always been like that. Except that I'm not a shrink. Or a social worker. In fact, I'm what they call a welfare mom!"

"Wow! Times must be so tough! It's really very kind of you, but I don't think I'm going to need any help with welfare money or unemployment and all the rest of it. I own a lot of property and I don't think I'd qualify for assistance. Anyway, I've taken up Thai boxing."

That was a curveball. She'd certainly gotten me thinking. It didn't seem like she needed a shrink at all! She needed one a hell of a lot less than I did, at any rate! Her ideas and her words were all over the place, but she was sane enough.

"Do you have kids?" I asked.

"No. My ex-husband was ashamed of me because of it. He's a big negotiator. Egyptian. I mean, he's a bigwig in negotiating. Good at his job. Physically, he's small. Not big at all. Honestly, with the life I lead, I've never had the time for kids. It's something my ex always understood, being a pretty nice guy, but he was ashamed of me all the same."

"Why did you split up if he was so nice?"

"He didn't want me to go to Sydney to do a story on heart transplants with this young journalist colleague of mine. I hadn't even told him I was crazily in love with this colleague. Hook, line, and sinker. It must have just felt off to him."

I was stuck for a reply. What could I say to all that? "Hmm . . ."

"Anyway, now I have serious problems making ends meet on a daily basis. It's been like that for a while now."

"I have a job I could offer you. It's short term, though."

"OK! I can edit and proof articles. I can give private lessons to history majors, art majors, or any other subject, really, as long as it's in the humanities. I can run writing workshops. I was a professional scriptwriter at one point. I've also helped people study for college entrance examinations. It's not one of my favorite things to do, and a bit of a step down the career ladder, but when needs must—"

"Actually, I wasn't thinking about any of that stuff."

Her shoulders dropped. "What were you thinking of?"

"A friend of mine is hoping to find a waitress because his main girl is currently in the hospital. I sometimes work shifts at his place, but I can't at the moment because I'm helping Véro out here."

"Waitress?"

There was a long silence. She eyed me suspiciously and seemed to be waiting for me to go into further detail. All of a sudden, her face brightened.

She broke the quiet spell with a loud, "I get it!"

Again, I had no response. How do you react to this kind of statement? What was there to get? She interrupted my bewildered silence.

"Is this some kind of new method?"

"What do you mean? No, it's not a new method! I don't know why you won't believe me, but never mind. I can't keep battling you like this. It's getting tiring! Why exactly do you need to see Rachel Amar again? Oh yeah, the burnout blues and all that bull, right?"

"Basically, I was shot to pieces following this investigation into something . . . well, something pretty dangerous, to put it simply. I reacted badly, and now I'm at a juncture between shame and fear and I've lost confidence in myself."

Finally! Now I was in familiar territory. I didn't have much confidence in myself either.

"And what sorts of effects has this had on you?" I asked. "Other than you not wanting to show up for work these days? Because all this seems pretty humdrum and ordinary to me."

"Well, other than that, I go out shopping quite a lot and buy tons of stuff on my different credit cards. Buy now, pay later. This is why I'm in massive debt these days. You wouldn't believe how far in the red I am on my checking account. And that puts me in a blind panic, because it means I have to start drawing money out of my savings and investments."

"Don't sweat it! There's nothing I don't know about being in debt. I don't have a magic solution or anything, but there is one thing I can tell you: when you're in debt, you get to stay in touch with folks! My old boss told me that just before he died. If you owe people money, they ain't going nowhere, right?"

I had no clue how to help her out of her sitch, but I didn't want to just dump her ass—it'd be like leaving a lizard out in the rain, or something like that, like my momma used to say. It would be just awful. So, I made some shit up on the spot.

"I want you to do everything I tell you, and to do it exactly as I say. You're going to go to the grocery store, just as everything's closing. Go take a look at those who *really* don't have any money and what they do when they have to eat. Then gather the ingredients to make a dish from your country without spending a penny, and come back here tomorrow and cook it."

"What? I can't even cook an egg!"

"That's exactly the idea. Go do something you've never done and get over this lack of self-worth! Allow yourself to just go with this, Madame Saccharine!"

"My name is—"

"Whatever, it doesn't really matter. Stop trying to control everything." I was pretty proud of my spiel. It turned out I was fairly convincing when it came to psychobabble.

She had what was obviously her grumpy face on. "You're very funny," she said. "You really are hilarious! And which country would that be?"

"What do you mean?"

"When you say 'a dish from my country,' do you mean Egypt, Russia, France, or some unspecified African nation?"

"It's up to you!"

"OK. I'll choose one. I'm willing to give this a go! I'm sure you're right about all this, but I find you very hurried. You don't leave much room for discussion."

"That's exactly what I am. Hurried. I don't have a lot of time. I need to finish cleaning this office. So come on. It's time to get out of here!"

She dragged her ass slowly out of the office and made her way to the living room, where I could hear her chatting with Gaston.

10

As I dusted the books on the shelves, I couldn't resist putting Linus Robinson on replay. I must have pressed the wrong button, because instead of Linus, I got a man sobbing his guts out. He was lying on the couch in that very office! OK, so Rachel Amar must film some of her sessions.

I was interested in what sort of advice she gave, how she went about her job, so I settled down into her comfy office chair, put my feet up on her desk, and watched away.

The guy was in pretty good shape and wore a black turtleneck sweater, jeans, and Nikes. He had a square jaw and piercing black eyes. Even though he was on the couch, I could tell he was fairly tall. He wore glasses, like the intellectual type, and seemed a gentle soul. But what did I know?

His name and the date of the session appeared at the bottom of the screen. Alexandre Laroche. His voice lacked energy. It was meek and irritating. He went on and on and on about how terrible he was at everything, how his life was one big failure. He moaned that he had no friends, no girlfriend, and nobody ever wanted to do anything with him. This went on for a half hour, but it could have been summed up in just one sentence: "I can't pick up women." And there was something about nights at the Carlton, a big five-star hotel on the coast.

What was that all about? I fast-forwarded a little and figured out he worked in some sort of Internet thing. He'd created a company and it was a big deal and he was a hotshot. He had lots of clients and organized swingers' nights for them, or sex parties . . . I didn't quite get it. Was that really a good way of winning new contracts? Probably. Anyway, despite all the sex, he dreamed of true love.

The session came to an abrupt end, the image froze, and then Rachel Amar's face appeared on-screen. Great! Just what I wanted to see.

Rachel had a closed face and a timid expression. She seemed reserved. Her hair was cut in a straight bob. She had an orderly style, a professional way about her, but with a soft look in her eyes.

She spoke directly to the camera in a serious tone. "Alexandre is currently blocked in an oppositional regressive phase and is suffering from suicidal tendencies. This anally retentive stage, in my opinion, will take a few years before it's finally dealt with. Unless he actually makes an attempt."

I let out a whistle. There were no two ways about it. This broad knew her stuff. She'd got it in one. Respect. It was a pity that everything she said wasn't going to actually help the kid any.

It was then that I figured something out. Rachel Amar, with all her brain-box knowledge, had a problem of her own.

The practicalities of it all.

I mean, once she'd deciphered what was wrong with someone, then what? With this guy, she was so sure of what she was saying and was obviously committed to him, but she wasn't providing any actual help. She wasn't intervening in any way. She was leaving him to talk too long, letting him do too much griping and bellyaching—hours and hours of it, by the looks of things. She didn't want to tell him what to actually *do*.

When he'd gone home and she was all on her own, filming her thoughts . . . Sure, she was great at what she did. No question. But with her patients? She was as good as useless.

I delved into her collection to see what other videos I could watch. It was the same old, same old with each film. One after another. Each one was someone with problems in life. They were people a lot like me and my friends—just the loaded versions of us. Rich whiners. Nothing like the screwball delinquents she had to work with in the court system. Nothing like the deranged criminals she talked about in her books.

I suppose she had to make a living, and dealing with rich whiners was the best option.

My stomach gurgled. I glanced at the time and realized I was running out of time! I'd have to find something to eat real quick and then scrub and polish the floor in the office before heading off to collect my chickadees from school.

Madame Gangrene (or whatever the heck her name was) was still yammering on and on with Gaston. They were also reading those middle-aged poems out loud. They'd underlined certain lines on Gaston's copies, highlighted some of the verses, and crossed words out here, there, and everywhere.

"We have to make the most dramatic passages really sing," she crooned.

My, my, my! Gaston had found himself a willing participant for his big opera project.

I pulled them out of their dreamworld so we could all grab a bite to eat. We finished off some leftovers from the fridge.

As we ate, Gaston read aloud the first poem they'd selected together. I had to repeat each line after him. He wanted me to start learning that shit already. This whole episode totally ruined my meal, let me tell you. I didn't enjoy a bite.

"I am the queen of weavers,
I am the queen of the weavers of peace.
My thread is held tight for the warrior that falls,
My thread is a shower of blood,
My thread is the thrown javelin.
I am the queen of weavers,
And I will weave a red thread.
Lances watered with blood are my trade,
My needles are blades,
I weave with arrows on the cloth of peace.
This needle rustles when swords are drawn.
Shields will crack,
The axe will dance,
The helmet will yield.
I weave with arrows on the cloth of peace.
I will move forward,
I will enter the fray when our friends gather,
I weave with arrows on the cloth of peace.
Our warriors will look upon shields of blood, broken
    skulls, dismembered bodies.
I weave with arrows on the cloth of peace,
There where floats the banner of the brave!"

So that's the poem?

I had to tell him, "It doesn't even rhyme, Gaston. You have no business going around calling that poetry. Even less business calling it a song. Get real."

I think I upset him.

"Yes, I thought it over for a long time," he said, "and finally decided on a poem that doesn't rhyme. We'll add the rhythm it needs once we have the music."

I continued reading the text aloud just to please him, but I knew he was on course to fail with this humdinger. Weaving women and rustling needles were no way to get views on YouTube.

After we'd all finished munching, I said, "I have some odds and ends to finish up with before I'm out of here."

I cleared away the plates and cups into the dishwasher and scrubbed down the office floor. I took the fifty that Amar had left Véro and we all skedaddled.

The depressed journalist had a bit of a bounce in her step! She'd reloaded her batteries. Recharged them? Whatever the phrase was. She waved warmly at us as she left the elevator. We went all the way down to the parking lot.

We had to get a move on.

11

After we picked up the girlios, I asked Gaston to drop us off at the supermarket so I could buy a few things. I was expecting a teenage boy on top of all the other human and feline mouths I already had to feed. That meant a whole load of food.

Before I stepped out of the car, Gaston slipped a photocopy into my purse. "I'm going to ask that you recite this to me tomorrow," he whispered, giving me an encouraging wink.

Oh, easy peasy lemon squeezy, I'm sure. It's not like I have anything else to do.

It was the wrong time of day to be grocery shopping. School was out, people had just finished work. I'd never seen crowds like it. There were kids everywhere—and not just mine. Sabrina was sticking close to me, helping push the cart. She had a very serious and grown-up attitude. I liked it.

My twinniebobs were running around like headless chickens. They couldn't have been more delighted. We don't often go to the big supermarket, and they love the place! They play hide-and-seek or hopscotch in the aisles, jumping around and hiding behind shelves. They adore the bright colors and the strange labels. There's nothing they don't like about it.

I grabbed what I needed to make refried beans and rice, and I threw it all into the cart. It's an incredible Haitian recipe that my good buddy Ismène taught me. I also threw in some pasta, dried beans, chickpeas, lentils, potatoes, flour, cans of tuna, and eggs. I didn't have much in the way of fruits and vegetables, but this was food to fill the belly. Food to stop us from starving. Food that didn't break the bank. I also had to get cleaning shit for Amar. I mean, that's what the money was for, right?

Checkout number four seemed the least busy. As I waited, I read some of the headlines on the newspaper rack. The kids caught up and joined me in line. There was a large photo of a rocker type on the front page of one of the local papers. He was pretty hot, with nice stubble and Johnny Hallyday eyes. The caption read: "The upcoming trial of Victor Falso, aka the Full Moon Pyromaniac, is set to begin."

I whispered, "It's that Full Moon Pyromaniac again!"

Sabrina grabbed me by the sleeve and cried out, "Thow me, Mommy! Thow me!"

She was hopping around. I gave her the paper just to calm her down, and she snatched it eagerly. She reads quite well these days, even if she doesn't always understand the meanings of the words. She sometimes reads the beginning of the word and invents the end. But I think it's kind of cute to do your own thing.

As she spoke, the twinnipats followed her every word. She started chanting, "Pirate Anorak! Pirate Anorak! He'th a pirate with a fanthy coat! It'th a big coat they wear in the north! Gathton hath one for hith tripth to Ithland and Greenland! Pirate Anorak!" The little ones joined in. "Pirate Anorak! Pirate Anorak!"

They went on and on for what seemed like forever. All three of my kids have a thing about inventing songs. They've all got a gift for it too!

I quickly understood why the checkout line wasn't all that long. The young Asian girl sitting behind the counter was in tears. She was supposed to be swiping and smiling, not blubbering like a loon! She sniffed and wailed, and whoever noticed moved away to join another line.

I listened in on her conversation with the customer at the front. The woman had a cart full to bursting, and it was taking ages. What it all boiled down to was some hopeless love story with a guy and she missed her family. She wanted to go back to South Korea, but her heart was breaking at the same time.

She was rabbiting on about all this between sniffles. Every couple of minutes, she'd get out a tissue from her pocket and blow her nose loudly. There were a few people waiting behind me now because the other lines had gotten too long. I noticed a little guy, a skinny, runty type who hadn't seen a razor for a good couple of days, with a rocker-style bandanna on his head and a few hairs remaining up top but nothing to write home about. He was rooting around in his cart, totaling the number of six-packs of beer he was buying. Something about him rang a bell. He kept giving me disapproving glowers. That's why I'd first noticed him.

Sabrina couldn't take her eyes off him either.

But then all my attention was drawn once again to the checkout girl. I really wanted to butt in, to reassure her, if only to get the line moving.

"It's normal to have lovers' quarrels at your age! Don't worry!"

But this just made the tears come faster. She cried out louder than any of us was comfortable with.

"Me Mathieu want me marry!"

I must have looked like I didn't have the foggiest, because Sabrina translated. "Mathieu wanth to marry her, Mommy."

Well, that cleared things up. Sabrina knows how to translate from any language. As long as the speaker is saying something emotional, she knows what they mean. She must have some sort of built-in software plugged into her heart.

So the girl's big worry was that some fella called Mathieu wanted to marry her?

"Hey! That's fabulous news!" I exclaimed.

12

The checkout girl told me her whole life story. I didn't understand much of it, though, because of all the bawling . . .

So my Sabrina explained, giving us all a running commentary.

"Her father thayth the'th a traitor to her people and that the'll end up being a hooker in Gangnam. What'th a hooker, Mommy?"

Whoa, there! I really didn't like that. First off, I don't like my kids using bad language. Secondly, how was I supposed to explain this particular profession to my little girl? I don't know if I'll ever be able to tell Sabrina the family secret—how Grandmommy Ruth went on the game after she managed to escape being hunted down by the Nazis during World War II.

"It's a bit like a nurse, sweetiepops. Or a nanny, you know? But for grown-ups. And Gangnam . . ." *It would have been easier if you'd just asked about Gangnam!*

"I know about it already. It'th in that thong! Tho, why doethn't her popth want her to become a nanny? A Gangnam-thtyle nanny?"

"Well, she didn't come all the way to France and learn French just to go back to her own country and be a babysitter!"

She seemed satisfied enough with this response. I turned back to the checkout girl.

"What's your name?"

"Saejin, pearl of universe."

"Thaejin, which meanth 'Pearl of the Univerth,'" repeated Sabrina.

"Yeah, I understood this time, sweetie." I turned to Saejin. "Listen, OK? Your daddy's just jealous, that's all!"

"Yes, but other problem? I pregnant."

By some miracle, I'd understood again. I think everyone in the line had understood, actually. The woman in front of me, as well as the customers behind, were all captivated. They had been following this conversation as if we were in the latest episode of some daytime soap opera—some were even making comments and giving their opinions.

After a few more exchanges and a couple of Sabrina's translations, I felt I was in a position to give some good advice to this poor girl.

The crowd was all hanging on my every word. The weirdo guy behind us was starting to lose patience, though. He was muttering. I think he thought I couldn't hear. But I've got great hearing.

"Is this some kind of joke? A hidden-camera gag? Are we all going to have to spend the night here or what? She's giving consultations here now! That way, she doesn't have to put it on the books. The tax man doesn't find out and the rest of us pay for it! Wow. Doesn't anyone earn an honest living these days?"

What was this jerk-off blabbering on about? Another one escaped from the asylum.

The woman he was talking to stared wide-eyed at him, eyebrows almost reaching her hairline. He was getting angrier by the second.

"Come on! Get your ass into gear, Amar! There's shit waiting for you outside. Your destiny! Get a move on! You're toast. Joan of Arc toast. The butcher's waiting for you."

He guffawed and the people around him said, *"Shhhh."* I wondered why he was talking about Amar. Was it a coincidence, or did he really know Rachel Amar? Did he think I was Amar? And what was the Joan of Arc talk all about?

People were sighing and tsking, but it was just getting him more rattled.

"That girl's been holding up this whole line for the last hour! I'm not making that up, right? She ought to just go back to Nam—then she wouldn't be having any more of her so-called problems!"

Everyone appeared outraged.

A woman screamed in his face, "She's Korean, not Vietnamese!"

Then it seemed like everyone got involved.

"Just hush up! How is she supposed to think clearly?"

"If you're in a hurry, change lines! Holy cow!"

He rolled his eyes and looked wigged out.

My turn in line had come by this point, and once the girl had scanned all the items, I realized the total went over my budget. I had to put a couple of cans back. It really wasn't a big deal. My welfare check was due any day, and I was going to earn quite a little windfall with all this housework at the therapist's place. Just in the nick.

I left Saejin with some encouraging words as I put my groceries in a big plastic bag. Once the conversation had come to a natural conclusion, I flounced out of there with my three babachicks hot on my heels.

Sabrina was asking me heaps more questions, but they didn't seem particularly important. I was only half listening. I was more concerned about the rice-and-beans recipe.

"Mommy, why did the man leave all hith thopping in hith cart without paying?"

"I don't know, darling."

"Well, I'm going to athk him, then."

"Girls, you know we don't talk to strangers, right? Especially if they offer you candy."

"Yeth, we know, Mommy."

"Candy! *Candy!*" the twins started to shout.

They're always a little bit behind Sabrina. Only a couple of seconds or so, but still. They're little. They don't always get it.

"What's with the hubbub, bubs? We've left the store now, kiddies. Listen to me now! We've got other things to be getting on with. Come on! Let's go!"

The two youngest ran ahead of me. Every now and again, they'd stop to scrutinize something on the ground, singing their little heads off as they did so.

Sabrina held on to my wrist. My hand was gripping our groceries, so my wrist was her only option.

"Mommy," she said, "I don't want you to worry, OK? You know I'm good when it comth to bad guyth, right? You jutht let me know if you need my help."

"Yes, my sweet pea. Same here. I can totally help you out too if you need it," I replied without really paying much attention. I was on autopilot.

We'd left downtown and were now venturing into no-man's-land, where my trailer is parked.

I happened to spot the weird guy from the supermarket. He was whistling and carrying a purse thing with a shoulder strap. What a sad sack! What a rudo! He must have lived in the housing projects farther toward the outskirts of the city. He was totally giving us all the once-over as he sauntered past us. Who did he think he was? Just as I was about to say something, he darted face-first into a street lamp. I actually heard a metallic twang as he crumpled down onto the sidewalk. We all watched as a whole pile of odds and ends fell from his special man-bag.

I started to wonder whether this freak had followed us home, but I tried to control my extra-strength paranoia. *Cool it, Rosie. He's just a nobody. It's a coincidence and nothing more. This fella must live around here and that's all there is to it. I'm loony for trying . . .*

Sabrina ran to the guy and helped him pick everything up. She's such a helpful little angel, that one.

We were nearly home.

"Come on, my girl!"

13

It was just as we were approaching the trailer that I spotted a miserable-looking teen, as lanky as they come, sitting on the cinder blocks that were supposed to pass for steps leading up to my front door. And he wasn't alone. A few feet away, a few other teenage boys were playing soccer with an empty beer can.

Oh, gee whiz! I'd totally forgotten to pick up Léo.

I spotted an empty bottle of vodka on the ground. Unacceptable! And these buddies of his seemed like a little bunch of losers. Riffraff! Check out my language . . . I'm getting old now.

The twins ran to Léo. They're both so in love with him. It's kind of cute. He's a real pretty boy, despite the fact that a smile almost never crosses his lips.

They jumped onto his lap and clung to him. There was no escaping.

"Hey there, Léo!" I shouted. "You been waiting long? It's nice of you to come and keep us girls company awhile!"

I was trying to joke with him, but he didn't laugh. He grumbled something and stood up with all the grace of a gangly adolescent. He was just your average high-schooler—mute, shy, and in a permasulk.

The other young fellas stopped kicking the can and stared at us. They didn't have anything to say either.

"Hey! Your moms never taught you to say hello, huh?" I asked them with a sunny tone, smiling ear to ear.

A few of them mumbled, "Hey."

One of them, the smallest, flexed his muscles, or what he obviously thought were his muscles. He must have considered himself the head honcho.

"And your problem is what exactly?" he asked me aggressively.

Léo appeared embarrassed.

I didn't know how to respond, so I came back with the same thing. "What about you? What's your problem?" He was attempting to out-stare me, so I added, "Do you want my goddamn autograph, you little dope?"

He scoffed. "Autograph? You're a freak show, woman! You been on *The Voice* or something? You don't even know who you're talking to!"

"Sure I do! I'm talking to a little ratbag! Piss off, dickwad! Go have your fun someplace else. And don't let me catch you around here again."

He found that hilarious. He wasn't going anywhere.

The others talked to him. "Come on, Dorian. Let's leave this bitch and her scrubby little kids alone and go see that package lugger. You know, that little wreck of a thing. We can punk her! It'll be awesome!"

I noticed that Léo pressed his lips together when he heard this last remark. His fists were balled up.

I had no idea who or what they were talking about. *Wreck of a thing? Package lugger?* Was this newfangled streetspeak? Whatever it was, Léo looked agitated to the max!

I unlocked my front door. Pastis was giving us the eye from the little kitchen window. He gave me the impression that nothing in the world could possibly worry him. As cool as a cat, like they say.

The twins ran into our little house as soon as the door swung open, and Sabrina hopped to my side. Since he looked like he didn't know whether he was coming or going, I told Léo to follow me in.

"Léo, come here!" Sabrina said.

"What?" snapped Léo.

"I've got a thecret. I know a man called Pirate Anorak! He wearth a coat and he hath loth of matcheth and lighterth. That'th real dangerouth, ithn't it? Léo? I thaw he hath a bag thing for them! A cathe! Very dangerouth!"

"What are you saying there, sweetie?" I asked.

She quickly replied, "Nothing, Mommy. I didn't thay a word!"

"Come on in, then. I want you all inside now. Hop to it! Twinniebobs, you already said hello to Léo, didn't you?"

In chorus, they said, "Heeeellllllllooooooo Lééééééééoooooooo agggggaaaaaaiiiinnnn!"

"Good girls! OK, so we'll all have a snack and then it's homework time!"

I put a big crusty loaf down on the table with a tub of margarine. I took a box of powdered milk out of the cupboard and put my red kidney beans to soak.

The kiddies forced Léo to sit down and butter their bread for them. He sighed, but I could tell he was enjoying it.

14

Weirdly, Pastis stayed by the window. He didn't want to take part in the little feast we had going on.

"Why isn't Pastis over here begging us for milk today?" I wondered out loud.

"It'th nothing, Mommy," garbled Sabrina before whispering something in Léo's ear.

"What?" asked Léo, which obviously bothered Sabrina. She couldn't handle not being listened to properly. "What are you talking about, Sabrina?"

She stared at Léo reproachfully.

Emma blurted out, "Léo, it's true what Sabrina is saying! There is a Pirate Anorak! He's for real!"

"Enough's enough with all this storytelling. It's time for you to get out your homework. What have you all got today?" I turned to Léo. "What about you? Do you have homework to get on with? How does that stuff work in high school? Do you have a notebook I need to sign?"

He murmured something and I didn't understand a word of it. I cleared the table and everyone got out their pencils and notebooks and got on with their work. This was great stuff happening here! Sabrina, as always, showed just how studious she was and applied herself 101 percent to her assignment. The babas drew circles and lines and colored the spaces between the words. Léo had a couple of worksheets with some math problems. He was definitely sulking, but he was at least making attempts to solve them in between pressing buttons on his phone.

I turned on the radio and set about peeling some onions. Soon enough, along came a couple of tears.

"You crying again?" asked Lisa as she started to cry herself. In sympathy maybe?

"Oh, it's nothing! It's the onions again! It's normal. I'll have pretty eyes afterward! You just wait and see! Who wants to try some?"

Loud screams and shrieks of protest filled the trailer as I shoved onion slices under their little noses. They howled like hyenas.

I went back to my little kitchenette and started browning the onion with some garlic in the pan. After a short while, a delicious smell filled the room. I added two mugs of rice and drained the beans.

"So do you have problems in math?" I asked Léo, trying to pull him out of his silence. "Shitty grades?"

As I shuffled past him, I tapped him on the head with my spatula. He shook his head and gave me a begrudging grin.

"Hey, don't mess with the hair! I'm not five years old, you know?"

"Oh, you can straighten it back up! No probs! So, your math isn't too hot. What about your French? Where are you at with that?"

"I got a D."

"There you go! Better than math, then!" I said, hoping he'd feel encouraged. I rolled my eyes, so he'd know I was just kidding around, but he didn't take it too well. He turned a bright shade of red and pushed away his books.

"I'm sick of all this bull. I don't like school! I can't handle it!"

The twinnos stopped tittering and watched him carefully. Sabrina was still sulking and wouldn't even look at him. He started to play with my kitchen knife while I hunted down a couple of coriander seeds Ismène had given me and were kicking around in a jar somewhere.

"You'll just have to concentrate a little more, that's all."

"That's exactly it, though! I can't! I'd like to get better grades. Of course I would. I'm not doing this on purpose. But my teacher doesn't seem to care whether I understand this stuff or not. If I ever ask a question, he says I should've been listening. What kind of teaching is that? The crappy kind, that's what."

"Listen, I'll go have a word with him. I'll go with Mimi and we'll see if he's as bananas as you say he is."

"Oh no, please don't go. We'll look like the Brady Bunch!"

"Well, I reckon Mimi would rather you were a Brady Bunch kid than a bonehead. I'm sorry I can't help you more with your work, but I'm not much use at all when it comes to math. All I can do is add up my change when I have some at the end of the month." And it's never as easy as I was making out.

"So you don't get it either? Your brain's fried too?"

"If I'd been more attentive in school, I wouldn't be where I am today. The only job I can get is as a replacement maid for a girlfriend. Still, I gotta do what I gotta do! And fish is what gets fried, by the way . . . fish, potatoes, mmmm! But not brains, OK? Not mine, anyhow. Not even with math! My French is pretty good—at least, I think it is, even though I had to repeat tenth grade four times. But I've read a lot of comic books, and I think that helps."

He stood up in a sudden burst of action.

"No more! I can't do it! I wanna quit school!"

"Oh, no chance of that, bud. You have to go. The law says so. Don't sweat it, we'll find someone to help you out with all this. I've got some good friends. Some pretty cute ones too! I'm sure one of them can get you all hot and bothered about math!"

He was kind enough to crack a smile at my sorry attempt at humor. Good kid. Deep down. I took this moment of light relief to ask, "So what were your friends saying about a *package lugger*? What does that even mean? What sort of packages? And a *wreck of a thing*? What's that? Can't I even kick it with the kids anymore or what?"

He gave me a suspicious look.

"Why are you asking me this all of a sudden?"

"Oh, I'm a busy Nelly! A nosy bee!" I could tell he didn't like my out-of-the-blue grilling, but I continued all the same. "And dizzy bodies like me can lend a hand with these sorts of things, usually . . ."

"Oh, really? How's that?"

"I don't know, because you won't tell me what's going on!"

There was a loaded silence. The little ones were still watching us. Sabrina was examining Léo—every word he spoke, every move he made. It felt like a secret was about to be let out of the bag.

"Oh, it's nothing. Just a chick."

"Well, is it nothing? Or is it a chick?"

He chuckled again.

"It's a girl. We see her sometimes after school, usually on the way back to our cribs, see? She dresses kinda all screwy. Like some old gramma. But I don't think it's really her fault. And she's so gorgeous, it doesn't really matter, anyway."

He blushed crimson as all the details fell from his lips.

This was love! A high school romance! Could it possibly be that young girl from yesterday? She did dress horribly. Like a tramp—I mean tramp like a homeless person, not a hooker. And she was so pretty, it's true.

Pastis interrupted this intimate moment of sharing and caring and jumped heavily onto my neck. *So* typical. My little Sabrina got all jellybags and came over to join us. She wanted some attention from Pastis too and tried climbing up my back to get it.

"Did you finish your homework, precious child?"

"No, but I want Pathtith to give me a quick cuddle. Why doeth he alwayth climb on your neck and not mine?"

"Because my neck is bigger. Pastis could easily fall off your neck, couldn't he? And you know he's super smart, right?"

I sat down and put Sabrina on my knee. She nodded with me, but I could see she was still upset. I think she was jealous that Léo and I were having a serious conversation that didn't include her, and she was just using Pastis as an excuse to sulk about it.

Emma had to have her input too. "Pastis jumped on you because he doesn't need to keep watch now! Pirate Anorak has gone!"

"What's with all the pirate stuff? Did I miss something?" I asked.

"Oh, jutht ignore her. Emma maketh it all ath the goeth along!" Sabrina said as she stared wide-eyed at her little sis.

"Not true! Not true!" Emma protested. "I never make things up! It's you! You're the one who told me about the pirate!"

Sabrina grabbed hold of Pastis's ears and pulled them. Apart from a little meow, Pastis didn't react.

"Naughty cat! Don't thcratch!"

"Sabrina, leave Pastis in peace! And be careful—he will scratch you if you annoy him! He's a real-life cat, not a stuffed toy!"

"Naughty cat! Don't scratch!" repeated Lisa.

"No, Litha. He didn't really thcratch me! You thaw that he didn't!"

"Be careful, Sabrina! He's scratching Sabrina!" shouted Emma, making everyone laugh. She hadn't followed what had happened, but wanted to protect her sister.

This unfaltering loyalty snapped Sabrina out of her moany-pony episode, and she stretched over the table to grab her books and resumed her homework from the comfort of my lap. I could tell she still had one ear open, though, to listen to me chat with Léo.

Léo had clearly thought all the cat-scratching business had gotten him off the hook, but I turned my attention back to him.

"So the packages?"

He sighed. "Well, this one time, we followed her and saw that she was dropping off shopping bags filled with . . . something . . . at people's houses. She'd go to a house or an apartment, knock, go in, and then come out minus a package."

So now I was sure. It was the same girl. What was I supposed to do? Tell him that I knew where she lived? And that she lived with a nut job of a man who seemed like a maniac crook? I just couldn't, could I?

"What do you think the packages are?"

"Dorian knows all about it. He's always suspecting people of transporting packages. He's been the same way since we were little kids—but he might be right this time. See, he delivers packages himself."

"What do you mean?"

"He never looks inside them. The guy he works for told him never to poke around, and Dorian's scared shitless of him, so he never does. Who would? He knows there's some heavy shit in there, though."

"And that's a job?"

"Yes."

"How well is he paid for that?"

"They pay him in dope. Shit. Grass. But he won't share the work. I wouldn't want to deliver packages, anyway. I saw how all that turned out for Jesse in *Breaking Bad*."

"You couldn't be more right, kiddo. That brain of yours is on fire! So, what's this girl's name?"

"Dunno."

"Does she go to school near here?"

"Dunno."

"Where does she live?"

"Du—"

"You don't know much! Does she have friends she hangs out with?"

"She's always on her own. But this one time, I was on my own too and I managed to talk to her. I asked her if she wanted to go to the beach and she said yes! But I dunno when."

"Okey dokey. And let me just check that I got this right . . . Your buddies went to see her tonight? I don't like the sound of that."

"Me neither. They're such a-holes. I'm worried they'll do something to her. And none of them are replying to my text messages."

I surveyed my fabulous little fam, my Mimi's boy, the homework spread all over my table, my pots and pans bubbling away, my beans all cleaned up and ready to rock . . .

I switched off the stove and sighed.

"All right! If it's the same girl I'm thinking of, I saw her yesterday!"

"That'th a thurprithe, Mommy!" declared Sabrina, who'd been following our every word, even the curses. "That'th life! Life givth uth unbelievable thurprithes! Ith it the girl we thaw yethterday, Mommy? Her daddy is a real nathty man."

"Come on! Let's go find out what's happening. We'll just take a peek, OK? You know what we could do? We'll ask her if she has a swimsuit for the beach. I think I know where she lives."

Léo's face lit up. As for Sabrina's . . . Well, her face was a picture! She loves going out on an adventure. Especially if it's unexpected, and especially at night. As for Emma, she'd go to the end of the world and back for Sabrina. And Lisa just sticks like glue to Emma. So we were all in agreement.

It was June, which meant it wouldn't get dark until much later. A hop, skip, and a jump and we were all outside, ready to take off.

15

Léo walked at a brisk pace and we had a hard time keeping up. I was in my heels, and the girls only have little legs! He didn't want to go where I thought she lived. I don't think he believed we were talking about the same girl.

"I'd rather we walked along her Tuesday route. I know it well," he said.

We arrived at an intersection. There was a big round fountain in the middle with a ton of old candy wrappers and other bits of litter bobbing around in it. Léo stopped and pointed at a house.

"She often comes here on Tuesdays and drops off the biggest parcel."

"And where are your friends?"

"Dunno."

Suddenly, a door opened and a girl sprang out of the house—the same girl I'd seen the day before.

She was wearing rags. A total mess. She had on a long knitted skirt. A woolen skirt in this heat wave! The long-sleeved green shirt wasn't exactly doing her any favors either. Nor was the weird headscarf she was wearing like a bandanna. Her hair was stunning, though! She looked like a Romany. But she must have been sweating her ass off.

She turned her head left to right before crossing the road.

Her almond-shaped hazel eyes appeared haunted. She bit her quivering lower lip. It was definitely the same hunted little gazelle I'd seen a day earlier. She was very pretty. She wasn't all that tall and was as skinny as they come. All legs.

"It's so weird that I noticed her yesterday, and she's the girl you've been thinking about!"

I started to approach her, to talk to her, but Léo, a bright shade of scarlet by this point, pulled me back by the wrist.

"No! No! We'll scare her!"

"But I thought you'd already spoken to her? You have a date, don't you?"

"Not now."

"OK, so we'll follow her."

And so we did. We were as discreet as a herd of elephants.

Léo stayed at the back. He didn't want to be recognized.

Our lack of stealth ninja skills actually worked in our favor—even if she'd seen us, she couldn't have possibly imagined we were following her. Who would think a broad with her swarm of kids could be up to no good? It also meant she probably hadn't spotted me the day before, either. Or if she had, she hadn't been paying much attention.

Sabrina seemed agitated. We were all careful, watching where we were going, trying our hardest not to lose sight of the girl, but Sabrina began trailing behind Léo, scanning behind us every couple of steps.

"What are you doing?" I asked, surprised by her weird behavior.

"Nothing, Mommy. Don't worry! Everything'th OK!"

Emma peered at me and gibbered, "Sabrina doesn't want him to attack us from behind!"

Like mother, like daughter. She was becoming a paranoid little freak too! What a pair we were. It was madness! What was she talking about?

"What are you saying, Emma?"

Sabrina marched up to the front to join me. "Nothing, Mommy. Don't pay any attenthion to her." Then she said to Emma, "You're mixthing everything up in your head!"

"Where is she? Where did she go?" asked Léo, suddenly sounding panicky.

The girl had disappeared. We thought we'd lost track of her for good, when we realized she was actually behind us.

"What you wanting with me?" she asked with an odd accent I didn't recognize.

I jumped half out of my skin and the kids all screeched.

Once my heart had stopped pounding, I giggled. The kids too—except Léo.

"You scared us half to death, sweetheart! You can't go sneaking up on people from behind like that."

She must have found it weird that we were laughing. She recognized Léo right away.

"You follow me why?"

"I wanted to a-ask you about o-our d-date! Tomorrow afternoon? I don't have c-class."

"No. Father no want this. Hit me if be late."

My feet were damn near killing me by now, so I sat on a little brick ledge.

What are you doing? Are you in school? What grade are you in? What are you carrying in those packages? Does your father beat you? Where are you from, dressed like that? I so wanted to ask her all these questions, but I didn't want to see her run for the hills. Léo deserved a chance with her. Young love deserved a chance.

"What's your name?" I asked.

She stared at me for a long time without saying a word.

"This is Léo," I added, pointing at the new man of the house.

"I know it," she whispered.

"Here we have Sabrina, Lisa, and Emma. And I'm Rosie . . . Cricri, actually," I said, giggling. "Don't worry. I'll explain the whole Cricri thing later."

She managed a smile despite such an avalanche of names to remember.

"What about you? What's your name?"

"Errr . . . ina," she whispered.

"What?"

Sabrina translated, "The'th called Erina, Mommy."

Erina nodded.

"Do you want to eat with us? I've got beans! We can ask your father if you want?"

There was no longer even a trace of a smile. Total freak-out. Erina's eyes wildly darted back and forth. She was scanning every direction, trying to spot the trap.

"Leave alone. Go. Go. Me return house."

She was choking up. Léo gave me the evil eye. I understood why.

"Don't worry!"

I didn't know how to deal with this. I'd sent her into a meltdown. I walked over to her to reassure her. She shuddered when I first touched her, but then relaxed and got closer for a hug. She started crying in my arms.

The children were all eyes—like they'd never seen anything quite so interesting in their lives. Lisa even blubbered a little.

"You're allowed to have friends, aren't you?"

She shook her head.

"What about the beach? You can go to the beach, though?"

Another shake of the dome.

"Do you have a swimsuit?"

More shaking. This father of hers didn't let her do much. Was it that insano from yesterday? The guy who'd tried mouthing off at us?

Her tears were in full flow by this point. I got out an old handkerchief from my pocket so she could blow her nose.

"We'll take you back to your place."

We all started trudging. It was like a funeral march. She stuck by Léo's side. The sky was darkening. I thought it was getting late for my babas to be out and about. They were usually in bed all snug as bugs in rugs by this time. It wasn't school vacation yet!

Erina whispered, "Me come tomorrow. Me say lie. Me do work quick in morning."

I couldn't tell her that she shouldn't lie to her father. I'd have done the same thing if I were her.

"I'll pick you up tomorrow at the fountain," said Léo. "At two o'clock."

16

We left her in the murky alleyway next to her house.

She gave us all a heartrending look and was still trembling as she climbed through the window to get inside. It felt as though we were watching a prisoner who'd been allowed to go out in the daylight for a couple of hours, but who now had to go back inside her cage.

Léo couldn't seem to tear himself away. And neither could I. The twinnies, who are usually to be found in pretty excellent moods, started whimpering. I couldn't hold them both in my arms like I used to. They were getting far too big for all those shenanigans. It meant I had to carry Lisa while saying to Emma, "It's your turn in five minutes, OK?"

No, it wasn't OK. She got herself into a tantrum and sat down on the ground. Sabrina put her arm around her. In the meantime, Léo took the opportunity to head over to the back of Erina's house and try to get a glimpse of her. I had the same inclination and followed him.

Despite having Lisa in my arms, I stood on my tippy-toes to get a better look. But there was some chiffony fabric hanging up at the window and it wasn't clear what was going on inside. We managed to find a couple of gaps and got a rough idea of the layout.

The handsome roughneck from the day before was sitting at a table. He'd taken his jacket off. He was wearing a short-sleeved white shirt and smoking a cig. Erina crossed the room to find refuge in what appeared to be a cubbyhole under the stairs. Surely not! She closed the door behind her, but just as it shut, a voice screamed out, "'Rina!"

From outside, the man was certainly easier to hear than he was to see.

He gabbled something in his own language that we didn't understand. How could we have?

Erina came back out of her Harry Potter room and started to rummage around in a makeshift corner kitchen with some pots and pans. As she left something to heat up on a burner, she set the table for the hot ruffian.

I'd seen enough. I absolutely had to do something for this miserable young girl. But if this guy was her father, what on earth was I supposed to do? Maybe I could speak to Borelli, my cop friend, about it? But I couldn't exactly go telling the po-po stuff, ratting her out, if I didn't know what the consequences would be. I risked doing more damage than anything else.

Borelli was a police lieutenant or captain (what do I know about these things?) and one of the people who annoyed me more than anyone in the world. He was also my savior. Still, I had to be careful. I mean, a cop's a cop—even if he had saved my ass a few times, there's no reason he wouldn't whup it too.

"Let's go home," I whispered to Léo. "We've got beans waiting for us. It's already way past the bambinos' bedtime, and you've all got school tomorrow."

Halfway back, I remembered it was Emma's turn in my arms and swapped them over. Lisa plodded next to Sabrina and we all traipsed along in silence. We were wiped out.

The inside of our trailer was cool because it sits in the shade of a huge plane tree and a cherry tree—but even so, it's nice to eat outside sometimes when the weather is that hot. So I got out the camping table.

My rice-and-bean dish wasn't the extravaganza I'd been hoping for. It was a flop, to be honest. Maybe I was simply too spent or, more than likely, too sad to put in the effort it required.

We were all feeling pretty down. I found the candy bars I'd swiped from Rachel Amar's waiting room, and this seemed to change the atmosphere. The kiddos were all over that chocolatey deliciousness—well, everyone except Léo, that is. His heart clearly wasn't in it.

When we finished the meal, the little ones put all the plates and cutlery into a bucket. I hadn't had time to figure out our water issue, so we'd have to go to the fountain the next day to wash it all up. The plumbing thing hadn't even crossed my mind. I had no idea what was going on with that.

As we headed inside, everyone cleared something from the camping table—a cup, a napkin, whatever. The rule is you don't leave the table empty handed. The smallest kiddies loved helping with housework and stuff. Sabrina participated too, but she was a lot less enthusiastic. Léo went toward the small room he'd be using as a bedroom.

A loud whistle stopped him in his tracks just before his door. It was me. I'm one of those loud whistlers. I do it with my fingers and everything. People are usually surprised. Léo spun around and glared at me like I was as crazed as could be.

"You didn't forget anything by any chance, did you?" I said.

I pointed outside at the table. There were still some pieces of cookware and crap left to tidy away or put in the bucket.

He dragged his feet as he slouched back outside to help finish up. Once the table was clear, I asked him to wipe it down with a damp dishcloth. There was still plenty of water left in the plastic bottles I'd filled earlier.

"We never have to do all this shit at the center," he moaned. "There are people paid to do all this. And dishwashers. Machines!"

"Oh well, welcome to the real-life club, budster!"

He sighed, but he helped Sabrina wash everything down while I brushed the twinnies' teeth and put them both in their pj's.

And then *whoooosh*, everyone was off to bed! I started telling the girlios a bedtime story, and, because there was a package-carrying princess in it, even Léo was listening. After a short while, I heard snoring.

I went back outside to pick up a few of the toys lying around, along with some empty cans of soda and takeout wrappers that Léo's buds had left behind.

Before bed, I washed myself down with some cold water from my bottle stash, then slipped between the sheets, feeling much cooler.

It was such a hot and sticky night that even my Pastis didn't want to sit on me. He slept on the table opposite the open window, a light breeze ruffling his fur slightly.

I went over everything I'd seen and heard that day. What an awful lot to process. What use was all that psychology twaddle I was learning if I couldn't do anything for Erina? How could I possibly help her?

My life had gotten a whole lot more complicated in just a couple of days:

1) I'd been put in charge of a teenage boy.

2) I was cleaning Véro's boss's place. This was great in that it would bring in some money, but not so great when it came to straightening my life out, managing the school runs and all that kerfuffle. Luckily, Véro's boss was out of town, so I'd be able to pick and choose my hours as long as I actually got the job done. And I absolutely had to find the time to do it properly. Véro trusted me not to mess this up.

3) A random girl who I thought to be in danger had made a sudden appearance in my life. This was never a good thing. It meant I had to do something about it. I felt concerned. Responsible, even.

4) I'd been thrown in at the deep end at Rachel Amar's. It wasn't only cleaning I was expected to do. Some cracked broad had gotten the idea that I was some kind of therapist.

And I couldn't even bear to think about Gaston's poem I was supposed to be learning by heart. There was only so far I could be pushed before having a loopy episode of my own. A burnout, as they call it. I'd have to make up some sort of excuse for Gaston.

Despite all this weird nonsense going on around me, I reflected, I still had my health. Then I dropped off and didn't wake for even a second until the sun came back up again.

Wednesday:
Fluctuating Current

17

The emotions of yesterday's events had worn us all out, but I woke up bright and early.

The last images of my dream were still very much with me, almost burning my retinas, which was weird, because I'd spent the night in vast, snowy wastelands. I'd been walking for what seemed like half a lifetime. Wow, Canada is one hell of a freezing country, even when your heart is all warm and fuzzy.

From the other side of a frozen river, a man had beckoned me. All of a sudden, he launched into the air and flew across to meet me, landing at my feet. It was Linus Robinson.

"Are you cold?" he asked, his velvety voice warming the cockles of my heart as he took me in his arms. My skin grew hotter as he held me. The snow started melting beneath my feet and before I knew it, I was knee deep in a pool of icy turquoise water. And then *pfffff*, I was all on my lonesome. No more Linus.

His departure felt brutal. It was as if I'd known perfect beauty just before it was ripped away from me and I was thrown into the void.

Mmmm. Linus Robinson and those big strong arms of his. The sensation had been nothing short of amazing. Exquisite. So perfectly reassuring. Terrifying but exciting. Just as I had touched upon this ecstasy, I was abandoned in the cold, left in a bottomless, loveless abyss.

The soundtrack to my Canadian adventure, obviously sent by my mother, was about snow and winter, hazy seasons or something. I didn't know who sang it. It sounded like Simon & Garfunkel. They were huge favorites of my mommy's. Were they Canadian? Probably not—I'd have to do some Googling. They were singing about winter and a patch of snow on the ground, but there'd been more than a patch in my dream!

I went bright red. Thinking about the song made me feel deliciously sexy. Thoughts of Canada and of the cold ice and Linus Robinson . . . Oh, no! No! Not that! Was I at that point already? Could this actually be love I was feeling? No. Not again. I had to get with the frigging program here! I didn't even know the guy! Never met him! All I'd seen was some lousy interview on tape!

But that's where I'd been caught! I thought back to the video. It was as if I'd been trapped in his magic web or some shit.

No! No! There was no way I was starting up all that claptrap again.

It was hard work, though. Giving up an addiction. Loads of folks are obsessed with chocolate, addicted to alcohol, even sports. Worse than sports, some people are addicted to work! *Work!* I couldn't believe it when I first heard it either, but it's true—workaholics actually exist. Maybe they exist in some parallel universe, though, because in my group of friends, well, we're more addicted to naps and siestas. Maybe it depends on the type of job you've got.

As far as I'm concerned, none of those addictions are really my style. What I suffer from is an addiction to love. I've known about this for a long time. Or at least since I started reading all that psychology crud. I always have to be in love. If I'm not in love, I feel like there's a huge gap in my life. Every time it happens, I swear it's for the last time. The disadvantages far outweigh the pluses. We all know this. When does a love story ever have a happy chirpy ending in real life? We all know about the divorce rates. But then, who cares about the facts and figures and all the evidence? I like falling in love. It's my guilty pleasure.

And this time, all it had taken was a videotape! Crazy crapola! Could it really be going down like this? I was such a little loser! But I recognized all the signs.

First, it felt like I was having a heart attack. I could hear my heart beating in my chest. And that's all I could hear. The rest of the world went silent. In fact, it seemed like it had come to an end, or had slowed down and everything turned to black and white. Only the man I happened to be in love with at the time stayed in color. Technicolor!

Rosie girl! You know nothing about this guy! And he's a shrink! a little voice inside me said.

But another voice was quick to respond. I have two voices. It's very annoying: *So, what's the big deal? It's a good thing he's a shrink! That'll do nicely! Plus, he's Canadian! How exotic!*

The stricter voice hadn't let up yet. *He has an accent, sure. So what?*

I (we) continued this inward debate. *A Canadian accent. That really is something.*

Is it? What's the diff?

One side really wanted to win this one. *Nothing. I love Canadians, that's all. They're nice people. If you ever bump into one, the Canadian will say sorry. I saw that in a TV series once. I guess they're all class acts.*

The harsher inner voice sighed and then shut up. So I'd won.

I got out of bed, feeling a little chilly. *Brrrr!* I stretched and dragged myself into the living area, singing all about the patch of snow on the ground and the hazy shade of winter. It was a great little tune, but a weird song choice given that it was already a sauna outside.

OK! No good moping around dreaming about Canadians all day! There were little people whose butts needed moving. And now there were five of us to share just the one bathroom—with bottled water! Grim! Plus a breakfast for kings had to be prepared. Well, last night's bread with a bit of strawberry jelly.

I did everything on autopilot. Like a robot. But a cool one with good fashion sense and heels. I wasn't doing much in the way of talking. I was still in fantasy mode. The bambinos were all singing as they got out of bed. They're very jovial in the morning. It was the Pirate Anorak song again. In a loop.

Léo was in a mopey mood. He told me that he couldn't stop thinking about his date with Erina. He was worried. I picked up a few odds and ends and shoved them in my purse—the container of leftover beans and rice from the night before and a swimsuit for Erina.

We all had a quick wash-down with what was left in the water bottles and headed out to school. Léo only came as far as the end of the street with us before heading off to the high school.

I dropped off my three babas at their respective thought-killing factories. I didn't bump into anyone I knew, which is often a blessing, and I headed straight over to Rachel Amar's place. I had to take the bus. Her apartment wasn't exactly in my neighborhood, and I didn't want to waste half a day getting there.

The Russian-African insano journalist was waiting for me at the door. She had a blue-and-gold robe on this time. She wasn't wearing a turban today. Instead, she wore her hair tied back tightly in a knot, all pulled away from her face. Her Longchamp bag had disappeared and she was now sporting a mustard-colored Hermès backpack. She looked incredible!

"It's you again!" I said.

"I realized I hadn't paid you for yesterday's session!"

"Yesterday's wh . . . ? Oh! I get it! It's this therapist claptrap again! I don't know how many times I'm supposed to tell you. Why won't you believe me? Take me at my word."

"I don't understand what you're getting at."

"I'm not a shrink."

"Oh, stop it with all this silliness. How much do I owe you?"

"I told you already! It's free of charge! Free, free, free!"

"I see. Is this also part of the new method? I have to exchange something, is that it? But what could I possibly give you in exchange? Do you like traditional African dress? Or Dior, maybe? How about a Hermès scarf? Would you like that? What about some Egyptian cotton sheets?"

She followed me into the building as she yammered on.

I ran over to the elevator. I was faster than her. The doors closed before she could get in. Good. I hoped she'd now consider her ass dumped. I'd had enough of all the bats-in-the-belfry weirdness the day before. No more shenanigans, please!

18

I stepped inside the apartment with a feeling of ownership. I liked it! Nobody had been there to mess the joint up, and, seeing as I'd done quite a lot the day before, I felt ready to target the rest. And there was still a ton! On Rachel Amar's note to my Véro, she'd mentioned something about wanting a deep clean, which meant windows, curtains, all that nightmare stuff. I wasn't going to get a second to mellow out, that was for sure, and there'd def be no time to watch Monsieur Linus Robinson tapes. I'd just have to remember him, being in his arms, the icy lake . . .

I headed to the office and Amar's computer. Véro (now me) was supposed to check her e-mails.

One was a message from her accountant saying Amar had to be careful. Her latest book hadn't sold many copies. She didn't have enough patients. She was spending too much on art and shit. Basically, she was in the red. Wow. Going broke was clearly an epidemic. And her accountant's advice? Amar should do a lot less research and write fewer books. Books didn't sell. She needed more patients. Patients paid.

There was also a message from some legal firm. It was from the lawyer who was defending the infamous Full Moon Pyromaniac. Apparently this guy was still doing the whole vow-of-silence thing. He'd taken the stand and written a note stating he wouldn't say a word unless in the presence of the author of *Psychoanalysis and Criminality*.

Amar had asked to be told if there was an emergency, but I didn't really think any of these e-mails were all that urgent. She was probably used to being broke by now, and if she wasn't . . . Well, I guess it's always better to find out these things as late as possible. As for the pyro guy and his lawyer, she already knew about all that. She'd said to explain she was away if he called.

I was secretly hoping Rachel Amar would show up earlier than expected. It would mean I could get to the curtain washing and all that spring cleaning bull without having to play the secretary, and it would also give me more time to think about what we were going to do to help Erina.

I'd only just gotten the espresso machine working when I heard the doorbell ring. It was that Trampoline woman (or whatever her name was!). She just wouldn't give up! She had a small box, wrapped with a fancy ribbon, which she held out to me as she stepped inside.

"This is my way of paying you in part—"

"How many times . . ." I eyeballed the box. OMG, that box smelled *great*! What was in it? My stomach growled a big *yes*. "What is it?"

"A few appetizers from Chez Ernest. The savory kind. I guessed you might like them. Also, I had an idea. You don't want me to pay for my therapy sessions. Fine. I'm going to cook for you instead! Like we talked about yesterday! I'll go to the market at closing. Do you like West African dishes? Traditional Russian food? I'll learn how to make it all!"

"Sessions? Multiple? No. It ain't happening."

She didn't respond. I was starting to feel angsty as I followed her to the kitchen, where she put the box into the fridge.

Seeing as she was there, and that I wanted to make it perfectly clear that I was a replacement maid and not a replacement therapist, I picked up a duster and started wiping down all the ornaments in the lounge and then in the office. One by one.

While I did this, she went and sat her ass down in the waiting room. She took a huge file out of her bag and started reading away. She'd taken an ornate paper knife whatchamacallit from the kitchen and was playing with it as she read from the file.

"I'm editing a study written by a colleague of mine who works in finance. It's supposed to be sent off for printing any day now. I got the job yesterday after our session. I made a few calls. This is all thanks to you! You're really very good at what you do, you know."

"What?"

By this point, I just assumed she was one of those compulsive liars I'd read about. Maybe she needed a real doctor.

Someone else was at the door. I startled when the bell rang, and the journalist peered at me over the top of her glasses.

"Are you going to get that or should I?"

I shrugged and went to open up, but she pushed me out of the way, overtook me with the letter-opener thing in her hand, and answered the door. A man, I'd say around forty years old, stepped inside. He was tall and wore glasses, a Lacoste polo shirt, and Nikes. He was the business guy I'd seen the day before on the video. He'd started some company and had been having loads of sex-swapping parties or key orgies or whatever they're called. He was the one desperately seeking love with a capital *L*. He looked all wound up!

He was obviously surprised to see us both there. He checked the name on the door, then stared drop-jawed at the journalist.

She opened her eyes wide and boomed, "What is it? Do we know one another? Is there something wrong with my nose? It's still in the middle of my face, isn't it?"

She was starting to sound like me!

"Are you new here?" the guy said. "Allow me to introduce myself. Laroche. Alexandre Laroche. I'm one of Doctor Amar's patients."

"Oh, aren't we all? Get in line!" the journalist replied. "And what's with the 'Are you new here'?"

He looked bothered by this. "I don't get your meaning."

She pointed to the living room with the letter-opening-knife thingy, but it got a bit too close to my face.

"Hey! Careful with that thing! I'm right behind you! You could have poked my eye out!"

"So, again, I don't get your meaning," the guy said. He spoke slowly, really trying to pin her down. He was evidently angry that she wasn't responding. I don't think he'd noticed I was there.

Madame Limousine (what was that name again?) gave him a holier-than-thou superstare.

"If you'd just like to take a seat in the lounge area," she said, "she'll be with you in a moment."

"What? Why can't I go in the waiting room?" asked Laroche worriedly.

She got screwball now. Real cross. As she headed into the lounge, pushing him in front of her, she whispered, "I can't get over it! They're all trying to jump the line!"

Speechless, Laroche allowed himself to be frog-marched. I bet he was wondering what the f-star-star-star was happening to him (I doubted he used foul language—he didn't seem the type).

She threw him into an armchair and shouted to me, "OK, so where the hell was I? I said I'd cook! So, I'll cook! You've got to do what you've got to do!"

"What the devil is all this?" he said. "I don't have the slightest idea what's going on here today. I really don't."

"You're going to drive me nuts! I wouldn't be surprised if you sent me over the edge!" she cried out, pointing at him.

"Hey! I will not allow you to . . . Where's Madame Amar? Huh?"

But the journalist stormed out of the room. She must have lost all interest. She shook her paper cutter at him as she flounced past and rolled her eyes.

Laroche looked speechless. He sat there like a little scaredy-cat, not moving a muscle, not uttering a syllable. He stared at me. He hadn't even noticed me up to that point. I took pity on the poor bastard.

"Don't pay any attention to that one," I said. "She wants a therapy session with me and I won't give her one, so she's wound herself up and gotten all hot and bothered."

"Who are you, anyway? And why have you got that thing?" he asked, pointing to my hand. "One of you is brandishing a paper knife! The other a feather duster! What is this? A cult? Are these your magic objects?"

He stood up hurriedly and marched toward the waiting room. He scanned inside and seemed surprised to see Madame Kerosene (or whatever she's actually called) standing in front of the sofa.

I was too.

"Hey, Madame Mezzanine"—I was just hoping for the best on the name front, to hit the jackpot at some point—"what are you doing in here? Weren't you supposed to be cooking or something?"

"Oh, I'd like to have my consultation first," she sulked. "I don't see why I should have to go after everyone else."

"What's your problem?" I asked.

"S-so sorry to interrupt you," stammered Laroche. "I'm a little taken aback, to be honest with you both. I don't usually bump into anyone else when I come here. The whole system is run very smoothly so that we never see the . . . um . . . the others . . ."

"Yes, well, we're bumping today. Sorry about that," I said. "We won't be bumping for long, though. What I suggest you do is as follows, so listen up. Go home and call the office next week to set up another appointment."

"What's going on here? Why's everything changing?" he asked, his voice quivering. With a voice like that, I could understand how he'd annoy the heck out of anyone.

"You don't like my style, then? Not happy with how I do things? Well, you're right. This isn't how shrinks should do things! And that's because—now, please listen carefully—that's because I'm not a shrink. So, please, just go home."

"Don't listen to a word of this," said the journalist. "It's some sort of new method."

He stared at her, then at me, then back at her before taking a very deep breath. He ran over to the sofa and plopped down on it as if he were running on impulses alone.

"OK, are we getting on with it, then?" he asked.

"Getting on with what?"

"The sofa thing . . . the couch . . ."

"Listen to me! There'll be nothing happening on that couch, because I'm not a—"

"This can't be happening! Am I dreaming? You can't just go ahead and do something like this without warning people first! I feel like I've been abandoned! I'm completely on my own here. What should I do?"

Another minute of that and I think he'd have started crying real actual tears. I knew I had to shut him up and shut him up fast.

"No, come on, you're not alone. You've got all your friends. You've got all those sex-party people."

His cheeks flushed and he glanced quickly at Madame Wolverine (or whatever . . .). She must have been very embarrassed, because she darted off to the kitchen. On her way out, she said, "Please, carry on without me. You can go ahead of me. I'll have my turn later. No worries."

I almost gave up. I almost sat down at the desk to give this guy a good therapy session. I just wanted to get it over and done with so he'd get out of there. But I went for the quickest route. I grabbed his arm. He flinched.

I pulled him gently toward the door. He wasn't happy, but he had to go along with it. I pushed him out into the hallway with no further comment and shut the door behind him.

I listened. I was worried he was going to start blubbering in the corridor and that the neighbors would hear, but after a while, I heard his footsteps as he scuttled away.

19

My cricket phone startled me with its loud chirping. It was Mimi. She wanted to hear everything that had gone on the night before.

Mimi! Jeez! What was wrong with me? I hadn't touched base with her at all! I put her mind at rest about Léo and told her the whole tale about the night before and how we'd all followed Erina around town.

Mimi hadn't gone under the knife yet. They'd postponed the whole deal by a full twenty-four hours at the last minute. She hadn't eaten a thing because she'd been expecting to go in for surgery. It hadn't happened, but instead of feeding her, the doctors had told her she still couldn't have anything to eat.

"I must have lost seven pounds since I've been in here. It's great! I can't cheat because I can't move and nobody will fucking feed me! You wait and see how skinny I'll be when I get out of here!"

I thought she was being really brave. I wouldn't have been so funny and chatty if I were in her shoes (or bed socks). She was tiring out pretty quickly, but I was glad I'd managed to reassure her about Léo.

My mind wandered to the water back at the trailer and how it might actually be simpler if we all bunked at Amar's place until I got the chance to figure it out. May as well. I could do the housework in the evenings if I didn't have enough time to get it done during the day with all my to-ing and fro-ing.

I headed back to the office and found the journalist lying on the couch—a delighted smile on her face.

"Are you free at lunchtime?" I asked her.

"Free? Why?"

"Because it's Wednesday. I have to pick up my kids from school. There has to be someone there to meet them at midday, but I can't do it. Too much work here. Could you go and fetch them for me? I'll call up the school and let them know you're coming."

"No problem."

"Also, could you drop by my place and make sure that a teenage boy named Léo comes home? He'll help you with all the kids. Then bring them all back here after that. Seeing as the boss woman isn't here, we can all sleep in this apartment and it'll save all this traipsing around. I think it's a pretty nifty idea!"

"That's fine. But then you'll take me for a session, agreed?"

"Well . . ."

"Great! Finally!"

"You don't give up, do you?"

"No! How did you guess?"

"Listen, that's all well and good, but I have to at least try to do some housework. The windows need cleaning, as well as the curtains, doorknobs, and light switches. Then there's all the ironing. Sitting on my ass listening to you harp on is hardly going to get any of that done, is it? I need this job. Well, I need the money, at least."

"I get it, I get it—you want to anchor me to reality. I understand your technique."

I let out a sigh and made a quick call to the kiddies' schools.

"What's your name again, please?" I asked her.

"Eudoxie Bintou Apraksine."

"I'm calling to let you know that Madame *exactly what she just said* will be picking up my kids today." They checked my telephone number, first off, and then I had to answer a ton of questions about my babies' dates of birth, as well as all the details about the lady in question. It took ages.

A *bing bing* sound let me know that I (Rachel Amar, actually) had gotten mail.

My stubborn "patient" was letting rip as she jabbered on and on in a monotone. "I don't know what it is that's driving me, but my brain is insanely active. It's like I can never switch it off. I wish I could be less of a perfectionist, say no sometimes, and find a way to balance my professional life and my home life. Not to mention my love life!"

"Yes, but you can't have it all, right? Nobody on this planet knows how to balance all that shit. Take me, for example: I can't even find the time to do a quick shift down at Tony's. He gets real busy just as I have to leave to pick up the kidders from school. And then, who's supposed to take care of them while I'm helping out Tony? If I pay someone to babysit, it'll end up costing me more than I can earn."

"Button it! I'm doing the talking here! I like your new method and all, but you can only push me so far." And off she went again. "I can't sleep at night. I have to find a way to . . ."

I sneaked a peek at Rachel Amar's laptop and noticed she'd received an e-mail from none other than Linus Robinson.

I felt the blood pounding in my chest. This was dramatic!

I had to read it. I had to read it now! It was my number-one priority and I had to get it done before attempting to start anything else. But my mother and grandmother had instilled good manners in me, and this meant I was stuck like glue to my chair, listening to Madame Windowpane. They'd both told me that you can't go reading shit when you're supposed to be listening to someone—especially when that person thinks you're their shrink. Well, they didn't say anything about the shrink bit. I added that.

I nearly crapped my pants when Madame Iodine (getting closer . . .), from her relaxed position on the couch, legs crossed, started cackling like a maniac, grabbing her sides as she howled and howled. She even started banging her fist against her forehead. Freakazoid of a woman!

"Ha-ha! But of course! Great! So that's all that's left to do! Incredible! Honestly, Madame Maldonne. You're amazing. A genius—really! Just look at me! I'm sure you can tell! I've totally transformed, haven't I?"

"If you say so . . ."

I wondered what she was talking about, as I hadn't done anything or spoken a word, but I could also sense that time was almost up in our fake therapy session and that I'd soon be able to read the message from my Linus. Wow, there I was already calling him *my* Linus. A man I'd still never met—and wasn't likely to!

What happened next terrified the living daylights out of the pair of us. I freaked out first because Madame Paraffin (?) had her back to the door and so it took some time to understand what was going on.

20

A head popped around the doorframe—Laroche!

His face was haggard, his marbled skin showed traces of red, and he was pointing a big kickass revolver at our heads. This was clearly an emotional time for him. His panic-stricken eyes moved from me to the journalist and back again to me at a frantic pace.

But Madame Tangerine hadn't seen a thing. She'd noticed my expression, but I guess she took it to be a response to her gratitude. She stood, sauntered over to me, and planted a massive smacker on my cheek.

With his wide eyes on us and his knuckles white as he gripped his gun, Laroche moved into the room. That's when my "patient" turned around and found herself with a gun almost touching her nose.

She cried out.

The sex-swapping man was trembling as he held up the revolver. The journalist was trying to form words, but nothing came out.

Laroche stuck his weapon under my patient's chin and looked like quite the pro.

"Madame Maldonne, there's definitely a problem here," she articulated slowly.

I needed to get this situation under control, but holy mother, I was frozen in fear. I had a big-time freak on. I was imagining my children without me, all alone in the world, wondering why I'd left them.

In a shaky voice, I managed to say, "Come on, don't lose your shit. Talk to me. Don't be afraid, Madame Margarine, this guy's a nice guy."

"If you say so. What about the kids? The kids I have to pick up from school?"

I eyed the clock on the wall.

"Yes, the kids will be waiting. You're late, Madame Clementine! Get your ass into gear!"

Gun Boy reacted to this by pressing the revolver further into the journalist's face without even looking at her.

"Where's the witch Amar? She got her own way, didn't she? She won! I'm going to kill myself! And I'm going to do it in front of her! That's why I came back! Where is she? You'd better tell me!"

I managed to keep my cool, even though I already saw myself in a pool of my own blood. I remembered an old film with Marlene Dietrich or Greta Garbo in the role of Mata Hari when she's just about to be executed and lifts an eyebrow, mockingly. I made the same move.

"Good one!" I said. "Well played. But you'll have to wait a few days before the big event if you want Rachel Amar to witness it. She's away on business and it'll be a few days before she's back. I'm sorry. You're going to have to take a rain check."

He stared at me nastily, so I gave it another go.

"Hello? Are you taking any of this in? Do you want me to sum things up for you?"

"You're Madame Amar's replacement?"

"No. Nothing like that. Do I look like a shrink to you? Can you not tell how old I am? I'm only just out of elementary school!"

"Age has absolutely nothing to do with status," he replied. "It's more your style that's the problem. You know. Your makeup, the colors . . ."

"Yeah, listen to me. You're pissing me off with your talk of how I look—like *you're* a fashion king or something. You don't exactly come across as on-trend. Just go back home, would you? Nice and quiet. I've already told you that Rachel Amar has gone to the US."

"I don't believe your story for a minute! You're making all this ridiculous nonsense up as you go along! It's a trap."

"I swear to you. I'm telling nothing but the whole truth."

He lowered his arm. He seemed defeated. I'd finally worn him down. I knew he'd never have the nerve to follow it through. Our little discussion had given Madame Limousine a chance to escape.

My telephone gave a little *diiiiinnnnngg-a-riiiinnnggg* to let me know I'd received a text message. I took a quick peek. It was Léo.

He was in front of the school gates waiting to pick up the girlios, but he needed my authorization. He gave me the number of the gate woman. I'm sure that wasn't her official job title, but all the same. I dealt with it and the babas were handed over to Léo. I couldn't have been more relieved that he was taking care of things.

After texting him where I was and telling him to bring the kids directly to Rachel Amar's place, I called the journalist. "You needn't bother picking up my kids now, thanks. Someone else is on it."

While these texts and calls had been going back and forth, Laroche had regained his strength. He was agitated again, but I also detected a sense of wariness. It was something in the eyes.

"I'm not into all this messing around. Rachel Amar's replacement will just have to do. Sit down at that desk. I'm going to lie down on this couch for a few minutes and you're going to listen to me."

I was beside myself.

He clearly didn't like the laughing. "What? What did I say?"

"Nothing. She'll take you. Don't worry . . ." whispered Madame Borderline, who had snuck back in, smiling nervously.

I couldn't believe my ears! I glowered at her. "Madame Margarine, please . . ."

"It's Eudoxie Apraksine."

"What?"

"My name is Eudoxie Apraksine."

"Isn't that what I said? Whatever your name is, I think you should mind your own business! Monsieur, I am not replacing Rachel Amar. It was a coincidence that you saw me in her office. Please let me explain. As I've already told you, I am the cleaner, the maid, the housekeeper . . . whatever you want to call it, but I'm not a therapist or a psychologist or a psychiatrist. There is a massive difference between dusting and curing brains."

Alexandre, eyes bulging, started howling like a Dementor. "Housekeeper? Seriously? My brain most certainly does need curing if you think I believe that! I'm sick of everyone treating me like I'm nothing! Like a turd! You don't think I saw the both of you having a session earlier? Maid! Ha-ha! You're too young to be a maid!"

"What? You're very judgy, aren't you? Since when has there been a right age for cleaning up someone else's mess? You've obviously never been to a cleaning agency! I'm way too young to be a shrink, but I'm more than old enough to clean shit up."

"That's so not the case. You could have skipped a couple of years in high school or college. This replacement could even be part of your training! Cleaner! What else have you got for me?"

He held up the gun again in front of my face. And that was it. I lost it. My fear disappeared out the window, as it often does during those moments when I maybe should be worried for my safety.

"'What else?' I ain't got nothing else for you, dickhead! I've been telling you the truth!"

"No, it's not the truth! She's a liar!" shouted the journalist frantically. What a racket. She must've been driven by fear, enthusiasm, or her deep-held belief that I really was a shrink. Or all three?

"She's fantastic at her job! She totally knows what she's doing. If your head's broken, she'll fix it. She's like a brain mechanic or something!

Absolutely marvelous! Get on that couch and your whole world will change, I guarantee it. I'm Eudoxie Bintou Apraksine. And you are?"

"Alexandre Laroche. Pleased to meet you," he said with a smile, holding out his left hand (not the one with the gun in it).

This Kerosene woman really needed dealing with. How was I going to get her under control? She was the reason my situation was going from bad to worse.

"You need to watch it, Madame Chlorine, because I won't just keep repeating myself. This must be the third time at least. Don't interfere with the setup here. I am not taking on the responsibility of dealing with a suicidal obsessive who's spent years in Freudian therapy and still hasn't acted on a single threat he's made."

"Oh, and that's how a typical housekeeper speaks, is it? Ha-ha!" cried out Alexandre Laroche, becoming more and more manic by the minute. "Not a very good cover-up. Or is it intended to be amusing?" he added frostily. "Sit over there. And I'll lie down here. I'll give you one last chance to try and get me to change my mind about how worthless I am. And if you can't do it, I'll kill myself right here in front of you."

"Jesus! I can't deal with this!" I shouted.

"Come on, Madame Maldonne, say you'll do it! Help him, please! Don't be so selfish! You can see how much he needs you!"

"Madame Plasticine, this is a big deal. A serious situation and I'm not qualified! In fact, I'm pretty sure it's illegal! I can't do it. Come on! Please!"

As we were speaking, Laroche had changed position slowly and was now able to grab the journalist and take her as his hostage.

"Enough already! You give me my therapy or I'll kill her before I pop myself."

"Madame Maldonne, I'd very much appreciate it if you could think very carefully before responding . . ." said the woman in a quiet, squeaky voice. "Don't forget that I promised I'd do all your cooking for you."

I sighed and sat down at the big desk.

"So you'll talk with me? You'll do this?" asked Laroche, surprised, I think, that his aggressive method had actually worked.

I nodded, but felt desperate about what was happening, about how I was going to get out of this. And now my kids were on the way. What had I been thinking?

Encouraged by his newfound success, he pushed Madame Guillotine out of the room.

"Get the fuck out of here! Leave us in peace!"

So it turned out he did use bad language, and she didn't appreciate it in the slightest.

"Young man, in my country, men show women more respect than that. How dare you address me in such a manner."

I wondered which of her countries she was talking about.

She turned to me. "This man needs you more than most, I would say! I'm going grocery shopping. There's a great little organic place near here. I'm going to make some mafé for us. It's a West African dish. Very spicy! It'll cheer you up! The market exercise will have to be for another day, I'm afraid. You eat chicken, don't you? I'm taking the keys! Be back soon!"

21

Things weren't A-OK with me.

It's one thing to give a friend a bit of advice in passing, to tell Véro or Mimi what to do with their lives, or to help out a Korean cashier in the supermarket, but from that to the bigwig sitting behind a desk with a patient on the couch? It was too much. Honest to frig. This had all gone way too far.

I really had to get a grip or this was all going to wind up one hell of a mess. And with the number of kids I was taking care of, I couldn't allow myself to get caught up in this kind of game.

Laroche cheered. "Yeeeehaaaaw! It works! That's wild!" He gave his gun a loud kiss. Odd or what? "These things are magic, don't you think?"

I shrugged as the front door banged shut. The journalist must have headed out to do her all-important grocery shopping.

"OK, so are you sitting . . . um, lying comfortably?"

He certainly looked like he was all snuggly, his revolver lying across his belly.

The doorbell rang again and we both reacted with a start. What was this? A slapstick? One character leaves the stage and another character enters. I exhaled deeply through my mouth.

"We're never going to get through this. When I think about all the work I have left to do!"

The journalist had come back. I heard Léo's voice.

"Come in, Léo!" I hollered.

"Coming!"

Laroche shoved his weapon behind his back and blocked his ears with his fingers.

"Can you put the kids in the living room, please? You guys can all watch TV for a while, if you like. I'll come and hang out in a bit, I've got somebody in here with me right now."

"Housekeeper. Cleaner," whispered Laroche. "Everyone always takes me for a moron, it's ridiculous . . ."

I heard Madame Aquamarine closing the front door behind her again. I stepped over to the office door for a second and watched as the horde made its way to the living room. I needed my cuddle fix, but I didn't dare leave the room because of the sex-swapping crazo. It just felt so weird that I hadn't given my babas a kiss after school. I had a ton of questions for Léo too.

"Mommy! Mommy!" screamed Lisa.

She started searching for me in every room, and it wasn't long before she found me. She jumped into my arms for a hug while Emma and Sabrina continued to explore the new pad. Léo followed Lisa into the office. He was carrying all the kiddos' backpacks.

"Are we camping here now? Your life is pretty mental! You're always on the move. I've gotta eat real quick. I have a date! I got a beach towel for Erina. You don't have a suit for her, do you?"

I winked at him and rummaged around in my bag before pulling out a fuchsia-and-turquoise bikini with a stunning glittery Tahitian flower print. He seemed pretty pleased with the goods.

"If you check the fridge, you'll see some leftover beans and rice. Just dump it all on a plate and reheat for a couple of minutes in the microwave. We'll all have dinner later. But before you go swanning off to the beach, you have to get your math homework done. I know you have some, so don't lie to me." Intuition.

"What? But I'll be late!"

"You won't! You'll do it real quick! Come on, get that butt of yours moving! Send me a quick message as soon as you get to the beach, OK?"

Laroche groaned. "Will you be finishing up any time soon? When were you thinking of starting our session?"

I threw my eyes to the heavens. Lisa whispered something in my ear. I noticed she didn't look too great and she was whimpering.

"What's up, sweetness?

"Frighty."

"You're frightened? Frightened of what, honeybun?"

"Pirate Anorak."

"What? What's with all the pirate talk still? Sabrina?" I shouted. "Where's my big girl? Sabrina? Come here, would you?"

Sabrina came in, giggling. "Yeth?"

"Why are you all talking about this Anorak man all the time? Have you seen someone hanging around?"

"Oh, it'th nothing, Mommy. I haven't theen anyone. Don't worry!"

Lisa covered her mouth and giggled nervously. "It's a man. He keeps bumping his head on trash cans and lampposts. He's a pretty funny pirate, but I feel jumpy-out-of-my-skinny. He's strange. Very bad."

I gave Sabrina the eye. The eye usually worked. The eye said, *Let's get to the bottom of this, or there'll be trouble.*

"The'th getting all mixthed up between the thtorieth I make up and real life," explained Sabrina.

"My Lisa! Don't be scared of someone who bumps his head on stuff! You're not spooked by Mr. Bean, are you? We all giggle at Mr. Bean, don't we? He's not scary at all!"

When she saw that I wasn't a bit bothered about the story with the clumsy pirate, she clearly felt reassured, because she wriggled around in my arms, which meant she was ready to be put down.

I set her gently to the floor, then called out to Léo.

"OK, Léo, I'm just going to finish up with this patient and then I'll come and take over with the tots!"

We were finally alone. Laroche and I. Let the therapy commence!

22

Laroche let out a massive sigh. "At long last!"

"Cool your horses."

"What, do you run a daycare center on the side or something?"

"These are my nippers and they need taking care of, OK? Normally, I'd have finished work by now, but seeing as I can't actually get any of my actual job done in this joint, I still have a whole load left to finish by the time I'm done with you. And by that, I mean cleaning, not shrinking!"

Alexandre Laroche seemed to be worried about all the noise and confusion, but he started to speak anyhow, spouting off some miserable tale . . .

"I don't have a whole lot to say other than I think I've reached the end of my rope. That's about it. I'm sick to death of spending a fortune on therapy that isn't getting me anyplace. It does nothing. Nothing. Nothing. That word pretty much sums it all up perfectly. I don't need a CV because I run my own company, but if I was to write one, do you know what I'd write?"

"Mmmm," I mumbled, trying my best to imitate what I'd seen of Rachel Amar on the tapes.

"Nothing," he said. "That's what I'd write. Nothing."

Sabrina moseyed in and sat on my knee. She studied Laroche with interest.

"What'th thith man talking about, Mommy?"

"His name is Alexandre. He says he's unhappy. He feels like he's nothing."

She nodded her little head. "I thee. You can continue!" she exclaimed.

"Oh, please don't mind my daughter," I said. "Go ahead."

And so he went ahead. And boy, did he go ahead.

"It's not even as if I'm a nobody. Being a nobody is still something. Me? I'm nothing. I'm taking up someone else's place on this earth. I don't even know why I've made all this fuss. Why did I insist on having this last session? I know there's no hope for me. I'm in way too deep. I have a total lack of desire, you see. Nothing. That's what I am. All I ever wind up doing is stuff that doesn't even interest me. Like the se—" He noted Sabrina. "You know, the things I do as part of a group . . . the parties. I don't know why, but I don't even feel anything there either. I really am at the bottom of the heap. An absolute nothing. And what happens when nothing disappears? Well, that's just it, isn't it? Nothing happens. Is there anybody out there who would miss nothing?"

"Of courthe not!" shouted Sabrina triumphantly. "Becauthe it'th nothing! Nothing can't be mithed!"

"Exactly," responded Alexandre with a sardonic smile, his cheeks burning up. "She knows what's she's talking about, this girl! Exactly! Nothing can't be mithed—uh, *missed*—by anyone!"

All this weepy, moody moping was getting on my nerves. Big time. The old gray matter was working like crazy, trying to think of something to say to such a sad sack.

"Oh no, no. It's hopeless . . ." he wailed.

I'd had it.

"Just stop! Stop! You've got to put a lid on it now, I'm afraid. I did not agree to this just so you can lie there and feel sorry for yourself!"

"Mommy doethn't like people who complain all the time!" explained Sabrina. "We have no time for complainerth! Mommy alwayth thayth the'th not the wailing wall! It annoyth her and the doethn't like it. It thtopth her thinking clearly. Mommy liketh to be happy all the time. Like a Thmurf! Thmurfth have fun all day long!"

"You mean Smurfs? So you think I whine, do you? *Put a lid on it?* You stop me and tell me to put a lid on it? B-but . . ." He spluttered and stumbled and then stopped. There was silence for a good few seconds, and then he asked, "What school of thought do you follow?"

"The elementary school down on Rue Macé. Why?"

I could see how bewildered he looked. He must have meant something else.

I forced out a laugh. "Hey! Just a joke! Wow! You're so uptight! For an orgy boy, you're a real stiff!"

"What'th an orgy, Mommy? An orgy boy?"

"It's like Georgie Porgie pudding and pie, kissing the girls and . . . you know, the nursery rhyme, from when you were a little tot?"

Laroche must have been really put out. I felt like giving it to him once and for all. He was seriously getting on my last nerve. It was just that I didn't want him to kill himself. I'd have felt so responsible if he went and did that. So I decided to try reasoning with the miserable little . . .

"I just don't think all this misery is going to get you very far in life!"

"Oh, really? You don't say! So? What do you suggest?"

I thought about it awhile. "I want you to do everything I tell you and do it exactly as I say. Stand up."

Looking defeated, he stood up, put his back to the wall and his hands behind him. Damn, where was the gun?

It was at that point that Léo stormed in, a notepad and pen in hand.

"I'll never understand this! I'm going to miss my date! You know what? This morning, in class, I listened real hard! I swear, Cricri! But I just don't get it. I must have fallen too far behind. It's way over my head! Anyhow, next week is vacation. It's too late to catch up, so . . ."

I suddenly got an idea. If Alexandre Laroche wanted to take the step from being nothing to being something, he could tutor Léo in math.

I asked him, "What were you before you did that web thingamajig?"

"You mean before my start-up? Before I became the French Bill Gates? I was an IT engineer. Why?"

"Ask him about your math problems, Léo!"

"It's Thales' theorem. I don't get it. I can't remember it," Léo said.

"Go ahead. Tell me what you think it is," said Laroche.

"Um, you've got a triangle ABC with points DE . . ."

At this point, I zoned out on all the stuff with right angles and proportions and theorems. Who the heck knows? Well, other than Laroche, anyway. But I zoned right back in when I heard Laroche say, "It's how they measured out the pyramids. It's just unbelievable, isn't it?" Now I was pissed! I wanted to know how the pyramids were measured out! But I guess I'd missed the boat on that one.

"I can't believe it!" Léo exclaimed. "I didn't get it at all with my teacher. Zilch! And with you, it's in the bag in less than two minutes! You're awesome! Respect!"

Laroche brought his hands out from behind his back. I think he was a little agitated by the shower of compliments. The gun was in his left hand.

Léo spotted it quick as a flash. "What is it? A Smith & Wesson? OK, so double respect! A math teacher who comes heavy! Wow! Cricri, you know the coolest people! It's like *Prison Break* in this joint—or a cowboys-and-Indians movie. I love all that!"

"They're not playing cowboyth and Indianth. Thith ith jutht how they do thingth at the thychiatritht'th."

"Hey, I have to go!" Léo said. "I got a date! Did I tell you? Ha-ha! I'll copy out the theorem later!"

"Wait, come here a sec."

I searched my pockets and found a few bits of loose change.

"Here's bus fare for you and Erina. You'll have to get a drink from the fountain on the way, because I don't have enough."

"Don't sweat it, Cricri. I've got more than enough. My mom gave me a ton of cash last weekend. I haven't spent any of it yet."

I felt my cheeks flush. I didn't know why, but I was touched that he understood I wasn't rolling in cash.

"You make sure you're back around six, OK? And you've got my number? Yes, of course you do. Call me when you get to the beach."

"See y'all later!" said Léo.

He hopped out of the room, and we heard the front door shut behind him with a clack.

I was really concerned and upset that Sabrina had seen the gun. I was worried about the effect it would have on her. Trauma much? As for the loon, I was scared he'd have another breakdown.

"Put down that stupid weapon! You're ridiculous! Aren't you ashamed to wave it around like that in front a child? You should be."

He gripped it tighter than ever. I breathed in sharply. I had to find a way to get him to drop it. I didn't even know if the stupid old thing had a safety on!

"Stand facing me. We're going to try to take a journey together. A journey into your past. It's like a role-play. I did it with some buddies of mine back in high school. They were big manga fans. But that has nothing to do with this. I used to like being the princess, but it also used to piss me off that I was never allowed to make any decisions. Anyway, let's go back and try to find out when all this first started, OK?"

"Thith ith a funny game, Mommy! I like being the printheth too. But thith boy in my clath thaid I couldn't be a real printheth becauthe I am too bothy."

"These things never change, my love. You'll always find there are stupid boys like him. Princesses are supposed to be bossy. And they're excellent fighters. You've seen *Shrek*, haven't you?"

"But she's an ogress, not a princess."

"She's both. And you're not bossy. You're the boss. OK, Alexandre, concentrate, please. You're your mother and I'm you at ten years old. Do you want to give this a try?"

He nodded, but I could sense the fear. It showed in his eyes.

Let's see if Linus Robinson's Oedipus thing works here.

"So, what's your mother saying to you? Come on! Go! Go! Spit it out!"

"Well, she was always saying to me—"

"No, no, not like that! You're supposed to pretend to *be* your mother!"

"Oh, I see!"

He acted weary and worn out all of a sudden, and then mewled in a high voice, "Oh no, Alexandre! What are you doing now? I told you not to touch that television set! You really are a good-for-nothing! When will you ever stop bugging us? Oh, well, we all have our crosses to bear . . ."

"I think hith mother wanted him to get out of her hair and go off to camp," reasoned Sabrina.

"OK, listen. We're swapping. I'm your mother and you're you at ten years old. You respond now."

Then the tears started and they wouldn't stop. He was shaking the gun as he blubbered.

"Mommy! Please! I'm sorry! I won't bug you anymore! Sorry, Mommy! You're right! I'm stupid! I'll get out of here! I don't want to bother you. You'll see! I'm going! But I love you!"

"Oh, no! He'th whining again, Mommy. Don't freak out."

I whispered, "When I think about how short life is and that there are some people who want out even sooner . . ." And then in a louder voice, "Very good!" I pretended I knew exactly what I was doing and that this was something I did all the time. "Take a few steps to the side."

He did as I asked.

"Great. Now who do you see in front of you?"

Laroche wiped his eyes, snorted, and then stood there speechless.

"This is my own method. Just go with it. There's nobody there now, right?"

"Right. You were in front of me before, then I moved, and now there's nobody in front of me. What's your point?"

"It's simple enough, isn't it? Who just noticed there's nobody there?"

"I did. Me."

"Perfect! Yes! We're getting there! You see? You're you! Alexandre whatever-your-name-is."

"He ithn't nothing anymore, Mommy?"

"No, he isn't. He just told us so himself. He's him. The difference is pretty obvious, because nothing is what's in front of him. Nothing. Nobody. Right?"

"Right! That'th real clever!"

"There you go! My work here is done! Now hop off out of here, because I have a pile of ironing to get through!"

In fact, what I was dying to do was to engage in an e-mail conversation with Linus Robinson. I'd had some great ideas on that exact subject during the role-play. What if I replied to Linus as if I were Rachel Amar? It wouldn't be that big a deal if I did. It might even be good fun! I just wanted to live out the fantasy a little . . . Everyone else seemed to think I was her, so why not?

"Hold on a sec!" Laroche said. "I don't get it. Do you expect me to believe this little game of yours has cured me?"

"That's exactly what I expect you to believe. This is a brand-new method. You'd be surprised how effective it is. It's come directly from California in the US of A! That's right! I read all about it in the dentist's waiting room the other day. You'll soon see the effects in your everyday life."

None of that was true. I hadn't read anything at all, but I felt like we'd spent enough time together as patient and doctor. It had run its course and we'd all learned something. I'd learned that dishing out therapy wasn't really my thing. I wasn't patient enough for patients. Like Shakespeare wrote, "We're all on a big stage and we've all got speaking parts." Something like that. He said it prettier. Well, my part wasn't here.

I heard the door open and close. Madame Adrenaline was back.

23

The journalist darted straight into the office. "Laroche? You all done in here? Could you please carry my shopping bags through to the kitchen?" She dropped a pile of brown paper grocery bags onto the floor and gawked at us both. "Are you finished up? Problem all dealt with?" she asked me.

Silence. Neither one of us answered.

"Well, does he still want to off himself?" she asked.

"I don't think he doeth now!" trumpeted Sabrina.

"I was so sure you'd manage to do something!" she shouted glee-fully. She nodded at me with what looked like great admiration. "You really are quite something!"

She was double pissing me off with all the praise.

"One session and see what you did! You saved his ass!"

Laroche seemed overwhelmed by all this, and he went from staring into the void to rolling his eyes into the back of his head. Was it some sort of fit?

"Ahhhh!" he moaned.

"Hurry, Madame Aspirin-or-whatever-you're-called! Go get some vinegar! He's having an episode."

All she did was relay my message. "Get some vinegar! Someone get some vinegar now!"

Sabrina ran to the kitchen and retrieved a bottle of balsamic vinegar. As Laroche fainted, he rolled across the floor like a rag doll, the gun sliding off in the opposite direction. Great!

Madame Submarine grabbed the vinegar and ran to pick up the gun. She stashed it in her purse. She sat Alexandre Laroche upright and made him sniff the vinegar. This woman was a fast worker! He opened his eyes and the first thing he saw was her face inches away from his.

"Hello there," he said, a wide smile on his face.

"Hello!" she replied shyly.

"You two go make friends somewhere else, would you?" I muttered. "I've got a trillion books to dust in here!"

I couldn't believe all the drama! What was wrong with these people? All I wanted was five minutes' peace and quiet so I could get back to Linus Robinson.

Laroche shook himself and stood up. He put his hands in his pockets.

"Sorry about the whole gun thing. I don't know what came over me . . ." He took some money out of his wallet. "Do you charge the same rate as Amar?"

Was this guy ever going to leave?

"You're as stubborn as a mule! I won't tell you again that I'm the maid, OK? You don't owe me a thing. This wasn't a real session. And that makes sense, doesn't it? Because you're not actually cured, are you? And in this game, there's no such thing as cured, is there? Haven't you ever noticed that everyone you ever meet is nutty in his or her own way? Every single one of us."

"I'm confused. But I think I get your meaning. You want me to go along with the method until we reach a conclusion. Until the end. Or when you say it's the end. So, what can I do to thank you?"

He clearly wanted a response for thanking me. But thank me for what? For the role-play nonsense I just made up on the spot? It was true that he seemed less jumpy. I thought about Léo and the issues the poor kid had been having with math.

"I have an idea! But it's not for me, OK? It's for my friend Mimi's kid. You know, Léo? The whole mathematical dyslexia kid or whatever. He's not so hot at that numbers stuff. Like me and his mom! I don't know if it's some kind of permanent mental block or whether maybe a few lessons would straighten him out. So, the two of us are going to cut a deal. After what I saw you do with him earlier, I think you could turn this kid's life around. The math side of it, at any rate. So if you help him out, we'll call it quits. What do you say?"

His grin told me he was delighted with this solution.

"Of course—it would be my pleasure."

And then finally—*finally*—they all got the hell out of there so I could have some alone time with Linus Robinson.

Dear Rachel Amar,

I found your e-mail address on the Freudian Psychoanalysis Clinic site that I know we both frequent.

As you may know, if you've had the chance to download my latest podcast on the site, I am currently touring France and have recently traveled down to the Côte d'Azur. It was not only to get a glimpse of the Mediterranean, but hopefully to enjoy this opportunity to finally meet with you in person. I was asked to speak at the Mouans-Sartoux Book Fair, and when I noticed that this village is near yours, I accepted the invitation with great joy. And so, here I am! I must admit, however, that I detest hot climates and know that I am unlikely to see a patch of snow whilst in France, unless I go very high up into the Alps. This is unfortunate, as I am very much accustomed to spending ten months of the year snowed in. Goodness, it's hot here.

Wow—he mentioned a patch of snow! Like in the Simon & Garfunkel winter song my mother had sent! I couldn't believe it. I thanked my mommy. She was in top form, as ever. How did she do it? Well, I suppose she wasn't right every time, but she impressed me on a pretty regular basis. She must have been trying to tell me that Linus and I were meant to cross paths. So Simon & Garfunkel were going to show me the way.

Thanks, Momma! You're spot on again! The same words in an e-mail— that's clever! You never even knew anything about e-mail when you were down here. Well done!

I continued reading Robinson's message:

I'm sitting at a beautiful terrace bar on the famous Croisette, overlooking the stunning seascape, and all I can think about is you, Rachel. I so admire your work. There is nothing of yours I haven't had the pleasure of reading. Even now, I have *Psychoanalysis and Criminality* on this very table next to my coffee. But you must be used to such declarations of admiration. I would like to meet you before venturing back to deepest, darkest Canada.

I will be staying in the area for the next few days. I hope to hear from you shortly. I would very much enjoy comparing my latest theories with yours. It would certainly make for an interesting discussion.

Sincerely yours,

Linus Robinson

I didn't know much about the latest theories on anything, but what I did know was that *my* Linus Robinson was in France! Not only in France, but in my neck of the woods! I absolutely had to see him! I'd get a copy of one of his books and have him sign it for me! I'd show up at the book fair that weekend. It would be the first time in my life going to something like that, and I hoped there'd at least be a few comic books there I hadn't read. That would be a real bonus!

I started singing in a French-Canadian accent: "Linus Robinson . . . Robinson . . . Robinson . . ." And I added a Simon & Garfunkel twist: "And here's to you, Monsieur Robinson, Cricri loves you more than you could know . . . ho, ho, ho . . ."

I pressed "Reply." I thought for a moment, then wrote, "OK. When do you want to meet up?"

And *whooooosh* . . . I clicked "Send."

24

The whole e-mail sitch had worked me up into a state of excitement. I jumped up from my chair and shook myself off from head to toe. I didn't know what to do next. I couldn't get over this. I was one brave little minx at times. A daredevil! Wowsers! But what was I expecting to happen next? Had I lost my marbles? How could I be so mental? What was I going to do now? Maybe I thought my life wasn't complicated enough as it was? What in God's name was I doing?

The doorbell rang again. What was with this place?

"Can't we just be left alone?" I yelled. "Is this a shrink's place or a what? What's all this in-and-out, in-and-out all the time?"

Someone opened up and the bambinos started screeching. Top volume. Lisa pushed the door open and scurried toward me, screaming at the top of her little lungs.

"Bean! Bean! Mr. Bean!"

"Oh, my little pie face! What's going on here? Are you hurt?"

"It's Pirate Anorak, Mommy! He's here! He just rang the bell! He found us! He wants inside here! Inside your boss's house!"

"OK, my little angel babe. Let's go and check this out. We'll see what this pirate has to say for himself, OK?"

She hid behind my legs as I made my way toward the entrance. There was a guy standing there in an electrical-repairman outfit. You know the type—blue overalls, baseball cap, high-vis jacket, messenger bag, and a huge toolbox. Weirdly, he had Band-Aids all over his face and neck, and his left hand was all bandaged up. I had the feeling I'd seen him before. Under the bandages I imagined he looked like our national treasure, Johnny Halliday. But a more tired version with shifty eyes.

The journalist placed herself at a fair distance from the front door and held her nose. She caught my eye and stressed in a low voice, "I know it's not very polite, but there's a weird smell coming from him."

The guy gave her the once-over and uttered in a mean, bitter tone, "Electricity. Electric boiler. Problem with it."

"You didn't fall in a public dumpster on your way over here, did you?" The woman had no shame.

The repairman seemed just about ready to lose it. He barked, "I'm not here to talk to you. My boss told me to come over. Need to fix the boiler. Where's the meter?"

"I don't know. Would you like some of my mafé? It's a traditional West African dish made with peanuts. I think it might cheer you up. You seem to be feeling a bit glum!"

"Don't eat foreign shit." He sniffed the air. There was no doubt about it, the mafé was starting to smell fantastic. "Definitely no African shit."

She glanced at me and squeezed out a smile—a smile I considered to be dangerous. I'd have been more careful if I were the guy, but he seemed lost in his own nasty little world.

"Really? I get it," she said. "I bet you'd prefer . . . cassoulet? Is that it? Tell me if I'm getting close."

"Shut your mouth, you silly bitch! You're wasting my time here! Don't you have something better to be doing? A bongo to play?"

We just stood there, our jaws on the floor. The journalist's initial shock turned to pity quite quickly—all credit to her.

"Oh dear. This is more serious than I first thought. You're clearly going through a very difficult period. You need some help. Some counseling could do you a world of good. And you know what? You're in the right place."

"Crap, just drop it, OK? Go back to wherever it is you came from, got it?"

She wasn't bothered by his ugly words. I'd never heard anything so disgustingly racist. She turned to me.

"Out of respect for you, I'm going to step away from this situation. But I want it noted in my file that I kept a hold of my emotions here. I think it shows some progress, don't you?" She turned on her heel and headed back to the kitchen.

"Bunch of savages," the repairman whispered to himself.

I couldn't believe how well she'd kept herself under control. I'd have gone to town on the guy and ripped him a new one. I missed Gaston. He had ways of hurting people that went far above my capabilities. You wouldn't think he was much of a fighter, but he could handle himself.

The very least I could have done was slam the door in his face, but I was working for Rachel Amar now. Seeing as I'd been doing whatever the hell I liked up to that point, I could at least get one thing right and have her boiler all fixed up for her by the time she got back. I felt obliged. It was more than an obligation I felt, it was guilt. She had some problem with her electricity and this foul pinhead was there to fix it. So I breathed in deeply and stepped over to him.

"What is it you're here to do exactly?"

"I was told to come to this apartment, madame. You're Amar, right?"

"Yes, well, this is where Madame Amar lives."

"OK, then show me where the meter is."

"The meter? I don't have the foggiest idea."

He started muttering to himself—thinking aloud, maybe? "She hasn't the foggiest idea. It's just a short circuit and it'll all be up and running again, I bet. Doesn't even know where the meter is, for fuck's sake. One of these days, the whole system'll just blow up in their faces! If it does, I ain't going down for it. No way!"

"Mommy, Mommy, don't let him in! It's Pirate Anorak! He's horrid!" boomed Lisa in a full-on cry.

Sabrina's eyes widened. "Of courthe it ithn't! He'th here to fix thtuff, that'th all!"

"Do you think that little brat could give it a rest? Insulting me like that?" the repair guy said, thrusting his chin toward my Lisa.

My hands tightened into fists. I'll only be pushed so far. Was this guy seriously going to try to insult my kids and expect me to stand by and watch? I had to force myself to act with reason: *If Amar has problems with her hot water and called the electric company, I have to let this guy in to do his job.*

I held my breath, screwed up my eyes, and said in the syrupiest voice I could muster, "Come in, monsieur. Don't pay any attention to my daughter. She's just a little imp, you know? She watches a little too much TV. Listen, I have a lot of work to do, OK? Could you search around for the meter yourself?"

And off he went in search of it, opening every cupboard in the place. Sabrina and I returned to the living room. It was like the waiting room at a train station during summer when all the train drivers are on strike, like they so often are in France. I was the only one supposed to be there. Actually, Véro was the only one supposed to be there! Instead, there was me, the kidsters, Laroche, and the depressed journalist whose name I couldn't remember.

"It's ready! Mafé all around!"

The journo put down a huge platter filled with her special mafé. It was covered in thick golden cream. Wow, it smelled delicious. The main ingredients of mafé are chicken and peanuts. I couldn't believe she'd pulled it all together so quickly and that it smelled sooooooooo goooooooooood!

"I bought some of the ingredients already cooked, but I made the sauce myself."

The babies nearly dove into it headfirst. They started eating from the platter rather than waiting for it to be served up.

Laroche gazed at the dish with interest.

"Why are you still here?" I asked him.

"First off, I don't think my session is really finished. Second, I'm waiting for Léo so I can give him his first math lesson. And third, I've been having a good chat with Bintou."

He threw our cook a sideways glance and she reddened.

"Bintou?" I said.

They both giggled like a couple of goons.

"Bintou, huh? That's new, isn't it? Since when have you called her Bintou?"

"Uh . . . ummmm . . ." he stammered.

Is something going on between these two?

"I don't think much of your explanations," I said with a smirk.

"Well, it's not just that . . . I actually think it's pretty cool hanging out here. It's a happening place."

I rolled my eyes. *"A happening place?* Who uses language like that? You're too old! Stop wasting your time around here. We're not happening. Nothing's happening."

"Don't pay her any attention," said the woman with the complicated name. "You know this is all part of her strategy."

I could have shoved her face into her mafé!

"That's enough, *Bintou.* If we're going with *Bintou,* it'll make life a hell of a lot easier. I've been having some trouble with your other names. Monsieur Laroche, stop listening to her, I'm not who you think I am."

Bintou simply smiled.

"You may not be who I thought you were," he said, "but it doesn't matter. You're doing the job nicely. I'll wait for Léo and help him with his math."

I sighed again. I'd sighed a lot already that day.

25

It sounded like the door was being kicked in. Léo was shouting, "Quick! Hurry! Open up!"

I ran to let him in. I'd never seen him so agitated.

"Erina came to meet me, but we didn't go to the beach because half her face was swollen. I ended up taking her to the pharmacy to buy her some disinfectant. When I started asking too many questions, she clammed up and wouldn't answer. In the end, I lost her! She went and disappeared on me! A bus went past and I guess she hopped on. I don't know how she did it."

"Don't worry, it's not like we don't know where she is. We know where she lives."

"Yes, but what good is that? We know that's where he beats her. Oh, I should have told you. That guy we saw is not her father. Well, that's what she told me. I'm going to rat him out to immigration. Did you notice she was limping? I think she has something wrong with her hip, or her stomach."

"Did she say something about it?"

"Yes, but it wasn't clear. I didn't catch what she was saying. She was talking about someone called Kholia? She seemed so worried! She sounded freaky desperate about the whole thing."

"What was she saying, exactly?"

"'Not Kholia. My fault. Too small. Go. Return him. My fault.' Something like that. In broken French." He was agitated, wringing his hands.

"OK, Léo, listen to me. We're going to have a think about all this and figure it out. We need to find out more about that nonfather of hers. And it's going to be hard work. I bet he's a trafficker harboring illegal immigrants. That's my guess. He won't be all that easy to trace. But we have to find her. And the bit about Kholia, about being too small . . . Is that a kid? It sounds bad. I'm going to finish up here and then I'm coming with you. We'll try to find her. And you know what? I'm usually pretty good at this kind of thing. I'm an excellent detective. You'll see. Ask your mom."

Despite the brave face, I felt panicky. What were we getting our sticky little noses stuck into this time?

Laroche butted in. "Come here, Léo, I want to show you something.

Léo tried to cheer up a bit. "What's your job, exactly? What do you do?"

Laroche looked put out and thought for a moment. "I invented a real hot piece of software that helps financial peeps earn shitloads of money. After I got that up and running, I created my company. We have an app that does the same thing as the software, and now I run and manage a financial-analysis agency. I buy and sell shares. I use money to make money, basically. I put people in touch with other people. Get my drift?"

He appeared embarrassed. I guess he was thinking about the orgies. I suppose it was one way of putting people in touch with others.

"Wow! I don't even know what half that stuff means," Léo said, then paused for a while. "So, actually, you don't really have a job? You move money around from one place to another, and while you're doing that, you take a cut. Is that right? I don't think I could handle making a living that way."

"Why not?" asked Laroche.

"I don't know. I like to see results when I've done something. Concrete results. Like, if you fix a car engine, the car works when you're done. See?"

"Well, I did invent that app," replied Laroche.

"Oh yeah!" exclaimed Léo. "That's cool! And do you work every day?"

Lisa and Emma started to recite the days of the week. "Monday, Wednesday, Thursday, Saturday, Monday . . ."

I left them all to it and went to find a stepladder so I could take the curtains down to wash. Léo followed soon afterward. He wanted to help me get through all my work as quick as possible.

I started with the office curtains. This seemed to be the only place in the whole apartment where I could be alone to think. Well, almost alone. Léo was with me, of course. The repairman popped his head around the door, spotted us, and then ran away again. Weird.

Léo was in a dark and mopey mood as he held the ladders for me, despite my reassurances. He seemed to already have forgotten about Laroche and the cool app stuff. I didn't blame him, though. He didn't say a word.

As I worked, I got to wondering what could have happened to Erina.

Lisa wandered in. She likes to know where I am at all times.

"You're not playing with your pirate anymore?" I joked with her.

"Don't make fun, Mommy. Luckily, Sabrina is keeping a watch out. But it's fine right now because the lady who made the nice food gave the pirate a real good kick. He fell down in the big bedroom and didn't get back up."

I was only half listening. I knew Sabrina had one heck of an imagination, but I hadn't known until then that Lisa was following in her footsteps. She has some talent! Was she making this stuff up or copying what she'd heard her big sister say? Sabrina came in with a giant smile on her chubby little chops.

"Ith everything OK, Mommy?"

She took Lisa by the hand and walked her out of the office.

"I told you not to bug Mommy! She hath a lot of work to do."

26

Léo was growing impatient. "OK, do you think this curtain thing might be wrapping up any time soon? We've taken them all down now! There can't be much else left to do!"

"You're right. Let me just get organized and put the first set of curtains in the machine."

"So, where are we going to start searching for her?" asked Léo.

"She must be hiding out someplace, and I bet she's terrified. She could be all alone with no shelter. She could be in a real mess. Or she might have gone home and now be at the mercy of her father. Nonfather! As if he ever deserved to be a father! And what was that tale about a little tot? We need to get all this stuff straight, Léo. If we don't find out what's going on, nobody else will."

I didn't say anything, but my thoughts turned to my Linus Robinson and whether or not he'd read my reply. Well, Rachel Amar's reply. Well, the reply I'd written on behalf of Rachel Amar. What a mess.

I found Bintou with Laroche in the kitchen. They were washing the pots together. I gave her the address of Sélect and told her to pay Tony a visit. She was to say she was filling in for Mimi.

"I mean, if you want to. Tell him that I'll be back as soon as I've finished up at Véro's boss's house. You should also explain that sometimes you'll be there with my nippers, so he's not too surprised when he sees you with them."

She turned her head to one side. "Got it. And this is all part of the method, right? My treatment?"

To make everything easier, I said, "That's right. Yes."

"But do you really think I can manage all that, Madame Maldonne?"

"Yes, I do. I think it'll be a cinch for someone like you. You could do it with one hand tied behind your back."

I turned around and marched back to the office.

Laroche, who'd left while I was chatting with Bintou, was lying back down on the nitwit couch. Cue more sighing from yours truly. When was this nightmare going to end?

"But—" I started.

"Yes, I know. Let's just finish our session, OK? I'm not exactly asking for the moon on a stick."

"No way! Just stop this. It's too late now! I'm afraid you've missed your turn for today. I've got stuff to do, and I need to get a move on. Pronto."

I could hear Sabrina fretting. Bintou was getting the kiddos ready. She had her big purse all ready to go. I was pretty proud of her. I asked her if she'd mind taking the girls to McDonald's right after her shift at Tony's. It would be a great way to keep them all busy while Léo and I looked into the whole Erina business.

Bintou was fine with the arrangement, but Sabrina started making waves.

"I don't want to go, Mommy."

"Why not? Don't you want to go play with your sisters?"

"No! I have homework I need to do here!"

"Don't worry," said Laroche. "I'm staying awhile. This is a great place to work, and I brought my laptop with me. That's if you don't mind, of course. I can watch Sabrina. Someone needs to stay with the electrical guy. I think you might have forgotten that there's still a man roaming around the apartment."

Sabrina shut up and looked surprised.

I had forgotten about the electricity man, for sure. Neat. This Laroche guy was a walking computer. He remembered everything.

"I'm staying with Sabrina. I have to defend her," Emma breathed.

"I'm staying with Emma," Lisa said, nodding shyly.

"No problem," exclaimed Laroche. "They can all stay."

"OK. If any more patients show up, tell them that Amar isn't here. Come on, Léo! Let's get out of here!"

"Wait, I'll come with you," said Bintou. "You can point me in the direction of Sélect."

27

Once outside, with Bintou on her way to Tony's place, I turned to Léo. I had to let rip.

"You and I need to talk. I need you to tell me everything that went on with Erina."

"I told you everything already!" He threw his hands up and breathed heavily.

"Just control yourself. I want you to tell me word for word. Maybe there's a detail you missed. It might help us find her."

We were in the middle of the sidewalk. He let it all out at super speed.

"First off, I had to wait awhile before she showed up at our meeting place at the fountain, right? She wasn't carrying any plastic bags or packages, so I guess she must have finished her rounds for the day. As she got closer, I noticed something was majorly up with her face. I ran up to say hi asked her what had happened. She said she'd fallen down some steps. I didn't believe it for a second. I felt like killing the whole goddamn world! I asked her again and again! I wanted to know how her face had ended up that way, and she just kept repeating the same bull that she'd fallen. She also kept saying that the date was a bad idea.

"I'm simplifying here. She's kinda hard to understand when she speaks. This all took some time.

"Finally, she agreed to come to a pharmacy with me. I bought some basic stuff to try and fix up her face a little. After that, we went to a snack bar. I wanted her to sit down while I cleaned her up. I disinfected the cuts and bruises. I did my best. I tried out a few jokes on her to get her to smile. She didn't.

"There was a guy sitting at a table nearby reading a newspaper, and I noticed she kept staring at the front page. She seemed real focused on the photo. I read the headline. It said: 'Shooting at Border! Child Found Dead!' And then something about a smuggler and a truck? The writing was too small.

"Anyway, she stood up suddenly and gave me a look like she knew it was the last time she'd ever lay eyes on me. She ranted, 'You no try see me no more! Never! Never! Agree?' But I didn't agree. I can tell you exactly how the conversation went—almost word for word! It's engraved on my heart forever. She said I was in danger. She said the lady and children were in danger too. I assume she meant you. It all came pouring out that she believed she'd be killed if she continued to see me. All she wanted was for me to agree not to see her.

"I explained there was no way I could agree. Absolutely not! I asked her why she felt this way and explained she could come with me. That there was no need to be so afraid. I wanted her to understand there are laws to protect people here, you know? But she just laughed. She shouted about France. I think she was using bad words in her own language to talk about this country. I tried to tell her about the laws to protect asylum seekers, but she started crying and said something about a French guy who works with Murrash.

Honestly, I couldn't get her to stop crying. I wanted to know who Murrash was. Was it her dad? She told me the whole story. Or some of it, at least. Murrash isn't her father. She says her father is a kind man, but not all that bright, apparently. Her father is back in her home country, and he trusts this Murrash guy, but Murrash is a liar. He's the bad guy. She says he takes kids. Kholia. I guess Kholia is some little kid. I think you're right about that. And she wants to save him.

"She was yammering away at top speed. It was hard for me to grasp everything she was saying, but she did say I'd never understand. She said I was selfish. That my life was great. That I didn't know what problems were. That we aren't the same. We don't have the same way of life. It was upsetting to hear. She told me I was just a boy. And that I know nothing about real life. I got so mad. Unhinged. I may not know much about life, it's true, but I know I could crack open the skull of whoever did that to her face. She wouldn't admit that it was that Murrash guy.

"In the end I promised her I believed her. I couldn't think what else to do. I suggested we go see a social worker together. But this just sent her way over the edge. I think she thought I was suggesting we go to the cops. She's very worried about the pigs. She spat on the floor at the thought of cops!

"That's about it. Everyone was staring at us, so we left, and that's when she told me I was too kind—kind, but stupid, like her father. And then she ran off! It took me a couple of seconds to realize what she'd done, and by that time she was off in the distance. She turned at one point to glance back. Then a bus stopped in front of me and I couldn't see where she was. By the time I'd stepped around it and dragged my ass over to the other side of the road, she was gone. I ran in every direction looking for her. But it was pointless. I headed over to her crib, but she was a no-show there too. I waited, but I got sick of hanging around and sick of the smell of piss. I was thinking maybe a rat would eat me. I cracked. I feel ashamed now."

"Well, don't," I said. "You did everything you could. We'll find her. You'll see. We need to come up with a POA. A tragedy. Like in the war, right?"

"Do you mean a strategy?"

"Exactly. That's what I said."

I thought the best thing to do would be to go see my law-enforcement buddy, Borelli. I trusted him and he trusted me. Well, there was this one time he suspected me of murder, but he'd always given me a chance. We were good friends. I sometimes thought our relationship was unlikely (and I often needed him to save my ass), but we were the winning team.

I wanted to tell Borelli about Erina and her story. He could be counted on to not let the immigration people know about her. He was a good guy like that. Plus, he owed me one. He knew I knew that he'd kept hush about some powerful bigwig who wasn't paying for the crimes he'd committed. So, Borelli needed to scratch my back. He'd be able to check out what the bad guy was doing and protect the girl at the same time. And that's just what we needed here.

Léo didn't want the cops involved at all. But in the end, he came to understand that from our side, on our own, there wasn't much we could do.

I called Gaston and invited him to Amar's joint for a big meal with Bintou, Laroche, and the bambolas. I also asked him if he could make his way over to the trailer in an hour's time to pick me up. There were a few thingamabobs I needed from home. He desperately wanted to know whether or not I'd learned the words to his poem. I stammered as I told him I'd explain everything later. I made a mental note to remember to call Mimi and wish her all the best for her surgery.

So we had an hour to go and see Borelli.

As we made our way to the cop shop, we looked up and down the streets, every which way, trying to spot traces of Erina. It wasn't the most organized search, but it was worth a shot. It wasn't like she was simply going to materialize out of thin air in front of us.

We went the same route she took on her deliveries, but she was nowhere to be seen. And we didn't uncover a single clue either.

When we arrived at the station, we were told Borelli was out on a call. Luck was clearly not on our side.

I thought about leaving a message for him at the front desk. But I don't really enjoy hanging out in those types of places, so I decided to leave a voice mail on his cell instead.

Yeah, I have the personal phone number of a big cop boss. Cool, right?

28

On the way to my trailer, we passed a newspaper stand. Léo grabbed me by the arm.

"Hey! That's it! That's the article!"

He showed me the front page of one of the local rags. There was a photo of a cargo truck and a stretcher with a body on it. The whole scene was surrounded by officers. I read:

Shooting at Border! Child Found Dead! Truck Containing Smuggled Children from Albania Attempts to Flee

Poor Léo was in a total state and I had a lot of trouble bringing him the heck back down again.

I didn't want him hanging around or even near the bad guy's place, especially on his own. And I didn't want to go back there myself either, at least not without the green light from Borelli. I told myself that we could make this thing a whole lot worse if we kicked up too much of a fuss in Erina's neighborhood or got this guy worried in any way.

Especially as he'd already clearly threatened me and said he'd do shit to me and my dolls if I went anywhere near his pad.

We went anyway. We just made sure we took a few precautions. We made our way to the shabby old building and did our best spying act, taking turns to peek through the filthy window.

Nothing. We couldn't even hear any noises coming from inside.

Just as we were leaving, ahead of us on the sidewalk, a hundred or so yards away, I spotted a flurrying movement. It was the looker. The nasty man. He had his stylish suit on again and he was making his way home. *Murrash.*

And he wasn't alone. There were three men altogether and a kid. A young boy, maybe around ten, with blond hair and little cheeks all smeared with what I guessed were jam and tears. He was weeping, following the adults but dragging his feet. The men appeared sour.

"That's him," I snorted, pointing at the suit.

"Do you think it's her father or not?" asked Léo.

"I don't know. She said not, didn't she?"

"What do you think we should do?"

"We can't do anything at the moment."

They spotted us. As the three men got nearer, I knew the good-looking bastard recognized me. And he knew that I knew it too! But he didn't do a thing.

We darted past the four of them and carried on. Just normal people walking in opposite directions on a normal sidewalk on a normal day. I felt relieved because, to be honest, the guy gave me the creeps, and I feared a little (a lot!) that if the three of them had decided to give the two of us a good thrashing, we'd have been easy pickings.

We suddenly heard footsteps behind us—someone running. When we turned around, we saw something that was quite simply unbelievable. It was Erina, sprinting toward the men and child. Just as Léo had described, half of her face was puffy and covered in bruises.

She didn't say anything when she reached them, but her demeanor was so defeated. Humiliated. The man raised his arm, almost automatically, to hit her, but he stopped himself. Léo was to the point of tears, his anger showing on every inch of his face. I was close to dying from the urge to scream out. That bastard needed a few hard truths—but I had to stop myself and literally hold Léo back with all my strength to keep him from getting involved. This was a crowd we didn't want to mess around with.

Erina took the kid's hand. The boy grabbed her like his little life depended on it. The men lost interest in the girl and child and headed to the house. They must have known that the children wouldn't have dared do anything else but follow them.

Erina scanned the scene, and her sense of anguish was palpable. She saw us at the end of the street. The look in her eyes changed—it turned lighter, more hopeful, and there was just that little bit more sparkle in them. It broke my heart. We started creeping toward her, but she gave us a panicky gesture. She obviously wanted us to get out of there, to leave her alone, to not interfere.

She ran with the little one toward the scraggy excuse for a house. The kiddie went first through the rotten window, and just before she was out of sight, she held her hand up, spreading her fingers. Five. Was it a sign?

She followed this up with a couple of other quick gestures and mimes. She was pretty good! We understood!

The fountain. Tomorrow. Five o'clock.

Phew!

The whole thing was like a weird dream. She was gone.

We headed around to the back of the house. We could hear the muffled cries of the small child. We peeked in through the dirty window, trying again to see whatever we could through the flimsy fabric.

The little boy was trembling in the corner. Scared stiff. Poor little mite. Erina was sitting next to him. The three guys were around the table chowing down on sandwiches. The food looked pretty good!

Murrash threw a piece of bread at the small fry, maybe in an attempt to stop his sniveling. He then continued to munch on his sandwich with a satisfied grin.

"You hungry, 'Rina?"

She nodded slowly.

"Come! Here you go!"

She scurried over to the table and held out her palm to receive the scraps. He handed her what was left of his sandwich. The others were in stitches. Murrash took her chin and held her face up. He directed her head to the other two men.

She was totally trapped. Totally under his control.

Léo was desperate to break in and help her.

"Smile, 'Rina."

She didn't react.

"She's very beautiful, you know? You can't really tell right now. What happened to you, 'Rina? How did you do that to yourself?" he asked, laughing.

She whispered something, but we couldn't hear.

"Stupid little bitch!" He shook her violently. "You're going to show Kholia your route tomorrow. All week, you'll do that. I want you to teach him a few recipes too. Understand?" He let go of her, but she was frozen to the spot. "Move! What are you standing there for? Get to bed! And take him with you!"

She took the little one by the hand and they both went to the space under the stairs.

Murrash grunted to his buds. "She'll heal up pretty quick, you'll see. She really is a stunner! I'm telling you. She's worth what I'm saying. You tell your boss that."

Léo and I stared at each other in shock.

What were we getting ourselves involved in? Should we go in and smash the place up? Would we get ourselves killed? Did we just have to swallow what we were seeing? Not make a move? Not intervene? Go home with our tails between our legs? Feel powerless?

I thought back to what Bintou said during our therapy sesh. She'd grumbled that she couldn't do her work, she wasn't coping all that well, and so she just let it all drop. She felt ashamed.

And me—Mademoiselle Rosie Maldonne—always with a brave face, not bothered, big mouth . . . I was doing nothing. I chose to protect my own little moppets.

I didn't have the courage. All I wanted to do was to protect me and my own. I had to keep my wits about me. I had to react calmly to what I'd witnessed and try to get through this latest episode life had thrown at me without getting killed.

Did this mean I was growing up? Was I becoming reasonable? Was I maturing? OMG! Was I getting old? And what if I did let things drop? Did it mean I was closing my eyes and ears to it all? That I was acting like everyone else? Acting with only myself in mind?

"Let's go back to the station and let the officers know what's happening," suggested Léo, his voice breaking.

"No! You know what she said! She's scared of cops! It won't be the same with my friend, Borelli. We'll wait for him to get back to me."

We got out of there.

All the way back to the trailer, Léo and I came up with a bunch of theories to try to make sense of what we'd seen and who the little kid was. I'd been thinking of them all as illegal immigrants, maybe, but I hadn't realized the gravity of this sitch. I'd had a friend from the Philippines who was in France without all the right papers. I hadn't ever really considered what it must have been like for her on a daily basis, the way she'd got into France in the first place, or the reality of her journey. But it looked like it had been even worse for these kids. They weren't just illegals . . . they'd been smuggled.

"It's just like the article we saw," I said to Léo. "She's as illegal as they get. She's been smuggled! God, she must have been through hell! Imagine the conditions in one of those truck thingies!"

"But why has she been smuggled exactly? What's she doing with those men? And the kid? Has he been smuggled over here too?" asked Léo.

"I'm sure of it! Maybe he was even one of those kids who crossed the border in the truck we saw in the paper."

"Life must be awfully hard where they're from, if they're willing to risk their lives coming here—even in conditions like that," reasoned Léo.

I knew about this stuff. It was a big risk. Many illegals know what they're getting into, but some don't. Many women and children are trafficked against their will.

"They're going from one hellhole to another," I snarled.

Léo added, "And I bet there are so many people profiting from all that . . ."

On that jolly note, we continued our way home in silence.

Léo was relieved to have found Erina but worried to death for her. He later explained how he didn't think he'd sleep a wink that night, that he couldn't wait to see her again the next day.

Gaston was already waiting at the trailer with his Jag. This bucked up Léo and his solemn mood. Not a lot, but a little. You show any man or boy a Jag and the results are pretty astounding. Something magical happens.

Gaston was going into great detail with Léo about what the car had under the hood (the famous MK2 engine—his precious "Mark Two") while I packed up some random clothes, toiletries, toothbrushes, books, and whatnot so that the squirts and I could spend a few days at Rachel Amar's place. I heard a bike bell. Weird. I glanced outside. The hood was now open, and all I could see were Gaston's and Léo's butts sticking up in the air, their heads stuck in the MK2.

Then I saw it was Antoine from Tony's place who'd made the ding-dong dangy noise. He rode up to the trailer and I stepped onto my makeshift stairs.

"Evening!" I said. "What are you doing around here? I don't think I've ever seen you in this neighborhood before! You get everywhere on that bike of yours!"

"I was looking for you! I'm having a big birthday party! Would you like to come along? Your kids are invited too, of course!"

"Heck, why the hell not?"

"I sure hope you'll come! You're such a funny duck! I'll let you know when it is, but it'll likely be a Sunday." His eyes darted around the place. He was a nosy one. "Well, your way of living is certainly original," he said, smiling gently. "And you're absolutely sure you don't want to buy a condo?"

That was twice now he'd made that rather heavy-handed joke. He could tell from a mile off that no bank would ever loan anything to the likes of me.

He rode off. Ding-dong, ding-dong.

I put the bags of clothes and shit in the trunk and taped a note to the front door. I wrote the address of where folks could find me if they needed me. I realize it's not the best idea to let burglars know you're not home, but there isn't all that much to burgle in our place.

I picked up Pastis and got into the back of the car with him. He settled on my lap within seconds. They say a Jaguar engine purrs, but I swear my Pastis purred louder that day. He was so pleased to see me.

29

As soon as we returned to Amar's apartment, I set Pastis on the floor and went straight out onto the terrace to prepare a litter box for him.

The crazy electricity ape had left, but everyone else was still there. I had a couple of squatters on my hands. Laroche and Bintou didn't appear to be going anywhere. The kids were there, of course. It was starting to look like camp. And now Gaston was joining us. Not to mention my Pastis. He climbed to the top of a dresser and stayed up there, checking out the scene below.

Everyone was in a pretty goofy mood, except for Léo and me—we still had the major frets for Erina. Someone had ordered some pizzas to go with the leftovers from lunchtime. I explained to the whole group (because nobody was admitting who'd done the ordering) that we couldn't eat pizza every night. It's not great to let pups get used to that kind of food. Bintou took the blame for it, although she wasn't my number-one suspect.

"I promise, Madame Maldonne, I'll make lots of vegetables tomorrow."

She'd made herself the family chef and she was taking the role very seriously. And I couldn't cope with her calling me Madame Maldonne all the time. I felt like I was about thirty or something!

At the end of the meal, Gaston offered those who wanted one a ride home, but nobody took him up on it. He came over to me, full of hope, and asked, "So the poem? How are you getting on with it? Have you managed to learn it all? I've got a nice little melody in my head, you know? I have a feeling that this is going to make you a star!"

I pulled out a note I'd prepared from my pocket:

Pleeze ecskuse Rosie Maldonne as she wuz unabal to lern the powem becaws tyme went veri fast and she had 2 mani things 2 do yesturday? Pleeze do not purnish her. Thanks fur yur conperhenshun.

He smiled, but I could tell he was crabby and maybe just a little sad. I don't think I'd have gotten away with it if he really had been my teacher.

"Cricri, you're not taking this seriously at all! It's a crying shame! You're going to have to put some effort into this. Put your back into it, girl, or we'll never get there!"

After some time, everyone but my nearest and dearest went home. The imps and I explored the bedrooms, but my babas didn't want to be too far away from me. Back home in the trailer, we're never more than a few feet from each other. I don't know what Freud and Amar would make of it, but I put the twinniesprogs in the big bed with me and a mattress on the floor for Sabrina. We were happy as pigs in crap, the four of us all in the same room.

Léo slept on his own, of course. I don't think he was used to such luxury, because he looked pretty impressed with the whole arrangement. A choice of bedrooms! I helped him make up his bed with some clean sheets and we chatted.

"You know what? I saw something totally crazy in that walk-in dressing room before we went out to search for Erina," he said. "I didn't want to tell you about it. I don't know why. I didn't want it to slow us down, I think."

"What did you see?"

"I saw a guy. He was lying on the floor. Knocked out, maybe? Freaky."

"Lisa did say that Bintou had kicked or smacked the electrical man. I thought she was just making it up. You don't think it's true, do you? OMG! I hope not! We could be in it deep! You can't go attacking people who come into your home to work! He's a public servant, isn't he?"

I went to take a look. There were several walk-in closets and cupboards and Christ knows what in almost every room! Nothing. Why didn't I know any normal children? My and my friends' offspring were all whack or something.

It was getting dark outside. Slowly but surely, I listened as my little ones' breathing got deeper and steadier. They all went to snooze land pretty quickly. This is the sound that usually sends me to sleep myself. I find it reassuring. It lets me nod off worry-free. When I hear it, I know that everyone around me is relaxed and safe.

But that night, I tossed and turned for hours. I couldn't stop obsessing about Erina. What was the solution? How was I going to find a way to help her? Would she really show up the next day by the fountain? Five, she'd said? I hadn't even bothered to check whether Léo would still be in class at that time. I was pretty sure he'd bail on it if he was! And I understood that. I wasn't going to tell him I was OK with it, but I got it.

Everything had taken a turn for the worse since filling in for Véro. What sort of a nightmare was I getting us all mixed up in? And what was with the taking on patients? Was I out of my freaking mind? I'd sunk to new lows. And I'd written back to Linus Robinson! What was that all about? Honestly. I'd fricking zoned. How was I going to get myself out of it?

All of a sudden, the answer came to me. Just like that. Out of the blue. The next morning, when I came back from dropping the bamberinos off at school, I'd close Rachel Amar's door and double lock it from the inside. People would assume nobody was home. I wouldn't open it to a single soul. Then, I wouldn't have to try and fail to say no to any of these freaks. There'd be no more consultations. No more inventing therapy on the spot.

No more messages to Robinson either.

I finally managed to fall asleep, but I remained agitated until the following morning. Nightmare central!

I dreamed I was on the stand in some sort of court case. All the people I'd given my not-so-nifty advice to were around me: Saejin, Bintou, Laroche, and others I didn't even recognize. They were talking amongst themselves, but I could hear parts of what they were saying.

"I was doing really well. I was feeling better until she came along and messed it all up for me."

"Me too!"

"Me too!"

"Every day, I feel closer to putting an end to it all."

"Me too!"

"Me too!"

"How come she just left us in the shit like this?"

"She's a cold bitch. Heart of stone."

Some of them were crying, some were hopping from one foot to the other, some were sucking their thumbs. Some stared at me reproachfully, while others begged me to do something to relieve the pain.

"That girl's got a dark soul!"

"She doesn't care—she left us in the lurch!"

"We feel a little bit lower every day. Every day!"

I woke up, shuddering, soaked to the skin. I noticed with relief that my kiddos were still in a deep slumber all around me.

My negative thoughts came back and it took some time again before I managed to drift off.

I didn't understand why I was so concerned about whether or not people were getting proper therapy when Erina's situation was infinitely more serious. That girl was in danger!

I hoped I'd have another Linus dream. It would be a massive improvement.

But the subconscious never does as it's told.

Thursday:
The Lover Who
Came in from
the Cold

30

The alarm clock came as a bit of a shock. I'd managed to get a fair amount of sleep, but it hadn't been a deep sleep. The only reason I'd nodded off at all was because I'd thought, *To hell with all the moralistic claptrap crapola! Stop being too hard on yourself!*

These people needed me.

OK, so I had no training as a shrink. And I didn't really know what I was doing. But the people I'd seen so far seemed to like what I was coming up with. I was helping them make progress in their lives. So why should I refuse to help? It was better than them having to deal with everything all on their own until the real psycho woman came back.

I'd been feeling guilty for no good reason at all. I should just keep on following my instincts.

I'd also received a reassuring message from dear old Ma. A love song. We've always been a romantic bunch in our family. All hearts and flowers and all that jazz. My mother sent me love songs more often than not, actually. It was a great number by Blondie! "Call Me" . . . *Cover me in kisses* or something. I can't remember the words, but the tune is amazing! Good pick, Mom!

We ate at the breakfast bar. It was all very high tech. I sang the song and felt pretty cheery. Sabrina was being a bit of a slowpoke that morning, though. I asked her what was up.

"My tummy hurts."

That worried me. My little girl is hardly ever ill, and when she is, she never complains.

"You need to go straight back to bed, big girl. Go and sleep. No school for you today. Climb into Mommy's big bed, OK? I'll come in to see you and take your temperature. I won't be long. You try to stay nice and calm and peaceful while I take the girlios to school."

Emma banged her little butt down on the floor.

"No. We're not going to school either. Not if Sabrina isn't," she said with a pout.

"What? You can't do everything exactly the same as Sabrina all the time! You're going to grow up to be free-thinking, independent women! And free-thinking, independent women have to go to school. Do you want to be free?"

"Yes. But we also want to protect Sabrina from Pirate Anorak," Emma continued.

"That's enough of that! You little ones are going to school and that's the end of the discussion! Period."

Emma turned into a hysterical were-hyena. That's the only way I can describe it. I'd never, ever seen her like that. She's always so soft, so easy, and here she was screaming so loud I thought she'd spew her guts. And it went on. And on. She rolled all over the floor. Kicked! Howled! A full-on tantrum!

I was furious at first, but the longer it continued, the more I felt sorry for her. I couldn't believe my little fairy girl (who was normally just about the sweetest thing on this earth) had turned into a monster. We were having a bit of a Hulk moment. I tried to put myself in her position. She really believed that her big sis was in danger. She didn't want to leave her to face it without backup. So, one day off school wouldn't be the end the world. Nobody would die. I mean, summer vacation was coming up in a few days, anyway. No biggie.

Lisa was gobbling down some cereal I'd found in the cupboard, keeping a close eye on Emma. Pastis joined the group and meowed desperately. He hates it when my chubbettes are upset. I've never known him to not want to get involved.

We all waited, hoping Emma would join us back in the real world. As she ran out of breath at the end of one particularly long squawk, I slipped in, "Are you done yet with these frantic antics? You can stay with Sabrina just this once, even though you don't have a fever. Tomorrow, you go back to school, understood?" Lisa dropped her spoon on the floor and gazed up at me pleadingly. I cracked with her too. "That goes for you too, Lisa. You're staying home today."

"No. I don't want to stay. I really like school. But I want to stay with Emma. I like being with Emma. I don't know what to pick. School or Emma? School, I think."

Emma charged into our bedroom to announce to Sabrina that she was staying home. Pastis ran behind her, not wanting to miss out on any fun.

Léo was just about ready to head off. He didn't look all that cheerful.

"Léo, I'll shuffle along with you some of the way. I'm dropping Lisa off at school, OK? Listen girls, I'm going now, but I won't be long."

Before I left, I found some vitamin C chewables in the boss's bathroom cabinet. I gave a couple to Sabrina and made sure I tucked her in really tight.

"I want you to be careful," I said to Emma. "You're going to be on your own now for about thirty minutes. You open that door to nobody. *No. Body!* I want you to both stay in this room. Don't go onto the terrace. Don't make anything to eat. Don't go into the bathroom. I'm counting on you, Emma."

I know, it sounded like I was trying to protect them from a horde of serial killers in some freaky movie or something, but you really never can be too careful with kids.

We took the bus. Léo got off a couple of stops before us. As soon as I'd dropped my Lisa off, I sped back to the apartment like lightning.

When I returned, Laroche was already in the stairwell, waiting for me. I didn't say a word. We walked up to the apartment together and I opened up, letting him go in ahead of me. He headed straight over to the living room and sat down in one of the big comfy armchairs. He got a laptop out of his bag.

I heard voices in the hallway. The little ones were playing with Pastis. I heard the dressing-room-closet-whatever-it-was door clack shut. I remembered what Léo had mentioned the night before and went to open it. There was nobody in there. Must have just been the wind. I closed the door again. Sabrina hopped up onto the bed. She was full of the giggles. Pastis jumped up to join her, lying across her little belly. He was purring his head off.

"Everything all right with you two?" I asked.

"Yes, Mommy, yes," both my daughters replied in unison. "The doorbell rang, but we didn't answer it," explained Emma.

"I get the feeling that you two little monkeys are as pleased as punch not to be at school, am I right? But I'm warning you, Sabrina— you have to let me work today!"

"Nice and quietly! Help people fix their sad heads," sang Emma.

I frowned. What an understanding she had of the world already!

"I have to do a lot of laundry. Those people who are telling me about why they're unhappy . . . that's not really my job. I help them because they ask me to. That's all. I'm good at curing them. Don't worry, Sabrina. A day off from school with Mommy will have you feeling right as rain again. You'll be cured too!"

I went to the kitchen to clean up the bomb site that had been left behind after breakfast. I kept on talking to her, not sure if she could hear me from so far away.

"Sabrina, listen to Mommy's funny song! *Inch'ballah! Mektoub! Hayah Katouv!* Yeah, yeah! Life's something you've got to get on with!" I was just spouting gibberish to make her laugh. Good for morale. "*Advienne que pourra! Qui vivra verra! Que sera sera*—whatever will be, will be . . ."

"Say, do you think you could turn the volume down a notch?" asked Laroche.

"No way! You think you're going to try and stop me singing as well as working? Do you want to put a muzzle on me while we're at it?"

Pastis, who must have heard my voice, came running into the room and jumped up onto the table to listen to me. At least I had one fan in that house.

I didn't hear that there'd been a knock at the door or that Emma had opened up. A voice made me nearly jump out of my skin.

"Excuse me, Madame Maldonne, but your little girl opened the door . . ."

It was Bintou. She wasn't wearing her African clothes but a very straight, tailored skirt and fitted jacket. She looked every part the businesswoman extraordinaire.

"Well, hi there, Bintou," I replied. "Please call me Cricri. It'd be a lot simpler."

The whole Madame thing was still causing me to break out in hives. How old did this broad think I was?

"Did you knock or ring the bell? Weird that I didn't hear a thing. Have you been waiting long? Did you eat breakfast already?"

"No. I'm here for another consultation. What do you think about what I'm wearing today? I haven't dressed like this in some time. Since I burned out, in fact."

I pushed Pastis out of the way. I knew that most people can't stand the sight of a cat on a dining table. I put a cup of coffee down in front of her as she took a seat.

The kids showed up.

"Is there something you two want?" I asked.

I put my hand to Sabrina's forehead and noticed that her temperature had gone down. The vitamin C was doing its job. No more burning out for Bintou. Now no more burning up for my baby.

"Can we watch some TV?"

The screen in the living room was so big, you'd have thought we'd all gone to the movie theater. They sat down on the big sofa and cuddled up together. I put a cartoon channel on for them.

"She had a tummy ache this morning and she was all clammy," I explained to Bintou. "I decided not to send her to school. I've been paying too much attention to everyone else and not enough to her. It's classic!"

Pastis jumped up onto my neck. There were a couple of strangers around and he wanted to show them who was boss.

I noticed something odd. Both my girls had their heads turned toward the terrace as if the show was happening outside and not on the big screen. I tried to get a look at what they might be seeing, but I didn't spot a thing.

"Is there something specific you'd like to talk to me about?"

"Um. No. I'll wait for our session." She was staring at the TV, her eyes glazed over. "Did you see that guy? That pyromaniac guy, Victor Falso? According to the papers, he's a massive attention seeker. He's been trying to recreate the world with a couple of fireworks or something. Like the Big Bang."

"You mean like a jazz thing? He's a musician?"

"No! Not big *band*! Big *Bang*! You know, the world started with the Big Bang? This guy has a serious God complex, I'd say."

"Oh yes. Wait a minute. I think I saw something about the Big Bang on TV. Those scientist brothers, the Bogdanov brothers? They were talking about it on TV. Wow! That's some serious shit! Didn't he do it at the library? Has he hurt anyone yet with all this fire nonsense? Burn anyone?"

"No, he's just interested in the actual flames. He doesn't want to burn anyone . . ."

Emma slugged over to me and pulled on the bottom of my shorts.

"Jutht leave Mommy alone!" Sabrina shouted. "I told you not to make her worry! You really are a baby! You believe everything I thay!"

Emma shrugged. "Mommy? Why is Pirate Anorak on the balcony? He's holding onto the edge of it! He's going to fall!"

"Well, yes, people can't go hanging on balconies forever. They usually fall." I studied the terrace again. There wasn't anything happening out there. "See? There's nobody on the balcony! No pirates out there! Not today!" I took her over to the sliding door so she could take a look for herself. "See? Nothing."

Emma seemed sad but still stared at me as if she felt superior. She obviously thought she was still right about the whole thing. Sabrina whistled. My tiny tot ran back over to join big sis. Sabrina made a gesture with her hands as if to say, *See, I told you so!*

I headed back to the kitchen. "That girl watches too much TV!" I said.

Pastis jumped down from my neck onto the table. He sat opposite Bintou and started a staring contest with her.

"Tell your pet to stop gaping at me like that. It's giving me the willies."

Pastis suddenly turned away from her and hissed in the direction of the terrace. At the same time, a massive crash could be heard coming from outside. Sabrina and Emma ran out onto the balcony.

"What now?" I asked.

They came back indoors, giggling like goons.

"Nothing, Mommy," squeaked Emma. "Two cars bumped into each other. An *askident*."

"God, another accident. People drive like morons around here. Pastis, stop giving Bintou the willies with those big greens. Say, would you like a piece of chocolate to go with your coffee?"

"No, thank you," she grunted, striding out of the room. Weird.

I got the curtains out of the dryer. It was time to get some ironing done now. It took a fair while.

I went into the office. Bintou was lying down on the couch. I stopped, mouth agape.

"What are you doing there? What is it you need my help with?"

She thought for a moment before responding. "Actually, I was wondering what I was going to talk about this morning. It turns out, you're right. I'm doing very well right now. I don't think I need any more therapy!" She gazed at me and a look of joy flashed across her face. "You're incredible. You really are the best. I'm going to tell all my friends about you."

So I'd done it. I'd sent this nutter over the edge.

She stood and started searching through her purse. I assumed she was hunting for cash so she could pay me.

"Stop with all the histrionics, Bintou. We made an agreement, didn't we? I'm not allowed to take your money. I don't have the right. What sort of misfit do you take me for? You're such a stickler! A stubborn ass! Imagine if I was going around saying I was a real MD, but I don't got no degree in medicine. Get it?"

She clearly didn't get it. "Then how am I supposed to pay you? It's important to me. I thought you were just joking yesterday! If you don't pay your psychiatrist, I'm pretty sure it doesn't work. That's what I've heard. Do you want my watch?" She handed over a stunningly delicate pink-and-gold wristwatch.

"Um, no, thank you. That jewelry doesn't look very shock resistant. I don't think I could wash the pots with something like that on. And who even wears a watch these days? Don't you have a cell phone?"

She was getting antsy. "But, but . . ."

"Do you really want to do us a favor?" I asked. "Keep making meals for us! I don't even have time to shop for food these days, let alone cook the gosh-darn stuff. Plus, I have a teenage boy who needs feeding now."

"Yes! That's it. Like we agreed already. I'm fine with that idea. It'll help stop the crazy. In fact, this is a way of my therapy continuing, right? I love your method. All right, in practical terms, how should I go about it?"

"Go down the street, turn right, and you'll come to a real nice bakery. Get a ton of croissants and *pains au chocolat* and anything else you think the dolls might like for their after-school snacks. That'll all need to be bought fresh every day. For lunch, you'll have to go to the supermarket and buy what you need for your own recipes. Like I explained."

"Meals from my homelands, right? So, today it's going to be a stroganoff. Do you think that'll be fine? Natacha, my grandmother's maid, used to make it with beef. We ate it a lot when I was younger. I still remember how she did it. And for anything I can't remember, there's always the Web. It'll be perfect." A soft expression crossed her face. She had calmed down. "Marvelous! Of course! I'm so grateful to you, allowing me to do the shopping for your family and everything. OK. I like the idea of being a cook for a while. It's fun. Madame Maldonne, you're very kind. Oh, look at the time! I'm supposed to be cooking for you and it's nearly the afternoon already! I have to get to the market now."

She ran out of the apartment in her shiny Gucci moccasins, wide-cut Hermès scarf, and sweet little cream Chanel coat, carrying a chic Vuitton purse.

I'd have to tell her again about the Madame Maldonne thing. I couldn't handle it.

31

I'd been so busy scrubbing the place down like there was no tomorrow, I hadn't even noticed Bintou had returned. But suddenly a smell from the kitchen teased my nostrils.

"The beef stroganoff is ready! Everyone come and sit down!" shouted Bintou.

And that's what we all did. Laroche, Bintou, Sabrina, Emma, and me. The meal wasn't the biggest of successes, but Pastis was a fan.

In the afternoon, I asked Laroche to help me put the curtains back up on the windows. It was one hell of a job. I hoped I was well paid!

It was just as I was hanging off the top of the stepladder that a phone call—the phone call that, unbeknownst to me, could change my entire existence into the love story of the century—came through.

I scurried down, with no clue that destiny was knocking, and snatched up Rachel Amar's landline.

A voice. OMG! *His voice!*

My Linus Robinson.

"Yes, hello, Rachel Amar?"

I closed my eyes, then opened them again. I was imprisoned by my own anxiety. This was a desperate situation. I had to try and hide how worried I was. Turmoil. Inner-conflict central! *Who am I? What should I do? Am I her or am I me?* My voice took on a military tone.

"To whom am I speaking?" I barked. (I mean, who even talks like that?)

Bintou was now in the office and was watching me with her mouth agape.

I paced in circles, shaking my hand at her, trying to shoo her out of the room, making silent angry faces (or at least trying to). This was an extreme show of emotion for me. I was shitting bricks.

Bintou hooted. "Are you sick or in love?"

"Shhhh!" I answered, pointing to the telephone, my ear, my mouth, the sky outside . . .

Linus Robinson started speaking again but much more hesitantly. "I'm, uh, Robinson. Linus. I left you a message a couple of days ago . . ."

"That's right," I replied in a dry, meanish voice. "Exactly. Of course. Linus Robinson. You left a message. I remember."

"Yes, um . . ." continued Robinson. "I wondered whether . . . I'm in France, you see. I've come for a book fair . . ."

"Yes, you said so in your message."

"Please excuse me. I'm repeating myself," he muttered.

I felt pity for him. He didn't know whether he was coming or going.

"No, no. It doesn't matter . . ." I said. My sudden change in mood must have made him feel braver.

"I was thinking, seeing as our current fields of research are similar in nature, maybe we could . . ."

As soon as "fields of research" were mentioned, I felt a cold wave rush over me. This was supposed to be a conversation between two psycho peeps at the top of their game. I needed a wake-up call. A bucket of ice water over the head might have done the trick.

"Our research, hmm . . ." I tried to buy some time.

"Yes, I wouldn't mind talking about your thesis, the one on crim—"

"No, no. Let me stop you right there," I said. This little game had to end. It couldn't possibly go anywhere good.

No, Maldonne, you're cracked! Why would you do such a thing? screamed one of the little voices inside my head—the reasonable one, the one my brain listened to, on occasion. *What are you going to do here? Think about it! This guy thinks you're a shrink. You're not a shrink! Say he did wind up falling for you . . . it wouldn't be the real you.*

Wow. It was all getting a bit complicated for my sorry excuse for a brain. The bossy voice continued. *Stop it with this charade! You're treating people who are sick! People who need to see a real psychologist! Now, that's one thing . . . But this man you're falling for actually thinks you're something else. It's too risky. You're going too far. There isn't a single good reason for you to carry on this game you're playing.*

Oh yeah? Well, I'm sick of being unhappy all the time, I replied with the few brain cells I had left. They were childish brain cells, but they were mine. *I want to meet him, touch him, see if he likes me too. If he'd be capable of falling for me.*

Oh! OK! So, just to sum things up here, you're doing all this for love? You're like a spoiled kid who wants more candy. You know that nothing good can come out of being so impulsive, so reckless, right?

OK, you're right! You're right! Maybe nothing good can come out of this, but I do have one good reason! I loooooooovvvvvve him!

Of course you do! Some guy you've never even seen! You know what? You could get in a heap of trouble here. A bigger heap, I mean! I'm talking serious difficulties.

That's enough! I'm not a total loser, you know. And I'm not stupid either! I know this doesn't look too hot. I know I shouldn't pretend to be someone else. It's identity theft or fraud or something, right? But I'm doing it for the right reasons! For romance!

Come off it! Aren't you sick and tired of these hopeless romances yet? They never amount to anything serious.

Yes, I know. This is more than ridiculous. It's impossible that anything could come of it. Firstly, he's going to know pretty much straight off that I'm not a real shrink. So if I'm not her, it won't work. But then, if he liked me and he knew I wasn't her, that would be great. What if he couldn't tell whether I was her or not? But I'm NOT her! It would mean he loved her, not me. Even if he liked my body, it would still be her he loved. And that would be worse—he'd love her soul because he wouldn't have seen her body. Unless he liked my personality too. I don't know what I'm talking about now. I'm getting lost here. The easiest thing would be to just stop all this crazy bullshit . . .

Linus Robinson continued on his end of the line. "Oh, but yes, I insist. I think both our subjects are very . . ."

I tried to resist, to grow up some, to not give in to my addiction. "No! I'm not the one you—"

"This polemic is so interesting, and yet, it all seemed so self-evident! You must allow me to insist on speaking with you in person."

"In person?"

"Yes. Why don't we meet?"

"Well . . ."

Too late. My imagination was on fire.

I could already see myself flying out of my little mediocre life into the arms of this guy for one minute, one hour, one evening of absolute happiness, where I could feast on him—a tête à tête with Linus Robinson *himself*, my idol, the star I could never quite reach, the dream, the most gorgeous, kind, intelligent man . . . maybe on the planet?

Bintou was listening in and seemed to be quite enthralled with just my side of it! Laroche was next to come into my . . . um, *the* office.

Bintou attempted some kind of sign language to let him know that something important was happening, and they both went extra quiet so they could concentrate on eavesdropping.

"I imagine you have a very busy schedule," Linus Robinson continued, "but maybe, just maybe, our meeting will allow us to explore the paths untrodden . . ."

"Yes. It could well be . . . uh . . . ummmm . . ." I stuttered as I battled images of us having cocktails served with crushed ice. Oh wow! Linus. Ice melting . . . Finally, I managed to pull myself together enough to utter (in the harsh voice I'd used at the beginning of our call), "I can't schedule a meeting with you right now . . ."

"It doesn't matter; I'll call you back. Speak to you again soon." And he hung up. No hanging around with this one. I imagined he knew how to sail his ship through stormy waters! He came across as being all shy, but Linus Robinson knew a thing or two.

I was in shock. The good news was that I hadn't had to make any decisions one way or the other. So I couldn't blame myself for a thing.

"Why didn't you tell *him* you were the maid?" asked Laroche. "Is he getting some sort of special treatment?"

"Oh, he isn't a patient," I answered, lost in my thoughts, not paying much attention to what I was saying.

"Oh, I see!" He smirked, rolled his eyes, and marched out of the room.

"So? Who is he?" asked Bintou, evidently on pins and needles.

The tears came. Out of nowhere, but boy did they come. "It was Linus Robinson. He's amazing. And me? I'm just a big fibber. I was so excited to talk to him and I don't know how it all happened. I told him I was Rachel Amar."

"Oh, don't worry! You'll tell him the truth next time!"

And that one little innocent sentence led me to make my big decision.

"No."

"What's that? No? No to what?"

"Rachel's the one he likes. The one he admires. For once, I'm going to do my own thing here. I'm not going to tell him that I'm not her. I know what I know. I've lived the life I've lived. And this life has taught me some shit. I'm always far too honest. This time, I'm going to do what needs to be done."

"But you're the one always saying we have to be ourselves, that staying true to ourselves is the most important thing."

"Bintou, do as I say and not as I do. I'm going to apply the rule of the ends justifying the means. And I have one hell of a good reason."

"Is that so? What's your reason?"

"It's between my therapist and me, actually. My self-therapist. I'm not actually seeing a shrink. If only I had the money! So I take care of my own brain, you know?"

"And how's that working out for you?"

"Well, this is where I'm at: I need to start learning to say 'I.' I need to say 'me.'"

"How's that?"

"Like this: I love him. I want him. I desire him. He's for me."

"Makes sense, I suppose," concluded Bintou as she left the office. "By the way, where I come from, we have a proverb: The zebra's shadow has no stripes."

32

I sat down (well, I almost collapsed). The tsunami of lust had taken away all sense of reason, reasonableness, and reasonability from me. Are those all words?

I'd forgotten everything my mother and grandmother had taught me about female honesty, how important it was for a woman to have a frank attitude, to be independent and strong and earth shattering and all that stuff. I was ready to do anything, even lie to myself, for just a few minutes with Linus Robinson—who I'd only ever seen on-screen. All I wanted was to have him gaze into my eyes with desire and admiration. But I was under no illusions! My time with Linus Robinson wouldn't last any longer than a few minutes.

That's when I remembered my mother's song from that morning: the Blondie classic! *Cover me in kisses* . . . Blah, blah, blah . . . *Call me!*

Amazeballs! I think that meant my mother wasn't dead set against this whole plan. At least, that was how I was choosing to read it. Or did she know he wasn't going to call me? Maybe that was it? Whatever it was, I felt protected by her.

My mother had always been on my side. As long as something made me happy, she was up for it. I think that's what makes a happy mother. A mother is only as happy as her saddest child. I've heard that somewhere. That means that if I am sad, my babes will be sad? Or if they are sad, I will be? Well, that goes without saying. I had to go meet this guy. Someone would wind up cheerful, surely!

Someone rang the doorbell again. Ever since I'd agreed to replace Véro, I hadn't ever heard as much doorbell ringing in my life. She hadn't told me that the job would be answering the goddamn door all day like a butler. I was supposed to be maiding, or whatever the official job title was!

I headed out of the office, but Bintou had managed to get to the door before me. Again. She opened up and the electrical-repair nitwit stepped in. Easy as pie. Not so much as a hello. He had a big bandage on his nose, his ankle was wrapped up in more bandaging, and he had what appeared to be a plaster cast on his knee and another around an elbow.

As soon as he set eyes on Bintou, he started acting up. He looked her up and down and said in a sarcastic but weak tone, "Oh, it's Aunt Jemima!"

Who speaks like that in this day and age? I was going to tell him that he needed to watch himself, but Bintou got there before me. Except she kicked him in the face rather than have a word with him about his attitude. He collapsed. Wham! Straight down on the floor. That's Thai kickboxing for you!

He didn't see it coming. How could he have?

She managed to push him (with her foot again, so let's call it a kick) to a corner of the hallway so he wasn't blocking the front door.

"Is this guy a kamikaze or what? It takes him a long time to catch on, doesn't it?"

I hesitated. My instinct was to help this inanimate man lying in a heap on the floor. But he'd asked for it, and I had other fish to fry.

Pastis turned up. He must have known I was thinking of frying some fish.

So it was true what my kids had seen the day before. Bintou had given the guy a good beatdown and they'd witnessed it.

I went back to the office with Pastis. He sat on my knee while I cleared my head and got over the trauma of the phone call.

It was then back to the spring clean of the century. I tackled every single doorknob in the place. I made them all shiny and new.

The alarm on my cell went off. I'd set it to remind myself to fetch Lisa. Whether you're a shrink, a maid, or an unemployed woman receiving government aid, there's always the school run. We're all equal when it comes to picking up our little darlings.

As I headed toward the door, I tripped over Electric Boy. His leg was sticking out a little too much. It was hard to get past him. He could have done with a few volts up the ass to get him going again.

As I checked to see if he was still alive, I had the slightest feeling of worry for the poor fella. But screw that. I was going to be late!

I left the building. There was no way I was going to keep Lisa waiting for the sake of that loser.

33

In front of the school, draped across the hood of the Jag, I spied Léo
(little show-off!) chatting with Gaston. I headed over to them, and, after
we'd done the kiss-kiss-kiss-kisses on each other's cheeks, we all climbed
inside the ride.

Gaston was flustered, almost giddy. He thundered, "I had Bintou on
the telephone. Wonderful! Marvelous! I found something out about that
truly exceptional woman! She attended one of the leading music schools
in the country! She's the most talented composer! Can you believe it? It's
splendid! I will write the tunes and sing them to her, and she will tran-
scribe everything—the score, the libretto. I have a meeting with them
later on today at your boss's place. We're going to work on it."

"*Them?* Really? Plutocracy?"

"You mean 'plural,' Rosie. With Bintou and Laroche."

"And what does Laroche have to do with this? Laroche? Seriously!"

"He'll be producing. Didn't he have a word with you already about
this? He knows a lot of people who would be very excited about invest-
ing in an opera."

I shrugged, not knowing what to say to him. This whole poetry
thing was going right over my head.

Back in the apartment, Monsieur Electrifico was no longer lying on the ground. He must have woken, got back on his feet, and left again. So he hadn't been all that hurt. Maybe he'd been playing it up? Making out it was worse than it was?

Everyone was in the living room. The TV was on, but the sound had been muted.

Gaston took a quick, slight bow and handed out pretty pink files to Bintou and Laroche. He was taking it all so seriously. He's so formal!

Sabrina was settled in the corner of the room, winding up a ball of nylon yarn.

"Well, then! Let's get to work," barked Gaston. "Have you learned the words, Cricri?"

"Gaston, listen up. It's very kind of you, but I haven't really had the time since yesterday."

He tsk-tsked. "That's not OK, Cricri. I'm working on my end. I've got the tunes, I've now got an excellent musician who can do the orchestration, I've found my money guy . . ."

"Why do you need a money guy, Gaston? You're loaded to the max!"

"Because this is a real project, Cricri! And real projects have investors. Don't you realize that? I mean, it's a dream come true! All the elements are finally coming together. You have to keep up, Cricri."

"Oh, don't stress. It'll be all right on the night," I replied grumpily. "We're still worried to death about that young girl, you know? Léo will explain everything to you, I'm sure."

Issue dealt with.

On the kitchen table, there was the biggest plate you could imagine, covered in pastries. Wowsers. And next to it, a huge bag with the word "Chacok" on it. That was an expensive clothing store. The real good stuff.

"Oh, I just couldn't resist!" mewled Bintou, her eyes lighting up.

She handed over the bag. It had a huge gift-wrapped box inside. I understood. *No way!* I didn't want that to all start up again. Why couldn't I just be left to do my job? I was there for a bit of cleaning. I just wanted to pocket the cash for it and sleep easy! Presto. Job done. Out of there. But here this woman was again trying to make me feel guilty or trying to buy my silence (or at least my shrink skills) with outrageous gifts.

"Is that for me?" I asked, taking the box gingerly as if I believed it had a snake inside.

"Yes!" squealed Bintou.

I sat my weary ass down. "Sorry, but I just can't," I said firmly, and I pushed the box to one side and grabbed a *pain au chocolat*. "Anyone else hungry around here?"

"We were waiting for you, Mommy!" bellowed Sabrina.

The chickies got all over those pastries like ravenous little pups.

Bintou was staring at the TV screen. "Oh, look! They're talking about that crazed fire man again!" She turned the sound up.

A police truck could be seen parked up in front of the city courthouse. There were officers standing around. They all appeared on edge. Jittery. One of them opened up the truck at the back and the famous (or rather the infamous) Victor Falso stepped out, shielding his eyes against the sun. He staggered a little. A TV crew was ready and waiting. They ran to meet him and stuck microphones and cameras into his face.

"This is André Peautini reporting live from the city courthouse. I am hoping to speak directly with the suspect who has come to be known as the Full Moon Pyromaniac. Victor? Victor? How do you feel on the fourth day of your trial? Do you think you might break this stretch of silence today and finally speak out in your defense? Why have you chosen not to say a word? Does your silence mean something?" His brow was furrowed. I guess the interviewer was feeling the strain. "Um . . . can I just say . . ."

Victor Falso stared straight into the camera. His look was intense. He didn't utter a syllable. The journalist stepped back, at a loss as to how to act. The accused waltzed past all the other journos, TV crews, and general rubberneckers and strode up the courthouse steps, escorted on either side by two cops handcuffed to his wrists (trying to keep up).

André Peautini wiped his brow and gawked at his team with an apologetic smile before pulling himself together and running over to a guy dressed in lawyer robes.

"Monsieur! Monsieur! When is the ruling expected?"

"We're a long way from that!"

The lawyer looked past Peautini and pointed at something. The journalist turned around to see what it was, and the man in the dress gave him the slip. Childish move, but it worked. The image cut and we were all treated to an ad for laundry detergent. I turned the sound back down again.

"I don't suppose you've thought about anything else that might help my particular case, have you?" asked Laroche almost timidly.

Bintou was sitting next to him, and it gave me an idea. There was an orange dishcloth lying on the countertop. I passed it to them. I got them to each hold an end of it. Pastis sat on the counter as if he belonged there. He was watching the scene unfold with fascination.

"Here! We're going to try and get you both out of your usual habits, set you on the right track again. Agreed?"

Two heads nodded vigorously.

"All righty, we can do this. I think you guys are friends now, am I right?"

More nodding.

"Maybe even a little more than friends?"

Pink faces.

"Can you see your relationship here?" I held up the dishcloth.

Still in perfect unison, they shook their heads. Vigorous shaking.

"Look, the thing is bright orange. It's pretty hard to miss!" I yelled, pointing at the cloth.

"Ahhhh! OK!" Now they understood.

"So, sit there and try not to let go of your end, OK?" I said, handing them each a side. "It's like not letting go of a relationship, get it?"

Léo walked in. "I can see you're busy, but I'm heading off now. Erina said to meet at five o'clock."

"You mean, that's what we think she said. But we're not sure, are we? We're not sure of any darned thing!"

"Well, I'm sick of waiting for the cops to show up and help—or show up, period. What are they waiting for? The right time or something? I'm going to the fountain, and I'm taking her away from all that. And if she's not there, I'll just show up at her place, break everyone's faces open, and leave. With her."

"And where will you take her?"

"I'll bring her here."

I thought about it for all of two seconds and reasoned: 1) we didn't have all that much to lose and 2) he was probably right. Waiting for the police to show up or expecting the situation to straighten itself out would take ages. Those weren't solutions. We had to take the bulldog by the horns. Did bulldogs have horns? What was the saying again? Whatever it was, we needed to get on this thing fast.

"I'm coming, Léo! I'll just finish up here and then I'm hot on your heels, sweetie! I'm up for punching a few people's lights out this afternoon. I really am. If there are two of us, we'll get the job done better and faster."

Just then, the telephone started ringing. My hand flew to my chest. I felt uneasy.

Laroche and Bintou didn't even notice how agitated I was. They were still holding the orange rag and staring at each other with big smiles on their faces, blocking my access to the phone.

"Let go!" I screeched at them. "Come on! Let go! We're done with the exercise."

I wanted to pick up the call quick, find out what was what, and then leave with Léo.

They wouldn't let go, though.

I let out an exasperated breath. The telephone continued to ring on the other side of them.

"OK, you can stop with the cloth thing. It's over. We've been interrupted too many times now, what with Léo and now the phone. Just let go. We'll do this some other time."

I tried to stretch out my arm across the cloth, but I couldn't reach the phone. So I gave them my evil eye. The pair of them traipsed off without letting go of their bit of fabric.

Still ringing. I picked up. I felt a bit doomy.

Laroche and Bintou were now over on the sofa, side by side, both still holding the orange talisman. I'd invented a powerful game there (by accident!).

"Yes?" I asked quietly.

"Yes. Hello. Um, please excuse me, it's . . ."

"Linus Robinson," I mouthed breathlessly. I pressed the mute button. I didn't want him to hear how stressed I was. I needed to compose myself.

I took a huge breath, pointed at Laroche and Bintou to stay quiet, and found the harsh military-style voice I'd used with him the last time. I needed something to mask my emotion, and this did the trick. Throat clearing followed.

"Is that you, Linus?"

"Of course, and is this Rachel?"

"No, sorry, it's not possible." I hung up, ashamed, silent. So, that didn't go too well. Grip-getting was called for. I glanced around, picked up my purse, and hollered out to whoever was listening, "I'm going out with Léo. I'm counting on you to take care of the children."

"Don't worry, Mommy, I'll play with the little oneth," said Sabrina. "We have a prithoner."

"Really? Who is it?"

"Oh, you don't know him. We're going to judge him."

"That's good," I replied absentmindedly. "But don't forget that we're against the death penalty in our family!"

"We'll thee. We haven't dethided who'th judging yet. We have the prithon part done, though."

What a bizarroid game they were playing. But I didn't have much time to think about it. Léo started pulling my jacket. He was getting frantic. I didn't want all the glittery bits on my jacket to go all over the floor, so I followed him.

Gaston caught up with us as we stepped out into the hallway.

"Wait! Where are you going? I can take you. It'll be a lot faster."

"That'd be great. We have to get to the fountain downtown. We're already late!"

34

Just as the three of us walked out onto the street, we bumped into Borelli in his old cop car. Why had his ride never been upgraded? As soon as he spotted me, he started on me (as was his usual style).

"Hey! I got your message yesterday, Maldonne! I passed by your place and saw your little note. Now there was a bright idea!"

"Thanks, Borelli!"

"That's not what I mean, Maldonne! Where's your head at? You're just as naive as ever! Let me explain: You're messing around with that little Albanian girl. There's trouble brewing. And you're a pretty recognizable woman. Especially around these parts. So, say you piss these guys off—just saying, it's not the sort of thing you'd do at all—and they head over to your trailer and you're not there. Fine! But just imagine someone had left some sort of a clue behind. Imagine someone had written a note explaining that you weren't there but giving the address of where you were staying. That would be dumb, don't you think? Deranged, even?"

"Christ! You're more paranoid than me!"

"If it makes you feel better, call me paranoid. Anyway, I took the note down. Just to be on the safe side."

He asked us to get into the car with him. The cop car! As if. He wanted to take us down to the station.

"Sorry, Borelli, but no can do. Not right away, anyhow. We have a meeting."

"Actually, it's an order, Maldonne. There'll be no discussion."

Léo looked nervous. Kids should be a bit antsy around the five-o, though, I suppose. I said to Gaston, "Could you go over to the fountain on the Rue Coste Corail and tell my friend to wait for me, please?"

"Of course!" replied Gaston. "Just let me know when you've finished with this nice police officer and I'll come pick you up!"

So Borelli took us to the station under the pretext that he wanted to explain to us exactly what we were getting ourselves into.

Once we got inside his teeny tiny office, he was super kind with us. Not what I was expecting. He offered me a cup of coffee and Léo a hot chocolate.

"Hey, Borelli, what's with the change in 'tude? You're being super nice! I'll have some of whatever you've been having! It's weird."

"Ha! And you think I'm the paranoid one? I'm the same as I ever was. Listen, we know each other well now, Maldonne. I've grown to like you. We've done some good work together, you and I. But, honestly, you're messing with me now." His voice turned harsh, almost bitter. "You're getting on my last nerve."

"Why the nasty talk, Borelli? I'm not a little kid, you know."

"Maldonne, you were the one who called me yesterday. It wasn't the other way around, OK? So you're going to listen to what I have to say. And it'll do you some good, understand?"

"Oh, come on! What's your problem?"

"I knew this was going to happen," snarled Léo.

Borelli paid him no mind and continued. He came across as being pretty stricto.

"When you spoke to me about that girl and her so-called father, I checked some stuff out. You're in some ugly business there, Maldonne.

Very ugly! It's something we've been investigating for a while. And we're advancing. That's partly due to you and the call you made to me yesterday. We know where they're hiding out now, at least. But things are heating up and I don't want you involved."

"Ease up! Let's keep things polite here, Borelli! What's the case, anyway? What are these guys up to?"

"Drug smuggling, human-trafficking rings . . . The list is long and it's all bad. Do you want me to continue?"

"Surely you're exaggerating!"

"Do I look like I'm exaggerating? These guys bring these kids over from Albania and Hungary. They promise all sorts of incredible stuff to the parents. Schools, mostly. Or they just take the kids as debt repayments. And then the nightmare begins for these children."

"What happens?"

"There's a ton of scams, but what you've got yourself involved in is the worst of the worst. Trafficking. It's very profitable. And there are a lot of buyers. You don't want to know. Very often, they're sent places to work. Unpaid, of course. I've seen it down here on the coast. Switzerland too. They're sold to the highest bidder. Simple as that."

"Never! Slavery?"

"Yes! Slavery! Sure, there are all sorts of prettily written laws in this beautiful and free country of ours. This and that has been abolished. That and the other is a crime. But this and that, and that and the other, are all still widely practiced."

"Jesus! I can't get over this! They're just tots!"

"I know. A lot of them are used for begging. They're the lucky ones, I guess. But another big problem we've been seeing is this mule business."

"Mule? What does that mean?"

"Maldonne! You must have heard of the expression, with all the TV you watch! They're called drug mules. It works best when the kids are little. They carry drugs, basically. Deliver them. Bring back money.

Nobody suspects them because they're so little. Innocent. They don't attract attention. Who would imagine a little tot with supermarket bags was carrying a load of class-A drugs? The poor mites have to do this on a daily basis."

"That's it!" yelled Léo, who hadn't opened his mouth until this point, but was now making a good attempt at deafening us.

"What's it?"

"That's what Erina does! I'm sure of it! Like Dorian! But I don't think she even knows what she's carrying in those bags!"

"The less she knows, the better it is for her, because when it comes to drugs, even minors are tried as adults, according to international statute. She'd be sent to juvenile prison. The fact that she was forced into it isn't really taken into consideration. Even if she can prove it."

"That's so unfair!"

"That's just the way it is. We don't live in a fluffy world of rainbows and unicorns and Care Bears and whatever else you imagine. I bet she'd be in a heap of trouble with immigration before we even got started on the drug stuff. She'd be sent back to her own country, through all the official routes, and as soon as she landed back there, she'd be arrested for having traveled illegally in the first place! These things are taken very seriously."

"And what happens to these nippers when they grow up? When they're too big for this mule work?"

"Well, that's when it gets really ugly, Maldonne. Especially for the girls. They're never really allowed to leave the network. They just have to work in a different field. They become hookers. There'll never be any shortage of work for them. Oldest trade in the book. More girls than boys go into it, but some boys too."

"OK, I've heard enough of these horror stories."

"No, you haven't, Maldonne. I haven't finished yet. I have to make sure you get my point here. I don't want to see you poking your nose into this. Think about your daughters and keep on the straight and narrow this time. Sex slavery isn't even the worst of it. Yes, it gets worse. Hard to believe, I know. If you're sold to certain people, well . . ."

"What?"

"Snuff movies."

"What does he mean?" Léo asked me.

I shrieked at Borelli, "Watch it! This boy's a minor too! What will his mother say if she knows we've been talking like this in front of him? He's too young to be hearing about such horrors! Drop it!"

Léo was just about to protest when Borelli snapped. "He's not too young, Maldonne. It's always better to have knowledge than not. This is going on all around us, and it's better to avoid traps than find out some other way. Knowledge is power."

I didn't know what to say. He was totally right.

"So, what's a snuff movie?" Léo insisted, staring at Borelli.

Borelli eyed us both nervously and then lowered his head. I don't think he could bring himself to elaborate.

We all waited for someone to break the silence. Each of us lost in our thoughts. I often say that the person who knows how to get me to shut my big trap hasn't been born yet, but I had to admit, right then I had nothing to say. There are no words for such things. I kept telling myself that we weren't talking about animals here. We weren't talking about some weird mutant race. These were human beings doing this. People like me. We had the same makeup. It's a cop-out to call them monsters.

Borelli stood, took a few steps, and then returned to his seat. He sat back down again. He banged his fist on the table and turned a bright shade of purple. He shouted, "I don't want to see you anywhere near these people. They're trash! Trash of the worst kind! Hello? Are you still with me here?"

"Yes," whispered Léo almost inaudibly.

"Yes," I sighed, trying to put a brave face on things.

He calmed down some. "Albania isn't the only place supplying these children. On the market at the moment, you can add Poland, Hungary, Romania, Ukraine, the Czech Republic, Belarus, and Russia. The Middle East isn't organized enough yet. They're too busy with all their wars. So, basically, Western Europe demands and Eastern Europe supplies."

"And what can we do about it?"

"It's delicate. Very delicate. But what can you do about it? Nothing! As for us, we're doing what we can."

"It's disgusting!" cried Léo. "Why can't you do your jobs? Erina hasn't done anything! She doesn't even know what she's carrying! She's being beaten. And there are a ton of people making money out of this! Lining their pockets! And there are folks here—cops, the government— who all know what's going on!"

"That's the way of the world," Borelli said. "It's been like this since records began. And it's always the youngest who suffer. Even though Erina isn't responsible for what's happened to her, she'll be paying for it for the rest of her life. When the authorities decide to go in for the kill, they'll sweep Erina up like she was nothing more than a grain of sand."

Léo flipped. "What are you going to do for her?"

Borelli spoke slowly, his tone reassuring. He was trying help Léo manage his emotions. "We should be able to protect her. We need to get her away from Murrash. Murrash destroys everything in his path. It won't bring an end to what's going on between Albania and France— we're a long way from solving that issue. But it should get Erina out of danger. You've put your finger on a network here. We need to find out how big it is. Well, how long's a piece of string, you know? But one thing's certain: if we don't go about this correctly, Erina, given her young age, might be sent back to her country, where the authorities could very well imprison her, or she could end up caught up with the same types of people and find herself back at square one. We may lose sight of her forever.

"Another possibility is that she could spend a few years in a deten-tion center here in France. Or even juvenile prison, in which case these men, or men like them, will pick her up when she gets out. And then it would be prostitution for her. We wouldn't be able to protect her in that scenario, because she'd be an adult. The best thing for her would be for us to find out if she still has family somewhere—a family who gives a shit—and take it from there. That's our best shot."

"But we can't just let these bastards continue what they're doing!" I cried. "It's not just her! They've got a little boy too! Even younger!"

"I didn't say I'd let them continue, Maldonne. I'm doing my job. I'm trying to work out the best-case scenario for your young friend and the boy. The scenario with the least trouble, the least collateral damage. And I'm trying to figure it out before it's too late. I can't change the world."

"Why can't you just arrest them? Or we could go fetch Erina nice and quietly and then deal with the rest of those bastards later down the line! She's waiting for us at the fountain!"

"We know the gang you're talking about, and we know what we can charge some of them with, but for the others, we don't have any hard proof yet. We need to find out who their boss is. They have a contact here in France, and we want a name. We don't have anything. No idea who it is. Nor how they're communicating. We can't listen in on any calls. They're always changing numbers, swapping lines—by the time we get a wire up and running, all the authorizations it entails, they've changed their phone. I know there's a guy in charge. Someone here in this one-horse town of ours. He's the one ordering all this. We need him." He glanced at Léo. "In any case, I don't want to see either of you hanging around this thing. Keep away from my case. It's too dangerous. I hope you realize that. Also, you could risk messing it up."

"But we're not just going to leave Erina and the boy with those evil pigs! They're the ones in danger! Not us!" yelled Léo.

"Hey! Cool it, young man! If you really want to help us, you're just going to have to let it go. And I'll help you out on my side. I'll let you know what's happening as it happens."

"Bull. It won't be enough." Léo sulked.

"OK, so if I need your help, I'll call you. How about that?" Borelli asked.

We stood up without giving an answer. I started hunting around in my bag, buying time. I didn't want to leave. I couldn't deal with being out of the picture. Borelli strode around his desk and held me by the shoulders.

"Get off my back, Maldonne. Give it up, would you? I'm warning you. If I catch you on my tail, don't bother coming to me for help again. Get your act together. Mind your own business and leave it to the pros."

"Let me go, Borelli! Just because you lent me a hand once or twice in the past, you think I'm your pawn or something now?"

I pulled myself free from his grip and marched out of his office, my head held high. Léo followed. The poor boy was worried to death.

35

We left the police station in the most depressed mood ever. As we plodded along toward the bus shelter, Borelli watched us from his office window. We sat on the bench in silence. A bus arrived, but we didn't take it. We looked at each other. Léo was waiting for me to talk first.

"Should we get a move on?" I said.

"What, you mean we'll go search for her?" he asked.

I didn't answer, but stood instead and trotted off in the direction of the town center and the fountain. With a little bit of luck, Gaston would have passed on the message to Erina and she'd still be there.

I didn't know whether Borelli was still watching us. I didn't care.

We slogged for a hell of a long time before we reached the fountain. There was a heap of tourists flocking about, but no Erina. And no Gaston. We waited for five minutes and then decided we'd be better off heading over to the Albanian joint.

As soon as we were in the miserable little alleyway, we crept up to the place. We went around the back, careful not to make a sound. The scrap of fabric they used as a curtain had been moved slightly to one side. We could see in pretty clearly.

Murrash was sitting at the table with two goony-looking friends or accomplices or gang members or whatever you'd call them. They were shitfaced. The main guy looked angry, on top of that. It seemed like they were chatting about something serious. I couldn't catch what they were saying. They must have been speaking Albanian, but Murrash was dropping in a few French words every now and again.

I managed to catch "She'd be good. That's what I've been saying all along!"

The other two protested.

"She's never been taken," he said at one point. What was this? Were they talking about Erina?

Whatever was being discussed, the three of them weren't agreeing. Murrash was furious as he spat out, "'Rina!"

She came out of her cupboard with the little angel we'd seen the day before attached to her skirt. Little Kholia. They were shaking with fear.

"You, sweetheart, you'll be worth the wait! If you fuck this up . . ." He ran his thumb across her neck. "This is what will happen to your dickhead of a father. *Capisce?*"

Erina didn't answer. She didn't cry either. Murrash certainly didn't care either way. He sneered along with the other two soulless bastards before threatening her some more in his loud, drunken voice. I only just managed to stop Léo from breaking through the window. We wouldn't have gotten anywhere. Three professional tough guys against the likes of us?

"Know what?" Murrash said. "You're making me lose face in front of my partners here! Running away all the fucking time!"

He lifted his fist, but one of the other two stopped him just in time. He must have wanted to protect his merchandise.

The little boy started to whimper.

"That's enough, let's go!" yelled Murrash.

He grabbed the little child's sleeve. The boy put up a good fight. He held on with all his might to Erina's skirt. He was in such a frenzy! A force to be reckoned with! But Murrash gave him a smack and stormed out of there with the boy. His two pieces-of-scum friends followed.

We ran toward the front to see what was happening, hiding around the side of the building so they wouldn't spot us. They used the door (I didn't know they could, since Erina and the boy always used the window), taking care to lock it carefully behind them and replace the boards. We had just about enough time to run into a nearby derelict outhouse. Risky business.

We watched as they slithered away.

Léo grabbed an old wooden crate from a rickety shelf and smashed it onto the ground. He took a piece of the broken wood, and a few minutes later, we came out. I think he felt safer with his new weapon.

We climbed the front steps and opened the window. Erina was too terror stricken to come out. Léo scrambled in while I kept watch. They came out together. She was a shaky mess.

And that's when the three of us beat it. I swear, I don't think I've ever sprinted that fast in my entire life. And I should know. I've done a fair amount of running. We didn't even look behind us. We had just the one goal in mind—to get Erina somewhere safe.

Jeez, we ran for it. I'm talking Olympic-level, maybe even medal-winning, speed.

Léo raced ahead, but a thought struck me. He didn't know where he was going. He just knew he had to get there fast.

We arrived at an intersection and I hollered, "Over here! This way! Follow me!"

We were on the road to Gaston's house, and we weren't all that far, but I was running out of breath. I stopped and tried to catch it. I reached for my cell in my pocket. He'd asked us to call, so now was as good a time as any. There was no point continuing on to his house if he wasn't there.

Before I even had time to dial, we saw the Jag. I waved like a maniac and Gaston stopped. Of course he did.

"What are you doing here? Why didn't you call me?"

I was still breathing like a sick camel, but I managed to say, "We were heading to your house! Well, I mean, we wanted to go to my house . . . no, to Amar's place. Oh, I don't even know, Gaston!"

"Amar's place. That's a super idea," chirped Gaston. "Everyone hop in! I'm always ready to give folks a ride!"

Erina probably didn't have the foggiest idea what was happening, but she didn't ask. The explanations could come later. Now, we had to get cracking. Our asses needed to be in gear. *Top* gear. She had to follow us. She had to have total trust in us.

Gaston just drove. No questions asked. Every now and again, I noticed he glanced in the rearview mirror at Erina. He was intrigued by her, I could tell.

We got there! Into the underground parking lot, the building, the elevator. I found the keys, opened the door, closed and locked it behind us. Aaaaaaaannnnnnndddd breathe! Phew! We were saved!

We took a couple of seconds to adjust to our safe haven, stared at one another—and cracked up! It wasn't a normal laugh full of good humor. It was a nervous, anxious, manic kind of snickering. But I guess it did us some good. Laughing has to be better than crying, right?

"Honestly, Cricri, who are you?" snorted Gaston between giggles.

Our howling slowed down and our breathing returned to normal. It all went quiet while we took stock.

I inspected Erina and the traces of bruising on her face and croaked, "Bintou, could you show Erina where the bathroom is, please? I think she'd like a little time to freshen up."

Léo looked at me gratefully and Bintou took Erina by the hand.

36

Just as I stepped into the living room, the telephone rang. Good God. Never a quiet minute.

I headed to the office to pick it up. With a hop, skip, and a jump, I managed it just in time.

A sexy Canadian accent said, "Rachel?"

"Uhhhh . . ."

"Listen, I'm in the neighborhood. I wondered if . . . if . . . it might be an idea. What do you think?"

"If what might be an idea?"

I knew. Of course I knew! I was sure of it! But I wanted to hear him say it, because I couldn't quite believe it.

"If I came to see you now. Then we could have a quick chat before I took you out for the evening. On a real date. So, what do you think?"

"Well . . ." I hesitated but succumbed. "OK, I'm on my way!" I hung up.

A crowd had gathered in the office. Everyone was standing around, but I couldn't actually see their faces. My eyes were staring into the distance.

"What did I just do?" I was flummoxed, to say the least. "I've got a problem here! Have I lost my mind or what? I just agreed to a date!"

I paced the office. Everyone started talking at the same time. Suddenly I caught a glimpse of myself in the mirror Amar had hanging on the far wall.

"No way! Look at the state I'm in!"

I pulled at my long hair. OMG. It was filthy.

Bintou decided it was time to get involved.

"Wait, Madame Maldonne, please. Let me help. There's no need to panic. I know exactly what you need. You don't want to go too sexy. You need to be classy with an intellectual twist. Something in linen. Yeah, that's right. Linen with a hint of silk. A dress. A nice little dress. Not too long, because you have stunning legs. You should take a look at what I bought for you! You'll like it and it'll do the trick, mark my words. We'll brush out your roots, cut off your split ends, change the color, tone it down with some conditioner, blow-dry it a little, and you're good to go!"

"What about the opera?" whined Laroche.

"Later, later! This is real life and it's happening right now!" replied Bintou.

I stopped listening as I ran out. The bathroom was where I needed to be. On the way there, I stepped over the electricity guy. He was sleeping in the hall. The others followed me and did the same thing. It was as if we'd gotten used to him being somewhere in the apartment on the floor. How many times had it been now? He was part of the furniture.

"Yeah, he's here again," Bintou said. "He wanted *me* to apologize! Can you believe that? I know I shouldn't have kicked him again, but I couldn't help it. It's like my foot has a mind of its own when it comes to this guy."

We crossed paths with Erina as she came out of the bathroom in a fluffy terrycloth robe. She'd washed up and put new dressings on her cuts and bruises. I smiled at her. I really would have liked to have spoken to her for a while, but we weren't on our own. We had an audience.

I took a couple of seconds to say, "Erina, you can sleep in my room tonight with my daughters. Sabrina will show you where everything is."

The twins pulled at her robe for her to follow them into the kitchen. They love nothing better than a houseguest, that pair. Léo went with them, and I heard him ask if she felt like a bite to eat.

I wasn't able to battle against Bintou's bossiness. She really is something else! Before I knew it, I'd been sat down, stripped, wrapped up in several bath towels, and given a full-on beauty treatment. She filed my nails into pretty shapes and straightened out my hair so it was smooth and glossy. Like I'd just stepped out of the salon! She didn't have the time or means to change my color, so luckily we didn't need to have that fight. Her argument was that my roots were brown, so the rest of my hair should be. She said a chestnut brown would be classy. I disagreed and argued that red was more stylish and it suited me and I looked gooooooood! It had said "Hot Red" on the box, and that sounded sexy to me! Hell yeah!

Bintou held out a Max Mara dress. I pushed it away.

"Where's your head at? Can you really see me in that thing? What do I look like to you?"

"You look like a psychiatrist," she declared in her straightforward tone. "A shrink with a well-heeled clientele."

"That's all well and good in your world, Bintou, but I'm not a shrink, I'm—"

"A maid! Yes, I know," she sang.

"No! It's not that! I'm me. That's who I am! And I don't wear dresses like that. I think it looks like it's from the olden days or something. I wear sexy shit! Mimi, Léo's mom, passes stuff on to me. Hot rags, you know?"

I stepped away from the hair dryer and rummaged through some of my stuff. I pulled out a pair of glittery shorts with rhinestones and a satin tank top with cutouts on the shoulders and sides. I slipped it all on and there I was, a super sex kitten. I felt like me! I turned to look at her triumphantly.

"You know the stuff you bought in all the pretty wrapping? I think it would do well for Erina. She doesn't have anything with her. And have you seen her clothes? Oh, the poor child."

My cell started chirping somewhere in the distance. Laroche sprang into the bathroom and handed it to me. Good thing I was dressed!

I sighed and picked up. "Yes? Is that you, Tony? OK, right, wait . . . Just a sec . . . I can't do anything right now because I have an emergency here, you see . . . Yes, I *knoooow*, you've got an emergency too . . . Hey, I sent you someone, didn't I? . . . Listen, Tony! I can't do anything! I'm on vacation, so you're just going to have to deal."

I hung up. Bintou and Laroche were openmouthed. That pair didn't get out much. I couldn't stop laughing. I felt tickled! Tickled pink! Sometimes it's nice to put yourself first for a change . . .

The doorbell.

Aaaaaahhhh! My makeup-artist-hairdresser-stylist got up to answer the door, but I stopped her in her tracks.

"No. Let *me* go."

I was dressed, the war paint was on, my hair was just about done . . .

I opened up. Linus stood there, blushing. I threw him my bestest, most dazzling smile. We gave each other the once-over, sniffed each other's asses (well, not literally), and stood in mutual appreciation. At least, I think it was mutual. He broke the spell.

"We have a date?"

Without responding, I spun on my heel and scuttled toward the office. He followed. A flurry of out-of-earshot whispers and mutterings coming from the kitchen forced him to turn his head in that direction. The whole gang had come out through the living room into the hallway to stare at him. Léo, Erina, Sabrina, the twins . . .

"Hi . . . hi there," gibbered Linus, surprise in his voice.

Everyone waved at him.

I made a sweeping movement with my arm and begged them with my eyes to do a disappearing act.

"Don't pay them any mind. I'm running a seminar at the moment. They're my students."

"Oh! How interesting! And you've opened it up to children?"

"You can never start too young, that's what I say," I replied.

I stepped over the Electric Wonder and Linus did the same. He didn't comment. Had he even noticed?

Just before we were both inside the office, the gossipmongers started. We heard every word.

The first shots came from Bintou. "Wow! Yankee Doodle Boy isn't half bad!" she squealed.

"What'th a Yankee Doodle Boy?" asked Sabrina.

"What do you mean by 'isn't half bad'?" demanded Laroche.

"Pleath! What'th a Yankee Doodle Boy?" insisted Sabrina.

"Oh, he's not my type," continued Bintou, "but I know a good pedigree when I see one. And he has definite sex appeal."

"But what'th a Yankee Doodle Boy?"

"Your fries are getting cold. Come on, Sabrina, finish your fries."

"No. Why won't you jutht anther my quethtionth? Nobody'th dealing with me! Nobody'th paying me any attention! I'm thick of it. My ideath never count for nothing. I jutht have to keep quiet. Thut my big cake hole all the time!"

A door slammed.

"Wait! Wait, Sabrina!" pleaded Emma.

I was cross, but I smiled at Linus Robinson, who gave me a perplexed grin in return. We stepped into *my* office!

I closed the door behind us. I don't know how it happened, but the very first topic of conversation we hit upon, or rather stumbled upon, was lying! The one subject I would have hoped to avoid. *What's my subconscious doing?* I wondered, throwing myself into the deep end.

"So, if we work with the idea of truth in a session, can the notion of lying also be tackled? Lying when lying down, so to speak. Hmm . . . lying down," pondered Linus, deep in concentration.

"Yes, I see," I replied, a bag of nerves.

In fact, I was lying right there, but not lying down (like I wished!). I wasn't even following what was being said. I kept saying to myself, *OMG! He's hot, he's intelligent, and he smells really good!* I was drooling a little bit.

I remembered some of what Amar had droned on about at the end of her film with Laroche. I repeated it like a little parrot.

"When you speak of lying, we must remember that the subject sees it as an essential form of protection. A barrier. It's very difficult to separate himself from this." Christ, my memory was on point!

Linus stared at me with admiration. His eyes were shining and bright. When I took a closer look, I even saw a hint of flirtiness. But at the same time, a voice inside me was screaming, *Impostor! You're such a poser! Rosie Maldonne! You know everything there is to know about lying! This is identity theft! You're a scammer! You'll pay for this!*

I think it's safe to say that Linus Robinson had no clue about the state I was in. He was under my charms. He liked what he already knew about me, or what he knew about Rachel Amar, and he liked what I'd just said . . . whatever it was.

"However, in your latest published work, you . . ."

He reached for a book on the shelf at the same time I did. I knew Rachel's latest book—that's about all I knew! Our hands touched. I felt an electrical charge pass between us, and I closed my eyes in ecstasy. Linus must not have felt it. He only noticed that I (Rachel Amar) had his book on my (her) shelf. This seemed to excite him more than the hand thing.

"Oh! You have *Resilience* . . ." he said, a little confused, maybe even intimidated.

"Of course!"

"And . . . have you read it?"

"I know it by heart," I lied.

He seemed delighted by this!

"And . . . what . . . what did you think of it?"

"OK! I'm starved! Should we go eat now?" I replied, opening the office door briskly. I might have come across as a little harsh.

The entire group of family / friends / patients / smuggled children fell inside the office. They'd been stuck to the door, eavesdropping to the max.

"What are you all doing? Have you finished your homework?"

They looked around guiltily. Bintou's punching bag (kicking bag?) was still on the floor, but stirring.

"Hey, are you still here? You should have finished by now, shouldn't you?" I shouted. How long was fixing this heater thing supposed to take? Pandemonium.

He opened one eye, sat up, and nodded, trying to pull himself together. He stared at me, pointed to the office, and fell back down face-first onto the floor.

"No. No way. Not you too. If it's a session with Rachel Amar you're after, you'll have to come back. I am not—"

"Rachel Amar, I am her maid . . ." everyone said in unison.

Linus stared at the whole scene in disbelief. He couldn't figure it out.

I smiled at him.

"They're all messed up. They love these wacko practical jokes. I never really understand them!"

Sabrina and the twinniebobs were standing just behind Laroche. I noticed Erina next to my girls. Her hair was tied back and she was wearing the Max Mara number. She was so pretty. Lisa made her way through the crowd and jumped up into my arms.

"Ith he a Yankee Doodle Boy?" asked Sabrina.

"Sort of! But, really, he's a Canadian. It's not the same."

"You can go out. Sabrina is watching the pirate," Emma said.

Sabrina was sitting on the electrical man's back, pinning him to the ground. He looked too exhausted to do anything about it. She had a flask or a bottle in her hand. God knows where she'd found it.

"He preferth a flathk, not a glath. It containth more and it'th more practical."

"OK, Sabrina. I think this is all a little over the top, isn't it? We shouldn't sit on folks like that, OK? It serves no purpose."

"Just leave it, leave it," muttered Floor Man.

What a loser.

I turned to Linus. "It was very kind of you to invite me out to dinner, but I don't think I'm going to be able to make it tonight. Something unexpected has come up. I'm sure you understand." I pointed to Erina. "This young girl is under my protection now and I don't want to leave her on her own."

"No, no!" Laroche, Léo, and Bintou cried out. "We'll take care of her. We'll do it! Don't worry!"

Linus's eyes pleaded with mine, brimming with hope.

I couldn't resist those peepers.

I caved pretty easily.

I gave the babas lots of snuggles, cuddlewuddles, kisses, and smoocherinos and told them they had to listen very carefully to the grown-ups. I said their special job was to be nice to Erina and to give her cuddlewuddles too if she wanted them. I told them they were to get to bed early and promised I'd be home by eleven p.m.

I pulled Linus by the sleeve. I couldn't help but feel a little guilty to be looking after number one. How come I was taking time for me all of a sudden?

Because I needed it. We left the apartment.

37

When we stepped outside, I discreetly looked up to the balcony. They were all there, watching us leave. Everyone except Sabrina and the electricity repairman.

We sauntered at a leisurely pace toward the beach. I wasn't very at ease in the neighborhood. It was too snooty for me. It reminded me of the time I took the kids to a five-star hotel for dinner. Very funny. But I had an idea.

There were so many great little joints on the beach that had delicious salads. There was no need to go to some high-class restaurant. And it could be super romantic too! Some of the beach huts had tables outside. We sat down in a little booth for two with an incredible view over the ocean. There were a ton of tourists milling around us, but we were in our own little world. It was the sort of thing I never did. It was crazy that people considered the beach huts low rent. They were the best places with the best views!

It was like we were the only people on the planet.

We sat in silence for a while. Linus studied me, and I sensed he was surprised at how easy the silence was.

I put my hand on the table. Linus timidly moved his forward. Our fingers lightly brushed. You'd have hardly noticed if you'd been watching. We smiled.

"This is one of the best days of my life," declared Linus, as straight and simple as lines come.

"Why?"

"Because I finally get to meet a woman who I have so admired through her books, admired for such a long time . . ."

My whole face burned.

"Not only are you one of the sharpest women I know, but you're so full of life and sensuality. You have a certain softness. You're also very beautiful. Be careful, Rachel. There's a strong possibility I may be falling in love with you. And it's the first time in my life this has happened to me."

"Stop, Linus. I can't take this. Don't throw that love stuff at me! And don't call me Rachel!"

He didn't even look shocked. "No?" He smiled. "And what would you have me call you, you delicious creature?"

"Cricri."

"Cricri . . . Cricri . . . Cricri . . ." he repeated like a lovesick schoolboy.

"Can I ask you a question?"

"Oh, yes. You can ask me all the questions you like, even the indiscreet ones. There are no secrets. I won't hide a thing from you. Understand? Not a single thing . . ."

"What if I hadn't written all those books? If I wasn't a shrink?"

"You are so anxious. You are asking me if I would like you just as much if you were someone else, but how can I answer such a question? You are you, Rachel. You know that your books are as much a part of you as these five beautiful fingers on this beautiful hand . . ."

He kissed my palm and a shiver ran all the way down my back. I let out a sigh of resignation and closed my eyes. I was going to run with this. It was all fake, but it made me feel deliriously happy.

After our meal, where we enjoyed French fries and *pans bagnats*, we walked to a high-class wine-cellar place and Linus bought a bottle of chilled prosecco and two very pretty glasses. Real glasses, not the plastic kind. We stepped over to the jetty and sat in front of the yachts. That part of town is famous for the monstrous yachts moored there. Some of them are bigger than houses and I don't know how they stay afloat. But tonight, they looked pretty, their strings of blue lights illuminating the sea.

We clinked our drinks together, our eyes shining with infatuation. Linus grew tipsy pretty quickly. He became dopey and charming. He started dancing on the quayside singing songs from *An American in Paris*. I giggled, sipping my drink. To tell the truth, I was acting like a total brainless bimbo.

I gazed up at the stars and full moon in the sky. Could it have been more romantic? We danced cheek to cheek even though there was no music, and that's when Linus Robinson leaned in for the kiss. Before allowing his lips to brush against mine, I whispered, "Linus."

"Yes, Rachel? I mean, Cricri . . ." he added with a silly tee-hee. "Hmm! I love how you say Linus."

"There's something I need to tell you. Um, well, to admit to you . . ."
"Already? Darn!"

He stopped me from speaking with our first kiss. The big long kind.

I can't really remember what we did after that. I just remember that we were on a cloud . . . a sweet-smelling, pink, lovey-dovey cloud.

We took a taxi back to Rachel Amar's place. Linus got out of the cab to wish me a good night. He gave me a deliciously sensual kiss in front of the door. The taxi driver beeped his impatience and I gave in. I melted. I looked Linus straight in the eye. He didn't have to be a mind reader. Linus paid the taxi and we got into the elevator.

We stuck to each other like glue all the way up and continued our kissing session for several minutes in the hallway before opening the door to Rachel Amar's place.

Lisa came to greet us.

Lisa? It was almost midnight!

"Lisa! What are you doing up? Didn't anyone put you to bed?"

"Yes, but I got up again to watch Sabrina lock Pirate Anorak of the Full Moon in the closet. Because it's the full moon tonight and he wants to burn everything again. I'm scared."

And that's when I got it!

"Pirate Anorak? Full moon? What are you saying, baby girl?" It suddenly clicked. They were trying to say *pyromaniac*! Sabrina had first started this whole Pirate Anorak business after reading the newspaper at the market. "Do you mean the Full Moon Pyromaniac? Is that what you've all been blabbering about all this time? I understand now! Yes, it's a scary story, all right! And you're seeing him everywhere! He's been in the papers and on TV a whole lot, that's why. Everyone's talking about him too much. It's all too much. It's not right. This kind of news is what traumatizes little kidlets. He's in jail now, sweetness! So you see? There's no need to be so shaken up, is there?"

"No he isn't! He's in your boss's closet! He wanted to set fire to everything and he wanted you in the middle of it. Luckily, I saw him, and Sabrina locked him in the closet with the key."

"Good job, my lovely one. Your sister has excellent reflexes, doesn't she? OK, off to bed with you now."

She went into the big room and I noticed Sabrina sitting cross-legged on the floor in front of the walk-in closet. She was holding a glass of water. The glass was much too big for her little hands. Who'd given her that?

"What are you doing with that glass, Sabrina? Come on! Off to bed! It's way past your sleepy time!

"Don't worry. It'th nothing. I wath jutht really really thuper thirthty."

Erina was already tucked up in the big bed with little Emma.

I put Sabrina back down onto her mattress on the floor and took a blanket out of the cupboard. I was going to need it.

When I'd finished up and switched out the lights, I went to find Linus in the living room. I took him by the hand and walked him toward the office. I made sure the door was firmly locked behind us.

And boy, oh boy, we got ourselves all wrapped up in that blanket and had ourselves a little unprofessional time on the couch. I finally got to do some of that lying down he'd been talking about.

Friday:
Hurricane, Tornado, Deluge

38

I woke up at around six the next morning in Rachel Amar's master bedroom.

The song running through my mind as I awoke didn't exactly predict good things ahead. It was that song about raindrops falling on your head. A golden oldie by some American crooner, I think. I can't remember the name of the singer, but everyone knows the tune.

Life was complicated enough without this being added to it.

But at least I could consider myself forewarned now. If my mother sent me this as a message, it meant there was trouble ahead. A storm was brewing. Maybe literally. There was no need to guess the hows and whens. I'd know soon enough.

A memory suddenly came back to me. In the middle of the night, Linus had left. I was cold, so I'd crept back to the big bed and got in alongside the twins. I remembered I'd been half-asleep.

I shivered as I dragged my butt into the kitchen and poured myself a large glass of water. I smiled thinking of my mommy's song. Erina had woken up at the same time and followed me. She sat down at the table. I grabbed the chair opposite her and she started chatting.

I sighed deeply. Whatever she had to say was certainly going to eradicate the lovely images I had in my head . . . Dreamy pictures of my night of excess . . . Things that were making me blush. Oh my!

But it all came pouring out of Erina in one long monologue. She spoke with some difficulty. But, even without my Sabrina, I managed to understand. Off and on. She told me all about her journey to France. It had been long. Exhausting. A nightmare.

Léo wandered in. He still seemed drowsy. "What are you two doing?" he asked.

"Erina's telling me things," I replied.

She glanced at him quickly and then continued her woeful tale. Léo didn't join us at the table, but he stayed in the room, listening to every word.

Her voice was without emotion. It had no particular tone to it. She would not stop talking. I figured it had to come out.

When Erina thought about Albania, she saw herself back in the mountains with her mother and father. Or going out on crazy runs with her beloved dog, Nico. For her, Albania was nothing but fond memories and happiness. When she'd left, she thought she would return home again after she'd helped her father pay back what he owed. She would be working off his debts. She crossed the border with other "accompanied" children. There were plenty of kids going through. Always escorted by a man, usually on his own. He would hand out bread and water at regular intervals.

All this in a truck. Days and nights of it.

Suddenly, she stopped talking. It must have been too difficult for her to continue. Léo and I didn't say anything either. What could we say? There was nothing to add.

She crossed her arms on the table and put her head down.

Léo glanced at me, but I couldn't think of a way to reassure him. This boy had been with me only a few days, but wow, how he'd changed. He was no longer the sulky teen prone to mood swings—he'd become a knight in shining armor. To the rescue! What was I going to tell his mother? She wouldn't recognize him when she saw him.

I took Erina by the hand and we plodded back to the bedroom. I imagined she'd need more sleep. I took a short nap alongside her.

A little later, I heard a huge kerfuffle coming from the kitchen. It was mainly Gaston's voice. He was all excited, hollering, humming, singing . . .

I snagged Rachel Amar's bathrobe (the softest, fluffiest thing you could imagine), wrapped myself up in it, and went to investigate. My hangover had started to kick in. I wasn't up for all this racket. I'd had far too much wine the night before. And romance. And other things. What I needed there and then was coffee. A short, strong black espresso.

Gaston was dancing around the kitchen doing some sort of mime? Who knew. Bintou was also all bright eyed and bushy tailed, sipping tea. Laroche was watching with intense concentration. They started a deep and meaningful conversation about the Icelandic poem—the heroic gestures of the saga, the rhythms, the characterizations. Go figure.

I tried to listen, but the yawns got the better of me. "What are you all doing up so early? What time is it?"

"Ten o'clock! If a person's not up and about by ten a.m.! My goodness!" chuckled Laroche.

"*Ten o'clock!* Why didn't anyone wake—" I stopped to yawn.

"You got in quite late last night, didn't you?" asked Bintou with a definite nudge nudge wink wink undertone to the question.

I turned pink. "Where are the girls? Did Léo take them to school?"

"He took the twins, then went off with Erina," explained Gaston.

"Erina went outside? Don't you know how dangerous that is? She's not supposed to leave! What about Sabrina? Didn't she go to school? Sabri—"

I hadn't even finished calling her name and there she was, making her way toward the table, where she sat down and picked up a giant piece of bread, which she then covered in Nutella.

Sometimes that one knocks my shoes off. My blocks? My socks? She surprises me, OK?

"But Sabrina . . ."

"Yeth, Mommy?"

"You're not at school?

"Well, you didn't wake me up thith morning, tho I jutht thought that you wanted me to thtay at home one more day. Like I did yethterday. Anyway, it'th thchool vacation on Tuethday, you know."

"You can't stay here all day long doing nothing with your little life! Did you have breakfast earlier?"

"Yeth, Mommy. It wath a good breakfatht. Much better than uthual."

"What did you eat?"

"Blinith with thalmon eggth that the lady made thpecial for uth."

"What lady?"

She pointed to Bintou, who was giggling. I smiled at her.

"That's fab, Bintou! You've done a great job. It's very difficult to get a kid to change eating habits. And you did it on the first try!"

"They all really liked the blinis," she replied.

Sabrina continued to plead her case. "Don't worry about what I'm doing with my little life today, Mommy. I'll play with my imaginary friendth. You know, like, Pirate Anorak. All hith thtorieth are pretty fun. I like making up thtorieth for him. You like it when I uthe my imagination, don't you?"

"Yes, OK, but you could do with coming back to earth at some point, sweetie. Back in the land of reality."

"I am in the land of reality, Mommy! I like to invent thingth when I play, that'th all. But I never lie. You know that."

The whole group was following our conversation with interest, probably wondering which one of us was going to win this particular battle.

"Point taken," I agreed. "I'll admit that you never lie. That's true. So, what are you doing now?"

"You mean in my game?"

"Yes."

"Well, Pirate Anorak ith hungry, tho I'm getting him a bite. Thingth are going OK at the minute. He theemth pretty calm. But I have to keep doing what I'm doing." She got very excited all of a sudden, rabbiting on and on. There was no stopping this kid. "Well, it'th the full moon, you thee, and it'th very dangerouth. He wanth to thet fire to everything. Thith meanth he hath to be watched all the time. Luckily, I have all my thtring and my yarn. He fell into my trap and now I've thtrung him up like a thauthage, Mommy! He wath thaying he wanted to burn thith houthe down and burn you with it. He doethn't believe that you're a real *thpykaya-kitht*! I told him you were, too, but he wouldn't believe it. When he knew that I knew that he wath Pirate Anorak, he got all nithe and kind with me. He wanth me to do thrinking on him now. I told him that theeing ath it wath the full moon, it would be better for him to jutht thtay in the clothet without any matcheth. He cried with happineth when I told him I'd go get him thome bread and butter. Bread and Nutella ith even better! He'th going to love thith! When I grow up, I want to be a thpykayakitht like you and help people'th headth get better. Tho, I'll take thith to him now."

And off she went with her big chocolatey sandwich.

I could feel the pressure already, and the day hadn't even gotten started. Raindrops were certainly falling on my head. It felt like it. Great big fat ones.

The gang looked to me, waiting for a verdict.

My brow furrowed. "I wasn't the same at her age," I spluttered. "She's so bright. She has such an incredible imagination. How can I win when I'm up against a girl like that? It'd be a crime to stop her having fun."

They all nodded.

Clack, clack, bang, bang. Someone at the door. So what else was new? Surely everyone was accounted for. It was too early for this. Rachel Amar wasn't just a shrink; she was running a drop-in center here!

It was Léo. He was back with Erina and the twins. They jumped up all over me as soon as they saw me, chirping loudly. Such giddy little kippers!

"Our teacher is away this morning. She'll be here this afternoon! Léo took us to McDonald's!"

They scurried off to find Sabrina. Pastis went with them, ecstatic at all the action.

"And you? Why aren't you at school?" I asked Léo.

He didn't respond but simply asked his own question, only aggressively. "Hey! What's going on here? You all stuffing your faces? Was breakfast good?"

The others stared, nonplussed.

"Why are you asking?" asked Laroche. "Did you do something to the food?"

Léo guffawed and pointed to Erina, who looked shy and worried. "No. We don't have time to be fooling around with food. What's wrong with you? We have to figure out a way for Erina to pay off her debts. If not, her father and her whole family are going to be in an insane mess."

"Let's just go over this again," said Laroche. "What is the exact problem? We can come up with an exact method—an algorithm, if you like—to solve it. How does that sound?"

"The problem is that Erina has been sold to pay back a debt owed by her father. The reason her father owed this money is because he wanted to send her to Italy for her studies. But now, she's being used to carry drugs. *Muling*, it's called. And when she's too old to deliver drugs, the guy in charge of her will sell her for . . ."

He stopped, too embarrassed to go on.

"OK, enough, Léo," I barked. "You're giving me a migraine. Can't you see I've just woken up? And my mother has sent me a very catchy song, but a song that might spell trouble. I'll spare you the details."

I think he was confused by my attitude. "Sorry, Cricri! I didn't mean to wake you up!"

A teenage boy apologizing. I'd seen it all.

"You didn't wake me; I was already awake. It's just that I haven't totally joined the human race yet. Don't worry about it. It's not your fault. Anyway, these guys can't do much about Erina and her troubles. These are just normal folks with normal folks' problems. They've come to see a normal folks' shrink so they can get on with their lives normally, like normal folks do. That's it! They don't need you ripping into them all! Because these people have been hard done by enough already."

Out of the corner of my eye, I saw Bintou waving at me, almost hysterically.

"Yes?"

"I absolutely have to say something very important to you."

Oh no! What now? All the housework was building up again. If I didn't clean this damned place, how would I ever get paid? I wouldn't, that's how!

39

Bintou stepped toward me and whispered, "It's about Erina. You can't keep her here. It would be very dangerous. I did a write-up about the child trafficking situation in Europe and I really wish I hadn't. I can't remember if I told you or not . . . I think that's where it all started . . . the burnout."

I gaped at her. "So is that what you think? That I have no idea how dangerous this thing is? Well, Erina's in a massive amount of danger too, so what do you expect me to do? Just throw her out on the street? Come on now, Bintou, let's think this over."

Laroche turned the sound up on the TV and yelled, "Hey, everyone! Victor Falso!"

"Who is Victor Falso? Is he famous?" I asked, trying to be polite. I wasn't really paying any attention to him, I was too busy thinking about what Bintou was saying.

"It's the arsonist. They're calling him the Mental Pyromaniac or something."

"Oh, right!"

"Well, it's almost comical now! He's taken the judge hostage!"

"What?" everyone shouted at the same time, as if this new twist in the story concerned them directly. I know local stories tend to be more interesting, but it's not like we knew the guy. I suppose we were in Amar's house, though. That made it a bit more exciting.

"Yes! Hostage!"

"But what for?" I asked.

"He says he's sick and tired of waiting for your colleague, Amar. He wants to see her now and he has threatened to burn everyone, starting with the judge, if he doesn't get to meet with her."

"Wow! So he's still asking for her. Why her? He's out of luck—she's not around. Won't be for a while, I imagine. Well, forget about him. I have enough worries. I'm going to go get dressed. I'm expecting someone."

I felt like the whole world and its dog were after me to solve their problems. Well, I just couldn't do it. I didn't have enough room in my brain to worry about everyone.

I headed into the hallway, but Laroche and Bintou intercepted me, eager to bend my ear. *Bend my ear.* What a weird expression.

"Wait up!" cried Laroche with unexpected authority. "Bintou and I want to finish what we started."

"Do you think the two of you might be going a little bit overboard with these demands of yours? I'm not even dressed! I haven't even had my breakfast! And while we're at it—Bintou, how are things going with Tony down at Sélect? The job?"

"Not that great. I didn't last long. Some drunken moron put his hand on my ass, so I kicked him in the balls. He rolled around on the floor in agony and Tony fired me."

"I guessed something like that might have happened. Oh well, that's the way the cookie crumbles."

"Should we do another exercise with the orange dishcloth?" asked Laroche.

I frowned, eyebrows meeting in the middle. "Lordy! What did I do to deserve this? It's loopy! You're all loopy! Are you trying to put an end to me? Is that what you want?"

I walked away and Gaston shouted after me, "Get a move on! We've a lot on our plate. I've brought a cassette and recorded a few melodies on it. I'd like us to try a few things out."

Laroche was upset about the whole orange-cloth thing. He followed me, hoping I'd give him instructions for another exercise. He wasn't giving up that easily. He was sticking to his guns!

"Shall I make more coffee?" Bintou asked anyone who was still listening, playing the role of hostess with the mostest.

I slammed the bedroom door shut, almost smacking poor Laroche in the face.

"Do you think I could maybe get dressed in peace?" I yelled.

The raindrops from the song were definitely falling. I could feel the pressure of them on my headachy head. The day was getting more complicated by the second.

I managed to grab a quick shower and then put on some proper maid clothes. An old pink tank top and some pink neon shorts from one of the bags I'd brought from the trailer.

As I got ready, I noticed the kidlets sitting on the floor, playing together quietly. They were speaking in muffled voices as they opened and closed the closet door. When they noticed that I was trying to see what they were up to, they locked the door to the big walk-in closet thing and left the room. I could see that Sabrina was smiling, trying to stop herself laughing, maybe.

I decided to have myself some quiet time in the office to catch up on some z's. Not for long, just a power nap in the big therapist's chair. Oh soooo comfy.

Around ten minutes later Bintou came in. I knew Laroche was sitting on the couch, waiting for some sort of session to begin, but I'd been trying my hardest to forget about him. She came in on her tippy-toes.

Her movements were very exaggerated. She was trying to let me know that the last thing she wanted to do was disturb me. On the corner of the big desk, she put a small tray with some buttered baguette and jam and a big cup of milky coffee, steam wafting up into my face.

"I thought that after that teensy-weensy coffee you had, you wouldn't say no to a frothy one! Was I right?"

I treated her to one of my widest grins as a thank-you. Laroche stepped into the doorway and held out the famous orange towel. Bintou took the other end.

I watched their little game as I gobbled down my yummy breakfast. Bintou, still holding the orange thingy and studying Laroche's eyes with great intensity (Laroche seemed to be in a bit of a trance by this point), suddenly said, "Can we just get back to the young girl a second, please?"

"Don't start, Bintou. Don't push me. You can't come anywhere near to understanding. Let me explain a couple of things. She's Albanian. She's hiding out here awhile. That's it. I've just given you all the information you need to know. I will find a solution. On my own."

"Madame Maldonne, are you sure everything is quite all right? I thought you were more reasonable than this. What you're doing right now is highly dangerous. It's more than that—it could get you all killed. I know that young girl. I met her when I was writing my report. She's in with Monsieur Charles's gang. He'll end up buying her, I've no doubt about it."

"What you were just talking about there? What do you mean when you say 'gang'? And who's Monsieur Charles?"

"There's this man who goes by the name Monsieur Charles, Madame Maldonne. I don't think it's his real name, of course. He's the one in charge of all the drugs around here. He has a legit business as a cover-up, so he can launder the money, but I don't know what kind of business it is, exactly. One of my sources arranged a meeting with this guy, and I went to visit him in his kingdom. A great big villa in the hills somewhere around Mougins. I was blindfolded on the way over there.

I've never been able to find the place again. I've traipsed up and down countless streets and I've tried searching online . . . nothing. The only thing I ever managed to find out about him was the address of a place he used as a rendezvous spot. But I don't even know if it still exists today. The man is just awful. Open your eyes, Madame Maldonne! You're going to have to wake up and smell that coffee I've just put in front of you! What kind of world do you think you're living in? He's had his eye on that young girl for some time now. The human-trafficking business is a big deal these days. Drugs, prostitution, you name it—he's into it all."

"Bintou, are you telling me that you know the big boss of this whole deal? The guy who's responsible for the pain of all these children? The slave master?"

"Yes! That's exactly what I'm saying!"

"That's great! You can tell me everything you know, every last detail, and then I'll pay this guy a little visit. We'll have a chat and he'll come to the understanding that early retirement is the only option for him. He'll forget all about Erina and everything will work out just fine and dandy."

"What! Madame Maldonne! This guy's as f-bleeped up as they come! He's sick in the head. He runs the whole system. He's emperor of it. The king! Think Tony Soprano, but without a soft, duck-loving side to his character, you know? He'll swallow you whole. You'd be nothing but an appetizer to him! And then he'll get ahold of your girl. Please believe me. It's as simple as that. And you know what? Consider yourself lucky if he doesn't do the exact same thing to you."

"Is that what you think? Shame. I thought meeting with him was a pretty neato idea. I'm serious. Maybe nobody has ever actually had a heart-to-heart with this guy and explained how the people who he's forcing into this work feel!"

"Don't be naive. Drop it, Madame Maldonne. And whatever you do, get rid of that girl. If she stays here any longer, he'll find out about it. And that means anyone in this apartment, any of us who have had anything to do with this, will pay for it very, very dearly."

"Ahem," murmured Laroche. "Not to interrupt you, but do you think we could concentrate a little?"

"Yes, yes, of course." She shook the cloth to show she was taking part in my made-up experimental exercise.

"Listen, Bintou," I ranted, paying no attention to Laroche. "You know a lot of shit and a lot of people, but you don't always give the best advice. I'm not getting rid of the girl. I'm going to do everything in my power to protect her and shelter her. Then, I'm going to put Monsieur Charles in the can. A business is hard to run from behind bars, or so I've heard. I've got cop buddies. You'll see. And Gaston's a hard-ass. I bet you didn't know that, did you? He's like a martial-arts expert or something. So you get me? This guy had better not piss me off. And he better not threaten me in any way, shape, or form. But first off, you're going to have to tell me where I can find him. How can I get a meeting with him? A sit-down! I'll lay a trap for the bastard."

She just shook her head with sadness in her eyes. It was as if she already saw me, flat out in a coffin, being lowered six feet. All she said was, "Fine. Just go ahead as if I'd never mentioned a goddamn word to you!"

She turned to Laroche, who looked to be on the verge of passing out. She pulled the orange dishtowel harder than was necessary, her fingertips pressed tightly together. I felt her rage.

40

What Bintou had told me did have an effect on me. She had me worried. I went and found Erina.

"Could you come with me a minute, sweetheart?" I asked her.

I decided she needed a good grilling. I took her back to the office and had her sit on the floor in front of Bintou and Laroche, who were doing their special exercise with the cloth. Did she know who this Monsieur Charles character was? Had she seen him? If so, where? She'd spoken to Léo already about some French guy. I also asked her all about what had happened last time with Murrash. What had he done to her when she'd gone home on Wednesday?

I beat around the bush awhile, because the last thing I wanted to do was make her all uptight. She made it easy for me, though. She knew what information I wanted and told me what she knew. She said her time with Murrash was coming to an end. The big French boss had taken a liking to her. Murrash was scared of the guy. So it was just as Bintou had told me.

Erina said she didn't understand how and why she was still alive. She thought it was because she was still valuable in some way. She could still be bought and sold. At first, Murrash had declared that he'd only sell Erina once Kholia knew what he was doing with the deliveries, but on Wednesday, she'd disappeared for a while and even though she'd gone back to him (because she couldn't handle the thought of leaving the little one on his own), he thought she was trouble and wanted her out of his hair as soon as possible.

He'd taken her by the throat and told her how much money he'd make out of her. He'd explained that if she ran away again, he'd kill Kholia and she'd have his death on her conscience for the rest of her life. Now she was beyond devastated at the fact that she'd saved herself and left the little boy behind.

At this heartbreaking moment in Erina's story, someone rang the doorbell. One of those long, super annoying rings where whoever is doing it doesn't take their finger off the button. Jerk.

Léo opened the door, and I heard a deep voice explaining who they were. *Cops.* I poked my head out of the office and saw there was a good mix. A fancy one in a suit and tie, two humdrum uniformed officers like you'd see out on the street, and my main man himself, Borelli, in a leather-jacket-and-jeans combo. "Civvies," do they call that? What a pretty sight they all made. Well, I imagined they looked impressive to Léo. I didn't actually see them until they'd all piled into the office. I could hear them coming a mile off, though! Cops always sound like they're galloping, don't they? Even the slow ones who've had too many doughnuts.

This group made such a racket stomping around the place. I was desperate to go check out what was going on, but I thought it better to stay where I was so I could protect Erina. They were looking for something, opening and closing every door they came across. They left the kitchen almost as quickly as they entered it. I heard the big chief cop (I'm sure it was him and I'm sure he had an actual title) say, "Not in there. That's the kitchen. Find the office."

And they all filed into Rachel Amar's big office. It was a huge room, but there were a lot of us in there all staring at each other. It was a serious standoff.

Bintou was the first to break the silence. "So, you're here for Maldonne? There she is! Her work is being recognized at last! Finally! She really is wonderful!"

What was she doing buttering me up like that?

I recognized the decked-out boss guy. I'd seen him down at the station ages ago. He was a bit of a looker and in great shape, but what I remembered most about him was that he was one of those gentleman types. He'd told Borelli not to make me wait. I'd appreciated that.

I slipped as far back in my chair as I could. I felt tiny, crowded. The guy didn't recognize me. Pastis jumped up onto my lap and from there hopped up around my neck. The chief commander or whatever he was stared at Bintou in surprise.

She accosted him. "Oh! Bertrand! I didn't see it was you! What are you doing here?"

"Oh! It's *Elmer*! How lovely to see you! Is your husband here with you?"

Elmer? Another name? Out with the Bintou, in with the Elmer. I was having a hard time keeping up with all these weird-ass names of hers. I didn't say anything. The chief man stepped over to Bintou.

"Bertrand! I already told you not to call me Elmer! It's not a nice nickname! And no, Naïm isn't here with me. He's my ex-Naïm now. So why are you here?"

OK. How do these two know each other? Why is her nickname Elmer? Ah, I get it! Elmer like the glue! Elmer's Glue! It's not the greatest nickname. But it's true that as soon as she gets an idea in her head, she sticks to it. Maybe it had something to do with that. I wouldn't be surprised. Actually, it suited her. I might start using it.

"Oh, so you're not clued in to what's been going on?" Bertrand replied. "She's needed at the courthouse. You know the pyromaniac who's been all over the news recently . . . Oh, of course you do, it's your job! Well, he's taken a judge hostage. We've been called in to deal with it. It's a pretty big emergency. And what about you? How have you been? Are you reporting on this case?"

"No, I had to take leave. Burnout. I'm feeling chilled out now, though. Especially when I'm here. I've been doing manicures, and hair, and the cooking! Helping out around the place, you know?"

"Really? And you're sure you're feeling OK?"

He looked down at the orange cloth between Bintou and Laroche, a puzzled frown crossing his face. He turned swiftly toward me, but got his jacket button caught on the dishcloth. It was ripped from their hands in one rapid movement before falling to the floor next to Erina in a miserable little heap.

"Good going! That exercise is over!" I shouted in anger at Bertrand, who didn't have a clue how much this might upset the pear cart or the banana cart—some kind of fruit cart. "Why have you been sent here? Why are you cops always so clumsy? Look what you've done! What is this? It's like a goddamn circus in here, I swear! Why can't I just work in peace?"

Laroche caught Bintou's eye. He smiled and reached out for her hand. They didn't need the cloth anymore. They seemed to be at peace, less agitated, and, dare I say it, happy.

"Out of my office!" I continued. "Out of here!"

"Sorry, Madame Amar," grunted Bertrand, "but you're coming with us."

41

It was at this juncture that Borelli finally chose to speak up. He coughed. "Um. Boss. It's not her, boss."

"What was that, Borelli?" howled Boss Bertrand. "Of course it's her. This is her place, her office, she's working in here . . . It's her. Wouldn't you agree? I mean, where do you think we're standing right now? Where do you think she's sitting? Where are her patients sitting? That's where shrinks sit, Borelli, and that's where their patients sit. You never been to see one, Borelli? You should . . ."

I didn't know it yet, but Linus, *my* Linus Robinson, had just arrived in time to catch an eyeful of all these shenanigans. He'd promised he'd be back, and he'd chosen this as his moment to show up. Linus Robinson looking in through the door at the multitudes sitting and standing around me. One of the bambinos must have let him in. He was standing next to Borelli. Right in my line of view, except I hadn't seen him yet.

"Excuse the untimely intrusion, Madame Amar," said Bertrand, "but—"

"Oh no! Not that again. Stop it right now! This masquerade has to end. It's gone on long enough. *Listen!* I. Am. Not. Rachel. Amar. OK? And while I'm at it, I'm not a shrink either."

Bertrand was stressing out. He ran his eyes over all the books on the shelves, at the desk, at me sitting in the chair, the couch, Bintou, Laroche, Erina. This was clearly a lot more difficult than he'd thought it would be. I followed his line of vision. Borelli . . . then Linus.

"Oh! Linus! You're here!" I bleated, blushing wildly.

"I told you I'd come by in the morning!"

Oh wow, that accent . . .

"Yes, but you didn't say what time! I'm not even dressed properly."

"So get dressed and let me take you out of here—"

"Ah, no! *We're* the ones who'll be taking you out of here!" cried Bertrand. "You're expected at the courthouse as we speak. The Full Moon Pyromaniac?"

He got out some sort of official card from his pocket. The two uniformed cops shook their handcuffs. Those boys were getting a little too excited for my liking.

"Fine! I give up!" pouted Linus.

"I suggest you don't take her in," said Borelli. "It's not her. I mean, she's not Amar."

"Listen up, Borelli, you're breaking my balls here," grumbled the big boss cop.

Borelli smiled, turned on his heel, and flung his arms in the air to show that he'd washed his hands of us all.

"What's that supposed to mean, Borelli? Don't start acting like a drama queen! What a diva!" the boss man continued.

"Is there a problem?" Laroche piped up, coming out of his trance.

"The lady you see sitting there," said Bertrand, pointing at me, "is trying to tell us that she's not the therapist here."

"That's right. We all know that. She's the maid, the housekeeper . . . Whatever," sighed Laroche, as if he'd recited it a thousand times that day already.

He looked utterly fed up with the situation. Bertrand studied him closely. There was one flabbergasted cop if ever I'd seen one.

"Ha! You see!" I yelled triumphantly. "Why don't you just listen?"

"Yes, well. OK, Madame Amar. And this isn't your office. And these aren't your patients . . ."

"What do you want from me?" I asked, trying to wrap it all up.

"Haven't you seen the news today?"

"No, sorry! I haven't had time for TV today. I'm a busy girl, you know? Oh yes! There are some people in this world who don't switch the TV on as soon as they wake up in the morning, OK? Those people do exist in real life, and I'm one of them! So your answer's a great big no! I haven't seen a thing. So what?"

"Well, that sure is a shame! Because if you'd been paying attention, you'd have seen that you're all over the TV news. The Full Moon Pyromaniac. Keep up!"

"Victor Falso?"

"Yes! That's him!" exclaimed Bertrand. "He wants to see you! He's taken the judge—"

"Ah! Right! Yes, I saw that on the TV this morning . . . Well, I was told about it. Because, you know, I don't watch TV. But honestly, I wish I could help," I explained patiently. "But. He. Wants. Rachel. Amar!"

"That's why we're here!"

"But. I. Am. Not . . ." I enunciated as clearly as I could. I wasn't getting anywhere and didn't like the way this day was unfolding. I desperately hoped that at some point these blockheads surrounding me would understand who I was and who I wasn't. Linus caught my eye. I could tell he didn't understand what game I was playing. Oh, but I wasn't playing a game!

"Rachel Amar! I know!" Bertrand finished, winking at Linus (who was perplexed, but smiling, at least) and at Bintou (*Elmer?*), who winked back at him.

"OK, I'm out of here now. We're both out of here. See you soon!" called Laroche. It must have all been too much for him. He linked arms with Bintou and started walking out of the room, but Bintou resisted.

"Wait!" She trotted over to me and stood behind the desk, just next to my comfy chair. She leaned in and whispered in my ear, "I'm giving it back to you."

At the same time, right under the noses of all the cops, she opened my desk drawer and, to my horror and surprise, calmly pulled the revolver (the one that had disappeared and that I'd forgotten about, to be honest) from her purse and slipped it into my drawer.

She stood up straight again and pronounced, "We'll be back when you're ready to give us a little more attention. It's like a zoo in here! Sorry, Bertrand—I don't mean the fact that you're here, of course. I just mean that the consultations here have been a little hit or miss recently. You should go wherever it is they need you to go, Madame Maldonne. Get it over with and then come back here. Back to what you do best."

"Madame what?" asked Bertrand.

Nobody answered him.

Bintou smiled at me encouragingly.

I didn't even dare look at Linus. I made a decision then and there: I was going to continue with the charade. Keep going as I had up to that point. Let destiny play its hand. Raindrops would keep falling on my head. But it's always been like that. Shit happens. Rain happens. What's the big deal? That's right. I'd just have to get on with it. Even the police weren't prepared to believe me when I told them I wasn't Amar. So what was a girl to do?

I stood up and walked to the door, followed by the police and then my poor, confused Linus. We bumped into Sabrina, who was tiptoeing down the hallway with a mug of hot chocolate in her hands.

"You're still here, my love? Léo didn't take you to school?"

"You know that! I've already theen you thith morning. And we dithcuthed thith."

"Oh, right! I'm getting all muddled up here, my baby! Days! Times! Nothing's in the right order. So, what are you doing with yourself, then? Where are you going with that big mug?"

"Nowhere. I'm thirthty, that'th all."

"I see. Fine!" As I was leaving, I said, "Bintou, could you take the little one's temperature, please? I have a feeling she's still burning up a little." I also whispered, "I wouldn't mind if you hung around, if that's all right with you? Please make sure that Erina doesn't set foot outside this apartment—even with Léo." I used my normal voice again. "And you never know, I might be back late, so could you make sure the twinlets are back at school by no later than one thirty? I can pick them up at the end of the day." I called out to Léo, "You hear that, Léo? Don't go off anywhere with your girlfriend, OK? Bintou is in charge of the babies."

"Cool!" shouted Léo.

"Anything you say, Madame Maldonne," said Bintou.

"What's with the Maldonne? That's not her name!" Bertrand said to Laroche, who simply smiled. "They're all funny in the head here," the boss cop muttered.

Gaston, who'd been watching and listening throughout the whole cop/lover visit, rolled his eyes and headed back into the living room to his favorite armchair. "I don't know what the heck is going on in this place, but an opera doesn't write itself!"

He was driving me insane! He could have stepped in and straightened all this out, but he was too obsessed about those songs of his.

Borelli simply stood by the front door, waiting, his arms crossed. I knew a Borelli sulk when I saw one. Bertrand did his best to ignore him. He turned to face me and said gallantly, "Madame Amar, after you."

I went to open the door, but stopped. "Listen, please. I'd like to have a quick word with my gentleman friend. If you could just give me five minutes?"

"And then we're off? Do you promise?"

"Affirmative! Cross my fingers and hope to die. I, Rachel Amar, personally give you my word."

I saw Borelli's eyebrows head up toward his hairline. They'd never have caught it.

"OK. I can wait five minutes. We'll be outside," snorted the commander chief of detectives or whatever. He nodded to Borelli as if to say, *Told you so, dickhead! It* is *Rachel Amar!*

42

Linus was holding me in his arms. Heaven! Looking into those eyes of his . . .

"I really don't know if I should go or not. I don't have a great feeling about this."

"I don't want you to think I'm meddling in something that's none of my business," Bintou prattled, even though she and Laroche had stayed behind after I'd asked everyone to leave, "but you can't actually refuse to go with them! You're the best. You know you are! You'll straighten all this stuff out down at the court. You'll be doing everyone a huge favor. It's the right thing to do."

I didn't say a word. I studied Linus's face, taking in every last detail. "Linus, do you remember last night when I wanted to tell you something?"

"It doesn't matter," he replied. "You're the only person I'm worried about. You. And that's it."

"Well, then you need to know this. That's what it's about. Me. Who I am. Me. I'm—"

"I love you as you are. I love who you are. I love *you*."

"Well, I've seen enough of this. I'm out of here!" muttered Laroche. "You people should get a room!"

"Don't pay him any attention. He's in the middle of his *transfer process*," I said to Linus as if I actually knew what I was talking about.

He nodded in agreement.

And then it happened. Karma. Something always happens. And this was my karma catching up with me. I deserved it. What could I do?

A key turned in the door. Someone was there, and that someone hadn't realized yet that the door wasn't locked. Or even shut. The door was pushed open.

And . . .

There was Rachel Amar.

Rachel.

Amar.

The real one.

I recognized her immediately. I'd seen her one time with Véro.

She was dragging a huge suitcase.

Pastis ran up to greet her. He rubbed up against her legs and let out a huge happy meow. Then he realized he didn't actually know who she was, got skittish, ran over to me, and jumped up to my shoulder.

Amar shook her head, backed up, and checked the name over the doorbell. She stepped back in, headed straight for Linus, and held up a can of pepper spray to his face. She didn't set it off, though. Maybe she recognized him. Wow! This wasn't going to go down well. I backed up toward the living room and kitchen. Maybe there was a hole in the ground in there—a nice big hole that would swallow me up.

I couldn't have been more ashamed. What was I supposed to do? All my worst nightmares had come true all in one morning. Rachel Amar was back. She'd caught me red-handed in her own apartment, pretending to be her, no less.

But more humiliating than everything wasn't that she'd find out that I'd dared to treat her patients with my own special brand of therapy, or that she'd know I'd been sleeping in her room with all my crew. It wasn't even that I'd been having my way with one of her favorite colleagues. No, no. What bothered me the most was that I'd failed my mission.

The place wasn't even clean. I hadn't cleaned inside a single cupboard and the ironing was nowhere near finished. In fact, the place was a fucking pigsty. And I hated that! I didn't live like that, so why had I allowed it to happen here? There was no way I was getting paid for this sorry mess! Pay me? I wouldn't have paid me!

I found refuge in Linus, who had followed me and who I was gripping onto as if my life depended on it. He had no idea what was happening. Poor baby.

Bintou and Laroche had now made an appearance in this latest act of the tragedy of my life. They were both startled to see Amar too.

"What are you doing here?" asked Laroche.

"No! Unbelieeeeevable!" cried out Amar.

She had made her way to the living room. Gaston (he was the only one who'd kept to himself so far) forced himself out of the big armchair with a grunt, dropped his notes on the coffee table, and scuttled over to see what all the fuss was about. The twinnies followed him, suddenly interested in the latest character in what was fast becoming a farce.

"Who are you?" Gaston asked.

"Rach—*Arrggghhhh!* Who are you?" Rachel Amar asked, her face burning hot. She was showing all the signs of being crazy pissed. Out of her tree.

"Gaston Contini, at your service," he replied, ever the polite, high-class gentleman. You've got to love him!

"Gaston Contini, the poet? No . . ." Rachel Amar spluttered.

Gaston smiled. He was flattered. I could tell. I reckon that if he'd had a mustache, he'd have been twisting it between his finger and his thumb at this stage.

"Yes. And you are Rachel Amar, I presume? Come, come, I'm sure you must be in need of a little pick-me-up!" he sang. "Allow me to prepare you a Spritz." And just like that, he took her by the hand and led her to her own kitchen.

I could tell Linus was as confused as a man can get, but he still wanted to stay by my side. He must have thought there was something he'd missed along the way, and he must have wanted to know who Gaston was and what he was doing there.

Borelli and the rest of the police gang reappeared. My five minutes were up. He was rather pleased with himself, gleefully glancing at his boss every couple of seconds. I imagined he was thinking, *I told you so!* (It was one of his fave things to say!)

Rachel Amar soon discovered the extent of the damage a family of four to five adults and four to five children can make in a kitchen. Total chaos. Livid doesn't even come close to describing how she looked. She violently pulled her hand away from Gaston.

"Christ! What the fuck? What the fuck have you fucking people done to my fucking kitchen?!"

Bintou dropped the very expensive Bodum coffeepot on the floor. *Whoooosh!* Bam! It smashed. The soft and comforting smell of coffee wafted through the room. The white marble floor was splashed and speckled with black coffee grounds. The same went for Amar's legs. They didn't look too hot.

I had somehow found the energy to jump out of the way just in time, leaving Linus standing there in shock.

"Nobody move! I'll clean it up!" I roared almost as it happened. I ran over to the sink to find a sponge.

"Stop that!" screeched Amar. "I want to know who you are."

Bintou stepped forward to speak. Brave woman!

"Leave it, Bintou," I said. "I'll explain everything!" I started stuttering and spluttering.

Linus stayed, observing.

Rachel Amar's eyes fired lightning bolts at me. I was taken aback by her fury and didn't dare look directly at her. Very un-me.

Laroche sat down at the table and started hammering away at the keyboard on that fancy laptop of his. He lifted his head to get up to speed every now and again.

Bintou was feeling the terror, it was written across her face, but she worked up enough courage to say, "Of course, Madame Amar, this must be difficult for you to process. We had a slight suspicion that you might be a little vexed about this when you found out, but you see, your patients all believed, or still believe, that Rosie Maldonne was your replacement. We assumed you were in agreement about this and . . ."

Well, she'd got me neck deep in it, but thanks for the help, Bintou!

"Replacement?" asked Linus. Could a man get more bewildered?

"What? Who? Rosie Maldonne? Who's that? Is that you?" hurled Amar, shooting daggers at me.

"Rosie Maldonne?" repeated Linus, gobsmacked by this latest revelation.

"Rosie Maldonne?" asked big-boss Bertrand, his voice sounding disappointed.

"Well, sure! Rosie Maldonne! Who else?" proclaimed Borelli, cackling wildly.

"This must be a bad dream. Tell me this is just a dream!" Rachel Amar continued. "Unbelieeeeevable! You've had consultations with my patients? You're the cleaning woman? Is that right? My maid told me someone would be replacing her. That's it, isn't it? I never forget a name, and I know she sent a message to me saying she'd be away for a few days but would send someone to replace her, a certain Maldonne. Rosie Maldonne."

"Y-yeeesss. That's me, all right." My voice was trembling.

"The maid? The maid?" continued Linus, who was now looking at me with some distance in his eyes, almost professionally, like a psychiatrist would. I was no longer the love of his life, but a weird little specimen under his microscope.

"Do you think you could just stop repeating everything I say like a human parrot man?" Amar quipped.

Everything had gone to hell. Raindrops . . . head . . . still happening. At least, that's how I felt.

I thanked my mom for the heads-up.

But I added, *Mom, do you think your songs could sometimes include the solutions to these predicaments and not just tell me that something crappy's coming up?*

43

Laroche raised an eyebrow and glanced at me. "So, it was all true," he murmured under his breath.

Gaston came and stood by my side, ready to support me and whatever I'd done. "I hope we'll be all finished with this hullabaloo soon. What is this? Class warfare? Leave her alone! So she's the maid. Is that punishable by death or something?"

"Yes, it was all true, Monsieur Laroche!" I squalled, close to tears. "And how many times did I tell you? It's impossible to count! And would you believe me?" I turned to Amar and managed to make eye contact. I felt a little stronger now that I had my Gaston with me. "I swear, Madame Amar! This is not my fault!"

I couldn't believe it was me talking. I've always hated whiners, and there I was whining and moaning like the best of them.

Linus spun his head quickly to look at Amar. It was like he was watching the French Open, following the ball.

"Rachel Amar," he muttered in a low voice. "So this is the real Rachel Amar?"

"Can I help you?" Amar spat. "Do you think this ridiculousness might be over with sometime soon? Or is it that you want an autograph or something?"

"Psychoanalysis and Criminality . . ." he whispered as if meditating on the words.

"It's true!" insisted Bintou. "She told us who she was. But, before seeing your reaction, I wasn't really sure whether or not . . . She's quite brilliant, though! You should have seen how she straightened us all out and our specific cases!"

"You! I didn't ask for your opinion on this," Amar said, pointing in Bintou's face. "And you!" She moved her index finger in my direction and smiled nastily. "I know how to deal with you!"

"I knew this was going to be a big deal," I said, wincing.

"This might be the weirdest thing that's ever happened to me," exclaimed Amar, getting angrier by the second. "I'm not sure I can actually believe it. Someone pinch me! Jesus! It's unbelieeeeeevable! And completely illegal, of course. Everything that's gone on here while Rosie Maldonne has been in my house is illegal and you're all accomplices."

Bossy-boy Bertrand jumped with a startle. "Please, Madame, I beg you! There are officers of the law here. We're certainly not accomplices. Please watch what you're saying." He took out his badge and flashed it, feeling the big man again.

"Scared of me causing a scene? Worried there will be a story? Well, there will be! And not a small one either!" It was only then that she recognized the words he'd spoken. "Officers of the law? Police?"

She grabbed his wrist to examine the badge and he gasped indignantly. Police officers aren't used to getting grabbed much.

"Well, that's just great! You're already here, so that'll save me some time in getting this fixed. I want to file a complaint. Or I want them all arrested. Whatever I can do, I'm doing it. It's as simple as that." As she continued, she became more confident as to what she wanted done with us all. "I'll see you all at trial, every last one of you. One by one. Those of you who are patients of mine knew that Madame Maldonne's real job was a . . ." (She didn't dare say the word *maid* again in front of Gaston.)

I couldn't take much more of it. "Just take it easy with all your *Madames*! I'm not a golden oldie, OK? Christ, how old do I look?"

"Sorry to be a further bother to you," said Commander Bertrand to Amar, "but you're going to have to make all these complaints at a later date. We're unable to deal with them here. We're on official duty. You'll have to go down to the station and file them formally. However, you're going to have to come with us, anyway. You're expected in court."

Linus was definitely looking at me differently. I took it hard when I first noticed it, but I was forced to admit that his look didn't betray disgust or sadness . . . it was worse than that. It was professional interest. Any trace of being loved-up was gone. That was hard to take.

"Rosie . . . Rosie . . . Rosie . . ." repeated Linus—and more than three times too!

"What's with this nutcase? Why does he keep saying your name? This is unbelieeeeevable."

I spoke so that only Linus could hear. "Call me Cricri. Like I told you to. I prefer it. Let me explain why."

He started with the repetitions again.

"Cricri . . . Cricri . . . Cricri . . . So there was at least a morsel of truth in what you told me . . ."

Pastis came running as he heard my name and sprang up into my arms. Linus stroked him softly. I closed my eyes. I knew there was no way I'd ever be able to relight his fire now. What was done was done. No going back. My fairy tale had crash-landed in the real world. In fact, it had crash-landed in a big bucket of icy-cold water.

Bintou went ahead and said what everyone else was thinking—she was maybe saying it to herself, but it was loud enough so we all got an earful.

"There's no way I want Amar treating me anymore. She's a nervous wreck!"

Rachel flipped. I actually thought she might bite Bintou. "I already told you! Your opinion isn't required! Who asked for it, exactly?"

Laroche didn't appreciate Bintou being picked on and finally found his voice. "Madame Amar, we've been obliged to put up with your rantings for a good ten minutes, and I would now like to ask you to go easy. Yelling won't change a thing here. I agree with you, this is all a bit nuts. I'd even go so far as to say it is a catastrophe. But you're the one who bailed. From your practice. From your patients. And you were gone for some time. Madame Maldonne here covered for you. I'd even say she did a good job. A better job than you. She cured some of your patients! That's what's 'unbelieeeeevable'! I know you didn't have many to start off with, apart from all the criminals you treat for free for your research, but now you have even fewer. But don't lose hope. You're still young. You'll find more. You'll pull yourself back up!"

Rachel Amar couldn't find her voice. She was choking up big-time.

"Stop that!" I cried. "Don't speak to her like that! She's incredible! She's a real pro! The best!" I gazed at Linus, tears welling up. "Isn't that right, Linus? She's the best, isn't she?"

Linus couldn't look me in the eye as he said, "Well, this is the woman who wrote *Psychoanalysis and Criminality*, isn't it?"

"Take my advice," continued Laroche, speaking directly to Rachel, "don't bother taking anyone here to court. You won't come out on top."

"He's right!" added Bintou. "You know what, Rachel? I'm afraid to say it, but if your patients are asked to take the stand, they might just say they were undergoing therapy with you for years and years with no particular results, and then got cured by your cleaning lady in just a couple of days. I'm a bit worried it might not turn out so well for you . . ."

Rachel Amar stepped back, horrified.

"There'd be terrible publicity, you know?" Bintou concluded, clearly pleased she'd found the right words for the job at hand.

Rachel Amar gave it one last attempt. "Since when am I going to let a hysterical nutter who has suffered more than one major breakdown, and a loser schizoid orgy-organizer, tell me where I'm going wrong in life, in my business? And as for you," she hollered in my face, "you're so fired! You little good-for-nothing!"

I had to stifle a snicker. It was the first time in my life I'd been sacked from a job for the right reasons. It was a bit of a shocker! I hoped I wasn't going to stay traumatized for too long.

Amar ran out of the room and headed straight for her office.

"All of you leave me the fuck alone and get the fuck out of my house!"

"Sorry, that's not going to be possible!" replied Bertrand. "And watch that mouth of yours. Borelli, go get her. You two, back him up."

Borelli ran after Amar, followed by the two street cops. I followed too. I don't know why. I think I wanted to see her getting cuffed. Even Gaston couldn't tear himself away from the action.

Rachel Amar screamed hysterically.

What was she screaming at? The police weren't exactly going to rough her up. We all ran into the office to check it out.

Sitting at the desk in Rachel Amar's chair was my Sabrina . . . in the middle of a consultation. She was listening most attentively to the wacktoid electrical repairman who was lying down on the couch, all wrapped up in yarn and string. The guy was worse for wear. He was in a sorry state—bandages, cuts and bruises, plus the string. The twins were using him as a play mat. They were sitting on his legs, cracking up, playing the real version of Happy Families that I'd given Sabrina earlier that week.

"What's this, now? As if we haven't all been through the mill enough?" sulked Borelli.

"Mmmm . . . Mmmm . . ." muttered Sabrina, nodding her little head.

And the repair guy was letting it all out, chatting away like he was never going to stop. "And she never ever noticed a thing! I did so much! And she never saw me. Never. I broke stuff, I climbed up the curtains, I turned the radio all the way up . . . Nothing ever worked! So, this one night, I went into her room and set fire to the curtains. And it was on that night, as I looked up at the full moon, that I understood nothing would ever amount to anything. She didn't care. She continued to snore as if it wasn't happening. As if the flames weren't creeping up the fabric. Her whole room ended up on fire, and nearly the entire house too. She almost died! But she just didn't get it. The next day, she told the firemen she thought she'd left a cigarette burning on a paper plate. Whatever."

He started crying. Rachel Amar and the rest of us listened in disbelief. We remained where we were, not wanting to disturb this improvised therapy session.

"I tried telling her it was me who'd done it, but she wouldn't listen . . ."

"Sorry to interrupt," Rachel Amar finally managed to say in a small broken voice. But she wasn't able to finish her sentence. She crumpled to the floor, completely done, her face in total misery. She stayed crouched down around our feet. The woman was broken.

Sabrina turned to her. "Madame, I know your cathe ith urgent, but can't you thee that I'm with thomeone here?"

"She's right!" barked the electric dude. "You blind? You need us to draw you a picture?"

Sabrina looked over at me. "Mommy, let me prethent my friend Teddy to you. Teddy Pirla. He'th the Full Moon Pirate Anorak. He'th here for me to fixth hith head for him. You know, like you do with people."

Gaston ran to get a glass of water for Rachel Amar. She looked grateful when he returned with it and she swallowed it down in giant gulps.

"Ahhhh!"

"There you go. It's OK. You're just in shock," he chirped.

She was in a full state of panic but seemed happy to be taken care of. "Who are you again?"

He'd already told her, but she was so mixed up that her thoughts were clearly jumbled.

"The poet. But I'm more of a chauffeur at the moment."

"Oh?"

"You need to pull yourself together. They're waiting for you in court. These gentlemen will take you there."

"Oh?" Rachel Amar said again, half-comatose.

"Yes, come on, everything will work itself out."

"Work out? For me? Do you really think so?" She stared forlornly at her big desk and the space around her . . . her life. Gaston placed her book into her hands: *Psychoanalysis and Criminality*. As she scrutinized it, the color returned to her cheeks. She stood and addressed the room. "I've just made a big decision. If I'm needed in court, that's where I'll go. I'm handling the Full Moon Pyromaniac case, you know, and I'll deal with all this when I get back."

Sabrina shouted, her voice almost earsplitting, "Pirate Anorak ith right there, I already told you!"

"This is no time for fun and games, child!" said Rachel, regaining her confidence.

"It'th Pirate Anorak!" insisted Sabrina. I could see the pity in her eyes. She turned to me, her voice pleading. "I wath his thpykayakitht and now he'th going to get all better, Mommy. Thith ith the real Pirate Anorak. You believe me, don't you?"

I believed her. Of course I believed her! I believe every word that comes out of that kiddo's mouth. And the twinnikits were on her side too. I should have seen it. She'd found the real Full Moon Pyromaniac and the little sweetsie hadn't wanted to add to my worries, so she'd tried to take care of the problem herself.

Borelli looked like he had a thousand questions.

"She means the pyromaniac," I explained calmly. "The Full Moon Pyromaniac."

It was the first time I'd seen Borelli so bewildered. He usually liked to play the role of Monsieur Know-It-All.

"This is how it's going to go down," Amar said. "I'll follow you officers, but I won't be coming *with* you. If the man in the courthouse has asked for me—"

"SSSSSTTTTTTOOOOOPPPPP!" hollered Teddy.

And that's just what we all did. Stopped and listened.

"Are you going to listen to this little girl or not? She's right! *I'm* the Full Moon Pirate Anorak Pyromaniac! You bunch of turdo 'tardos! How many 'mistakes' do I have to make? How many signs, errors, clues do I have to leave behind at the fires? When will you take a good look and actually *see* them? Pack of crappy cops!"

"Oh, come on now. Unbelieeeeevable! Keep it together. Who gave you permission to speak to us as if we were nothing but dogs, huh?"

"He doethn't mean it. He'th jutht fed up that he never geth any attention!" explained Sabrina.

"It seems he has a persecution complex based on profound paranoia," Rachel said, tapping her cheek. She looked at him. "OK, so it's you? You're coming with us, then. Are you ready?"

"No," mumbled Teddy moodily.

"What do you mean? Why not?" asked Rachel.

"No! Not with you! I want to go with her," he yelled, pointing to my eldest cherub-face.

Rachel marched toward the exit, each footstep quicker than the last. I heard her whisper, "Sometimes I can't take any more of these nutcase social misfits!"

I heard someone coming down the hallway. Heavy footsteps.

Bertrand stuck his head around the doorway and looked at the sorry scene in front of him. He didn't seem too impressed. He eyeballed Borelli. "What's this goddamn freak show in here?"

Borelli tried to give an explanation using all the correct cop words. "It appears there's been a misapprehension or a miscarriage of justice, possibly in conflict with the arsonist case, monsieur."

Bertrand blew out his cheeks. I guess he'd had more than enough of us all. "Fine! Get the real shrink and whoever this guy is in the back of the police van. Do it now. We'll see what Judge Amblard has to say about all this. If he's not already dead."

Borelli cleared his throat. "There's a complication."

"What a surprise! A complication? Here?"

"This guy won't leave without the little one. Sabrina Maldonne-Mendès."

More cheek blowing. "Fine, so we'll take the kid. We should have left this place ages ago! Hurry! Quick march!"

Is this cop out of his fucking mind? They're not taking Sabrina anywhere!

I opened my mouth just to draw more attention to myself, because I hadn't quite gotten enough yet. "Um," I said, "my daughter's not going anywhere without me. Sorry."

"Wonderful!" clamored Bossypants Cop sarcastically. "Put the mother in the back of the van too."

Outside, a super classy undercover car was parked nearby. This was used for the commander copster and Rachel Amar, since they were the most important people there, obviously. The rest of us rabble got shoved into the back of a standard police van. Sirens on for the riffraff. Top speed.

As we turned the corner, I arched my neck to look at the building, hoping to see *my* Linus. Hoping to see him searching for me. Waving at the van as it sped away.

"Cricri! Rosie! Cricri! Rosie Maldonne!" he could have been shouting, not knowing what name to use. I might even have seen him hail a taxi to follow us.

Nice little daydream.

But it wasn't going to happen. It was hard to let go of romance. Especially for a love addict like me.

44

We drove so fast in that mean machine of a van that we arrived at the court before Bertrand, Amar, and the fancy car.

There were people all over the place in the courthouse. Every seat in the public gallery was taken. People were even sitting on the floor. I could see journalists taking notes, police officers eating sandwiches or drinking takeout coffee. The atmosphere was very casual. The seats where the jury and the judge were supposed to be were abandoned. Ghost town.

Standing to one side were armed guards, all geared up with special helmets and protective suits. I think they must have been an elite shooting squad. They were standing near a little wooden door. I guessed that was where the hostages had been taken.

When we walked in, people started to surround us. "That's her! There she is!"

"The shrink? What? That redheaded Betty Boop?"

I turned to see who they were talking about. There was nobody matching that description behind me, so I guessed they were talking about me.

"And who's the Frankenstein man with the little girl? This is a whole entourage, not just a psychiatrist! Why does she need so many people with her?"

The uniformed cops with us pushed the crowd out of the way so we could get through to the door. Borelli knocked on it loudly.

"Who is it?" asked an oldish-sounding voice from the other side.

"Well," Borelli said, "some of Rachel Amar's staff have arrived as requested by your orders, Your Honor, monsieur, Judge Amblard. We don't have the full team yet."

We heard lowered voices.

The judge spoke. "We want everyone except her to step back. When we open the door, she must come in, and then we'll close it behind her. I want to make it clear that a gun is being pointed at my temple. I am being forced to give you these orders. Please follow them with precision."

Borelli coughed. "There's another one. A new one."

"What does that even mean? A new what? I have a goddamn revolver pressed against my head, just in case you didn't know . . ."

"Sorry. Please explain to your captor that this is in his best interests."

"Who is this speaking?" demanded Judge Amblard.

"This is Lieutenant Borelli."

"And who's coming in?"

"I can't say. I don't want all the journalists to hear."

The journalists who'd managed to hear Borelli started booing him. His behavior clearly wasn't media friendly enough.

"Everyone back! Stand back!" Borelli shouted.

There was silence and then the judge said, "How many of you are there?"

"At the moment, one woman, one man, and a child. Oh, and three police officers."

"Wait, I'll ask."

Silence again.

"It's fine, but the police can't come in," the judge said after several minutes of whispered debate.

The door opened slightly, and a hand reached out and pulled me in. The very same hand then pushed Borelli out and slammed the door in his face.

The big bad man, aka Victor Falso, who hadn't spoken to anyone in days because none of the people he encountered were the oh-so-wonderful Rachel Amar, double locked the door with a big brass key behind us.

At the same time, he was holding on to the judge by his cheek. The judge actually seemed like he didn't mind. At his age, he'd more than likely seen and been through worse than that. In the corner of the room, I spotted the defendant's lawyer, biting his nails down to the quick.

When he saw me, Victor Falso threw his arms around me and started wailing. He clearly hadn't taken a good enough look at who he was clinging to. He suddenly seemed embarrassed. He stepped back and looked behind me, as if expecting someone. That's when he saw Sabrina and the other potential fire starter. He went and sat down a little farther away, morosely. But he still seemed like he was in control. The man was on high alert.

Nobody was paying much attention to Sabrina or the psycho repairman.

"Monsieur, this man here says he's the pyromaniac—" I started.

"Thith ith *my* cathe," interrupted Sabrina. "Ithn't that right, Teddy? You're my cathe? You're my Pirate Anorak?"

The judge barely even glanced at Sabrina and her Pirate Anorak.

"Finally! Madame Amar! At last!" the judge said. "You're certainly one sought-after lady!" He stared at me. I didn't quite see a wink, but there was a randy sparkle in his eye. He gave me the once-over and spent a bit longer than is normally considered respectful gawking at my legs, shorts, and cleavage.

Oh, I hoped this one wasn't going to be another villain in this farce of a play we all seemed to be in. Another crazy who wouldn't take me at my word. He wasn't going to make the same mistake as everyone else, was he?

"Uh . . . I'm not . . ." I faltered, unable to put a string of words together.

"Yes. The defendant insisted on seeing you and now I understand why!"

"You know, I'm not—"

He just spoke over me. Rudo.

"This is all so exciting. Yes? You were saying?"

Victor Falso stood up and glowered at the judge. This guy was a nut. A hard one, at that. He still was in no mood for talking, or so it seemed.

"What now?" said the judge.

Falso pointed at me and shook his head. I was a no-no.

The judge rolled his eyes. "What seems to be the problem this time? Is this not good enough for you? Have you changed your mind? Unhappy now that Rachel Amar has finally turned up? Maybe you want someone else, is that it? A speech therapist, perhaps?"

The accused pyromaniac continued to shake his head vigorously, almost wildly!

"Cat got his tongue," muttered the judge. "This was once a pretty cut-and-dried case, but we gave in to his whims. I don't suppose you could shed any light on this?" he asked me.

"Yes, I think so. It's pretty simple, to be honest, monsieur. Mistaken identity—that's all this is. I'm not Rachel Amar. My name is—"

The door sounded like it was about to break off its hinges. Someone (or someones) knocking like mad. Like they were out-to-lunch mad.

45

We could hear yelps and hollering and God only knows what going on outside that door. I guessed it was all the journalists getting a bit over-enthused. I could hear the busy cameras—*click, click, click.*

Bertrand's voice cut through the noise. "Coming through, coming through."

And then Rachel Amar's voice. "Let me pass, please. I'm Rachel Amar."

And then my Borelli. "Are you deaf or what? There are people coming through here!"

I said to Victor Falso, "It's her! It's the real one this time. Let her in!"

His eyes lit up and he got out his big key to open the door. He pulled the same move he had with me, hauling in Rachel Amar and shoving back Borelli.

We were only in a small antechamber, like a court waiting room, and it was starting to get crowded.

Rachel Amar glanced at Victor's gun. "Could you move that thing away from me? I can hardly work well with something like that stuck in my face."

"What is this nonsense? Who are you?" the judge asked Rachel Amar.

"I'm Rachel Amar. Let me introduce you to . . ." She turned toward Teddy Pirla and then looked a little awkward. "What's your name again?"

"I'm not telling you," Teddy-the-Real-Pyromaniac sulked.

"Fine. It doesn't matter what his name is," she continued. Amar wasn't about to let a little thing like that stop her. "This man is the real Full Moon Pyromaniac. He admitted everything to this small child here."

"And who might this small child be exactly?" asked the judge, astonished.

"She's my daughter," I said.

"You have a daughter, Madame Amar?" asked the judge. He must have felt the need to get to the bottom of things. A lot was going on, and if he didn't interrogate correctly and add all this new information to what he knew already, he was going to get lost.

"No, no, no!" replied Rachel Amar excitedly. "There can't be two Rachel Amars! Please try to keep up! *I* am Rachel Amar. The one and only. It's me."

Victor had followed every word down to the last syllable. He was gawking at Teddy with increasing interest.

I got hold of my little Sabrina and squeezed her tight before adding, "She's right, you know. It's what I've been trying to say for some time. She's not me. Well, I'm not her. Well—"

"One moment, one moment, please. I would like to understand this properly. Please start from the beginning. And you there, pyromaniac man . . ."

Teddy and Victor both looked up and said in unison, "Who? Me?"

Those words meant Victor Falso's vow of silence was broken. He bit his bottom lip, then shouted out, "Hogwash!"

The judge appeared disturbed by this and turned to pyromaniac number one. "Yes, you, the pyromaniac we've arrested. My pyromaniac. I mean . . . Oh, what am I saying? You! OK? You! Are you a pyromaniac or not?"

"No. The shrink's right. I've never set fire to a single thing in my life."

"Because it's meeeeeeeeeeeeeeeeee! I'm the pyromaniac!" yelled Pirla. He certainly had a pair of lungs on him.

But nobody was paying much attention to him. Again.

"What do you mean you've never set fire to anything? What, nothing at all?" the judge asked Falso.

Teddy, a ball of nerves by this point, started slubber-blubbering like a baby. "Saaabrrriiinnnaaa! It's starting all over again. They're not listening to me!"

Sabrina stepped into the middle of the room and screeched, "All of you! All of you! Thtop it! Would you jutht be quiet? Lithten to him! Thith man ith the real Pirate Anorak!"

I looked at my little one in admiration. Having such intelligent little critters can be a tough job.

"The little girl's right," explained Rachel Amar. "That's him, all right. Intense paranoia sitting alongside a persecution complex. He fails to take control of his impulses and possesses an extreme fascination for fire. His need to set fire to objects and buildings arises from a desire to release excess tension. It's what's called monomaniac incendiary perversity."

Here we go again. She loves all those labels, and while she's giving everyone's feelings a brainy-sounding name, she's losing sight of both the real problem and *how to help these people. How are you supposed to get ahead in life with all those names and terms stuck to you?* I thought we were making some progress, however, and I was starting to get an idea of why Amar's methods weren't too hot. At the same time, I still loved hearing all the technical terms for people. All that analysis was nifty stuff!

I don't know where I found the courage, but I managed to say, "You got some mighty big words there. And so? Now we know what he suffers from, but what are you going to do about it?"

"What did you just say? Unbelieeeeevable! B-but what and who . . ." stuttered Rachel, coming undone.

It seemed like the judge couldn't care less what was going on between us two Rachel Amars. He simply saw it as a disagreement between expert witnesses. He turned his attention to Victor and Teddy.

"OK. Very well. Now then, where were we?" he sighed.

"That's exactly what I'd like to know," grumbled Falso. "We're all a little sick of this, right? We need to get it moving."

"Turns out you're something of a chatty fellow after all," the judge said to him, holding out his hand. "What effect does speaking actually have on you?"

"Oh, it's liberating, that's for sure," Victor said. He looked totally out of touch with reality. Strung out! Speaking, it seemed, had transformed him. The drama had come to an end. He was indifferent to what was going on. As he continued to speak, he placed the gun he'd been waving around all day in the judge's open palm. "It's nice to be able to say something when you know exactly what it is you want to say. For example, I wouldn't mind a drink right about now! What about you?" he asked Teddy.

"Sure would," he replied.

The judge sized the pair of them up. "Sorry, my little ruffians, no can do! First of all, you"—he addressed Teddy Pirla—"if you really are the pyromaniac, there's not a lot I can do for you. You'll be doing a long stretch. And you, my friend"—he looked at Victor Falso—"with an armed-hostage situation, kidnapping, obstructing a judge and officers of the law, and creating misleading evidence . . . you'll be in the can for some time too, I'm afraid." He raised his voice as if to let us all know he was in charge again. The big boy was back. "So let's get on with it! Come on!"

He stood up and glided toward the door, and we all followed. The whole troop. Teddy Pirla was clutching Sabrina's hand, and Victor Falso was watching them both carefully.

The lowly lawyer with the nail-biting issue lifted his head, interested in the sudden movement and the fact that something might finally be happening. Was it nearly his time in the courtroom spotlight?

46

As the door to the courtroom opened, I surveyed the scene: a majority of the police officers were in snooze mode, the journos were ready for action—any action, and the mega-armed special forces super-stylish cops were ready to get trigger happy at the drop of a hat. A nervous cop jumped up, on edge. The elite shooty cops looked on the ball.

Judge Amblard was the first to exit the antechamber with Victor's revolver in his hand. (It wasn't actually Victor's—it belonged to the security guard who'd been on duty that morning.) The defendant's snively little lawyer squeezed past us all and slipped out of the building without so much as a kiss-my-ass. Guess he didn't want the spotlight after all.

The judge watched him, unmoved, and then stopped in his tracks. He suddenly seemed drained, his eyes reddened. He lifted his hand up to quiet the crowd and spoke to the armed super pigs.

"Please, officers, put away your weapons . . ."

They did as they were told, but some seemed pissed off about it. They'd been tightly wound and ready for a good blowout.

"Ladies and gentlemen, I have a statement to make," the judge continued in his haughty, official-sounding voice. "Thanks to the intervention of two highly talented specialists in their field, Rachel Amar and her associate, Rosie Maldonne, the following has been brought to my attention. There has been a dreadful error in terms of suspect identification."

Victor stood behind him, looking wigged out and tiny compared to the judge. Teddy was nearby, holding Sabrina's hand. I wasn't all that pleased about this hand-holding business, but Sabrina seemed to trust him. I didn't, though, not wholeheartedly. I mean, the guy was a racist frootloop who'd been pulling mental fire-starting tricks all over the place.

Rachel Amar just wouldn't let it drop. She wasn't going to let me get the better of her. The broad was all over me like a rash, up in my grille, talking in my ear, stopping me from getting in on whatever was happening around us. I always like to know what's what, and I was failing to get the full picture because she wouldn't shut up. The judge was talking and I couldn't catch a word of it. I made sure I was standing next to my baby girl, just in case Teddy Boy decided to do anything wack.

"As far as I'm concerned, you see," Rachel said to me, "the cure is nothing more than a bonus—"

"Get out of my face!" I said.

"Listen, you've been going around psychoanalyzing people with your cheap tricks, and it won't fly with me. I actually know what I'm talking about. I can see right through you."

I felt a sense of calm wash over me. "Really? I don't think so. I think you're scared."

She was losing face. "Wh-what? How's that?"

"You know full well. Maybe you're afraid that I'll shrink your head! You're afraid! But what are you afraid of? Success? Curing your patients? Reaching your goals in life?"

Her eyes widened. It was as if she'd been hit by a wave of truth. She stammered, "Fe-fe . . . fear . . ."

The judge was full of emotion. He was really giving his speech everything he had. I started listening again.

"Destiny often chooses to take the long and winding road. How could we possibly know that the day the Full Moon Pyromaniac set alight his final blaze would be the same day a child, tossing and turning on the tumultuous rapids of life, would uncover a talent that would liberate this man? Fate often deals us the strangest of cards!"

The journalists were exchanging concerned glances. They didn't have the foggiest clue what was happening. How could they?

I heard one of them whisper into his cell phone, "I can't dictate any of this to you. We can't use it—it'll never make copy. It's too obscure!"

"It's odd that I never considered, over all these years, that I might actually be afraid of something . . ." said Amar, her voice trailing off dreamily.

"OK! That's enough! We're done! You'll have to zip it!" I said, making a sweeping gesture with my hand.

But she went on, anyway. "I can't believe how your remarks might have really set the ball rolling . . ."

"Um . . ."

She was speaking with more and more confidence. "What's so fascinating in these cases, you know, is that . . ." And she leaned in to whisper a ton of professional secrets to me in a dull voice. The problem was 1) I wasn't listening and 2) I wasn't listening. First off, there was a hell of a lot of noise in the room, and second, I wasn't interested in what she had to say.

But I didn't want her to lose all hope or her fear to get any worse, so every now and then I nodded and threw in a couple of "Hmm, hmms"—but I was really listening to Judge Amblard. I'd missed the beginning of his speech because of her and I wasn't going to be missing any more of it. The guy was on fire (not literally, despite it being a possibility in this case).

"In truth, my dear brothers and sisters, let me tell you this! He is a wise man who presides over the destiny of even the most insignificant of his sheep, and even wiser he who guesses his intentions . . ."

"I'm sorry, I'm not following a word of this. I just don't get it," the journalist said into his cell phone.

"Dear Rosie, please!" cried out Amar, making me jump. "It is OK if I call you Rosie? I have a proposition for you."

47

The judge beckoned some police officers to him. A group approached with Borelli leading.

"Well done, Maldonne," he mumbled in a muted voice, giving me a begrudging thumbs-up as he walked past. "Well played."

They cuffed Teddy the fire-starting repairman and Victor the false pyromaniac (Falso indeed!) and off they went. They had some difficulty separating Sabrina and Teddy, but as soon as it was done, I pulled her toward me. Mine, all mine.

The worst yelp I'd ever heard suddenly echoed around the courtroom. I was sure there'd been plenty of screaming in that place over the years, but this sound was gut wrenching to hear. It was our Teddy, nutball extraordinaire, who was blubbering and wailing like nothing I'd ever known. All the cops, rubbernecking members of the public, robed lawyers, and important court people, as well as the journos and photogs, stood staring, flabbergasted.

The desperate yelps disappeared with the pyromaniac (and the ordinary maniac) as they were hauled out of the room and down a long corridor to . . . well, the cells, I guessed.

As soon as we were outside in front of the courthouse, the whole world and its dog came for us. There were TV broadcasters, crowds of onlookers . . .

"You must listen to my idea!" shrieked Rachel Amar, catching hold of my arm. "I'm sure you'll accept. What would you say to us writing a book together? On the Full Moon Pyromaniac? I think my bank manager would be pretty pleased about it, at any rate. Because I don't know about you, but I'm always in the red."

"I don't even bother saying it anymore. I don't know when I was last in the black."

"So, you see? It's a great idea, isn't it?"

"I have to admit something first. And when you hear this, you won't want to have anything to do with me again."

"What now?" asked Rachel, sounding wary.

"I fell in love with your colleague, Robinson . . ."

"But why should I even give a damn?" she replied, exasperated by my weird-ass behavior.

"All things considered, Madame Amar, I don't think book writing is my thing. You'll have to do it on your own. I don't even know that Teddy guy. It's my daughter who knows all the details on that one."

As we slowly climbed down the steps, I looked up to the sky and felt a sense of freedom. Wow! The bluest of blues! I took Sabrina by the hand and made sure she was holding on tightly. With Rachel at my heels, refusing to give up on the book idea, I marched straight ahead.

"I-I have another idea, but I dare not ask you about it," stammered Rachel Amar, letting out a fake giggle like a prissy teenage girl.

"I get why everyone thinks you're such a brainiac." I said. "These ideas of yours are coming fast and furious, aren't they? Unbelieeeeevable!"

"How would you feel about being my mentor?"

I knew by this point that she'd gone beyond reason and was maybe unhinged. "Ha! I'd love to be your mentor!" I squeaked sarcastically.

I don't think she got my ironic tone, because she seemed to mellow out some. Did she actually believe I was going to do it? We all wound up, naturally, in front of Gaston's Jaguar. He was double parked, patiently waiting for us.

He lifted up his nose to greet us. His head had been buried in a book, as usual. This time, it was a notebook in which he was furiously jotting down his opera ideas. I was disappointed not to see Linus. So he hadn't been able to forgive all the lying. I thought it showed a distinct lack of kindness on his part. They were only little white lies. His feelings clearly weren't strong enough to power through our first minor hiccup.

The paparazzi cameras were still going off all around us. Flash photography—what a nightmare!

I was getting ready to hop inside when the shit hit the fan.

Big time.

48

Directly in front of the courthouse, with a heap of cops, newspaper folks, and half the goddamn town watching, *they* nabbed us. *They* took us. As simple as that. Sabrina and me.

I didn't see it coming. None of us did. It was me they wanted, but Sabrina just got caught up in it all because she was holding onto me so tightly.

So this huge tanklike metallic-gray car came to a halt right next to me, its tires screeching, accompanied by the smell of burning rubber. By the time I'd lifted my head to check it out, I'd been picked up by giant hands (hard to say how many, but at least four) and hooded. Sabrina was still holding onto me as I tried to fight them off. The two of us were thrown into the back of the tank like we were no more than a couple of sacks of grain. The door was slammed behind us. I heard the motor turn and whoosh . . . we were off.

My mother's song came back to me. This was more than a couple of raindrops, and the day was far from over. We were up crap creek without a paddle, and I'd had enough of it all.

"Where are we going, Mommy? Who are the naughty people? Are they baddieth?"

Luckily, Sabrina was up close, right next to me. I couldn't see her because of the bag (or whatever) over my head, but I could touch her, feel her, hold her in my arms. I was too petrified to dare take the bag off and risk the consequences.

I stroked her hair. "Don't worry, my big girl. We'll find a way out of all this."

"Zatknis!" screeched a harsh, aggressive voice from the front of the vehicle.

Oh no! Was that Russian he was speaking? It couldn't be! It hadn't all started up with our Russian friends again, had it?

"You guys aren't Russian by any chance, are you?" I asked.

"Shit yorrrrrrray mooottthhh!" continued the same voice.

"Mommy, he uthed a bad word!"

"No, I don't think he meant to, darling. It's his accent, sweetie. Just listen to the way he rolls his *r*'s."

For that, I got a crack to my skull.

Calm down! Don't get your panties in a wad. Analyze the circumstances here. Don't let these guys get to you. You have Sabrina with you and you need to protect her.

It was a Russian accent.

If this is the Russian Mafia again, at least I know what I'm dealing with, although I have no clue how they've gotten mixed up in this story. I can handle it, though. I know what I'm doing here.

"Um, monsieur?" I put on my sweetest, girliest voice.

He didn't answer.

"Do you know Piotr and Marco? They're two friends of mine."

They whisked off the hood. There were two guys sitting up front and three of the bastards lolling behind us. I didn't know any of them from Adam.

"Marrrrrrco and Piotrrrrrrr?" one of them asked. "You know?"

"Of course I know them! They're both buddies of mine! I know them well!"

"You wrrrrrite file on them, analyze theirrrrr psychological prrrr-rofiles, call them crrrrriminal. You rrrrrrrresponsible they prrrrrison. *You grrrrrrass.*"

What in the fuck was this all about now?

"I didn't write a word about them. I can hardly even write my name half the time."

"Psychoanalysis and crrrrrrriminality," the guy boomed.

Psychoanalysis and Criminality. Rachel Amar's book! Could this get any more bizarroid? I doubted it. Lordy, lordy.

"Rrrrrachel Amarrrr wrrrrote book," I explained, using the same accent as them in an attempt to communicate better. "Rrrrachel Amarrrr grrrret psycho woman. Not me. Me maid. Me no good."

"No. You Rrrrachel Amarrrr!" he insisted.

"Listen, people have been making the same mistake from the out-set, and I don't know why. It seems everyone wants me to be Rachel Amar, but the truth is that I replaced her usual housekeeper. That's it. It really is. I ended up staying at her house with my kidsters because there was a lot of cleaning to do and I live far away. But I'm not a shrink. I'm not in the slightest bit shrinkified. I didn't even finish high school. I took tenth grade about four times and then flunked out! I can't even remember. What do you want with Rachel Amar, anyway?"

He understood me. His response was to point to his temple with his fingers and mouth the word *boom*. I was glad Sabrina hadn't seen it.

The pack of badasses, front and back, started chewing the fat. It was half in Russian, half in French, and I couldn't keep up. They weren't just passing the time of day. This was some serious discussion and they were furious.

Nobody bothered to take any notice of us while all the talking was going on. I scanned around me. We were on high ground, a hill or mountain, surrounded by pine trees. It looked like Estéral. Somewhere near Mandelieu or La Roquette. We weren't far from home. I was try-ing to think of a way I could hold Sabrina in my arms, open the door quietly, slide out, and roll onto the road without injuring ourselves and before any of these Russian asses got overexcited with a gun. But I suppose those things only ever work in the movies, right?

I held Sabrina very hard, found the door handle with my fingers. and waited for my intuition to tell me when it would be a good time to go. *GO!* But a huge mitt took my fingers off the handle and released it. The door opened and Sabrina and I were pushed out. I swear the car didn't even slow down.

All I can say is, I figure being thrown out of a moving car is worse than a kick in the gonads.

49

It happened so quickly, I didn't have time to think. Luckily, my reflexes were good enough to hold Sabrina tight to my chest as we fell. My body helped cushion her. Instinctively, I made sure I fell on my back. I had to do what I could to protect Sabrina. My right arm and shoulder took most of the blow.

We were lying on the side of the road, not moving. It took me several minutes to realize what had happened. Good news: we were away from the bad boys. At least they hadn't pushed us out of the other side of the car into oncoming traffic. Be grateful for small mercies. Earth, dry grass, and soft leaves had helped cushion the fall. Not a lot, but every little bit helped.

Bad news: I'd lost a shoe. I didn't take the news well. It was a golden peep-toe, wedge-heel beauty of a shoe! Honestly! I could have died there and then. Those dickheads really had no idea how long it takes a girl to find a shoe that hot. And at that price? I had to take a few minutes out to mourn.

Second piece of bad news: my wrist was swelling up and turning a dirty purple color. It was starting to look like a party balloon.

The second piece of good news (and this far outweighed all the bad news put together): my Sabrina didn't have a scratch on her.

"We're like *The Indethtructibleth*," she squealed. "We can jump out of flying carth and not even hurt ourthelveth!"

"You're right. I guess they could make a movie out of this strange life we lead, Sabrina!"

"Yeah, but we could do without all the bad guyth, though, couldn't we, Mommy? They're thearching for Madame Amar tho, they can do that magic."

"What magic? What are you talking about?"

"Make her do a dithappearing act, Mommy, like with magic thowth."

"Where are you getting all this from?"

"They thaid it in the car! You never lithen when people thpeak."

"Oh, they said it, did they? When was that?"

"In the car! Didn't you hear them?"

"Yes, yes, of course I heard them. What did they say, exactly?"

"They thent my friend Pirate Teddy Anorak to make her dithappear in a ball of flameth. Like in a magic thow, you thee? The thent them both to prithon. That'th what they thaid, anyhow. They all came over from Ruthia on purpothe to get their guy back! Now I underthtand my friend Pirate Anorak a bit more and thome of the thingth he thaid."

"Like what, honey?"

"It'th because of them, Mommy. They were hith prithon buddieth. People he met inthide. They told him that he could go off with them and thet off pretty fireworkth everywhere if he thtarted with Madame Amar. That'th really bad of them, becauthe Teddy knowth that fire ith bad, but he liketh fire. He loveth fireworkth. He didn't want to keep thetting fire to thtuff. He jutht wanted thomeone to like him. And now nobody ever will, becauthe of them."

"And you managed to get all that from what they were talking about in the car?"

"Yeth, you know when they were all arguing? They thaid loth of really nathty wordth about Pirate Anorak. They thaid he wath garbage and that they weren't thurprithed that he'd got the wrong woman. They thpoke about Madame Amar a lot too. They were going to make her dithappear. Give it to her good and proper. Have themthelveth a little party afterwarth. That'th what I underthtood. What were they going to give her? Why would they have a party for thomeone they were tho angry with, I wonder?"

"I don't know, Sabrina. People can be very strange sometimes. Their ideas don't always make sense. They're not as logical as we'd maybe like them to be."

"I know, Mommy. That'th why they need to be helped, ithn't it?"

"Exactly. And that group of baddies certainly needs help. But it won't be us helping them, agreed? We need to help ourselves first. Because I'm starting to get worried about the twins, OK? And Léo and Erina! Oh, I dread to think!"

I sat upright, nursing my wrist and feeling very sorry for myself. I always try to keep a brave face on in front of the kidders, but we're all allowed a break every now and again. To let rip. That's what I figure, anyhow.

"I can't believe this! Where in the heck are we? And I've only got one flipping shoe! How am I supposed to get home?"

"Hey, you're like Thinderella, Mommy! Why don't you jutht call Gathton? He liketh coming to the rethcue."

"They have my bag in that car, and my cell's in the bag, my sweetie pie."

"No, I got tonth of thtuff out of your bag and thtuffed ath much ath I could in my pocketth."

And out came my wallet, elastic bands, hairpins, toothpicks, a lipstick, supermarket receipts, hand cream . . . And my cell phone! Yeeeaaahhhh!

We came back down to earth with a bang, though. Dead battery.

Back to square one. This was going to be hard to get over. My little Sabrina had been so brave. The disappointment was gutting.

She wanted to cry. I could see it on her angelic little face. I didn't want her to lose confidence in herself. She'd done an excellent job! She's very intelligent, but she can be a little fragile and sensitive. She's not always so sure of herself, despite the heroics.

So we started making a move (except I wasn't moving all that fast, more like limping with only the one shoe). We just had to get to a house. We needed people. Or a person. Anyone. We needed another living soul. We really were up in the mountains, the middle of nowhere.

It took us almost an hour to find some buildings that at least looked like they were inhabited by humans rather than sheep. And in the middle of the little hamlet, a teeny-weeny drugstore! No way!

50

We headed inside. It was a little store that was all things to all people. Books, newspapers, canned goods, cigarettes, baguettes. The only clerk behind the counter.

He had his head stuck in a giant book. He didn't move, sitting in a comfy chair, with a long-haired spaniel-type doggy by his feet. He was a nice-looking guy, an Italian type with curly black hair, dark eyes, bronzed skin. His T-shirt said, "Professional Lazyass." What a case.

He lifted his head and glanced at us. He actually seemed a bit pissed off that we were bothering him. It must have been a good book.

"What are you reading?" I asked politely.

"War and Peace," he grunted. "What do you want?"

I stretched over so I could get an eyeful of the front cover and I saw the title: *Lost Treasures of the World* by Joseph Caron. Not exactly *War and Peace.* Oh well. Over it. Moving on.

"We've had an accident. Can I make a call?"

I was expecting to have to fight tooth and nail to get this guy to let me use his phone, but then I noticed his head moving up and down, checking me out. After this routine that I'd grown so accustomed to over the years, he gave me a cheery smile and put his book down. He stomped over to the fridge and offered us a cold drink.

"I'm Rémi. What's your name?"

I hesitated and then croaked, my breath catching a little. "Hmm . . . Cricri."

He had a deep voice. "Very original."

This guy was coming on to me but gently, in the old-fashioned way. I hadn't seen an attempt like that in eons.

He pointed to his phone. He wasn't exactly big on the small-talk front.

I ran over and picked up the receiver. I was out of luck. Gaston wasn't picking up. Or maybe he didn't have any battery left either. That seemed possible. The call went straight to voice mail. Everything was all just so annoying. One fiasco after another.

There was no point calling Véro, Ismène, or Mimi. Their numbers were in the cell memory, not in my brain's memory. I couldn't phone my "patients" either. Or Rachel Amar. Or Borelli. Perish the thought!

"Why don't you jutht call the polithe, Mommy? They can take uth back to our trailer."

Rémi had already dialed and he passed the phone to me. Nice! I asked for Borelli, I told him I had vital information for him, but that I was stuck up in the mountains with no way of getting home and that Sabrina and I were in danger.

"Oh! Finally! It's you! What was that ridiculous spectacle? A way to evade questioning, or was it a real kidnapping?"

"Is this some kind of joke, Borelli? Is that all you have to say to me? Me and my daughter were just carted off by a bunch of crazies!"

"OK, Maldonne, I'll send a car. I hope whatever information you have for me is worth it. But I'll say this. I've had it with you!"

I explained where we were. We had to wait twenty minutes.

Rémi got out a first-aid kit, massaged some homeopathic cream into the cuts on my wrist, and then bandaged it gently. He was quite the nurse!

My face was his next port of call. He disinfected the scratches with witch hazel. It stung, but not too much. I was coping fine. His eyes were close to mine, very close, too close, dangerously close. We could smell each other and we smelled good.

I turned away and picked up a Snoopy comic book from the shelf behind me. We needed some distance between us. He packed up his medical bag and put it away. I could feel him keeping an eye on me, and I could sense his smile.

Borelli's car showed up. I shook myself down and mentally prepared for what lay ahead. I put the comic back. Shame. We all said our thank-yous and good-byes.

Rémi shook my hand. I felt that he maybe squeezed a little too tightly and held on a bit too long.

As quick as you can say "Jumpin' Jack Flash," we were in Borelli's office. He shook his head slowly when he saw me.

I think we might be OK this time. Everything seems to be in order. The raindrops have stopped falling now and things are getting back to normal. I'll just have to explain everything to my old best bud here, and then I'll be on my way. He just needs me to shed some light on a few odds and ends. Easy.

Amar and Gaston were at the station too. No Linus Robinson, but that was no real surprise. What was I expecting? I guess he'd hit the road and gotten as far away as possible. Like a rat out of an aqueduct—as my favorite Monty Pythons would say. I had a gift. A gift for getting mixed up with Russians, hostage crises, Albanians . . . Linus was better off as far away as possible from this gift of mine.

Gaston looked like a broken man, but when he caught sight of us, he changed before my eyes. His sparkle came back!

Borelli ranted for a good ten minutes before actually asking me any important questions. Or even any unimportant questions.

"I knew it was all just too good to be true!" sighed Borelli. God, that guy can be so fatalistic. "I knew you had something up your sleeve. And I knew we'd have more trouble from you."

"That's not fair," I whimpered in as quiet a voice as I could manage, not wanting to aggravate him further. Yet I still had the audacity to ask, "Do you think you could stick this cell in the outlet there, please? It needs some juice."

Borelli rolled his eyes, but connected it to a charger he found in his drawer and plugged it in.

I really needed him to hurry things up. It wasn't the right time to be spending the night down at the station—especially as I had to move everyone out of Amar's place and finish up Véro's work. I mean, I really needed that money.

Before taking down my statement, Borelli gave a passing female officer a special kind of nod and a wink, pointing to my shoeless foot with his chin. I was in a bad state around the old feet.

"What are you up to there, Maldonne? Is this a new way of drawing attention to yourself?"

The girly cop came into the office with a pair of trainers or baseball boots or whatever they're called. There was no way I was putting those monstrosities on my feet. *Not a chance.* They were a size too big, anyway! But I guess that was better than a size too small. They had bits of pink on them, so at least there was that. I love pink. The color of roses. Like my name.

I had to put them on. I didn't want to cause any more trouble.

51

As Borelli interviewed me, I was finally able to put together a few pieces of the puzzle. Sabrina did a lot of the talking, because she'd been right! My little baby had been right all along about Pirate Anorak and everything!

After what seemed like endless discussions and explanations, Borelli said, "Kevin, could you read back the statement to us, please?"

Kevin was a young trainee. He'd been typing like an insano on the computer keyboard since the beginning of our interview. There were lots of boring details at the beginning: "The hereunder do solemnly declare" and all that bull.

The statement then went over all the main questions that were asked of us—our names, professions, addresses—followed by our responses. Simple enough. Toward the end of the report, there were fewer questions—it was more of a monologue from my little princess. There weren't many interruptions from Borelli. It was better to just let her speak. Out of the mouths of babes and all that. She was the key to the whole thing.

The statement ended up being a pretty interesting read in the end:

Mademoiselle Sabrina Maldonne-Mendès declares that she noticed a man matching the suspect's description following her mother. She found the suspect to be amusing at first. She considered him to be clumsy, as she had witnessed him banging his head and falling. However, after listening to the news on the radio, Mademoiselle Maldonne-Mendès remarked on some similarities between the suspect and the Full Moon Pyromaniac, as the media was referring to him. Once in closer contact, at a later stage, the suspect often spoke of flames, burning cars, and setting people on fire, which confirmed her suspicions. She also had the opportunity to study the suspect's bag, where she found a collection of matches, lighters, and small containers of gasoline. She recognized these objects because she had seen similar paraphernalia at the café-bar, Sélect, where her mother sometimes works.

The gentleman in question spent some time at psychiatrist-psychologist Madame Rachel Amar's apartment, where the mother of Mademoiselle Maldonne-Mendès (Madame Rosie Maldonne, hereby present) was fulfilling her role as a replacement housekeeper.

The man had entered the building dressed as an electrical repairman. His intention had been to set fire to Madame Rachel Amar's apartment, but he had been too disturbed by the number of people at the residence.

Mademoiselle Sabrina Maldonne-Mendès took it upon herself to guard the suspect, alongside her younger sisters, and did not go to school. They were helped in this by one of Madame Rachel Amar's patients, who had an altercation with the man in question. Twice, she attacked him physically. Mademoiselle Sabrina Maldonne-Mendès was successful in detaining the suspect in a walk-in closet using nylon yarn (which remains in her possession). She fed him meals at regular intervals.

This morning, the situation unraveled when Mademoiselle Sabrina Maldonne-Mendès agreed to treat the suspect following psychology methods she had witnessed her mother using. For the record, it should be noted that Madame Rosie Maldonne, although unqualified, had been giving clinical consultations to Madame Rachel Amar's patients during Amar's absence.

The suspect agreed to follow this treatment and developed a certain affection and trust with Mademoiselle Sabrina Maldonne-Mendès. According to her analysis, the suspect formed an attachment to her.

As the report came to an end, Rachel Amar, who was listening from the doorway, said, "Stockholm syndrome."

None of us took any notice of her.

52

So what had my little girl been up to? After Kevin had finished reading us the report, I had a little chat with her. Sabrina gave me the lowdown on how this had all started. The others listened patiently.

Apparently, she'd only gotten really worried when she'd opened up the closet to give Teddy Pirla a hot chocolate. That's right! I remembered that! She'd been carrying it down the hallway earlier in the day! Teddy had been mean to her, to start out with. He'd fallen on her feet as she'd opened the closet and blamed her. What was his problem? I needed to have a word with that guy. Being mean to a little kid who was just trying to help out?

She explained how he'd cried *a lot*. But he had appreciated the stuff she was pilfering for him from the kitchen. Cheese, chocolate, all sorts of goodies. She was worried she wasn't really getting anywhere and that she'd soon have to come clean with me about who she was hiding.

He was still acting pretty moonstruck (ha!) and threatening her. When he'd called me a "snooty bitch" and said he'd "burn me down to the ground," Sabrina devised a plan of action. She knew I liked my plans of action, and girls like to copy their mothers.

She said he'd used a lot of really bad words, and that he must have been very unhappy, because "happy people uthe happy wordth." And so she got him to talk through his childhood with her. Bless that little baby's cotton socks. She thought she could help him, that she'd make it better. Oh, to be innocent again!

She went on in some detail about the hot chocolate bit of her story. I think she thought it was important. It was what had initially relaxed him and gotten him to agree to her "treatment."

That's when she'd led Teddy into my office. She wanted to use the couch with her patient like she'd seen her mommy do. Once inside, Teddy had started snooping around the room, and that's when he'd found Bintou's gun. The one she'd put in the drawer just minutes earlier. He'd grabbed it and started giggling.

Sabrina had asked what he was doing. She was probably getting worried at that point. She wouldn't have liked the idea of her patient having a piece in his pocket. Obviously! Who would?

He wouldn't give it up, though. Apparently, he'd declared, "He who laughs last laughs longest." Sabrina didn't know what it meant. I'm not sure I did either.

And then Sabrina's work began.

He stretched out on the couch . . . and that's when she tied the nylon yarn a bit tighter.

53

So Kevin had a bit more writing to do at the end of that statement of his! There was one question on everyone's lips . . .

"Where is the gun now?"

Actually, the cops should have had more than that one question—you know, like whose gun was it? What type of gun was it? Where exactly did he find it? Blah, blah, blah . . . It was Laroche's gun, but nobody asked. Nobody wanted the details. I raised my eyebrows at Borelli. Nothing. He told Sabrina to go out into the corridor and grab a drink from the vending machine before coming back to sign the finalized documents. Sabrina left to join Gaston and Amar, and Kevin headed off to make copies. I stayed on my own with Borelli.

"So Pirate Anorak was the pyromaniac all along. Wow. Teddy Pirla." I sighed.

"Yeah, we've got one copycat nutcase who's obsessed with your psychoanalyst friend and another arsonist maniac who is clearly narco-leptic, from what I've heard. I wonder what will become of him."

"That's not even your department, is it? You don't work much in narcotics, do you?"

"You really should invest in a good dictionary, Maldonne. I said *narcoleptic. Narcolepsy.* Oh, forget it."

"Whatever. And the Russian Mafia was behind it all again. Incredible."

"How do you know that?"

"Well, they're the guys who picked us up. I didn't want to mention it. I didn't want to say much in case Amar was listening (which she was!), because I didn't want to scare the living daylights out of her. She'd be a wreck if she knew they'd been after her all along. And all because she'd given her expert opinion on a few lowlifes. They thought I was her. That's all it was."

"You were supposed to be making a truthful statement, and there seem to be lots of details missing. Why Pirla?"

"He met them in prison and they sent him in to do their dirty work. They wanted to throw a wrench in the works with Amar. Well, more than that. They wanted her burned alive."

"OK, what is it you're saying here, exactly?"

"Listen, it's pretty simple, Borelli. I thought you were more on the ball than this. All the members of the Russian gang in France were put in the can. The Russians sent in reinforcements, OK? And now the network is being built up again. And the boss of the French branch is giving all the orders, probably from inside! They saw that Pirate Anorak was dying to be in on it all. He likes a little action. Some attention. And a bit of fire! More than a bit! And now he's been caught. So they're trying to get their act together now. It's a matter of honor. Things are going to heat up for Amar here. I'd say all that was pretty clear, wouldn't you? Christ, you're not too bright today, are you?"

"Seeing as it's you, Maldonne, I'm not going to take the bait. But if you speak to me like that again, you'll be sorry. Let me remind you that I'm an officer of the law."

"And?"

"You can't speak to a cop like that!"

I shrugged. Borelli was having a little meltdown, throwing his weight around.

He continued, "But I'm a good egg, you know? And I'm going to give you the benefit of the doubt, because even though your arguments are never very logical, you often hit the nail on the head. I don't know how, but you do. So, Pirate Anor . . . Teddy Pirla is going down. I'm willing to put a mole on him inside. See who he hangs around with. See if he has any Russian friends . . ."

"It's no good. He won't have anything to do with them. Didn't you hear Sabrina? He was so touched by her therapy that he now wants to control his whole goodness-gracious-great-balls-of-fire side."

"Great balls of fire? What are you talking about now?"

"It's a song. Oh, never mind. Teddy Pirla doesn't want to set fire to shit anymore, OK?"

"Fine. So I'll put Amar under protection until I find out what's going on with the Russians, OK? The easiest thing would be if she didn't stay at her own place. Some of those guys she helped put inside will have made parole by now. Also, it would be easier if you gave me everything you know next time I ask, instead of just letting your daughter give the official statement."

He stepped out to go get the others. I wanted to say that it would actually be easier if he'd asked the right kinds of questions in the first place. We'd been kidnapped, for frig's sake!

Everyone signed the (half-finished) report. I kept quiet as much as I could, because I didn't want to annoy Borelli any more than I already had. It worked. He released us all back into the wild.

I (also!) hadn't mentioned to him that Erina was staying at home with us . . . I mean at Amar's place. I didn't want him to have another fit. And that's exactly what he would have had.

I had a long to-do list. At the top of it was to get some cleaning done, which meant I needed Bintou to take care of the twinniebobs that night. I had to ask Gaston if he could help move us all out the next day, and I also had to arrange a visit to see Mimi with Léo. Oh, and there was figuring out the whole Erina issue and finding the mysterious Monsieur Charles before he found us.

It would also be nice if I found the time to see Linus Robinson again. We needed a little alone time. I wanted to explain some things. I couldn't tolerate the idea of him heading off to Canada with such a bad impression of me. I'd been an impostor, a usurper, a charlatan.

Before leaving the station, Borelli mentioned that Rachel Amar's address had been found in Teddy Pirla's phone. He was right, then. It was safer to keep Amar away from her apartment for the time being. I asked Gaston to take her home to his castle. I was sure he could help cheer her up.

To my great surprise, Amar didn't protest. Not even slightly. She was more than happy to be told exactly what to do. She had gotten herself into a deep discussion with Sabrina about the methods my little one had used to break Pirate Anorak. She seemed captivated by what my baby had to say on the subject.

Great! I can finish all my chores back at the apartment, pack up, and get ready to move on out of there tomorrow.

54

So Gaston and Amar headed off in the Jag, and I took the bus back to Amar's place with my Sabrina. My wrist was still hurting me, but the cream had helped. I didn't know what was in that magic concoction that the handsome Rémi had used, but it had certainly done the trick.

School pickup time for the twins had come and gone, but I was sure Bintou had picked them up. I just had to make sure she'd stay around that evening, so I could finish up the cleaning.

Obviously, it didn't all go as planned. I don't know why things never go as planned for me. It's like someone cast a wicked spell on me at some point and forgot to uncast it. My mother's song was playing in my head at full volume: *Raindrop, raindrops . . .* I needed to ignore it. But I wasn't really a head-in-the-sand type of person.

As I stepped out of the elevator and reached the front door, it all began.

I'd just put the key inside the lock and turned it when I heard screams coming from behind me. Before I'd even had time to spin around to see what was going on, someone pushed me in the back. I went flying into the apartment and landed flat on my face, some of my weight falling onto the bad wrist. *Ouch!* I yelped and yelped. The pain was baaaad!

Sabrina shrieked. Léo ran from the kitchen, followed closely by Laroche. I felt relieved to see them both. I managed to stand, grab my Sabrina, and look behind me.

There were three baddies. And how did I know they were baddies, apart from the violent push? They were wearing pantyhose on their heads to hide their features.

It was all very *Point Break*. Oh, no, they wore masks in that. Well, it was the same idea, anyway.

They pointed their whopping great big guns at us.

"Hey, brainboxes! Do you think this is a bank? Are you whacked up on Scooby Snacks or what? There's no money here!"

Just as the words came out of my mouth, I wondered if Amar might, in fact, keep some cash around the place. Maybe she was hiding a big box of gold somewhere? Who knew? She'd been charging huge wads of cash for her shrinkage for years. Maybe these guys knew something I didn't.

Yeah, right.

Whatever was going on, these guys weren't about to let me in on it.

Laroche was saying the same thing over and over again. It wasn't helping much, and nobody was giving him any answers.

"What's going on? What's going on? What's going on?"

"Shut your fucking mouth!" yelled one of the stocking heads. He then turned to me and screamed, "Where is she?"

God. It was Murrash's voice. I recognized it. They'd come for Erina. Still, there was no need to speak to Laroche like that. It annoyed me.

"Hey you! Just because you've got a gun doesn't mean you should forget your manners, understood?"

And for that I got the butt of his gun smashed into my chin. He was strong. I landed back on the floor with a thud. As I fell, I let go of

Sabrina. She roared out in my defense, "Leave her alone! Thith ithn't right! It ithn't even clever!"

Oh no. I was worried for her. She shouldn't have been taking those guys on.

"Sabrina, go with Laroche, honeybun."

Laroche grabbed Sabrina and threw her behind him.

"Erina isn't here!" I shouted at Murrash.

"Simmer down, Maldonne," Laroche said to me. "They have a network of informants, these people! Don't try to outsmart them."

Well, at least he wasn't calling me Madame! He sounded like Borelli. Bigging his part up.

"I'm not doing any simmering!"

"I think it would be in your best interests to just do as he says!" said Laroche. "It would be the most prudent and intelligent—"

"You! What's with all the ass licking? You don't know me! I have my own way of doing things, OK? This is all part of my strategy, my—"

And with that Murrash gave me a good kick in the ribs, stepped over me, and nodded to his buds to go search the apartment. The nod must have also implied to break everything they came across, because that's what they did. A nod can say so much, can't it?

So the housework had been bumped off the to-do list. The place now needed renovating, not cleaning. I decided not to argue it out with these men. I didn't want any more thumps or kicks, nor did I want my Sabrina in any more danger than she was already in. I tried instead to follow Laroche's advice.

We all watched as Amar's armless, legless blue statuette girl started wibble-wobbling. If she fell, at least nothing would break off her. There'd be nothing to stick back on. We should be grateful for small mercies.

Léo suddenly took it upon himself to head-butt Murrash—but I don't think he had much experience in head-butting. Murrash moved at the last second, and poor Léo's skull cracked into the wall. He fell down like a sack of crap. He was out cold.

I didn't know whether Erina was still in the apartment or not. I hoped with all my heart that she'd left or found an excellent hiding spot.

But one of the buffoons came back to Murrash, dragging her by the arm. I had my answer, then. She hadn't left the apartment and she'd been in a shitty hiding spot.

When she saw Léo passed out on the floor, she tried to rush toward him, but the thug pulled her back violently. Murrash gave a second nod and one of his buds frog-marched Erina out of the apartment.

Murrash pointed his gun at me and took the safety off. At least, I think that's what he did. We see that sort of thing all the time in the movies. We always understand exactly what's happening in films, but it's harder to figure out in real life.

Sweat started running down my back, and my teeth started to chatter. I was sure I would have put up a better fight if Sabrina hadn't been with me, but I had to put her first.

Laroche was the next person who spoke. "Um, I really would advise you not to shoot. You've done all right for yourself so far. You got what you came for and no harm has come to you. No bloodshed."

The third thug grabbed Sabrina and pulled her toward the front door. Where did he think he was going with my baby? She fought tooth and nail. Literally. She squirmed, she bit, she scratched, she screamed. She was making some raucous noises! But he held onto her. He put one of his huge paws over her mouth, and they disappeared down the hallway outside.

I threw myself onto Murrash, but my hands and legs were tied together with tape before I even knew it was happening. Laroche wasn't in any position to make a move either. Murrash was holding him by the cheek.

"If you call the cops, I'll kill them," Murrash hollered. "Next time, blood will be shed. You," he continued, staring at me as I lay tied up on the ground, "you'd better not interfere in our business. All that's finished now. If you want to see your little girl again . . . alive . . . you'll keep a low profile. Mind your own fucking business."

I was beside myself with rage. I couldn't even hear what he was saying. All I could see, playing over and over again in my head, was that bastard's big hand over my Sabrina's mouth.

They tied Laroche and Léo together, back to back. And someone gave me another sharp kick to the head. I saw stars dancing all around me and then nothing.

55

The three of us stayed for some time in those positions. Tied up. Nowhere to go. For how long? It's impossible to say with any precision.

I think my neurons had been kicked out of sync. There'd been a short circuit in there somewhere. Everything had switched down. I needed a reboot. If I hadn't lost consciousness for at least some time, I think the stress would have pulled me under. *They had my girl!*

When I finally came back to the real world, it hit me just how big a disaster everything was. Léo was still out for the count, and Laroche was tied to him, traumatized.

This was what empty felt like. Silence.

Those bastards had disappeared as quickly as they'd arrived. They'd taken Erina and the apple of my eye. My Sabrina.

My feeling of powerlessness had gone, and in its place was pure fury. At least I was still alive and kicking. That meant I could go get my baby. My wrist felt hot. I could feel it burning. I could also sense that my neck was bruised and my ribs were killing me. Happy times!

I hoped Léo would get his act together. I needed him ready for action. He had to be in top form.

It wasn't looking good. In fact, as I examined the three of us, all lying on the ground in various states of injury, it looked pretty bleak. Catastrophic.

This had been a shit day from start to finish. The shittiest.

Except it wasn't even over!

Everything that had happened so far came back to me in an accelerated flashback: everything Erina had told me, the arrival of the police, Amar coming home, Linus finding out the truth about me and then splitting, Sabrina and Pirate Anorak, the courthouse hostage negotiations, our Russian kidnapping, making my way through the mountains with just one shoe, pretty-boy Rémi and his flirting, Borelli and the statement, the pink sneakers, and now out-and-out war with Murrash, who'd taken my love.

That's exactly what it was. A declaration of war.

He'd gone way beyond too far. There'd be no coming back from this.

I sensed that Léo was regaining consciousness. It took him a few seconds before he realized that he was tied to Laroche.

"Don't move. You'll just make it worse," I said.

We didn't have time to go into a big discussion. We heard voices outside. The little ones and Bintou.

When they came in, they saw us all on the floor.

I really didn't want the twins to see us all in this state. They were going to be scarred for life if they had to live through any more of these adventures.

But those two had incredible natural capabilities. They were bouncer-backers if ever I knew any! They hopped from me to Léo, howling loudly. "What are you playing? Robbers? Like Sabrina?"

"That's exactly right! And you're the cavalry, OK? You're here to save us just in time! To the rescue!"

Bintou untied us all, muttering as she did so. "I warned you something like this would happen. These guys don't mess around. You're in it deep, aren't you?"

They weren't going to beat us.

"Are we going? Let's go!" I howled.

Laroche and Bintou looked at us, and Laroche reasoned, "I think we should go about this intelligently. That's how we'll win this thing. Throwing yourself out of the frying pan and into the fire won't do anyone any favors."

I couldn't deal with talk like that. Laroche sounded all wet. But I had to keep it together in front of my two youngest daughters. Whatever happened, I couldn't let the panic set in (it had, though, in a major way!). I just had to act like everything was normal, for their sakes. I didn't want them to find out that their sister was missing, that she'd been taken.

I took a deep breath. "I read you loud and clear. No messing around this time. No fear. I'll send those stinking bas—blockheads to the hole for good! We need to do this right. We can't hang around too long. We need a plan, sure, but anything could happen in that time. We need to make a move soon."

"No!" screamed Léo. "That's all just bullshit! I'm off!"

The girls roared with laughter. "What a bad word!" Emma said. "Mommy! He said bullshit!"

"Yes, but there's no need to repeat what he said, is there?" I explained in as nice a way as I could. To Léo I snorted, "Cut it out, boyo! Watch what you say in front of these babies. We need to keep our wits about us! Stop with the hothead bull!" I headed to the bathroom. "In the kitchen, all of you. I'll be there in a minute."

The scratches on my face needed cleaning. I also put some chamomile lotion on my neck to help with the bruising. It had started to swell. I needed some of Rémi's cream. The bandage on my wrist was still holding out, so I left it where it was.

I went and joined everyone in the kitchen. "I don't know about you, but I'm hungry. So we're going to eat."

It was important to keep up appearances, and when the poppets came home from school, the ritual was that we always had a snack. Period. So that's what we were doing.

As soon as the kids were each settled with a bowl of cereal that I'd dug out of a cupboard, we had our war council. It was just a figure of speech, because the fact of the matter was, we didn't have much of an idea of how to move forward.

"This time, it's over," Léo kept saying ad nauseam. "If we don't go now, I'll—"

"Wait," I told him. "You'll see that Laroche was right."

"Oh no! Come off it, Cricri! Next you'll be telling me that we're going to call up your friend Borelli. I'm sorry, but what has he done for us so far? That moron is totally useless. Plus, Murrash told us not to call the cops or he'd wipe everyone out. We need to get over to that hellhole house of theirs and try to find them."

"People can't be wiped out," reasoned Lisa. "Is he a people eraser?"

"Where's Sabrina?" asked Emma.

What could I say? My lip trembled. "She went out for a stroll with Erina . . ."

But Emma had already dragged Lisa off her chair and they'd run off to play horsies through all the rooms.

That's when I decided it was the right time to grill Bintou. She'd actually met the big boss. So she was the one who we needed to convince to help us. If we could find this Monsieur Charles, we'd maybe find Erina. And if we found Erina, we'd maybe find Sabrina. A three-for-one deal.

"But Bintou's going to help us find them again," I said, looking at her.

"No, I'm not! It's out of the question," she exclaimed. "I don't think you actually understand. You never even tried to understand. I know these people. I know Monsieur Charles. You've shat in his begonias, OK? And he doesn't like it. I'm sorry for the expression. I know it's crude. Let me just say, you guys are lucky to be alive! I know you've been roughed up pretty bad, but that's nothing! So take my advice on this and call the cops."

"No! You can't be saying what I'm hearing here!" yelled Léo. "Who are you, anyway? Why should we be taking such crappy advice from you? You're a journalist! You journalists are all the same! No balls!"

The twins ran past and Lisa tsked. "We're going to tell Sabrina about your bad words, Léo! She doesn't like it!"

"Yes, Léo. I told you once already. Watch what you're saying."

"You've got no balls, balls, balls!" sang the twins. Oh jeez!

He was right, though. I spoke my piece. "We can't do that, Bintou. The police are already on this, but we're not leaving it up to them. You know, they're all a bunch of . . . useless men with unmarried parents." I tried to use code to avoid certain words in front of the babies. I didn't want them to know how serious the situation was with Sabrina. "So we have to get organized. You're the only one who knows stuff that might lead to their whereabouts. So you're going to help us, and that's the end of it."

She shook her head. "Sorry. This is my life."

WTF.

I insisted some more. The least she could do was point us in the right direction. It wasn't much to ask.

She caved in to the pressure, finally. I've always been good at pressure. I also took the opportunity, now I had her where I wanted her, to ask if she'd take the girls to my trailer and babysit until I got home. I needed her to cook their dinner and put them to bed. I didn't know what time I'd be back.

But one thing was for sure, I wouldn't be coming home without Sabrina.

Was Bintou OK with staying with them? There was more than enough room for everyone.

She accepted all my demands, though she sulked about it. She had a long face when she sulked. Like one of those high-class horses.

"I want you to stay by your phone and that lap machine thing. Laroche, is that all right with you?"

"No probs," he replied. "I'll stay with Bintou and the girls. And I'll keep my laptop and cell with me."

With that, we all left.

56

Once we were outside on the street, Bintou asked, "So, what is it you want me to do, exactly?"

I explained my plan. With her help, we were going to find Monsieur Charles and kidnap him. Léo approved enthusiastically.

But Bintou busted out laughing. "Oh, you're going to kidnap him just like that, easy as pie?"

I opened up a tote bag I'd brought with me so she could see the contents. Laroche's gun was wrapped up inside a piece of fabric. His pistol, his revolver, whatever you want to call it. A killing machine with bullets. And I intended to use it. I'd found it under a cushion on the famous couch in Amar's office. Pirla must have shoved it under there before he'd had to leave with the cops. Thanks to Sabrina, I'd thought to look there.

"With this thing, he'll listen to me. He won't mess around with us. He'll do exactly what I say, and he'll be quick about it too!"

She surveyed us closely. I think I saw something like pity in her eyes. "And then what?"

"Then we'll get what we want. He'll let Sabrina and Erina come home. He'll call his minions and they'll bring the girls to us. Listen, we'll just see how it goes, OK? We'll improvise."

"You really are dense," said Bintou. "You'll only have one option. You'll have to take him down. It'll be you or him, believe me. Do you think he won't have his gun on him or something? If you don't kill him, he'll search all four corners of the earth to find you. And he'll find you. And he'll make you pay. He'll kill you and anyone who's with you. And quite honestly, Madame Maldonne, I imagine you'd have some difficulties killing a person, wouldn't you agree?"

"Stop calling me Madame Maldonne!" This was now becoming a sore point.

Léo was walking around in circles, getting overexcited. "So, what are we doing?" he asked, his voice rising. He was smacking his fist into his palm and cursing (again!). He was whispering to himself like a madman. "All that for nothing! For fuck's sake! Bastards! I'll never see Erina again. There's a chance she's dead!"

Bintou looked at him and let out a long sigh. "Here's what I propose," she said. "I'll show you where they were hiding out when they were doing their . . ." She was obviously embarrassed to be talking like this in front of Léo. "Their . . . well . . . when they were selling different things. So it may be that Erina's there too? Sorry, Madame Maldonne. I really can't show you any more than that. I have no desire to see you in a body bag. It wouldn't help anyone, least of all Sabrina. Where I'm taking you, if it's still used for what it was used for, is dangerous. So you're going to have to tread very carefully if you want this to work."

And she strode off down the road. Were we supposed to follow her? Léo tried to keep up with her (boy, was she striding!) and I moped way behind with a twin holding each hand. I had to more or less drag them so they wouldn't do their famous stopping trick every five minutes. Laroche stayed at the back. He was the slowest, because he had his computer bag and Pastis. I was proud that my boy was being so cooperative.

We left the old quarter, crossed the main street with all the shops, and started making our way through a neighborhood with lots of old vacant storefronts that had been left to rot—people who'd gone out of business. The residential buildings were a little worse for wear, to say the least. Basically, the whole area could have done with some sprucing up.

There were garages and key-cutting joints that hadn't heard the sound of a motor or cutting machine in years. There were some real-estate signs dotted around the place. Some of them were showing artistic impressions of what was to come. Some of the old buildings were to be knocked down to make room for giant new structures. It all looked very pretty. Flashy, but pretty.

Not far from a church, Bintou turned down a street and disappeared from sight. By the time we reached that street, I'd lost her.

"Hey! Pssst!"

We all turned our heads at the same time. She was waiting for us behind some kind of warehouse or shed. The sort of place you'd expect to find heaps of electrical stuff and grease.

She whispered, "Listen up! This is where the fun and games end, OK? No more bullshit! I'm not ready to leave this mortal coil just yet, not now that I'm feeling a heck of a lot better about life. Nor should you. So, you see that old body shop over there? That's it."

She pointed to some 1970s-era building. It was dirty—as if the windows hadn't been cleaned for decades. The shutters were all busted up. On the ground floor, the storefront was protected by a rusting security grille and padlocked doors. There was a small parking lot out front, but no rides.

"This is the place. Well, as far as I know, it's here. I can see it's not abandoned. They change their places often, from what I understand, but this one is still being used."

"How can you tell?" asked Léo. "There aren't any cars or anything."

"Exactly! That's one of the signs. All the cars are parked farther down the road. From out here, the whole place looks like it's empty. But can you see that little circle just below the 'For Sale' sign above the door?"

"Yeah?"

"It's a camera. That's why I'm not going any nearer than this."

"I'm going in," declared Léo.

Bintou whispered, "I'll leave you guys to it. Let me take the girls to safety. I have no problem letting the cops know what's what if you don't make it back tonight."

I gave her the key to my trailer-sweet-trailer, along with the directions, and warned her about the water issue. I told her about the plastic-bottle deal. I gave my twinnies big kisses and told them to be just as good and clever as they always were and to listen to Bintou no matter what. She took each of them by the hand and scampered off as quickly as she'd come. Laroche followed as best he could.

"Christ, she could enter the Nice-Cannes marathon, couldn't she? She might even win the thing!" I said. "Anyway, it's up to us now, kiddo. We need to get this raid of ours thought out. We can't leave any traces."

I was overcome by a wave of extreme cold. It froze me to my core. Rage had given way to an intense need. A need to get this thing right. There was no room for mistakes. Failure was not an option.

The body shop joined onto two decrepit-looking garages, which themselves neighbored a crusty old house. We could try to get in through one of the adjacent buildings. It was maybe a way of avoiding the camera. The place was surrounded by houses, sheds . . . streets and streets of urban decay.

"OK, you ready?"

Léo was about to head straight for the front door, but I pulled him back.

"No! Not that way! Do you want to get us wiped out from the start? We'll go to the other side of that house thing there. Or we could try to be tricky about this. Like dress up as the mailman or a pizza-delivery boy." I think he was embarrassed for me. "Yeah, I know," I said. "Not one of my best ideas. OK, forget what we said earlier. Major change of heart. I'm calling Borelli."

I dialed his number, but of course he didn't pick up. Not only did he not pick up, but the darned thing didn't even ring. I got his voice mail. What good would that do me? I hung up and sent a quick text to see if that might get his attention. Nope. No answer. What was the point of having a cell?

We'd just have to figure it out on our own.

We made our way around to the back of the body shop, taking the long way around, past the garages and the house. There was a gate leading to a little yard. Well, *yard* might be an exaggeration. Let's just say a patch of scrubby land. There was a lock on the gate, but Léo managed to bust in pretty easily.

"OK, we should be able to climb up to that window and jump onto the roof of the first garage. I hope I can manage it. This wrist is acting up pretty bad."

One thing I was pleased about was that I was still wearing the pink sneakers. They were as ugly as sin, but much more practical than my usual stilts.

Suddenly, Léo froze. We saw movement. Someone was sneaking around back there! A white suit. *Murrash.* He was leaving the body shop by a back entrance. Little Kholia was with him, tottering in front as they walked, and he was holding my Sabrina by the hand.

Sabrina!

My instinct was to run to her, but Léo stepped in front and blocked me. He turned to put a hand to my mouth until I calmed down some. Then he let me go. A pretty daring move on his part, but it worked.

I wasn't feeling that cold sense of dread. I felt ready for this. I was back. My inner rage was back. I saw red. But I wasn't thinking straight. I wanted to get the gun and take Murrash out, but I couldn't find it . . .

"What are you looking for?" asked Léo. And he showed me the gun. He'd taken it from me! Little pickpocket . . . or pickpurse?

I jumped on him. "Give that back! I'm going to kill that dog! I'm doing it now. Enough with the messing around!"

But he was taller and stronger than me and had already shown me that he was prepared to use his muscle. "Cricri! We have to be smarter than that. There's no point going for him now. First of all, he's probably armed too. Do you want him to kill one of the kids?"

His words hit me like a cold shower.

Murrash had his back to us. We were crouched down in a bush so that he wouldn't spot us if he suddenly turned around. Sabrina didn't seem like her normal self. She seemed floppy, dazed . . . just weird. She was just following the guy. No energy. Doing as she was told. That wasn't like my girl.

"OK," I said in a lowered voice. "You're right. I can't go in guns blazing. I have to do this safely. Let's follow them. There's no point hanging around here. We know that this is where they're staying. We'll come back."

"But . . ." Léo mumbled almost inaudibly. "What about Erina?"

How it hurt to hear those words.

It was hard to speak, holding back the tears. It was almost as if I couldn't quite catch my breath. But the words ended up coming out clearly and precisely. It was as if I'd stepped outside myself. I only had one image in my mind: Sabrina running to me, jumping up into my arms and laughing, with Murrash in the background lying in agony in a puddle of blood.

"Listen, stay here. Climb to the top of that garage and try to stay out of sight. Keep a lookout for any unusual movements. Whatever you do, don't go near the body shop or the house. Put your cell on vibrate. We'll stay in touch and keep each other in the know, OK?"

"OK."

"Promise you won't try and go in there without me."

He swore. Quickly. Too quickly and too easily for my liking. I was sure that as soon as I turned my back, he'd try to get into that house. What on earth would I say to his mother if anything happened to him?

Maybe he'd be our lookout and take his role seriously without attempting anything stupid. I couldn't follow Sabrina and stay with Léo. But someone needed to keep an eye on things here.

"There's a chance that Erina isn't here. So risking your life for no good reason would be bonkers. I think it'd be nice if you were alive when we found her, what do you say? Did you see what he was holding? A plastic bag. *Capisce?* Understand? I'm going to get the kids and make sure that bastard's picked up. And then things will really heat up for Monsieur Charles. If we ever find out who he is. If Borelli does his job right, Murrash should sing. We'll get a handle on this trafficking thing. If Monsieur Charles is behind this group of thugs, I'll have his ass. I swear it. Nobody takes my daughter and gets away with it."

"Make sure you don't do anything without backup. You need to watch your back. The kids' backs too. Be careful out there."

"OK. And don't you go inside that place until I get back."

So we both made promises we knew we couldn't keep. It meant we could go our separate ways with confidence. Fake confidence.

I squeezed Léo's hand and followed Murrash and the kiddos. I kept a safe distance. I couldn't risk him seeing me just yet.

57

As I followed Murrash, I prayed to Saint Expeditus—my family's special saint. He was a Roman soldier turned Christian. He saved my Jewish grandmother from the Nazis. Well, that's how the story goes, and I believe it. Saint Expeditus keeps an eye on the women in my family. I know this to be true. He's the saint of desperate causes. And that's what we are! I light little candles for him in church whenever I pass by. Well, whenever things get really bad. What's good about him is that he's usually quick to answer my prayers. That must be one of his tricks. To expedite. It means to act quickly, right? That's what my mom told me.

At the same time, I also prayed to the cosmos, Buddha, and my guardian angel (we all have one, apparently) that the bag Murrash was carrying contained what I hoped it contained. Snow-white powder. Snow-white powder that would see him behind bars. Drugs that he'd had little people carrying all over the neighborhood for him. I hoped we could catch him in the middle of a deal, and then he'd really be in for it.

We'd nearly reached the center of town. I recognized Erina's route. Sabrina hadn't noticed I was following her. She would have under any other circumstances, but she was so passive with Murrash, so weak, and Kholia was exactly the same. He was plodding along as if he didn't really know what he was doing. That prick must have given them tranqs or something. He needed them to follow him without making a fuss.

Murrash stopped off in front of a smoke shop. Someone slouched over to them. Was this the infamous Monsieur Charles? The two men chatted awhile. They were as shifty as they come. The pair of them nervously looked left and right. Furtive. They definitely had something to hide. He handed over an envelope to Murrash, who slipped it into his inside jacket pocket, then rooted around in the plastic bag and pulled out a parcel wrapped in brown paper and string. No, it couldn't have been Monsieur Charles. Must have been a client.

They went their separate ways as quickly as they'd met. The drug buyer ambled off into the distance, and Murrash headed inside the smoke shop. I took this chance to give Léo a quick call. I told him where I was and how far I'd followed them, and reminded him to maintain a safe distance from the house and body shop. I explained what I'd just saw. The deal.

"So there you go. What should I do now? If there really are drugs in that bag, this is the time to get the cops involved. I have to do it now before he sells the whole thing. All I want to do is grab the kids and run as fast as the wind. What do you say?"

"Sure, do it. If you want to feel a bullet in your back."

"*Grrrrr.*"

"Where do you think he's going next?"

"I think he's doing Erina's regular route but he's deviated a little. We're near the train station."

"Good. That's good. The station," said Léo. "Let's hope he's taking the train somewhere. A public place. Out in the open. It would be the best place to tackle him. There are bound to be police or security guards at the station. You need to make sure the cops see what he's carrying. Find a way to draw their attention to him. Good luck. I can't do anything to help you right now. I'm still on the lookout here. If they come out with Erina and try to make a getaway, I'll shoot."

He chuckled. This was worrisome. It wasn't something anyone should be laughing about. I kept my mouth shut.

He continued, "If you manage to get into the station, call me. Let me know what's happening."

As we hoped, Murrash made his way to the station. And the place was swarming with cops and soldiers. As I passed the Chinese fast-food joint just in front of the entrance, I decided it might be the best place to make my move. It was one of those now-or-never moments: a young cop was directing traffic, two armed cops marched up and down the sidewalk, two soldiers chatted at the crossroads, and the cherry on the cake—a riot van full of army boys parked up ahead. Everyone was out in force! I just had to calculate the right moment.

Two cops were striding in my direction when I started hurrying toward Murrash and the little ones. My heart was pounding. Murrash still hadn't seen me.

When the cops were only a few yards away, I took a deep breath and threw myself into action. I pushed Murrash as hard as I could in the back and looped my leg in front to trip him. What I wanted more than anything was for him to let go of the bag and for the cops to see what was inside. Then it would be game over. I know it wasn't the best plan in the world, but I was in full-on panic mode. The situation called for something urgent and I didn't know what else to do.

Murrash was surprised, to say the least. He fell to his knee, but kept hold of Sabrina's hand. Seeing him on the ground like that gave me a deep sense of satisfaction. I took my opportunity to kick him as hard as I could while he was down.

Kholia clearly couldn't believe his little eyes, although the way he looked at me was still mournful. Sabrina's face, on the other hand, showed a spark of joy, but it was as though she were keeping it hidden. She didn't fight to free herself from his grip.

She said in a switched-off voice, "Ith that you, Mommy? What are you doing?"

"Let her go, you asswipe!" I grunted, trying to pry Murrash's fingers from Sabrina's.

I'd almost done it when a powerful hand grabbed me by the scruff of my neck and hauled me up. It was one of the cops, a young one. He politely helped Murrash to his feet. Wrong one!

"You could have hurt this gentleman! Watch where you're putting your feet!"

I was shocked that the cop had taken that motherfucker's side! What the hell was this? Since when did the bad guys get helped to their feet by the pigs while the heroine of the story is given a good dressing-down?

Murrash pulled himself together. Now there was a guy who wasn't even the teeniest bit bothered by the presence of the law. He stood upright and then kept on walking, Sabrina in one hand, the bag of drugs in the other, and the little boy up front. Sabrina turned back to look at me but didn't make a peep. It was the opposite of what I would have expected her to do.

The young cop seemed satisfied with the way it had turned out.

I stood dumbfounded for all of five seconds and then I screamed at the top of my lungs, "Hey! Where the fuck is that dumb fuck going? Don't let him get away! He's got my daughter! He's a notorious drug trafficker! A people smuggler! He trades in children, I'm telling you, and he's taken my girl!"

The cop raised his eyebrows at me condescendingly. "What are you talking about, lady? Why are you screaming like that? Give it a rest! Leave the poor man alone! He hasn't done a thing!"

"Are you fucking deaf or something? Why aren't you listening to what I'm saying? He's a drug pusher! He pimps out young girls!"

"If you don't keep the noise down, I'm going to have to call for backup. You can't go shouting out things like that about passersby!"

Murrash had acted like he didn't know who I was . . . like I was a total stranger. And that's when it became clear. His game was better than mine. He was light years ahead of me.

He'd walked into the station cool as a cucumber.

The cop gave me the once-over and shook his head. He took me for a crazo! I couldn't understand it. Oh well, I didn't need someone like him on my side. I'd be better going solo! I followed Murrash, but made a big detour so that dimwit boy-child cop couldn't see what my intentions were.

Murrash was continuing to act like he was just a normal guy with a normal couple of kiddies. He went and bought tickets at the counter, and then they all sat down quietly in the waiting room. His attitude was ultrarelaxed, but I knew what was really happening.

He was worried. He was holding it in as best as he could. What he clearly wanted more than anything was to knock me off. He kept sneaking a peek at his watch. He wanted to be on that train. Whichever one he was taking . . .

I felt a deep sense of desperation. I couldn't stop the waves of guilt. I'd tried and failed. There was no room for errors, but I'd made one, anyway. And the lives of Sabrina, Kholia, and Erina were on the line.

I was a shit. Worse than nothing. And now Murrash had seen me.

I was out of sight for a few minutes, but I could see the worried expression on my little daughter's face. She was searching the crowds. She seemed more alert, as if she was coming out of her stupor. Maybe he'd told her they were going home, but now that they were at the station, she knew something wasn't quite right.

The next train to arrive was expected in ten minutes and it was headed for Italy. Was that where he was going? His escape plan? Had he gotten fake passports for the little ones?

I kept my eye on the waiting room, but made my way to a corner so I could use my phone without too much background noise.

"Yes? So?" asked Léo.

I spoke with gritted teeth, keeping the volume down as much as I could. I told him what I'd tried and how it had all gone so spectacularly wrong.

"We've fucked up!" cried Léo. "He's going to get away and Erina's going to die!"

"Listen up, Léo. This isn't exactly helping, OK? You have to keep it together. We won't get anywhere with that attitude."

He was silent and then said, "Didn't you say Laroche might be able to help us? He's got his laptop, right?"

"Yes, but what do you expect him to do?"

"I have an idea. I'm going to call him." And he hung up.

58

I waited for Léo to call back, my eyes not moving from my baby. The waiting room was glass paneled, easy enough to see what Murrash and the kids were doing. I watched as he stood and took them out of the room. They went back into the main hall, probably to look at the departures board. Jesus!

He had zero fear! He smiled and made eye contact with me! The prick! He took something out of his pocket and it shone as the light hit it. A knife. He brought it up to his throat and mimed slitting his throat. His eyes didn't move from mine. I'd never been so threatened in all my days. He put the knife back in his pocket.

I shook from head to toe. A knife in his hands was worse than a gun in mine. Plus, I didn't even have the goddamn gun. There weren't any metal detectors in the train station. Why not? There were international trains, for chrissake! Shouldn't there be border control and customs and all the rest of it?

As I stood helplessly, fretting about the lack of security, there was a massive crash of thunder. I looked up through the stupendous glass roof of the station and saw several forks of lightning. The visuals were quite spectacular. The atmosphere changed. Everything darkened. *I can't believe this! Even the weather is against me!*

Kholia seemed drained. He sat down on a seat. Murrash stood nearby in his expensive white suit. He still hadn't let go of Sabrina's hand.

She was preoccupied (this was a good thing), looking all around, staring into the face of every person who passed. She was searching for me. Bless her! I was hiding behind a newspaper stand only a few feet away. I didn't want to draw too much attention to myself. There were several things I could do at this point, but I needed the element of surprise.

I looked through the papers, magazines, and books. There was my eldest daughter. Was I about to lose her? In just a few minutes, the train was going to arrive and she'd be headed to the other side of Europe! What could I do? Follow them? Get on the same train? How, with no money?

An announcement came over the loudspeakers: "Attention. Your attention, please. Mesdames, messieurs, your attention, please. The little boy Kholia and the little girl Sabrina Maldonne-Mendès are asked to present themselves immediately to a member of the staff. Please note that they are to be quarantined by the Department for Infectious Diseases. They are traveling with a gentleman in a white suit. Caution. Caution. These children are in imminent danger and must not be allowed to travel."

Murrash looked beyond shocked! He scanned the area around him like a hunted dog (which was exactly what the bastard was). He'd lost his cool way about him, that was for sure.

My cell made a little *ding-dong* sound. I had a text message.

So? Did that work?

It was from Laroche. How had he done it? The mind boggled! The guy was a whiz! Léo must have told him what to say. In any case, they'd come up with this story—an emergency. It had certainly grabbed the attention of the crowds.

I replied. `Yes. Medikal mesaje brodcast in stayshun!`

Sabrina must have known I was nearby because she'd heard my dinging phone. She was searching for me, turning her head this way and that, but I was still blocked behind the magazine and book racks. She was trying to pull away from Murrash.

Another text message: `That was just the start! A test. Get ready!`

I thought, *What can he possibly be doing now?*

Murrash was not letting Sabrina escape his grip. Kholia had heard his name but didn't know what was happening. He stood up and glanced around. He was starting to look more alert and interested. Sabrina continued to try to pull away from Murrash.

Two soldiers were making their way toward the three of them. A third one stood a short distance away and spoke into a walkie-talkie. They formed a triangle around Murrash and the little ones. Two police officers approached Murrash and asked him the children's names. Something was finally happening!

"Peter and Maria," said Murrash, barely flinching. "Why are you asking? Oh, the announcement? Nah! Nothing to do with us! Ha! If my kids were ill or infectious, I'd be running down to the hospital with them, not waiting for my train! My children are the picture of health, as you can see!"

"You're not my father," croaked Sabrina.

But she wasn't forceful enough. The drugs he'd given her, whatever they were, were still having an effect. She wasn't her usual sharp self!

Kholia was looking panicked. He was pale and red-eyed, the most fretful skinny little thing. Surely the cops would notice something was amiss.

"Are you sure everything is OK here, monsieur? We can take you to the hospital with an escort vehicle, you know? If you want to, of course."

I stood up and walked so that I was behind the cops, but the kiddies could see me. I gave them a wave. But they were worried. They were shaken by the uniforms, the noise, the hustle and bustle. I wasn't even sure they saw me. How could I get their attention?

Sabrina's eyes finally reached mine, and within a tenth of a second she got it. She understood that I was trying to go unnoticed and that she was to pretend she hadn't seen me. She knew we only had one chance at this and it couldn't go wrong. We were far from safe, despite the cops and the soldiers being right there. Murrash knew what he was doing. He still held all the power.

And it was at that exact moment that he spotted me. I could sense his fury, but with the cops still in his face he couldn't do a thing.

Thunder still growled overhead and the entire station was cast in shadow.

"Yes, yes! I'm positive everything's OK! Thank you so much for your concern. You're very kind, but you've made a mistake," asserted Murrash.

And just like that, the police and the soldiers all moved away. What the . . . ? Murrash was going to get away with this! I couldn't think fast enough. How was I going to save Sabrina and Kholia? How was I going to stop Murrash from escaping?

Rage and desperation flowed through me in equal measure. And those emotions forced me to act. I ran for it! I threw myself on Murrash and pulled Sabrina's arm, hard. He held on—his grip was incredible! Sabrina was trying to help me, pulling away, but she didn't have her usual energy. She wasn't screaming, biting, and kicking like she should have been. She was so weak, she just peeked up at me with hope in her eyes. She needed me to do it for her, to free her from Murrash.

The plastic bag! I made a grab for it and managed to take it from him. I started hitting him with it, but it was pretty light. Murrash hopped from foot to foot, trying to dodge my moves, but he still didn't let go of my girl. The young cop from earlier was suddenly back on the scene. Jesus!

"You again?" he hollered. "What are you doing now? Why don't you leave this poor man alone?"

Was I dreaming or what? How could this guy have even passed his pig exams? How could they let a young boy this thick in the head join the nation's police force? It was ludicrous! Why couldn't he think this through? See it for what it was? There'd been cops questioning Murrash minutes earlier, an announcement, and now I was attacking him. Why couldn't he do some goddamn police work? I think it was the suit—Murrash looked rich and cool and classy! He certainly came across as a more reliable character than me in my pink sneakers and neon shorts.

"I don't know what this woman wants with me! She's stolen my sandwiches!" snapped Murrash, pointing to the plastic bag in my hand. "She must be very hungry."

"Sandwiches! Now that's a good one. You're quick, I'll give you that!" I yelled.

"It'th Mommy," said Sabrina weakly. "She'th here to thave me."

They weren't listening to her. I was, though. I smiled at my baby to reassure her. She gave me a sleepy wink in return.

How I wanted to scream, "This is my daughter and this bastard has kidnapped her!" But I was too afraid of being taken for a loon again. If I was stopped, or hindered in any way, by the time I proved I wasn't mental and that Sabrina was my baby, it would be too late. I couldn't risk being arrested.

The young officer had really gotten on board with what Murrash had told him. "I want you to give this man his sandwiches back. I'll have to take you down to the station if you refuse," he said in a stern tone. It was almost as if he were just out of cop school and trying out different voices.

He grabbed my wrist, the unbandaged one, and pulled the bag from my hand. He gave it back to Murrash without even looking inside. I tried to speak out, but there was nothing I could do. Murrash trudged away, muttering a few thank-yous to the officer, who held me back.

Just then, Kholia pulled the bag from Murrash's hand and threw it to me.

"This is ridiculous!" snarled the cop. I don't think he'd ever come across so much trouble over a bag of sandwiches.

"Do you think you could stop acting up, you little rascal?" Murrash said.

This guy was an Oscar winner. He didn't even shout at Kholia. He kept his cool and played the doting father. Murrash walked over to the bag and picked it up.

"I can't do this anymore," I whispered, meekly.

He ran toward a tunnel heading to the international platforms, dragging both kids with him.

I couldn't even follow them. Babycop was still holding me back. A voice announced the imminent departure of the train to Rome.

"If you're hungry, Madame, I could buy you a sandwich," said the cop.

I looked at him in anger. I'd almost lost the will to live. I couldn't stop the tears. "Do you realize what you've done? Can't you see he's leaving with my daughter? That bastard!"

More thunder and lightning above. It felt like it was closing in. The atmosphere was heavy.

"Take it easy, please. If this is a custody issue, there are courts for that. You can get a case against him, if that's what you want to do."

Murrash disappeared down the tunnel. It took every ounce of strength, but I tore myself away from the Muppet officer and ran toward the staircase leading to the same platform as the tunnel.

As I got to the top of the steps, I just saw the tail end of a white suit disappear onto the train. He was several cars away from me. I wanted to follow him, but there were two railway workers there asking to see my ticket.

I exploded. "Ticket? My ticket? So this is how it's going to end, is it? My fucking ticket!" I scanned the horizon, looked left to right, hoping to find a solution in a detail that had escaped me this far.

Another announcement—this time the voice was so soft, in stark contrast to the violence of the words being spoken.

"Attention, attention, this is a state of emergency. Suspected terrorist threat. All passengers must leave the station immediately. Please use the nearest exit."

The atmosphere changed in an instant. Passengers looked to each other for support. They were in shock. I could smell the fear. It was as if nobody wanted to be the first to move. At the same time, the station became weirdly silent. All conversations stopped. Everyone was listening for further instructions.

"Passengers aboard trains must depart. I repeat, depart all trains and make your way out of the station using the nearest exit."

People instantly started moving, but nobody was leaving their luggage. People were taking everything with them, and it was slowing things down. Others were scrambling to get past them. I was worried there'd be a stampede. Folks were hopping off Murrash's train in a dazed state.

I couldn't believe my ears.

The thunder above was suddenly drowned out by the sound of an engine turning, rotor blades. It sounded like the whole French army was landing at the station from above.

When I peered up, it wasn't thousands of helicopters, but just one, circling overhead. Wow, those things can make some racket.

Hordes of people were now running toward the exit in a wave of panic. Within a few minutes, the platform was practically empty. A few people were still getting off the train. I was the only person not going anywhere.

Soldiers started running up and down platforms. Then the cops started running. Finally, the remaining members of the public started to run.

It was as if the whole world had forgotten me.

But where was Murrash? There was no way he could have gotten past me. I headed to where I thought I'd seen them get on the train and spotted them through the window. They were stuck between two very old women with a lot of bags. Sabrina and Kholia managed to squeeze past the lady in front of them and jump down from the train.

I ran toward my baby and she jumped up, wrapping her arms around my neck. We didn't have much time for a big reunion. I put her back down, grabbed each child by the hand, and marched as silently and calmly as I possibly could back toward the main hall. I simply tried to do what everyone else was doing. Numbly get out of harm's way.

The tears were falling from my eyes, rolling down my cheeks, and dropping off my chin like two miniwaterfalls. Nobody was taking Sabrina away from me ever again. Murrash couldn't do anything now that the station was full of officers and soldiers. It was too risky.

I turned around and, in the distance, saw the most beautiful of sights—Murrash was being arrested. It was like being at the movies.

I watched as a gang of soldiers dragged him along the floor, dirtying up that pretty white suit of his. Five slow minutes passed. They dragged him around and searched him. I didn't know how and why they'd stopped him. Had he dropped his drugs? Was it a random ID search? Did they think he was a terrorist? Had Laroche played a part in it? Told them about the suit? I didn't care. I was just glad I wasn't in his place. They weren't treating him too kindly.

I ran over it all in my head. *Wow, Laroche pulled this one of out the bag! A terrorist attack! Who'd have thought of that? You'd have to be pretty gutsy to try that in this day and age!*

The tears were still coming, but I was smiling through them. As we scuttled outside, I started singing a little song to distract the babies from all the frenzy around us. I made it up as I went along.

"Come ooooooooon! That baaaaastard's going to have to explaaaaaain himself, yeeeeeeeah! I hope he's having a heeeeeeell of a tiiiiiiiime of it! Baaaaaaaastard!"

"Mommy! That'th a thtrange thong. A thong with curthe wordth in it? Not nithe."

I felt reassured. Everything she'd been through and she still had her morals. No foul language in front of my sweetie.

We were standing in front of the station with hundreds of other people. Most of them were waiting to get their trains, but I was sticking around for safety. I wanted to be where half of France's cops were. I spotted my old cyclist buddy, Antoine, on the sidewalk. He was looking at his watch—must have been waiting for a friend. It was going to be hard to find someone in all this kerfuffle. I waved at him and he waved back. He didn't even seem surprised to see me with another kid. Maybe he didn't know the boy wasn't one of my own. Old men don't usually keep track of these things. I smiled and turned to leave. I judged enough time had passed. We made our way across the road and sauntered down the street.

We went as fast as we could without drawing any attention to ourselves. When I felt like we'd left the danger zone, I sat down on a bench to catch my breath and calm down.

The weather was acting crazy. A hot wind had come from nowhere, and the thunder continued with the occasional bolt of lightning. It felt so weird. We could still hear the helicopter in the distance. It felt all apocalypsified.

I called Léo and explained that things weren't looking too good for Murrash and that the children were now safe with me.

"Don't you go anywhere! I'm on my way," I added. "I won't be there right away. I need to rest up a minute and take the kids to the trailer."

I wanted to go to Léo right away, but the children were my priority. They were exhausted. I was too! In fact, it felt like my legs had turned to jelly. I stayed sitting on the bench for a few minutes. I examined the sky. What a strange menacing color. I had to find a last bit of energy to power through, and I thought about what my next steps could be.

Little by little, the noises around us quieted down. The helicopter had flown off and people were dispersing. There were no more sirens. An armored vehicle sped past us and I caught a glimpse of Murrash's ugly mug in the back. He was sitting between two uniformed blue meanies. Oh! I liked that! He didn't see me. I cracked up. It was a sense of relief mixed with nerves.

I rested another ten minutes or so and made a few phone calls. The first one was to Borelli. Miracle of miracles, he picked up. Then he tried to put me off.

"This isn't a good time, Maldonne! It's pandemonium here!"

I didn't react as he probably would have expected. I was very blasé about the whole thing. "Yeah, I know. You've got some Albanian fella in, don't you? All powdered up? Weapons? Suspected terrorist, right? Take it from me, Borelli—put him straight in the clink. He's a trafficker. You don't even have to go anywhere near the terrorism thing. It'll be harder to prove. He's a dealer. Big time."

He was flummoxed for a few seconds and then said, "Fine. Drop it now, won't you? You always have to meddle. You'll end up paying for this, Maldonne. You need to learn to listen. A little discipline is what you need! Damn it! The guy was armed. So he's being treated as a suspected terrorist. End of story. OK? So what is it you want with me, anyway?"

"I'm going to give you an address, and I want you to come out on a rescue mission."

"What address?"

"Just an address, OK? Like a storage place, a body shop or something. Somewhere to hide shit. What do I know? Anyway, I saw Murrash coming out of there. Your Albanian. I'm sure once news spreads of his arrest, they'll all come scurrying out like the little rats that they are. You'll see! You'll be able to pick up some real cases down there! It'll be full to brimming with evidence."

"Chances are we won't find anything. We need to question the guy we've got here. And we need the big boss, you know that! We need whoever's running the show. But look, if you're giving me an address . . . Well, I don't really have a choice. I'll have to check it out or send someone down there."

"Oh, stop overthinking everything! Just get off your ass and go see what's what, you big shillyshallyer. The place could be full of drugs! *Passage Legoff.* It's a body shop."

"You're fucking this up, Maldonne. I might not be able to get my hands on whoever's running this because of you! I'm sure he's not where you're saying he is. And he might even know we're on our way."

"Or you could end up with the organist and not just the monkey grinder!"

"And I suppose this works two ways?"

"Yes, it does!"

"What do you want, Maldonne?"

"Erina. I think she's there. I want you to hand her over to me. No declarations made to anyone. She doesn't exist in your files, agreed?"

"I don't know about that, Maldonne. I can't promise anything. I'm not working on this case alone, you know?"

"You could let her go and pretend she escaped, couldn't you? Shit almighty, Borelli! Use your imagination! It's not that hard! I'm asking for a favor! Just this one time!"

He hung up.

I was livid. *I really can't count on that guy. After everything I've done for him.*

The adrenaline rush and its soothing pain relief had come and gone, which meant that I could now feel my wrist, my head, my ribs . . . the searing pain.

The sky was lit up by fork lightning, the thunderclaps directly above our heads. Kholia was scared stiff. He jumped up onto my lap and put his head on my shoulder. Sabrina smiled at him.

"Oh, it'th nothing," she said. "When you thee lightning, the cloudth are thrilled about it and they give it a round of applauthe! That'th all it ith!"

"It's going to rain kittens and puppies any second now!" I declared.

The little ones rolled around laughing and the wind went up another notch. *Sirocco*. That's what they call it. A warm and violent wind. The skies blackened further.

The kittens and puppies weren't there yet, but they were on their way.

59

As I regrouped, I wondered whether I should just head straight to the body shop with the kidlets. No, it was far too dicey. Going back to that place with these two little precious beings was one of the worst ideas I'd had in a while. How much more shit was I planning on getting in? The best thing to do would be to find these babies someplace safe to stay. My trailer would do just fine. So off we went.

When we arrived, Bintou had set up a dining table out front. All the windows and doors were wide open and flapping in the wind. It was a good idea to air the place out. The children ran around, giddy to be reunited and to make a new buddy in Kholia.

On the big plastic table were the remains of their dinner: pizza and chips. *I told everyone no more pizza!* But it wasn't really the best time to complain about diets. My children were safe and sound, and that was all that mattered. Everyone was content. The twins had their mommy cuddles and were following Sabrina around as if their lives depended on it. How they must have missed her!

The most delicious smell of melted chocolate wafted from the front door. Bintou came out and bellowed, "Dessert's ready! Oh, Madame

Maldonne, it's you! Great! Just in time for cake! You've brought Sabrina! That's just wonderful."

She was trying to remain confident, but I could see she was relieved to see me and emotional to see Sabrina.

"And who's this little one?" Laroche appeared behind us with a steaming chocolate cake still in the baking pan. He was holding it with the famous orange dishcloth. I couldn't believe it.

"There you are, Laroche!" I said. "Wow! You are a force to be reckoned with, my friend! Unbelievable!"

He blushed and gave me a little wink. "Hacker. It was my first job, if you can call it a job," he revealed. He set the cake on the table and rubbed his hands together, laughing. "So, how did it all go off?"

"It worked! I'll give you all the details later. Basically, the message about the infectious illness slowed him down and then . . . Well, it was spectacular! Total meltdown! Soldiers, antiterrorism squads, men in black, you name it, they all showed up. It was like watching a movie. An exciting one."

"Yeeeaaahhh!" cried out Laroche.

"I hope you didn't leave any traces behind!" I said. "And you know what? I still need your help."

The babas had all ventured back to the table, attracted by the sweet smell. Bintou was dishing out the choco delight. Wow! It looked incredible. I stared at it greedily. She cut me a piece and I wolfed it down in about two seconds flat.

"Léo is hiding out. He's keeping watch. We think we've found where Erina is. I have to go help him. So I need you to stay with the girls . . . and the boy too, of course!"

I cut another two pieces of cake and stuffed them into my pocket. "For Léo and Erina."

Just as I said the words, a huge droplet of water plopped down in the middle of the table. The little ones squealed and took hold of Kholia.

"It's raining! It's pouring! The old man is snoring! Come! Quick! Come and hide!" they giggled and sang.

They pulled their new friend into the trailer. Ah! I got it! I'd been trying all day to find a metaphor for the song my mom had sent, but I think she actually meant for me to take it literally. I felt better. Literal rain was easy enough to deal with. She just wanted to warn me. She might have been worried I wouldn't be dressed properly. Moms are like that.

But I was just about to set off to find Léo, and I wasn't going to take an umbrella with me no matter what my mom thought. It would slow me down. Maybe a waterproof coat? Nooooo! It was far too warm for a raincoat. I couldn't deal with the long sleeves. There was just no way. *But thanks, anyway, Mom! You're more reliable than the weather forecast.*

"OK, I'm out of here." And then I turned to Bintou and explained, "This little one hasn't had a wash in some time. Maybe you could take him along to the fountain to get cleaned up there? And the others at the same time? It might cool them down! And I'd like them to be clean for school tomorrow."

"Tomorrow is Saturday," said Bintou. "There is no school."

"You're right! I'm losing it!"

"Also, there's no need for us to go to the fountain. I've fixed your water, Madame Maldonne," said Laroche. "There was a blocked pipe, that's all."

I couldn't hold back. I ran up to him and gave him a bear hug. "You thought you were a 'nothing,' remember? And now look at all the good you've done! You've been an 'everything' to me!"

He blushed and smiled.

"We'll put them to bed soon," Bintou said. "If you get back late, we might be asleep. Unless that bothers you, of course. We'll go as soon as you get home."

"I hope we'll be bringing Erina back with us! Léo and Kholia can sleep in the same room and I'll put Erina in with the twins. Sabrina will have to come into my bed. I feel this need to just be with her . . . to not let her go."

More big drops of rain fell. Giant drops! Each one like a cupful. Bintou and Laroche scurried around the table, clearing up the plates and glasses, the leftover food, and the chairs. They were very helpful people to know!

"Bye, then! See you later! I can't be sure, but if everything goes as planned, I'll be back in less than an hour. If it floods, and let's be honest, it doesn't look good, make sure you don't float away in this trailer!" I joked.

And under what was fast becoming a ferocious downpour, I headed to the body shop and Léo.

60

I was soaked to the bone by the time I arrived. The storm had certainly come, and this one didn't do things by halves. It was bucketing down. I didn't think I'd ever seen anything like it in all my born days. I looked around the garages and at the back of the building, but I couldn't find Léo. There wasn't a single cop in sight either.

Why didn't people ever listen to me? One thing I did understand was that my mother was right to warn me about the weather. But this was more than raindrops falling on my head. Maybe I had the wrong address? I was blinded by the amount of water falling. No, I knew it was right.

I didn't know what my next step was going to be. I also had another problem—my feet were getting drenched. There was water running down the street, gurgling around my sneakers, above the soles. It was almost like I was standing in a stream.

Every time I heard a car, my heart skipped a beat. I wanted more than anything for Borelli to show up and lend me a hand here! I wanted to be sure he was going to arrive on the scene! I was feeling it, though. I really believed he was on his way.

But in the meantime, what was I supposed to do about Léo and Erina? I wasn't sure whether it was better for me to wait for the five-o to come do their jobs (and for me to shelter from the rain someplace) or break into the shithole of a building myself and find out what in the frig was going on.

What if Borelli didn't show? What if his boss hadn't given him the green light? What if the bad guys sent for backup and they all made a run for it and took Erina with them? And what if that all happened right now, and then it would be too late for me to do anything about it?

And what if Léo had been taken prisoner too?

There was only one solution, as far as I could see. I had to get in there.

But the rain wasn't quitting and the water around my feet was rising. It had gone past ankle deep. This was getting ridiculous. I had to reevaluate. The current felt strong. By this point, it was more than a stream—it was a river. What was going on? Shit started floating past me—garbage, leaves, branches. The water was getting muddy and dirty. This was a serious deal!

I waded across the street and behind the buildings, as far as the gate leading to the non-yard. I opened it up.

The water wasn't going anywhere. It went as far as the eye could see and was now up to knee level. How could this happen so quickly? It was one of those flash floods! God Almighty! I held on to the gatepost. The water now had such a pull on me that I was terrified it would carry me away if I slipped. I held on with everything I had. I couldn't comprehend how this had just come from nowhere.

This had to be the wildest shit that had ever happened.

In a matter of minutes, the whole area had turned into a natural disaster zone! I should never have made that stupid joke about the trailer floating away! It wasn't funny in the slightest.

And that's when I thought I must be hallucinating: I glanced back to the street and several cars that had all been neatly parked just moments earlier were now floating slowly away! Fucking floating cars doing some crazyass waltz in the middle of the road as they knocked into each other and spun around. If the current could move a car, what chance did I have?

I climbed up onto the wall that surrounded the scrappy bit of yard, and from there I scrambled onto the garage rooftops. The water could maybe carry away a car or two, but it would have problems moving a building. I slid along the surface, but I still couldn't see any sign of Léo. I made my way to the body shop and managed to slip through the first-floor window. Thank God I'm athletic. Wow! It was dry in there! Phew!

I was shivering all over, even though it wasn't cold. It must have been a reaction to all the water and the emotion of the day.

I didn't move a muscle. I was waiting for something terrible to happen. Something terrible was bound to happen! If this place was full of baddies, they weren't exactly going to be too thrilled about me coming in through the upstairs window.

I scanned the room. It was a biggish place. Pretty nice! The way it had all been set up on the inside was a shock after having seen the scruffy mess on the outside. I guessed this was where the boss boys hung out, not just your average badass.

After a few seconds, I thought, *Either there's nobody here or they're as deaf as dormice or they've heard me and now I'm trapped.*

I took a couple of deep breaths and decided to snoop around the place to try and find stuff out. That's when I heard a voice and saw a furtive movement out of the corner of my eye.

I flattened myself as much as I could against the wall. A little farther along, I saw a built-in cabinet. I crept sideways, opened it up, stepped inside, and crouched down. I left the door open a crack so I could keep an eye out.

Footsteps. The same voice. Someone was talking on a phone and he wasn't speaking French. He was about as noisy as an elephant. He was certainly not making any effort to hide his presence. He'd come in to the room and was speeding around as he barked down his cell, stopping to look out the window at the raging deluge outside.

He hadn't seen little old me. I just had to hope there was nothing he wanted in the goddamn cabinet. I held my head in my hands. The ostrich move, I call it. I gritted my teeth together to stop them from chattering. And then I chanted in my mind. *I'm invisible, I'm invisible, I'm invisible, I'm invisible . . .*

He slugged right past the door. He was a big man, but I couldn't see his face. I could smell him, though. Sweaty bastard. He moved away and his voice faded. I stuck my head out for a better look and spotted a big pair of black boots as they left the room.

Thank God!

It must have been a living nightmare for the cops, with this hurricane thing going on outside. I couldn't exactly ask them to come to my rescue now. There must have been a whole load of people in greater need.

A hurricane or a tornado or whatever it was on the Côte d'Azur? What was the world coming to? This sort of thing never, ever, ever happened here! I imagined what it must be like downtown with all the sirens and panic. It would be a bit like *Miami Vice* but with fewer competent cops.

The guy on the phone sounded like he was panicking, even though I didn't understand what he was saying. I came out of my cabinet and went to check out where he'd gone. He was in a hallway that wrapped around a large rectangular platform with doors leading off it. They call it a mezzanine, I think. I stood in one of the doorways. The mezzanine overlooked the body shop below. The whole of the downstairs was now flooded. I peered down and watched as all sorts of different pieces of machinery and engines and God only knew what bumped into each other below. It was car-part soup down there.

I tried to assess what the bad man was doing. He was just a couple of yards away, but luckily he didn't spot me. He was too busy with his phone call and too preoccupied with the mess below. Maybe he'd just learned that Murrash was going down? I hoped so. Or was it something else?

I had to get out there for a better look around. I needed to find 1) wherever they were hiding Erina, if Erina was really there, and 2) wherever they were keeping Léo prisoner, if Léo was really there.

The man shuffled into a nearby room. This was my chance to start making my way around the building. All these rooms needed checking out. I squished out of there, leaving huge puddles behind me. I could sense that he'd stopped. No more footsteps, no more talking.

Oh crap! He'd heard me! Well, he'd certainly find me if he wanted to! Just follow all the water and that's where I'd be.

61

I slipped inside the nearest doorway. If the guy came back, I didn't want to be standing there like a fucking twit. If I was in a room, there at least might be someplace to hide or something I could use in self-defense.

It was a pretty bedroom that had had a woman's touch at some point. A bed with purple satin sheets, delicate lighting, a pretty armchair with floaty fabric. It was sweet. Sexy. Ah, I knew what this place had been used for!

I spotted a bedside lamp made of some sort of metal—copper, bronze, steel, I don't know—but it was heavy, so it was mine!

I stood to the side of the door, ready to pounce. I froze as the handle turned and the door slowly opened. Shiiiiit! What was I going to do?

It was him. He pushed the tip of the gun through the door and then his big frame followed. He inched into the room, but his back was turned to me. Thicko.

I let out a yell—a real war cry! "Léo! Erina! Don't come out! Stay where you are! Stay!" Then I smacked the man's hand with my lamp, using every bit of strength I had. A good effort!

He hollered out in pain, and his gun dropped to the floor. I kicked it and it slid far away toward the bed. I was doing a mean-ass job and I was more than a little pleased with myself! I let out a victory whoooooop (well, in my head).

He bent down to look at his hand. It was messed up. I gave him a kick in the neck. I didn't want to kill him, but I needed him seriously out of the game. It didn't really work. In fact, I bet it was no more than a tickle for him.

He shook his head and slowly turned to face me.

I couldn't risk him seeing my face, so I jumped on his back and tried to smack him in the eye with the base of the lamp. The angle was awkward. It wasn't the great success I'd expected. I just couldn't manage it. He flicked me off him and threw my makeshift weapon in one direction and me in the other. Ouchy.

"Watch it, would you! That really hurt. Throwing me around like a goddamn laundry bag."

The lights went out. Christ. The luck I have! Total electricity failure was exactly what I needed. But it was no surprise, given the rain out there.

The two of us stayed still for a couple of seconds while what had happened sank in, and then he gave me a cracking kick in the side. I slipped along the floor, my head smacking into a hard object. I only understood what it was when I felt it with my hand. It was his gun.

I didn't see whether he'd noticed me grab it, but the next thing I knew, he was running out of the room to the car wash below. What a heavy-footed buffoon he was!

I pulled the safety off the gun, Clint Eastwood–style. Then I pulled the trigger. Maybe I'd gotten a little overexcited. The sound was immense! It nearly burst my eardrums. The gun had been pointing upward, and now big pieces of plaster were falling down on me.

I wanted to show him who was boss. Maybe that had worked.

I stood up and left the room, but I couldn't see him down below. I could hear someone splashing around down there, though. It sounded like he was swimming. Surely it couldn't have gotten that deep? He must have been trying to make it to the exit. The noises certainly made me wonder about my exit strategy.

Léo and Erina were somewhere in that hellhole and I had to find them. It would be a bonus if I could find them before the cops arrived. It was true that there was a good chance the police wouldn't be coming now because of the flooding, but what if they did? I had to make sure Erina wasn't around.

I called out to my babies over and over again, barely pausing for breath. I searched every room upstairs and held up my cell phone through the door like a flashlight.

And that's how I found them.

They were holed up in the same room, an office, as far as I could tell. Both were tied to the same table. It must have been some time since the place had been used as an office. There were cables, boxes, mouse pads, monitors, and God only knew what, strewn all over the floor. Total health hazard. Could it be the rain that had done this? No, we were still upstairs. Dry as a bone (well, I wasn't, but still). There was no paperwork that I could see, and no actual computer or hard drive or whatever you call it either. All gone. It might have been handy evidence. If it had been there in the first place. My cell light wasn't doing the best job, so maybe I'd missed something.

The kids recognized me right away when I shouted, "Hide and seek! Coming, ready or not!"

After untying them, I fumbled through the room, opening drawers and grabbing anything I could find that I thought might come in useful at a later date. I got a ton of paper clips, rubber bands, some rolls of sticky-backed plastic, and an old cell phone. I pocketed it all. There was some good stuff for Sabrina.

From below, surprise of surprises, we heard Borelli yell, "Just stay where you are, dumbbell!"

Then some weird noises followed. Hollers. Insults. A shot.

Christ. The big boys had arrived.

Léo couldn't stop laughing. "Oh, Cricri! You know how to keep folks waiting, don't you?"

Borelli called again from downstairs. "Maldonne? Maldonne? Was that you I heard a couple of seconds ago? Did you find them? Where are they?"

62

Borelli had arrived just in time to catch the bad boy trying to swim out the front door. I hadn't heard any car engines, but maybe they'd come in a boat? No exaggeration. The rain really was that bad. Had they come on foot? Waded in?

I put a finger to my lips to silence Léo. I tried to listen in on what was happening downstairs, but with the rain hammering on the roof, it was next to impossible. I signaled to the teens to follow me.

I put my head around the door and could just make out Borelli ordering his men to search the building. His arms were flailing around like a maniac.

I headed back into the room and placed the gun down in plain sight on the desk. I wiped my prints. I've seen as much *CSI* as everybody else.

We all left the office and stepped onto the mezzanine. I listened for Borelli. I could see light from a flashlight below. Beams moving around, searching. Cops didn't have to rely on stupid cell-phone light.

I moved in the opposite direction, back toward the room with the window I'd used to get into the building in the first place. And that's how we got out.

We found ourselves up on the rooftop of the double garage. In under two seconds we were all drenched. It was how I imagined it would be inside a washing machine. That's how wet we were.

"Let's try to find someplace to hide until this downpour stops."

There were no oink cars outside. There were plenty of civvies' cars, though. The rainwater level had gone down some, and I saw cars floating on their roofs. Cars that had somehow managed to get locked together. Cars stuck in manholes. Cars on top of each other. But no drivers. They'd done this to themselves—or, more accurately, the rain had done it to them. Nobody, cops or otherwise, would be getting through this mess anytime soon.

So we weren't getting a ride out of there! Oh, who cared? We hadn't come in a car.

We waited a little longer.

Léo explained how he'd used the same window to get in the building once the rain had started. He'd been searching for Erina when the nasty-ass bumped into him and threatened him with a gun.

Erina nodded to back up the story. She was looking toward the body shop with worried glances. The poor thing was so agitated. We could still see flashlight beams through and around the building below. The cops were going over the joint with a fine-toothed comb.

I thought I heard something. A scream. It was difficult to know where it was coming from in all the commotion. We crawled along the roof to check out what was happening behind the building.

On an adjacent street corner, a whirlpool water-vortex thing had appeared. It was horrible! There was a man on the very edge of it, hanging on to a window frame. The water was a powerful torrent around his legs, almost waist high. He was screeching. The water was going to carry him off!

"*Hilfen!* Helpen me! SOS!" He had a weird accent. Not French. He looked washed out (no pun intended). He was pale and terrified.

341

I gaped openmouthed at Léo and Erina. "That guy's not going to be able to hold on! What should we do?"

Just then, three people came out of another ground-floor window in the next building. Two men and a young woman. They made their way to him. The three of us scooched down the metal drainpipe and doggy-paddled the short distance to join them.

"Did you just hear shots?" the woman asked me.

"No," I said. "It was the thunder. Don't worry about it right now. What are we going to do about that man? He won't be able to hold on for long. Maybe he can't swim!"

One of the men took charge of the situation. I didn't usually like that, but there you go.

"I know what we can do," he announced. "Human chain."

He knocked on a few of the houses along the street. We needed more courageous neighbors on our side. Not everyone felt like opening their doors to let more water in, but some accepted. Léo, Erina, and I were already about as wet as a person can get. So what was a little more? In for a penny, as my grandmother would have said.

We all linked arms to make a human bridge so we could cross the "river" to reach him. Luckily, the cars all seemed to be staying put. It didn't look likely that any of them would be swept in our direction.

It was pretty hard work for me. My wrist was killing me, but my neighbors on both sides were linked to me by the elbows, so it wasn't bearing the brunt of the operation.

It was incredible to see people who'd never had anything to do with one another linked together to save someone they had probably never met. In times of crisis, people can really surprise you! The kindness of strangers. There was one mission here: save the guy with the weird-ass accent who nobody knows. He looked over to us with hope in his eyes. I was praying we'd be able to get him to safety without the chain breaking.

We did it. The first link in the chain wrapped his arm around the guy's waist. They gripped each other. The rescued man was sobbing and sobbing.

By the time we got him back to where the water was less of a danger, we started chuckling with relief. We were amazed. It had only taken a couple of minutes and a few helping hands (or arms), and we'd maybe saved the guy's life.

It turned out he was a German tourist. Could any of us speak German? Nope. He kept saying, *"Danker shern! Danker shern!"*

There was an old grandmamma who lived a little farther up the street. She called out to us that she had cookies and hot coffee for everyone. Sounded great. Most of the human chain went back to their own homes, but the German guy and the three of us joined the old dear to warm up and dry out.

She lived in a second-floor apartment. More importantly, she had cookies. You've got to love anyone who has cookies. Ah! I had cake too! I took out Laroche and Bintou's cake from my pocket. It was sludge. Just brown mud. You couldn't pay someone to eat that.

We decided to wait inside the lady's house until the rain stopped. But how long might that be? Noah went forty days and nights on that ark thing, didn't he? Or was that the number of thieves Ali Baba hung out with?

Whatever. We were in it for the long haul.

I looked out the window sometime later (it felt like days, but it wasn't even an hour) and noticed that the river had become more of a gurgling brook. It was still raining, but nothing like the earlier downpour.

"OK, it's time to bust a move," I said, eyeballing Léo and Erina for support. If we waited too long, we could wind up with the cops on our back. They were still milling around the body shop.

Our new German friend came out with noises that sounded like, *"Ik bleiber ein venig langer. Passen zee owf zik owf."*

Hmm. It sure sounded nice, but none of us had a clue.

His voice cracked when he added, "Danken you. Danken you very much."

We nodded, shook hands with the old lady who'd sugared us all up so well, and then left.

63

What a mess things were outside. It was truly devastating. There was mud all the way up the walls of the buildings. Some people had opened their front doors and were standing in eight inches of muddy water *inside* their houses. The ground was sodden. We were still ankle deep in places.

As we climbed back toward the center of town, the water level descended. Folks were out on the streets checking what damage had been done to their property. The thunder continued to growl ahead. It was getting farther away, though, and the lightning bolts less and less frequent. The rain was still coming, but it was nothing to write home about by that point. Just a good, strong, steady rain.

Around a half an hour later, the rain had gone.

It was as if the town had been hit by a tidal wave. It had started and finished in under two hours. It came, it kicked our asses, it went.

We crawled through the streets. They were destroyed.

Léo told me that just before he'd climbed through the window, he'd seen at least seven guys make a run for it from the body shop. Some of them went off on foot carrying bags and briefcases, others made their getaways in cars. Big black cars that had been parked farther up along the street. Big black gangster cars, by the sound of it. Why did they always have to have those cars?

"I guess that was when they arrested Murrash, then," I said. "They must have somehow gotten word and then scrammed."

"Could be. I thought they'd all gone. That's why I decided to climb in through that window, check the place out, see if I could find Erina. Because I hadn't seen her leave, I could only assume she was still inside. That's when I came face-to-face with that guy. I tried to put up a good fight, I really did. But I never stood much of a chance. He worked me over pretty good. When I came to, I was tied to that table with Erina. I'd found her! And then you came along."

So that's how it had all gone down.

Léo stopped talking. We picked up the pace. As I saw street upon street and house upon house of utter destruction, I became worried about my trailer. It was the king of trailers, but I didn't know how it could have withstood a torrent of that magnitude.

Erina and Léo didn't have anything left to say. They were shattered. I'd really hoped for the happiest reunion ever, but in the end, it was one hell of a sorry walk home.

My brain started going over some of the shit we were in. I didn't have a degree in psychobull, but you didn't have to have gone to the Sorbonne to know that Erina wasn't ready for our everyday life. We were all about rice and beans and loud babies and a trailer and rolling in the aisles and singing our heads off. *She really needs someone who knows how to help her through all the trauma she's been through. We're too crazy a bunch to deal with this. Bingo! Rachel Amar! That's who I need.*

I was going to take the two teens over to Gaston's place, as there wouldn't be enough room for everyone in the trailer, but I needed to see my own babykins first. And Kholia. Oh, the poor little boy. We all had something to go back to, even if it meant salvaging whatever we had from the water and mud, but Kholia had nothing. Truly nothing.

I tried to reach them by phone. It went straight to voice mail. Maybe Bintou didn't have any battery left. It was always a possibility. But it was same with Gaston's phone and Laroche's. Oh crap. I couldn't handle it.

"Come on, gang! We need to go faster!" I yelled. I'm a good yeller when I need to be. I startled the pair of them out of their lethargic state.

"What? How? Why?" asked Léo.

"I can't get through to them on their phones. None of them are picking up! I'm a basket case here! I have to get to my trailer. I need to see my little ones. Then I'm going over to Gaston's. I'm going to leave you two there. Is that OK? I don't think I can even begin to explain how whacked out I am after all of this. It'll be a goddamn miracle if I make it to the end of today in one piece. I feel like giving up, I really do."

They didn't have anything to say in response, but they were now almost running. Spent, but running. And they were doing it to help me out. Bless them. As we neared the site of where my beloved trailer was parked up, I could see immediately that something wasn't quite right. Jeez.

I saw all the concrete blocks around my pitch, but my trailer was on its side. On its goddamn side and totally covered in mud!

"Sabrina! Sabrina! Bintou! SAAAABBBRRRIIINNNNNAAAA!" I screamed.

No answer. I ran. I clambered up the side of the trailer to get to the front door, which was now faceup toward the sky. I did this with just the one hand. I don't know how, but when you've got kids, you find super strength from somewhere.

I peered down through the door. *DOWN!* The interior was soaked. Ruined. Oh nooooo! What was I going to do? My beautiful trailer! Oh, fuck the trailer! Where were my girlios? I'd only just gotten Sabrina back! How could I have lost her again? My twins! My girls! I jumped down.

"Sabrina! Lisa! Lisa? Emma! Where are you?"

I was calling out in total desperation and not getting anything in return but silence. Silence with the odd clap of thunder.

Then I heard some scrambling and a loud bang. I looked up. It was Pastis glaring down at me. I could tell he was cross.

"Meeeeeooooowww!"

He was perched on the trailer. It must have been interesting for him to see it from this new angle.

"Oh, Pastis. My boy! You're here! Oh, Pastis! Where are the girls?"

I heard a window opening behind me, a shutter being pushed outward. And then the twins. My twins' gorgeous little faces.

"Mommy! Mommy! Are you coming? We're in here!"

They were inside the old railway building behind my home-sweet-trailer. Up on the second floor. They clapped their little hands together. They were as pleased to see me as I was to see them.

Pastis jumped up to the window so he could show me how to do it. There was a special method. But I knew it. I'd had to do it in the past more than once. It was pretty easy once you knew how.

So Erina and Léo joined me as I climbed up to the second-floor window and squeezed in. We'd been through our fair share of windows that day.

Everyone was there. Oh, I didn't have words for the elation and relief I felt. Bintou and Laroche had decided to get up into the railway station as soon as the rain started growing really heavy. It was Laroche who'd insisted, apparently. He didn't trust my trailer. As soon as the big-time thunder and lightning came, he climbed up to the second-floor window with one of the light mattresses from the twins' room. Bintou carried a couple of bottles of water. And off they all went. They were a pair of bosses! They'd thought of everything.

The little ones were so excited. Sabrina and Kholia were fast asleep on the mattress. The tranquilizers they'd been forced to take had made them finally succumb to sleep.

We all caught up on the latest events.

We noticed that none of our telephones was working properly. I needed to get to Gaston's. I guessed that's where we'd all be staying. A sideways trailer was no place to be.

I picked my Sabrina up in my arms, even though I was running on empty and she was fairly hefty for such a little one! She woke up, but I couldn't even contemplate the idea of putting her back down again. Léo put Kholia on his back, piggyback style, and we all scrambled outside. Laroche had his car with him. They must have picked it up on the way back from the body shop. And it was a nice ride. Just what I expected, really. A seven-seater Volvo or something. Classy. Upper-classy.

There was room enough in it for everyone (OK, some of us were sitting on others). Three adults, four children, two teenagers, and our feline companion. Ten in total. If we'd really wanted to do this properly (and legally), we'd have needed a bus. But who was going to be checking on us today?

It was turmoil on the roads. The town was on its knees. Garbage piled up, mud everywhere, a stench like mold but ten times worse, people looking lost and lonely, others crying and haggard. It was like a zombie film. And it had all happened in such a short space of time. That's what I couldn't get my head around. It was worse than anything I could have imagined.

We went a few hundred yards and then had to abandon the car. All the roads were blocked, and Laroche and his super wheels wouldn't be free to move again anytime soon.

Laroche and Bintou wanted to stay with the car (and each other!). The rest of us continued to Gaston's place on foot. I still had my Sabrina in my arms, and Léo carried Kholia. Erina was holding hands with the twins. What a trooper. Pastis was running alongside us. I swear he's really a dog. The twins had taken to the whole disaster zone very well! They were full of beans, singing and chattering.

As selfishly as ever, I had my fingers crossed the whole way that Gaston's castle wasn't a giant mudslide. I just wanted to get inside and leave this sorry world behind for the night. I wanted to be clean and dry and safe.

I texted Gaston, just in case the networks came back or whatever it was that had gone wrong with the phones.

```
Yo! C U l8r. In a cpl of minits.
```

But it took quite a while for us to get to the sleepy castle . . .

We finally made it. When I saw Gaston's big fancy gates, my heart sang.

64

I rang the bell.

Gaston ran down the driveway to greet us and open up. He'd been around the bend with worry, because he'd received my text message and had been expecting us much sooner.

His house had been hit by the floods too, but only the cellar had really seen any damage. Water had gone through the vents. The foundations were pretty high, the water had lapped around the porch, but that was as far as it had gotten. The damage in the cellar was extensive, though. There was water five feet deep down there, and it wasn't going anywhere for the time being. All his stuff in the basement was floating around. Tons and tons of books.

I was so upset and emotional, I fell into his arms.

Yes. Me!

I had been holding it all back. The fatigue, the trauma of it all. I didn't want anyone to know how much of an effect it had had on me. What I wanted more than anything was to go straight up to bed. But we all needed a shower. We were a smelly bunch.

So that's just what we did. After their showers, I put the kids in Gaston's clean stuff—it worked fine as pj's. Gaston had made up the beds as soon as he'd received my message. He's great like that. Perfect, in fact. Always.

The big guest room felt like mine. There was enough space for me, Kholia, and the girls. Our own little piece of heaven. He told me he'd done the same for Léo and Erina. What a godsend.

As soon as the chillykins were wrapped up, tucked up, and storied up, I took off my damp clothes and enjoyed a hot shower. I found a big sleeveless shirt in one of the drawers. It was the perfect nightdress. Just my size.

I threw away the dirty, wet wrist bandage and delved into the medicine cabinet to see what Gaston had in the way of first-aid supplies. Not much. I went downstairs and straight to the fridge. I rubbed some butter into the bruising. This was something that Ruth always told me to do. She'd picked up the tip from her mother before her. Butter was supposed to be a big help when it came to bumps and bruises.

My stomach was telling me I was hungry, but the rest of my body more than hinted that tiredness was the biggest issue. I said good night to everyone who was still awake and then joined my girls and the new little addition. I bumped into Rachel Amar on the stairs. Her glasses were on the tip of her nose, a book in her hand, and a curious, inquisitive expression on her face.

I heard Gaston say, "Ah! Rachel! Just in time! We need your opinion on something here. You know Léo and Erina, don't you?"

I felt relieved. Gaston was there to take some of the weight off my shoulders.

I entered our room and got in the big bed next to Sabrina. Pastis had joined us too. Of course he had. He perched up on my hip, enjoying the vantage point.

And I let it all out. The sobs came. They didn't stop. I didn't know whether I was crying simply because I was shattered, out of relief to finally be somewhere safe, or because I was stunned by what had happened with Murrash. Maybe it was the emotion of being with my babies again, or the fact that Erina and Kholia were with us . . . or all of those things.

Maybe my heart was broken. I hadn't heard anything from *him* in a while. Would I ever hear from him again? Doubtful. Not now that he knew I wasn't who he'd thought I was.

Pastis didn't often see me cry. He pawed his way up to my face and licked my tears. Salty goodness. He let out a shy little squeak and purred into my neck to help soothe me. His gentle noises reminded me of that day's song. I couldn't remember all the words, but I fell asleep trying.

I'd totally forgotten about my stolen goods in my pockets . . . and the gangster cell phone . . .

Saturday:
The Fear

65

I would have liked more than anything to have a lazy morning, but I had too much work ahead of me. There was no school that day. That was one good thing, at least.

A distant aroma of coffee floated up my nosey holes. That nice song by Andy Williams was playing on my brain stereo . . . *Speak softly, love . . .*

Why would my momma send me that? What did that have to do with anything? Was Linus going to come and find me? It was a nice little song and I sang it well, even though the words were a bit tricky. English has never been my forte. I wondered whether or not Gaston might put a similar song in his Icelandic extravaganza.

I was sure it was from a film. Something real famous. Oh, it was on the tip of my tongue.

I thought about my ruined home and the effort it was going to take to get it all back in order. I had to get on that ASAP. I didn't want to take advantage of Gaston's hospitality. I wanted to be back at my place, quiet, with my little girl-gang and my kitty.

I was going to have to get my ass back to Amar's place to straighten it all out. Maybe she'd pay me enough so I could buy what I needed to return my trailer to its former glory.

That gorgeous smell of freshly roasted coffee got me out of bed in a flash. I could feel it was early. Gaston is an early bird, though, and would have been up and about since the break of dawn. I scanned the room. No kids. I entered the kitchen and discovered I was actually the last one up.

Gaston had already been out to buy fresh baguettes. We all enjoyed the perfect breakfast together *à la française*: coffee, crusty bread, butter, jam, and hot chocolate for the little ones.

The kiddies, bellies full, headed out into the backyard in their make-shift pj's to make the most of the sunshine. Pastis knew the grounds well and joined them. The adults (teenagers included) all stayed at the table to discuss what was to be done about Kholia and Erina. Gaston was just like me. For him, it was out of the question that the authorities be told about their whereabouts. There was not a chance we were going to let them wind up in a detention center. We'd heard stuff about those places. Not good stuff either.

Rachel Amar thought the authorities should be told. I knew it. She wasn't one to rock the boat. She admitted it, at least.

"Sometimes, the boat needs a thorough rocking, Rachel," said Gaston. "There are moments in life where breaking the law becomes one's civic duty."

"Like when people hid Jews in their attics," I added.

"I understand what you're saying. Just know that your consciences and personal moral convictions make no difference if you're acting criminally in the eyes of the law."

"I can live with it," said Gaston.

"I can live with it too," I added like a little parrot. "If I'd spent my life respecting the law, I'd be pushing up daisies by now."

Gaston looked at me proudly. I didn't know if it was actually true, but it sounded impressive enough.

Rachel intimated that, although she didn't really support our decision, she was bound by professional confidentiality and wouldn't say anything to the cops. That was the very least we could ask of her, right? That, and also to help Erina with some post-traumatic therapy. She needed to do that too.

The other subject on the table was the state of our respective places of residence, and what in the name of Jesus we were going to do about it.

Just before we tackled the matter, Bintou and Laroche showed up.

"We wanted to come earlier, but we had to do a little shopping first. You people have nothing to wear!" cried Bintou.

Jeez. Their arms were weighed down with expensive-looking bags and boxes, all wrapped up with satin ribbons. Bintou had been downtown and attacked all the classy stores. They'd been flooded too, and so everything had been going at knockdown prices. Oh God! Let me just say, those were some butt-ass ugly clothes.

But as my Grandmommy Ruth always used to tell me, "Never speak to a gift pony in the face and beggars can't choose nothing." All our clothes were rotting in the trailer. And everything we'd been wearing the day before was lying in a heap on Gaston's bathroom floor. I'd been too pooped to deal with it the night before.

I called the twins in and put them in their new little outfits. Dior pink organza dresses with black patent Mary Janes. Sabrina was next. She had a taffeta skirt and a top from Kenzo, like a ridiculous little bride. Kholia had a three-piece suit from Junior Gaultier (you know, just in case he had a wedding to go to that day). And for Léo and Erina? Matching tennis gear from Lacoste. No rackets. Thank God.

"For you, I thought Gucci was more your style," said Bintou proudly, handing over a long dress. "Plus some sparkly moccasins, of course. I noticed that you like anything a little shiny, am I right?"

Flat shoes? WTF? And a dress that didn't show my thighs? A first for me! The colors were bright and the shoes were gold, but when I put it all on, I felt like a nun.

I didn't want to pee on her parade, though. So I put on a brave face. She added with joy in her voice. "I bought doubles of everything! So you'll all have a change of clothing! The prices were incredible. I've got underwear and swimsuits too! You never know! Maybe you'll all take a trip to the beach later."

I raised an eyebrow. I really feared the worst on the underwear front, but I kept my mouth shut. This getting-older business was doing me good.

Once we were all in nice clothes and the thank-yous had been expressed, the babes went back to the yard to play in the mud. Dior's just so practical for that. And we all went down, me in all my finery, to check out Gaston's cellar.

It was a sorry sight, so much of his collection of books floating around down there, including poetry books he'd written as a young man that were no longer in print. I really felt for him. We stood on the stairs listening to the *glug glug gloop gloop* sounds of his belongings sucking up water like sponges.

Disaster.

Gaston didn't like to show much emotion. He's that sort of fella. He wouldn't have complained, anyway, though, because he knew I didn't have much to go home to. We'd all been affected by this. What had happened to me was more serious, I guess.

I got the distinct impression a part of him was secretly walking on air, because it meant we'd all be staying with him for a while. I guess this small pleasure compensated in some way for the loss of his precious books.

"We've got a lot on our plates, peeps!" he said. "Here's what we're going to do. I'm going to head out and buy a water pump. We'll get it up and running and then go to the trailer to see what damage we can repair back there. You are insured, aren't you, Cricri?"

"Insured schminsured. Nope. I've never insured a thing. Well, the girls had to be insured for something at school. I did that."

"That's a big pity, Cricri. All right, I'm off!"

He seemed motivated, excited even, about all the work we had ahead of us. Not me, though. It gave me the fear.

We'll never do it. How are we going to get all that water out of the cellar? That place is enormous—it'll flood the street! Then there's my place. Cleaning it? Getting all the ruined stuff out of there? Fixing stuff? With Gaston and Léo? I wouldn't exactly call that pair master builders! And then all the stuff at Amar's? That apartment has been trashed! It isn't humanly possible. This might just be the end of me. They'll be scraping me off the floor by the time we're done.

I advised Rachel Amar not to go back to her apartment just yet. She seemed pleased to be in Gaston's company, so it was no hardship. She needed to unwind after all the stress. She knew Murrash had trashed her place when he came for Erina (but nothing about the Russian scum, although she might have suspected). I didn't want her to see her home in such a sorry state. And because I had every intention of being paid for my work, I was as eager as pie to get stuck with it. Well, once we'd put my trailer back together and deflooded (what's the opposite of flood?) my beloved Gaston's cellar.

She divulged that she'd be more than happy to stay on a few more days. I got the feeling she was just letting everything wash over her and enjoying someone else making all the decisions. Plus, she was fascinated by our lovely Erina. Personally and professionally. She wanted to analyze her background and help the girl. She still had a major beef with Bintou and Laroche, though. She'd hardly spoken a word to them. I guess she must have felt betrayed.

Later on, as I grabbed our dirty laundry (I was trying to be a good little houseguest) from the bathroom, I came across my stolen goodies from the body shop. *The cell phone.* I took it down to the others to ask their advice. Did they think it could be of any use? Laroche was on it! Full-time geekio. He got it up and running with a mini UPS wire, or USB cable, I didn't really know the technical ins and outs of it all—just that he's a magic man when it comes to that stuff.

"There's only one number in the memory," he said.

"Oh yeah! I heard about this on *The Wire*! It's a common dealer trick! They change their cells all the time. Borelli mentioned it too! I wish there was a way we could find out who it belonged to."

"Usually, if there's just the one number, it's the boss's."

"Monsieur Charles? Do you really think so, Cricri?" interjected Gaston, back on the ball now that he'd put his opera saga away for a while.

"Monsieur Charles himself! But how are we going to get our hands on the prick? We can't call him, can we? Ha! Can you imagine?"

"I'm going to try to geolocalize him," declared Laroche.

"Geo what? Ah! You mean find out where he is? You can do that too? This is just amazing! The skills!"

"It's my specialty," he muttered, seemingly self-conscious in front of Bintou.

"Great! So, while Gaston is getting his special pump and you're geofinding people, Léo and I will go to the hospital and visit Mimi. She must be wondering what I've done with her son by now. And the blasted telephones haven't been working. I bet she's worried sick if she's been trying to get ahold of us."

I entrusted them with my bambinos, and Erina, Léo, and I set off to see his momma.

Luckily, the hospital is on pretty high ground and they hadn't been too badly affected by the weather. The electricity had been on and off, like in the rest of the town, but they had backup generators.

Mimi's operation had been a success. Her left wrist was in a splint and she'd been told to stay lying down as much as possible to help with her back pain. She'd be allowed to go home in two days' time. She'd need Léo to help her with all the day-to-day stuff. There wasn't much she could do in the way of shopping, chores, and the rest of it, and she'd been told to rest up. Doctor's orders.

"The world has turned upside down on me, Léo," she muttered. "I couldn't have been more excited about the idea of spoiling you for a while, and now it's you who'll have to take care of me. I can't even fasten my own buttons. I can't use a knife and fork. I'm ridiculous. And cooking? You can forget about it!"

He sounded embarrassed. "Please, Mom, it's nothing. I'll be glad to help you out. You know that. I like being useful."

I knew he'd be up to the task. She had a good son in Léo.

66

Gaston was back at the castle before us. He'd already gotten the pump into action, and the water was spilling out into his garden—as if it needed any extra! Better out than in, though!

He'd even taken the time to pick up a few groceries. Saint of a man.

We had scallops with roasted ham and polenta with a spicy sage sauce. Paradise on a plate. The munchkins were in ecstasy, not to mention Pastis. It's not every day we eat like that, let me tell you!

"My grandmother used to say there was no use not working on a full stomach, so this is just what we all needed, Gaston!" I said.

"I think she probably said that there was no use *working* on an empty stomach," replied Laroche.

"No. Not my Ruth. And I like to say it the same as her," I explained.

What I meant was we'd all eaten well, so we could now get some serious work done. Isn't that how it came across? And we could start with my trailer . . .

"It doesn't matter how it's said. We need to be off now. I want to go back to my pad and see what can be rescued. Sorry to love you and leave you! Come along if you don't want to be left!"

"I didn't want to say anything while we were enjoying that wonderful meal," said Laroche, "but I've managed to locate the number. I mean, the person whose number it is."

Everyone's eyes were on him . . . and then the questions started. All of us spluttering and stammering at once.

Léo was the most frantic. He was fretting half to death that the big bad was still out there. The guy who had his eye on Léo's Erina.

I wasn't really any less frantic. If this Monsieur Charles existed, he was going to pay the price for what had happened to my Sabrina. Even if he hadn't given the direct orders, he was behind it. Nobody messes with my babies. I'd have his bones for breakfast sooner or later—and the sooner the better. If we got to him, we could crack the whole network! Smash it into smithereens.

I decided that the trailer could wait another hour or so, and Gaston, Léo, Laroche, and I went off on the trail of a little red dot flashing in a grid on Laroche's laptop. It was all very James Bond.

We decided to go on foot. Laroche said it would be easier. No one-way streets to bother us. We headed in the direction of the city center. Laroche was in the lead. So far, so good. As he took a combination of lefts and rights, down small alleyways and through strips of public parkland, I realized that we were not all that far from Sélect. And that's where we ended up. Of all the places.

The coincidence was loopo insane. Léo couldn't get over it either. I mean, that was where his momma worked!

I stepped up to the front of the gang (we were a bit like a super cool gang by that point). I pushed the door open.

Tony was the only person in the joint. He was standing at the bar, cleaning a glass with a cloth. The TV was on, but there was no sound.

Normally, on a Saturday afternoon, the place is packed to the gills! You can't move in there. But with yesterday's awful flooding, it seemed that nobody had much of an inclination to be partying it up in a bar. They were more than likely at home, cleaning up the damage.

But if Tony was the only person there . . . and the little red dot . . . that meant . . .

No! I looked at my old friend, feeling devastated. *Tony? No. Tell me it's not true. Not Tony! Not him! No!* I was bugging out. Brain overload. It just simply couldn't be true. There was no way my Tony was the big boss of a trafficking, druggy, child-slavery ring.

Could Monsieur Charles be Tony? No! Impossible!

But what better cover? What better location? He was like Gus, the chicken guy in *Breaking Bad*! It was perfect! A traditional little café-bar, busy, a bit scruffy, rough around the edges, cheap beer, little concerts on a Saturday night . . . Who would ever suspect? What could be more banal, normal, run-of-the-goddamn-mill?

Tony smirked at me and winked, but then he must have seen my face and his expression turned to one of concern. "Whassuuuup, chica? Do I have something on my face?"

I was still too stunned to speak. As I stood there like a loser, he looked me up and down, head to toe, taking in the whole sorry sight.

"What's the deal with the outfit? It's not Mardi Gras, is it? Someone could have reminded me!" He spotted my bandaged wrist. "Oh, Cricri girl, what's with the arm? What did you do now? You badly hurt?"

He looked to the others behind me. "Yo, Léo! How's your mom doing? I haven't had time to call up the hospital yet. Not today, anyway."

Next he spied Laroche. He gave him a bit of a jealous glare. He never likes it when I bring a guy to Sélect. "Can I get you anything?"

Still no replies from any of us. We didn't know where to take this thing next. I glanced around and noticed Emma's Princess Sarah doll in her Superman get-up. She was sitting nicely on a bar stool, like a very miniature customer.

"Oh, you found the doll?" I whispered. I'd lost all the power in my voice.

"Yeah, I was hoping you'd show up. She must be missing it. Don't forget it this time," he replied.

"Thanks." I dawdled over to the stool and slipped it into my purse. "Does your phone work yet?" I continued, just for something to say, buying time.

I didn't know what to do, but I thought it might be worth a shot to get Borelli on the line. He'd be better equipped than me to deal with this right now. Finding out that one of your best friends in the world, not to mention the greatest boss ever, is a criminal mastermind was too much. Even for me. I was sick to my stomach.

"No," he answered. "It hasn't been working since last night. The electricity has been a big pain in the ass too. My cell wasn't working either, but I got a text about five minutes ago, so I guess the network's back up again. And even though I'm on the latest deal with 4,634 giga-megakillerbytes or whatever, I still don't have the Internet up and running. Not on my computer or my cell. I don't know when they'll get it all fixed. I suppose it'll take some time."

His words seemed to cause a panic. Everyone except Gaston got their little talkie boxes out to check if they had a connection or not. It was almost an automatic reflex. When did we all become so cell obsessed? What a world! Mine was still out, but Laroche and Léo were managing to get a weak signal. We'd had no difficulties with Laroche's lappy thing on the way over, so it must have just been this part of town. Also, Laroche must have had the best phone and computer stuff that money could buy, I was pretty sure of that.

"One of you call Borelli if you can get a signal. Léo, you have his number!"

Tony examined me and then his eyes moved to Léo. He was waiting to see what would happen next. But Léo didn't even question me. He typed in Borelli's number, glancing at Tony nervously as he did so.

"Monsieur Borelli? I'm calling you on behalf of Rosie Maldonne . . . Yes. At Sélect, do you know it? . . . Could you come? As quickly as possible, please. It's an emergency."

Gaston spoke up. "Could I have a little glass of *rosé de Provence*, please?"

I think he was a little slow on the uptake and hadn't figured out that Tony was our guy. Red-Spot Guy. He took his glass and went to sit at a table near the open window. I think he needed some air after the long walk.

"It doesn't look like you were hit too badly by the storm. Not much water made it this far, huh?" asked Gaston.

Tony didn't respond. He was too busy staring at me, a worried expression on his face. The tension was unbearable. Gaston was in another world. I hoped it was somewhere pleasant, for his sake.

That's when Laroche got out the cell. *The* cell. The *badass* cell. He banged it down aggressively on the bar and stared at Tony.

Tony came across as being mega nervous. "Hey, you all seem a bit on edge. What's the story here? I think I've missed an episode." He was trying his hardest to give Laroche the hairy eyeball in return. "I don't believe we've been introduced," he said.

Laroche slowly picked up the phone and pressed a couple of buttons. He was calling the boss. If the geothermolocomoco was right, Tony's cell would ring any second.

Léo and I held our breath. Could this have gotten any more dramatic? We waited for the first ring, hypnotized by Tony's every blink, twitch, gesture . . .

And that's when we heard it. A little tune coming from far away. It was that song from *Carmen*. The Toreador Song, according to Gaston. What did I know? It sounded real screwy in such a heavy, tense, murky atmosphere.

My first thought was that Tony's cell was in a jacket hanging up at the other end of the bar, or tucked away in a drawer somewhere. But just then, I noticed a half-empty cup of coffee on the shiny bar top. And then I heard the toilet flush, and a tap running . . .

Someone was there. In the bathroom. Someone else was at Sélect. Someone other than Tony.

My legs were doing that wobbly thing again. The emotion was too much. I stepped back and plunked my ass on a table, not taking my eye off the bathroom door. It was either that or drop to the floor. Léo and Laroche had the same reflexes as me and were now staring at the door marked "Toilettes."

The door opened and out walked Antoine, the cyclist. He came toward us with a cell phone in his hand.

As he noticed us all looking in his direction, he gave us his usual jovial smile, but then I saw the worry flash in his eyes. The shoe dropped. The cell in Laroche's hand, his own ringtone singing loudly, and our bizarre behavior . . . all of us fixated on him.

Antoine pressed a button on his phone, and Laroche said slowly and calmly, "Call refused."

Antoine made out like he hadn't heard and went back to his barstool. He finished his coffee, threw a two-euro coin down in front of Tony, and headed to the door.

"Leaving already, Antoine?" I asked, my voice still weak. "Or should I say *Monsieur Charles*?"

He stopped, turned to me, and tried to get a staring contest going between us, but his eyes were soulless, devoid of any feeling. Shark eyes.

Then he made a run for it, bombing out of the bar.

Léo lost it. Me too. We both jumped on him at the same time. It must have looked like a slapstick comedy as my head and Léo's smacked into one another. I heard the crack. Léo fell to the floor, but I hung onto Antoine's back, clinging like a limpet to a rock. I'd already had a little training at the body shop, and I knew Antoine wasn't as strong as the greaseball who'd thrown me across the room the day before.

"You bastard!" I shrieked. "You're not going anyplace. You pricks had my daughter!"

Tony so obviously didn't have a clue what was happening. He'd never seen me like that, although he knew I had a certain, um, character. Laroche, who was not exactly the best street fighter, as far as I knew, was trying to get a punch in, but wasn't quite managing it. He was seeking out the best angle. He never found it.

Monsieur Charles slipped his hand into his jacket pocket and pulled out a revolver. I should have known he'd be armed.

"Let me go or I'll shoot all of you fuckers!"

My only response was to grip even tighter. I hoped, I expected, that someone would help me bring him down. Why was I still on my own here? But now that the piece had made an appearance, the others were even more hesitant than they'd already been.

Panic flowed through my veins as I saw Tony bend down under the bar and pick up a bat. Antoine spotted him and didn't take too kindly to the idea. He was spinning around with me still attached to his back like an oversized, brightly colored backpack.

"Tony! Keep out of this, I'm telling you! Put that back or I'll take you down. I mean it. Not just you, the whole fucking group of you. In an instant. Whacked. What choice do I have? You meddling fucks! Didn't you know? When you dig in shit, you wind up stinking! I know what I'm doing here. You'll each get a bullet and I'll take what's in the cash register. Not that I fucking need it, but it'll be easy pickings."

"Don't be stupid, Antoine," snapped Tony. "I don't know what it is you supposedly did, but don't make this worse for yourself. Come on . . ."

Antoine's sinister laugh filled the room, and Tony quickly understood that this old bike boy wasn't who he'd always claimed to be. I closed my eyes. I sensed that it was all going to end up very bad. His comment about digging in shit had gotten me scared out of my tree.

Monsieur Charles flung his hand backward and caught my chin— a momentary lapse in concentration on my part. I crumpled to the ground.

"Big mistake," said Monsieur Charles, pointing his gun at my Tony.

What he didn't see was Gaston coming from behind like a sneaky sneaky ninja man. He must have sensed a movement, but it was too late. As Monsieur Charles turned around, Gaston did some kind of oddball scissor move around his neck. I don't think I'll ever get over how much of a kickass Gaston is. Nobody would possibly ever expect it. Especially a move like that! Both men fell to the ground. The gun flew across the floor and went under one of the tables. Monsieur Charles was still down with Gaston's thighs wrapped around his neck. He was being choked! Death by thigh!

I wondered how long Gaston would be able to hold him in such a position. I ran to the bar, grabbed a bottle of Campari from the nearest shelf, and rushed back to them. Using my good arm, I smacked Monsieur Charles over the head with it, with all the strength I could muster.

He stopped struggling. His head had gone purple, and blood was pouring from him. I nearly peed my pants! Had I killed him? Oh no, it was just the Campari. That stuff looks and smells like blood. Grim. Gaston released his leg grip and stood up proudly. What a useful old fella to know. I've always said as much.

"What on earth is going on here? Are you all high? What the hell was that?" asked Tony, in shock.

"I know this man probably seemed innocent enough to you," Gaston said, "but he's one of the naughty ones, I'm afraid. Cricri will fill you in."

"Antoine? With his bike and his shorts . . . going around minding his own business? No!"

I wasn't listening. I'd just understood my mother's song. It was from *The Godfather*! That's right! Here he was! Another one! I was getting good at catching godfathers! My momma had done it again.

I ran to Léo to check on him (he was OK!) and asked Tony for some string. The fake-ass real-estate agent got tied up Sabrina-style, and as

I finished, in walked Borelli and a beat cop. Just in the nick of time. *Not.* Thanks a lot.

"But . . . I can't . . . Jesus Almighty! Having yourself a good time again, Maldonne? Arrest them all!"

And so once again I was back in Borelli's office having to explain myself.

I didn't care, though. I had Emma's Superman princess in my pocket for luck.

67

It took a while to give Borelli the full story. The big problem was that we didn't have any proof to back it up. Just a phone with a number in it, which really didn't mean much. We couldn't prove where we'd found it or anything.

Borelli simply let us go. I lucked out there. Because I guess breaking an innocent old cyclist's skull open and then tying him up could get you into quite a lot of trouble in most places. Borelli explained that he was backlogged with work and couldn't be bothered adding another file on me to his pile. More luck.

I couldn't believe we didn't have anything on Antoine! Jesus! The only thing I could think of was to get Erina and Kholia to make a statement, but the cops would whip them off to a center in seconds. It wasn't an option. I'd handed them the (or yet another) real-life Godfather on a silver platter. It was up to the dicks to sort it out now. Borelli would just have to do the job he was always claiming to be so good at.

As soon as we were out of there, we headed for my trailer. Jobs to do! Tony wanted to come with us. He'd already closed his café, and he reasoned it might as well stay closed for the rest of the day. Besides, with all the flooding, folks were staying away anyhow. Tons of other shops and cafés were shut, so he didn't see why he shouldn't follow suit. I think he just wanted to hang around and check out my trailer.

Bintou joined us. Erina stayed with Rachel Amar at Gaston's place. They were on babysitting duty.

Between us, we managed to push the trailer upright again. One less thing to worry about! There was a huge dent in it, but it was around the back, so you'd have to know it was there. I wasn't too worried. It was looking the worse for wear, to say the least, but it was still solid, and once we'd put it back on its blocks, it was safe to venture inside.

We brushed the water out and threw away everything that was ruined beyond repair. We bagged up all the refuse and left it on the sidewalk. The local authorities were sending out garbage trucks to collect everyone's trashed lives. I know that sounds exaggerated, but it's how it felt. I had to get rid of all our linens, most of our clothes, our mattresses. It was back-breaking work and one hell of a cleanup, which was not easy with my wrist.

Gaston went to pick up the car and bring back some heavy-duty plastic trash bags from his house. It made the job a lot easier. It was heartbreaking. Truly. Bags and bags of memories. The kids' schoolbooks, letters, comics, the carpets! I tried to get as much of the irreplaceable stuff as I could out in the sun to dry, including a couple of photos of my mom and my grandmamma.

We managed to save some clothes. They were all thrown into the trunk of the Jag. I could launder them and they'd maybe come back all right again.

The dishes and cutlery were fine—just very, very dirty. Easy enough to take care of. Anything electric was a goner.

I sponged, emptied, washed, mopped, cleaned, and then did it all over. Oh, the kiddies' toys! My aching heart! So much had to go!

I found an old leather bag that had been my Ruth's. I'd forgotten all about it! It was full of papers, letters, postcards, diaries, tickets, bills, photos of people I didn't know. It was a little pack of treats and treasures. There was even a small brass key in there. I didn't know what it opened. I'd often wondered. Everything was sodden, but I couldn't bring myself to throw any of it away. Out into the sunshine it went.

The last thing I got to were my personal documents, which I kept in a big box. There was a heap of sentimental old stuff in there too. Things from the births of my daughters, adoption papers, all my momma's documents. My family heritage. Everything. I couldn't bring myself to look. I spread it all out on the plastic table outside. It would dry. I prayed it would dry. I couldn't bear to think of the alternative.

We eventually got to the stage where my trailer was "clean," an empty box. The electricity hadn't come back on, though, and it stank. Oh well! I cleaned up the dishes, pots, and pans and put them back in the cupboards. I also collected the bits of paper that had dried and found new homes for everything. I certainly had plenty of room now!

We stood outside and took stock. We sensed we'd accomplished something. And we had! The next time I did any cleaning at my place, it wouldn't take too long, that was for sure. There was next to nothing left. Silver lining and all that.

Bintou gave me a good tip about burning herbs to get rid of the smell. I couldn't wait to try it out. She divulged how eucalyptus leaves were a gem too. I'd seen a ton of them in Gaston's yard. I'd do it the following day.

The Jag was so full of stuff that I wanted to try to clean back at his place, there was only one seat left. It had to be for the youngest member of our gang, Léo. Gaston said he'd stop off and pick up some fruit on his way home.

The rest of us returned to the enchanted castle on foot. Laroche and Bintou. Me and Tony.

As we walked, I couldn't help but feel down. My spirits were low and I felt shattered. Tony picked up on this and told me jokes to try and buck me up. He's such a pal. When his jokes ran out, he told me about a couple of funny movies he'd seen recently. He made me giggle a few times, but my heart remained heavy.

There was still no news from Linus Robinson.

So much had happened, and my mind hadn't really been on him all that much, but my brain was starting to catch up with reality now. I guessed I'd deserved it. That's what you get when you try to fake-ass your way through a situation. When you're not yourself. When you pretend you're someone else. When you're a big liar masquerading.

Tony only joined us part of the way. He had decided earlier to head back to Sélect. He wanted to open up for the evening. He didn't like losing business, however little of it there was. An afternoon off was more than enough for my Tony. Bintou and Laroche had been invited to dine with us.

When I met up with my babas, they told me what a great afternoon they'd had. Pastis was up in a tree. Oh, the life of a cat! I gave Emma her Princess Sarah doll. Smiles all around! Even Erina seemed peppy. She was in the backyard with Léo, chatting away.

I hung up the wet things that were already in the machine and started sorting out the muddy clothes. Maybe we'd have something presentable to wear the next day!

We ate what was left of the fantastic midday meal, with raspberries and watermelon. Delish. If I ever have the blues, they soon disappear when I'm with my little ones. The evening wound down with a game of Monopoly.

The group was split into teams. Emma was with Gaston, Kholia with Erina, Lisa with Léo, and Sabrina on her own (now that she's all big and can read, she has more of an independent streak). I watched the fun.

Laroche and Bintou washed the pots and put everything back in the cupboards. Rachel Amar kept to herself in a little corner, scribbling away in a notebook.

Sabrina was on a winning streak! She had houses and hotels all over the board. My little brainiac. Suddenly she dug around in her pocket and got out her Happy Families game that Antoine, alias Monsieur Charles, had given her. She was fast fancying herself a real-estate mogul. She turned the cards over and started placing them on the board. Little "For Sale" signs everywhere.

"I'm thelling everything," she announced. "I'd rather uthe the money for other thingth. I don't want a big pile of houtheth. What'th the uthe? A perthon only needth one houthe, don't they?"

Shit. That was it! Why hadn't it come to me earlier?

The houses. Real estate. That's what Monsieur Charles did! All those places on his books! The houses, the shops, the apartments . . . they'd be full of drugs, weapons, girls. I'd seen a sign outside Murrash's place and outside the body shop. That's how he was getting away with it. That's where the evidence would be! There were "For Sale" signs all over that cruddy part of town.

I cried out, "'For Sale!'"

"What?" said Léo. "You're not even playing, Cricri."

"Are you selling your station, Sabrina?" asked Gaston.

I shouted, "Monsieur Charles! The houses. That's his cover! All those 'For Sale' signs! That's how we can tie all this together! This is how we prove the links to Murrash and all the other baddies! Through his agency! He must have the keys to half the places in town! He can store anything he likes, almost anyplace he likes. Goods, people . . . all the evidence that's not so easy to hide. Oh God. I've got it! He's going down!"

I called up Borelli to explain what I'd known all along, but which had taken some time to come out of my frazzled brain. He was a lot colder with me than I thought he would be. Probably because there I was, doing his job for him again. He promised he'd examine any evidence and that it was an interesting lead. *Interesting lead?* It was his proof! He explained how he would organize a systematic search of all the empty properties on Antoine's books. Well, thank God for that. I didn't like to imagine what he'd find, but Antoine was sewn up. Job done.

The Monopoly game went on forever. They always do. Does anyone actually know how that game ends?

I fell asleep, but I think everyone gave up in the end because my Sabrina was too far ahead. As always. She's the best.

Sunday:
Shiny Happy People

68

I woke up extra early on Sunday morning. Nothing playing on the mind-radio. A bit of peace. Maybe Mom thought she'd give me a rest. I'd had a packed week.

I put my own clothes back on. They'd all dried on the line outside. What a relief! Flowery shorts, a skimpy tee with a glittery pattern . . . back to my normal self.

I found Rachel Amar glugging down coffee in the kitchen. She smiled at me and served me a big cup of the delicious black stuff.

We had been mulling over what to do about the Albanian kids, and she told me she'd come to a decision. "I've been in touch with a friend of mine who works for the local authorities. The best solution here would be to send the children home to their families. That's the long-term goal. I've decided to focus my research on trauma faced by economic migrants, particularly minors. I will take care of the children until we can find a way to get them home. I want to be of some use here. I know something's happening with the Russian gang and that they're after me. I pick up on these things, Rosie! I've been assured that I'll have full police protection until the situation has calmed down. I'll

Alice Quinn

be able to do my research at the same time as taking care of these little people and ensuring they're out of harm's way."

Speechless. I'd had no idea what to do with the latest additions to the gang! Not an inkling. This couldn't have gone any better.

Gaston had been eavesdropping. He entered the room and told us that he knew very little about Eastern Europe but had always been fascinated. Was there a subject he wasn't fascinated by? He explained how he now planned to go on a tour of Greece, Italy . . . and why not Albania? They could travel with him when the time came. That would certainly avoid deportation and all the potential issues it might entail. Another heroic move from Gaston.

"But that's for later, of course. I'm sure that Léo and Erina would be delighted to learn a little about the Impressionists in the meantime. I haven't been to the Musée des Beaux Arts in quite a while. I'm going to take them both down there today. Would you like to come along, Cricri?"

Fits of laughter followed from yours truly. "I think I'll skip it, thanks!"

Rachel wiped her brow and uttered, "If there's air-conditioning down there, I wouldn't say no."

I was sure they'd all have a super time. It just wasn't my thing. Never was, never will be.

Before they left, I asked Gaston about the eucalyptus leaves in the enchanted garden, and he showed me where the best picks were, tucked away in the back.

Léo wanted to see his mother, so they all agreed they'd visit her on their way back from the museum.

The girls were playing with Kholia in the grass. He'd definitely become a favorite.

As for me, I made a mental to-do list. As soon as I'd fixed up Rachel Amar's place, I was going to head over to Sélect and pick up a few shifts.

The summer season was about to start, and Tony would need a lot of help, especially since Mimi was out for a while with her wrist.

The fact that Erina and Kholia were now going to be with Rachel Amar was a big worry off my plate.

Victor, Teddy, and Murrash were under lock and key. Monsieur Charles would be picked up soon enough. Borelli was on it. He'd get it taken care of, I was sure.

Once Antoine was brought in, the whole network would collapse. Borelli had a lot of baddies to deal with. He'd be a busy boy!

Linus Robinson had gone off to follow his own destiny and left me to follow mine. I was back at Go. Well, with my love life, at any rate. It was sad, but as my Sabrina always says, "That'th life!"

No more thinking about Canada for me. Over and done.

Time to spend some precious moments with my little ones. That's what weekends were all about. Sunday was picnic day in our world. We needed some time out after our week, and what better way than to head off somewhere nice with something yummy to munch? As I breathed in, I felt a wave of Zen flow over me. Sunday . . . reeeeellllaaaaaax! The sun was out, and you'd never have known we'd all just survived a tornado or hurricane or whatever it was. It wasn't too hot either. Not for me, anyway. It was just right!

The beach was the best option for us.

I found swimsuits, towels, and a big beach bag. I got some munchies together from the kitchen. Gaston had a good little snack stock: bread, tomatoes, tuna, watermelon. I turned on the radio.

The local news station was reporting on the state of our beaches. They were all no-go zones because of flood damage. The water was polluted, and there was garbage and mud all over our beautiful sandy shoreline. It would take a while for everything to get back to normal. That put an end to my plans.

Damn. I'd have to move on to plan B. Did I have a plan B?

I suddenly felt weary again. Friday's events and the shock of what had happened at Tony's place were catching up with me.

The kidlets were still enjoying the backyard, and Pastis was flicking lizards around out front. I felt alone and a little abandoned. Linus must have thought I just wasn't worth it.

He was right.

Maybe if I'd told him the truth and not gone around pretending to be someone I wasn't, I might have stood a chance with him.

I felt discouraged. I had a picnic basket good enough for Yogi Bear and nowhere to go. One of my faves came on the radio. The R.E.M. classic "Shiny Happy People." What a most excellent song! Something to cheer me up. I started dancing around the kitchen. I cracked up. Momma! She'd put this on for me. She knew I needed a boost.

I made a new plan. We'd finish up in the trailer, take the eucalyptus leaves, and have ourselves a little exorcism back there. The walk would do us all some good. After that, we'd head back and enjoy our picnic in Gaston's beautiful enchanted backyard.

Seriously, why was I even thinking of going anywhere else? We had exactly what we needed right there.

I got my pack together and off we went.

My thoughts turned to Linus again as we strolled along. He was the most perfect man on earth.

No, he wasn't. He'd been a dick.

No. I was the dick.

Had his reaction been totally normal? To just dump my ass like that? Did he feel cheated?

Was I going to get over him?

Jeeeez! Out! Out of my brain, Robinson! Your loss!

The girls played in the mud while I got some of the eucalyptus burning in a wok. A bit of gas, a bit of oil, and *whhhooooooossshhh*! It smelled like minty fire.

I heard a motorbike in the distance. The roads had cleared up some and traffic was now getting though.

Someone was talking to Sabrina.

A man shouted, "Is something on fire in there?"

He was right. I was starting to choke! The minty fire had turned to minty smoke, a cloud of the stuff. I headed to the door, spluttering.

Next to Sabrina stood a real cutie—a Mediterranean type with curly black hair, dark eyes, a helmet in his hand. His T-shirt said "Professional Lover." Quite a sight. He gazed at me, his delightful eyes winning me over in a second.

"Well, well! I've been searching for you!"

Rémi. Drugstore Rémi himself. Wrist-fixer extraordinaire and rescuer of Russian kidnap victims. It seemed ages ago . . .

He ambled slowly toward the trailer.

"How's the hand doing?" he asked in a husky, sexy voice.

I replied warily, "Good. Very good. You certainly know a thing or two about bandaging. What are you doing here?"

I wasn't expecting what came next.

"I brought you Snoopy. It seemed like you hadn't quite finished with him, right?"

I didn't think my heart could stand it.

I gave him my widest, bestest smile.

About the Author

Photo © 2014 Chris Melek

Alice Quinn has worked many jobs, from theater hostess to waitress, and has traveled the world, often relying on her wits to make ends meet. After the success of her first novel, *Queen of the Trailer Park*, in her native French, she quit her day jobs and now makes her living writing full-time. She lives in the South of France with her two teenage children and several cats.

About the Translator

Photo © 2015 Kirsten Claire

Back in 2001, after studying philosophy and French at the University of Leeds and realizing that writing a decent essay on Kant's categorical imperative didn't leave her with a great many career options, Alexandra Maldwyn-Davies decided to move to Paris, where she embarked on her career in translation. She's worked on popular video games (*Game of Thrones, In Memoriam*), top-rated apps (Human Defense), bestselling fiction (*Queen of the Trailer Park, Queen of the Hide Out, The Boy Who Dreamed of Flying in a Cadillac*), and seductive travel guides (*Fermes-Manoirs du Bessin*). She has steadily built a successful freelance French-to-English translation business and can now boast that she does what she loves every day of her life: telling people's stories. Alexandra lives in rural Finistère with a motley crew of thirteen rescued dogs and cats.

Made in the USA
Middletown, DE
19 November 2016